The Guardians
of Erum

AND THE

Calamitous Child of Socotra

A. ALI HASAN ALI

Publishing permitted by UAE's National Media Council
Permit number: MC-01-01-9623856

"Self-Publisher"
A. Ali Hasan Ali
+971508130033
Abu Dhabi, UAE

Book age group: +17 (The age group that fits the book's content is
classified and determined according to the age classification system issued
by UAE's NMC.)

...

Inspired by Arabia's pre-Islamic ancient history, traditions, religious beliefs,
and local culture and folklore.
Most of the locations described or named do exist as tourist attraction sites
in modern-day Oman or Yemen—except for the City of Wadi Erum, which
is believed to be buried under the sand dunes of the Rub' Al Khali Desert.

ISBN: 978-9948-34-462-9

To parents who have suffered the pain of losing a newborn.
Stay strong.

PART ONE

ERUM

1

Behas the *saher*, deceiver of all weak minds, master of all sorcery, necromancer and conjurer, alchemist, and lord of the *jinnic realm*, was widely known as the worst of mankind. But controversially, many ignorant minorities perceived Behas as a man of righteousness and heroism! Villagers, farmers, and cities had given him many titles and names based on their encounters with him.

However, you must know that none described him well, for no humans or *jinn*, unseen creatures, knew what exactly his true intentions and doings were. While most believed that he served the *Majlis of the Jinn*, a council of elderly *jinnic lords*, men debated whether they were envious jinn that opposed the world of man or benevolent ones that protected it from incomprehensible evil. You must also know that Behas himself justified his actions with the belief that he was bound to protect humanity from the evils of the jinnic realm, something he found hard to explain. He had tried on many occasions, but he had failed to convince everyone as a result of his wrongful actions, and even those who believed in him did not fully comprehend him.

The tale I am about to share with you is merely a minor example of the many stories that are told about Behas and his mysterious activities. This one occurred when he reached his late forties, and a special child was born—a calamitous child.

. . .

Long ago, on a calm night in the early years of ancient Arabia, Behas entered a palm-farming settlement near the southern tip of the Arabian Desert.

He snaked his way between mud-walled farms in a palm grove, moving towards his next victim and dragging his dark blue cloak over the wet path with effort. To his luck, the clean air helped him breathe deeply and withstand tiredness. He kept his cloak open, exposing his chest to the dry air as well. Beneath it, he wore his regular dark pants and a scarf wrapped around his waist and across his weak chest. It was a wicked night, neither dark nor bright, half lit by moonlight and half shaded by thick dark clouds. Behas walked in the shade of those clouds. It was not that he feared being seen by anyone; he simply preferred walking in shadows. And he believed that even if he were to be seen, no weak farmer would dare to keep him from his victim, so he walked with confidence.

His bizarre, sinister dress reflected his identity; one would know him even if one were seeing him for the first time. Other outlawed wizards and *jinn masters* like him tended to blend in and try to hide who they were. Yet he challenged his opponents to come and get him if they could.

New evil is born, his all-knowing jinni had warned him. A jinni, or jinn in plural form, is a supernatural creature that dwells unseen in our world, revealing itself only to men who are able to tame it or bind it to their wills.

Another! Behas had thought in confusion when he first heard. He had to perform a necessary task: He had to kill that newborn. A calamitous newborn, he believed. *This is the third calamitous newborn in only two decades!*

Behas, guided by his all-knowing jinni, reached the victim's home. It was a tiny single-roomed farm hut made entirely of dry date-palm leaves, or *areesh,* as they're called in Arabia. Behas stood at the door and pulled out a tiny pouch from his cloak. In it was a single dry, dead black worm. With two fingers, he pulled it out, held it near his mouth, and whispered a few words. Then he licked it and placed it near the bottom of the door. "Make no mess this time," he whispered sharply. With that, he summoned his second jinni for the night.

The dry worm came to life and slowly crawled into the hut. As it did, it grew bigger and bigger, until it transformed to a long black snake. This was Behas's second type of jinni, a transformation jinni. Unlike any other kind of jinn, these ones could easily transfer their souls into a dead being and bring it to life once their master allowed.

3

Moonlight shone between dry palm leaves of the roof, and more came through a small door at the back of the hut. That blueish gleam of moonlight gave the snake enough sight to check the surroundings as it lifted its head. A man slept on the floor on the right side of the hut, and a woman with a child on the opposite side.

The victim and its parents.

The snake moved as silently as that night itself towards the mother. The transformation jinni knew from experience that it did not want to strike the child first, as that would wake up the mother and create panic. The task would be easier without disruption, and the last thing the jinni wanted was to fail its master, Behas.

The snake reached the first target. For a moment, its venomous fangs hung inches above the sleeping mother's neck. The bite was slow and gentle; the tips of those fangs pierced her skin without being felt, like a mosquito's bite on a summer night, but with rather deadlier effects.

The woman had no senses, felt no pain, as she was killed by a jinni in the form of a snake. Panic or fear did not even exist in her final dream.

Behas, outside, sensed that so far, all was going well. *Painless night.* He sighed, annoyed that he had had to travel seven days just to stand at a door while his snake jinni had all the fun. He did not even get to see anything.

After leaving the mark of its fangs on its first prey's neck, the black snake crawled silently onward. It lifted its head to peek into the small bed, made of dry palm trunk, where the child lay. It paused to stare at his sulking face; the child seemed to be having a nightmare. *Time to end your fears,* the jinni thought.

But before it could draw its sharp fangs again, the small door at the back of the hut burst open! Moonlight shone brighter from behind the shadow of a young man standing at the door like a guardian angel. The snake froze in shock, but the young man moved without a pause towards it. Barely catching his breath from a long run, he smashed the snake's head with a rock he held in his hand. He had come prepared.

The rock smashed the soft bones in the snake's head, splashing blood on the hard, dusty floor. The wretched jinni had trapped itself in a vulnerable being and died with it.

The banging of the rock ended the child's nightmare, but he erupted in loud, distressed cries. The young man hurried to pick up the child. And as he stood to leave, he found its father staring back at him in disbelief.

It took a long second for the farmer to digest the scene before his eyes: a dead snake and a pool of blood below his motionless wife. His senses came back to him slowly as he realized that he wasn't dreaming, and a stranger appeared to be holding his child.

"Who are you?" He felt a bit angry and scared; kidnapping newborns was common in Arabia, and the stranger before him could be a thief. "Put my child down, now!"

"I, I will." The young man set the child down and stepped back in surrender as he saw the father coming towards him. But before the father moved any farther or said anything else, the front door of dry rachis fell hard on the dusty rug between them.

Behas filled the doorway with his height and long cloak. The father found him gloomier than the young thief he had seen first. Behas ignored the two men at first; his eyes fell on the sleeping woman and his headless snake beside her. "Again! One can never rely on a brainless transformation jinni," he said with a sarcastic frown.

The two men stared back at him with equal fear and confusion.

He pulled out a sharp dagger made of white bone—a single bone, carved elegantly from grip to tip. A jinn master usually carried it for cutting plants and skinning small animals, but not for fighting other men.

"A saher!" cried the farmer. *A dark sorcerer!* The situation was worse than he had thought at first. The unusual and sinister figure of Behas was revealed to be a jinn master, not a thief.

"Who are you two? Leave now," he pled as he stood between his child and the two unexpected invaders. He now thought that the young thief he had seen first was probably an apprentice sorcerer as well. His wife remained unconscious, and he began to think that they had killed her. The dead snake and the pool of blood made him feel that he had woken up to a nightmare. Nothing made sense; there was only an overwhelming feeling of anger and fear.

"I will leave," Behas said, sounding polite rather than sinister, but after a mere second, he gave an evil grin and added, "but only *after* I take your child."

The cries of his scared child and the body of his deceased wife ignited more anger. The hopeless farmer did not care about his life without his family. "You will not touch my son." He sprang towards Behas, grabbed his wrist, and pushed him out of the hut. Behas couldn't stand against the strong farmer, and while he was being forced backwards, he felt the weak bones in his wrist about to break. He couldn't hold on to his white dagger any longer, and as he moved backwards, he accidentally stepped on his cloak and tripped, falling on his back. The warlock's cloak covered his eyes as he fell and he felt the weight of the strong farmer above him, crushing his bones and lungs, pressing his body flat to the ground.

He used his free hand to remove the cloak from his eyes and tried to push the farmer off him, but with no result, as his arms were much weaker. That night, he did not summon any jinn to fight for him; he either had come not expecting a fight or had thought that no one would even dare wrestle him and beat him. Hopeless and out of strength, he looked to his right, searching for his bone dagger. It was not far, but before he could reach for it, the father picked it up and held it firmly, ready to strike.

"Wait," Behas yelled as he grabbed the farmer's wrist in a desperate effort to stop him. In a weaker position and with little time to improvise deception, the old jinn master had to tell the truth, in hopes that the father would understand. "I am here to *save* you from evil. I am here to save your child."

The farmer pulled his hands hard to free them from Behas's weak grip, then stuck the tip of the sharp bone in the jinn master's neck. It wasn't sharp enough to cut him, but Behas felt its pressure. "Who are you?" the father asked, reasserting his superior position over the intruder. "What evil are you saving my son from?"

"My name is Behas. And your child will not be normal," he said in a choked voice. "His soul will be used by other jinn masters. They will use his blood for their gain and will cast evil upon other men."

The farmer didn't pay full attention to the fact that he was holding a dagger to the throat of the most wanted warlock ever, as he was also reminded that his child was in the hands of another intruder. *My child!* He began to worry, as he could no longer hear the boy cry. His heart plunged. He had to save his son, but before he left to look for him, he had to end the situation he had on his hands.

"You are nothing but lies, Behas. I know what kind of man you are," the farmer spat out, pointing the dagger at Behas's face. "You are the only evil I should keep away from my son." With a sudden movement, he drove the bone deep into Behas's neck.

Behas felt the sudden pain of the bone being pressed deep into his throat. The shock of suffocation made his body react automatically, trying to push the father's hands away, but his weak muscles failed him. He tried to breathe air into his lungs, but he couldn't.

The farmer held the bone firmly, staring down into Behas's wide-open eyes. He saw fear and suffering in them but offered no mercy, even as it occurred to him he should feel guilt at the fact that he was killing another man. He could see nothing but the dying Behas under his arms. He held the bone until there was no more struggle. The saher's heartbeats slowly faded, then stopped completely. The most feared, most wicked, and most wanted sorcerer, Behas, was now mortal. *I killed him,* the farmer thought with relief, shock, and pride. He had never killed a man before that night. *I killed Behas!* But he failed to notice one important detail: No blood came from Behas's neck!

The thrill of killing faded as soon as he remembered his son and the other intruder. He jumped away from Behas and ran inside the hut to find his son. The sight of his motionless wife forced him to pause; he stared at her for a long, sad moment, wishing he had saved her. He crawled up beside her, pushed the headless snake away, and checked her neck to find the markings of the snake's fangs. "Forgive me," he wept after he kissed her forehead one last time.

In Arabia, it is believed that the dead can hear and understand. When people lose their loved ones, they can still express how much they loved them. The farmer promised his wife he would save their son and keep him safe. "No evil jinn will touch him."

He stood and went out the back door of the hut, but he saw no sign of anyone there, though the wet ground revealed traces of footsteps. He grabbed an *atala*— a wooden pole with a sharp rock tied to one end, which was used to cut the dead fronds of palm trees. It was similar to a spear but with a round tip instead of a sharp one.

The farmer moved quickly, following the marks on the ground to the end of his farm. He tucked his long hair behind his right ear to uncover it, then heard the echoes of his child's cries. *Not far away,* he thought as he jumped over his wall of rocks and mud and began to run along the narrow paths between the farms.

Only I will protect you from evil.

2

Back at the hut, Behas's corpse started to move. His heart started to beat again, and his soul sparked life through his whole body. Behas had only one soul, but he felt like it had left and a new one had taken over. It was all nothing but a faint, but he felt that he had died and was now coming back to life.

His lungs could hardly get the air they needed. Behas grabbed the white bone protruding from his throat and pulled it out. At once, his lungs expanded, allowing the air to burst in and fill his weak chest to its limit. He hadn't bled, and there were no marks or scars, no pain—nothing! It seemed as if nothing had happened. As if it had been an illusion. But it hadn't. Behas knew that, he felt it—he had almost been killed. Strangely, though, he felt more powerful now, as if he were in a new, stronger body.

"You are getting better at this," Behas told the third jinni he summoned that night—a protection jinni—as he stood up. "I *feel* better."

. . .

Jinn are not all the same; they have different types of skills or powers, and only a few were known to men at that time. Behas had encountered only twelve types and could keep fewer than that as his servants. Most jinn masters would have only one jinni as their servant; more rarely, a jinn master would own two or three. But Behas was different than all the other jinn masters. He was the only one to easily capture and summon jinn without effort at any time he wished, and he had a special tool to do so, which I will tell you about later.

The three types summoned by Behas that night were as follows. First, he called an all-knowing jinni. These jinn use the stars to gain knowledge and predict the immediate future. They continue to serve many soothsayers even today, using various rituals to learn about others and predict their lives. Next, Behas called a transformation jinni. These jinn can transform from their true form of smokeless fire into scorpions, black cats, black snakes, or even humans if they reach their highest potential. They are the most vulnerable type of jinn, but also the deadliest. Finally, as I have told you, Behas summoned a protection jinni. These can protect their masters from severe injury or pain and are widely used even today by stunt men. Jinn masters use them for stunts such as walking on burning coals or lying on sharp glass, but their origins and the limits of their skills are not well known.

As far as Behas knew, they couldn't bring people back from the dead, but they could prevent death from happening. Behas kept such a jinni around all the time as a precaution, but he never fully trusted him. He even called his protection jinni Gaddar, which is Arabic for "perfidious." Tonight, Gaddar had saved Behas. Some other time, he might just…betray his master.

…

"Speak, Zuhal," Behas said to his all-knowing jinni, who had helped him reach the evil child. The night had been going well, until someone had interrupted and killed his snake, and the child's parent had almost killed Behas. As a result, the child was still alive. "Where is the child now?" he asked the jinni.

Zuhal, the all-knowing jinni, used the stars to see where his target was. "The child moves," came a sharp whisper from behind the warlock's left shoulder. Behas had never seen Zuhal, only heard his answers like a wicked thought or whisper from the back of his head. "The child moves…on the path to Wadi Erum."

Behas opened his eyes wide as he remembered that the palm grove he was in was close to the *wadi*, or valley, of Erum, the biggest city and the capital of Erum's sheikhdom, or dominion. His night couldn't get any worse. His jinn wouldn't be able to enter the wadi with him because of its protection spell, leaving him vulnerable. If the child reached Wadi Erum, his mission tonight would end in failure.

He looked up at the stars, focusing his gaze to find the path to the wadi. It wasn't easy with the palm leaves arching above each other over his head, but he found the way. He lowered his head, locking his gaze on the end of the farm, behind all the palms. "Who took the boy?" His tone deepened as he asked Zuhal about the young man who had dared interrupt him, kill his jinni, and steal his prey.

"I cannot see him; he comes from many places. He must be an occultist; only they know how to hide from the stars," answered Zuhal. This was not a definite answer but merely a guess—a guess that seemed to anger Behas even more.

Without speaking, Behas tightened his heavy cloak with the scarf he had around his waist and across his chest and shoulders. *Time to kill.*

Now, he had to run after his prey.

Looking around, Behas wished he could summon a flying jinni to carry him above the farms before the child got away. But to do so, he would have to slaughter a male desert hyena or a female albino donkey as an offering to the magnificent Lord of Flying Jinn. These two animals were not likely to be found between palm farms, and especially not around Wadi Erum; the city opposed dark magic by forbidding wizards and sorcerers from owning the barns and farms they needed to raise and plant the ingredients for their dark sorcery and conjury.

Now Behas had only his legs to carry him and his stamina to help him reach the child before it entered the wadi. That city would make a jinn master's task extremely difficult. Behas began to run through the narrow paths between the palms. He could not fail now—the thought of it brought bad memories. He ran on steadily, trying to stop the evil consequences that he claimed to be the only man to comprehend.

3

The child's father's name was Fada, Arabic for "emptiness." In Arabia, many names are given based on, or relating to, an event at the time of birth.

Fada was born while his parents were traveling through empty flatlands on a dark night with no moon. The emptiness of the land and sky, and the absence of light, gave him his name.

Many Arabs also believe the power of a name affects one's future. A name can bring a bright future or ensure a dark one. In Arabic, *fada* is also the name for the galaxy above—or, more precisely, for the empty space between stars. The galaxy was majestic but also distant. It offered both mystery and knowledge. It had everything in it but was also known to be empty. Like his name, Fada's personality and life had two opposite sides to them. They were either whole and complete or empty.

Fada had always felt alone. Although his parents had lived with him a long time, he had never had siblings. And although he was a talkative and diplomatic person, he had barely any friends. Now, when he thought life had blessed him with a family, it had taken them away from him!

. . .

Fada, or Fad, as he was called, ran wildly after his crying child that night, and as he did, he remembered a moment eight days before, when the boy was first born, and a sign of bad luck had appeared before him. He had been sitting under the shade of the palm trees outside his hut, on a rug made of dry palm leaves, waiting for the news of his newborn to arrive. It had been a misty evening in August. The sun setting at the horizon had spread promising lights over him as it slowly faded away, leaving him wondering, as he stared above him at the dusky sky behind the palms, which star his son would be born under.

Most of the men on the farms had finished picking their ripened dates and traveled south to Sumhuram, one of the main port cities facing the Arabian Sea, and the second biggest city in Erum's large dominion. Its main port, Port Rori, was the biggest port in the whole dominion of Erum. It took two days of travel to reach from Wadi Erum. There, farmers from all over Erum sold their harvests, with the boats sailing between Africa and India.

Fad's farm had produced less this year than the previous year, another sign of bad luck to many, but he had still joyfully picked some of his harvest and entrusted it to a neighbor who would sell it for him in the southern port. He would have had his father take his harvest, but his old man had already left for Sumhuram with his own dates to sell. Fad did keep a few in the palms to make dry dates later and store them for the year. He missed the trade season in the south, where he traveled with his father every year, but he had decided to stay behind this year to see his first child. "You shouldn't stay; come with us. Your child will be born whether you come or not," his father told him. But that had not convinced Fad; the excitement of seeing his first child had kept him from traveling with his father. He had not yet known if the child would be a girl or a boy, but in Arabia, having a boy as a first child brought pride to both the mother and the father. They were both in their early thirties. And Fad and his wife, Nada, had had a strong feeling that their first would be a boy. They'd seen many signs like her belly being oval and the way the child kicked, or that she always craved salty food and lost her appetite for sugar. Thus, they decided to name their baby Dileel, Arabic for "proof." They were that sure it would be a boy!

Sitting alone, thinking of everything he had from family to trade, and waiting for a messenger to arrive with good news, he had noticed two young girls and a boy racing towards him. He had recognized them as his wife's relatives. The last glare of the sunset had shone on their wet and cheerful faces, and he had seen good tidings coming his way. They had probably run for an hour, as the farms were a bit far from the city where his pregnant wife, Nada, was staying as she waited for her child to be born.

He had stood up, tucking his long hair back and smiling, as the boy beat his sisters and reached Fad first. The girls were not far behind, but seeing him stand with excitement, one of them shouted while running. "It's a boy! It's a boy!" Her voice reached him faster than her little brother. And as they finally stood before him above the dry rug, the little boy had spoken quickly, spilling every word he had in his mind in one breath. "I came first! I am faster. It's a boy. You have a new baby boy."

The eldest girl had seen the happiness in Fad's smile, and as she came last, she had said, "Your baby boy and your wife are in good health, Uncle Fad. They are all waiting for you in Erum."

He had thanked them, lifted the little boy and kissed him, and rewarded all three of them equally with the bronze coins he had prepared for whoever brought him the great tidings of his first child being a boy, in accordance with tradition.

He had then begun walking quickly and in great excitement towards Wadi Erum, where his wife was staying at her parents' house. He had reached the birthing place after sunset and had noticed an unusually large owl sitting in a tree not far from the house. In Arabia, the sight of an owl is believed to presage bad luck. A bit of fear did pinch his heart at the sight of it, but he had ignored it. His smile had never left his face as he continued on his way to see his first child, Dileel.

...

But now, as he ran between the farms, searching and following the echoes of his crying child and chasing after the thief who stole his first beloved son and pride, he felt himself to be running in a strange nightmare instead. He cursed that owl, and he cursed the fact that he had allowed the young thief to run away with his son. But who would blame him?

4

We were late; we were almost late! Yam thought as he ran through the narrow paths between the palms with a crying child in his hands; his run now wasn't as fast as it had been when he'd first come to save the child. He remembered the words of his master, who had sent him to save the child. *Go quickly… Save the child… Do not be late… Do not fail.*

...

Only a few days before, Yam had been running away with a small sack of raisins he'd stolen from a docked ship preparing to sail out of Port Rori.

"Can I have a few?" Yam, a twenty-two-year-old man, had asked a trader after helping him carry his goods onto the ship.

"I gave you enough seeds to plant your own. Now get off the ship. The sails are all set. If the boat departs and you are still onboard, you know the captain will throw you in the water," the tradesman said, trying to scare away the young porter. His childish face might have been the reason why the tradesman did not take him seriously, thought Yam. He did in fact look like a fourteen-year-old instead of a young man.

Yam had noticed the anchoring ropes were being lifted and the bridge man was shouting his last calls to those not traveling to debark from the ship. Without a second thought, Yam had swiftly grabbed a sack and run towards the bridge to get off the ship.

"THIEF!" the fat tradesman had shouted, alerting the men on the boat to catch him before he could escape.

Yam had noticed that the man on the bridge had blocked the path with his broad shoulders and stood ready to catch him. He had decided to jump off the side of the ship. Yam had landed neatly on a sack of dry beans placed on the wooden pier below. He had flipped and fallen on his back, all the brown beans scattering below him. And before he could stand, he had seen two boatmen running towards him. He had managed to get to his feet and sprint away in the other direction.

He wasn't always a thief, but he had not liked the greedy tradesman's cheap reward of six grape seeds after Yam had spent his whole morning helping the man carry his goods to the ship.

He had noticed the men after him weren't giving up and getting closer to him. The sack he had stolen wasn't too heavy, but he decided to get rid of it so he could run faster, and so he had thrown it far out to sea. He hadn't cared to have it as much as he cared to escape; he had stolen it only to spite the tradesman. He had run faster without the sack, and the men after him had stopped chasing him and had instead tried to retrieve it before it sank deeper in the water.

. . .

Tonight felt similar, even if it was more of a rescue than a theft. The child was a bit heavier than the sack of raisins, and most certainly not to be thrown away, and this time Yam's enemy was more dangerous than boatmen.

The snake could have bitten the child first. He felt fortunate to have reached the child in time.

After running a long distance, he could see the end of the path, the last line of palms and the flat plains behind the farms. He could feel from the horizon's glare that morning would soon be nearing, but it was still dark. He feared that Behas had already killed the father, flown above his head across the farms, and was waiting for him at the end of the path. He well knew that Behas wouldn't be killed easily; his only way to save the child was to run fast and reach Wadi Erum, a safe city where a wanted conjurer like Behas could not mingle unseen or unstopped.

As he neared the end of the path, he saw a white horse standing there, fully equipped and ready to go. Yam had reached the farms with the help of the horse's rider, who was now out of sight. *Where is he?* He stopped, looking back over his shoulders in search of the rider. The child had stopped crying but still whimpered. Yam's worst thoughts of Behas reaching him now seemed more real.

He searched his surroundings one last time. There was no sign of anyone, and the child began to make a louder wailing noise, which sounded to Yam like a warning that danger approached and worried him even more. He heard heavy footsteps from behind a short palm, so he decided to act quickly.

He turned to climb the horse, but it refused to respond to anyone but its original master. Yam struggled to handle the child in one hand and the disobedient white horse with the other.

"Leaving without me?" The rider came from behind him, moving quickly to calm the horse.

Yam did not bother to ask where he had been. "Quick. Behas is here; I saw him. The parents have been killed."

The thin rider, with no more words, mounted the horse and helped Yam up behind him with the chosen child they had been sent to save. He was fully aware that they weren't safe until they reached Wadi Erum.

Before the horse could gallop away, they were stopped by a shout from behind.

"Wait!" Fad had reached them just in time and was relieved to see his child safe.

Yam and the rider turned their heads to find the source of the shout. The rider, seeing a long-haired farmer with a spear-like tool in his hand, pulled out an Arabic curved dagger.

Fad pointed the spear's round tip at Yam. "Give me my son," he demanded while barely catching his breath.

The rider stared at Yam with confusion. "I thought you said Behas *killed* the parents?"

Yam ignored the rider's question, for he was confused to see the father alive himself. "Calm down, master. We seek no harm to you or your child," he said. "My name is Yam. I was sent by Erum's Prime Sheikh to save your son from Behas. I was the one who killed his snake. But I couldn't risk leaving the child and waiting for another trick from Behas; I had to take him with me and run. The orders we have are to take your son to the High Palace. Be assured that the sheikh will be pleased to know that you too are alive and well."

Fad felt reassured by the words he heard, and more by what he saw. The rider's brown belt and the straps around his white cloth, the unique dagger in his hands, and his full figure resembled those of the chosen guards and soldiers who served the prime sheikhs, the sacred lands, and the great people of Erum. They were known as the Guardians of Erum.

He lowered his spear, trusting their words. What they said made sense to him. If they had wanted to harm his son, he would have been dead next to his wife, and if they were stealing the child, they wouldn't have stopped for him.

Yam paused and stared at the dark shadows between the palms behind Fad. "What happened to Behas?" he asked. Then he switched his gaze to the farmer. "How did you escape him?"

"Behas is dead; I stuck his blade in his throat."

Impossible! Yam thought. His heartbeats quickened with the fear rapidly spreading through his veins. He now sensed that Behas would get to them. *He can't be dead.*

Yam hoped he would get an unexpected answer to his next question. "Was there any blood when you killed him?" he asked, his eyes searching for any bloodstains on the farmer's hands or light-colored wool tunic. *Just as I thought. No blood. We need to move faster before he can reach us. He is certainly still alive.*

The farmer did not notice it, but he spoke confidently. "Of course there was blood. His wrecked body is lying there in my farm."

He probably didn't kill him, but he can delay Behas until we reach Wadi Erum. "Then I'll say this, master: Bring his head to my master in Wadi Erum, and you will be well rewarded by the Mountain Queen."

The Mountain Queen! Fad realized that Yam was not from Wadi Erum—he was a Noorian, part of a guild of occultists that opposed all dark magic and wizards associated with the summoning of jinn, or so they claimed. This made Fad feel calmer about where his son would be going, but more mystified about the child's nature. Before he could ask, *What's wrong with my son?* they were both interrupted.

"You can't kill him at night. He must have used a protection jinni. These jinn, as I have heard from my friends, are stronger at night. A jinn master like Behas must surely have one." The rider interrupted them to remind them that Behas was more deceptive than one would think and was known to have powerful jinn. He sheathed his dagger, pulled it off his sash, and threw it to Fad, who grabbed it with his free hand.

"Listen, farmer. We know it's your child, but be assured he will be safer with us. The orders we have are to take him to the High Palace, and we cannot be delayed any further." The rider spoke with his superior guardians' tone now. "Go back and bury your wife properly. I am sorry we couldn't save her as well. And if Behas *is* dead, remember you will be rewarded by Erum as well."

The rider continued to direct the confused father, who seemed about to delay them with questions that would be better answered later. "By noon, come to the High Palace, show the guards my dagger, and ask for me by my name, Baaz. They shall bring you to me. I will take you to the Chief Guardian in Erum. Now, we have to go."

"Wait! I will come with you now," cried Fad, but the rider seemed to ignore him.

"Your child is safe with us. See you in the city," Yam added before they galloped away.

Fad froze in his place, watching the horse gallop away with his newborn child. He wasn't sure now if he should follow them or go back to his farm, as he remembered the two bodies lying back there. One he hoped would be alive, but was most likely dead, and the other, which he hoped to find dead, was more likely to be alive after what Yam and the rider, Baaz, had told him.

Suddenly, his thoughts were interrupted by the sounds of a man running up from behind him. Before he could turn around to see where the sound came from, the man's shadow passed him and continued to move towards the path the party on the horse were on, heading towards Wadi Erum.

Behas! He recognized the dark cloak flying towards the horse. It had to be him. *They were right. The saher is still alive.*

Fad quickly began to chase Behas in hopes of stopping him again, but the warlock moved much faster. He appeared almost as fast as the horse carrying the two men and child ahead of him.

Fad couldn't keep up and started losing sight of both the party on the horse and Behas, but he continued to run on the same path, hoping he would see them from above the hills. He knew that the city was almost an hour away, but with how fast he saw Behas running, he felt sure that the jinn master would catch up with them before they could reach the borders of Erum.

5

Behas's protection jinni, Gaddar, helped him run. He felt no loss of stamina or pain in his legs as he ran wildly and unnaturally behind his target, as if the jinni itself were running behind the horse.

But a trained horse can sense if it's being followed while it's running. This one pushed its head further out to gain more speed. Baaz, alerted, peeked over his shoulder and saw Behas running behind them. The jinn master seemed far away, and the rider trusted in his horse's speed. He felt that Yam, behind him, didn't need to know, as he was already busy holding tight to the child and the horse.

The rider kicked the horse's belly, giving it the traditional command to go faster. He also loosened his grip on the reins, releasing its head to allow it even more speed. Moving this quickly while there were two men on the horse was a bit risky, but the wadi wasn't far. He could see the blur of its shadow on the horizon, and he didn't want to risk Behas getting closer to them before they reached it.

Yam felt that the horse's gallop was now faster than ever, like they were flying with each step. He had always enjoyed the rhythm of a galloping Arabian horse, but tonight, being *on* the horse, clutching the rider in one hand and holding a child tight in the other, felt dangerous and unpleasant. He kept his head down the whole time, wanting to ask Baaz to slow down but also fearing Behas was still alive. He only prayed they would reach the city soon.

Behas suddenly started to get tired and noticed the horse was galloping faster. Gaddar must have betrayed him again. He decided to stop to catch his breath. "I guess I am getting too old to outrun a horse," he said, mocking himself for his jinn to hear and prepare themselves for his orders. "Zuhal, your turn," he said, barely catching his breath. "Stop them."

Although Zuhal was an old all-knowing jinni, Behas used him for almost everything else his other jinn did not do. Zuhal was wise enough to find a way to perform the task, to direct Behas to the best way of doing it, or to tell him which other jinn could accomplish their master's wishes and demands.

Behas had no clue how Zuhal could do it. Nor did he care. He trusted his wisest and creepiest jinni to deliver.

Without revealing himself, Zuhal whispered in Behas's ear, "With pleasure, Master Behas."

Baaz looked back from his shoulder again to find that Behas had stopped and was growing farther away. *Good, he's tired.* He thought they were safe but felt he shouldn't slow his horse until they reached the city.

But then, all of a sudden, the horse lost its balance and flipped while galloping at its highest speed, tossing everyone off its back and far from each other into the darkness of the last hour of night!

Zuhal enjoyed being tasked with evil doings. He had no ability to transform into a physical being, but unlike many other jinn, who unwillingly remained invisible, he had the wisdom to choose when to reveal his true form.

All he had to do that night was manifest in front of the horse to scare it while it was galloping at speed. In the darkness of night, the horse was easily overcome by fear.

Its riders fell, scattered and unconscious in the dark, as Behas approached them effortlessly.

...

Jinn cannot be seen in their true forms, at least not by our human eyes. It is merely impossible. Unlike we humans, who are made of physical matter, they are made of smokeless fire, a form of energy like sound waves or light waves. We cannot see the energetic form of the waves, but we can hear them or see their reflections on other objects after our minds translate the information received by our eyes. So it is with us and the jinn.

The *inns* and *jinn*. *Inns* is Arabic for "humans," which literally means the unhidden, or the revealed. The Arabic word *jinn*, on the other hand, literally means the unseen, or the hidden.

The all-knowing jinni, Zuhal, could possess weak minds and place images in them. That is what he did to the horse, playing a trick that made it scared of what it thought it saw, a hideous beast standing in its path.

...

Yam's eyelids felt heavy as he tried to open them after the fall. Everything had happened in a single second. He had held on to the horse tightly, trying not to fall, until he suddenly found himself gliding fast towards the ground.

When he was almost unconscious, his ears were assaulted by the loud sobbing cries of the child, who was clearly in pain. Luckily, the baby was wrapped well in thick cloth, and Yam had held him tight and protected him when they fell. "Hang in there, child," he tried to whisper to him.

Yam tried to stand, but the pain in his legs, waist, and back kept him from doing so. He struggled to sit or even to move the child closer to him. The sobbing made him more nervous. He checked the child to see he wasn't injured, but he found a slight scratch on the boy's left cheek. The boy was crying in pain. "Don't worry, child; we will be okay," he tried in an effort to calm the frightened child down. Honestly, he too felt frightened, and he remembered his own mother and how she would calm him down when he felt afraid or injured.

Yam wondered how he would continue to carry the boy to the wadi, and he became more concerned. To add to his worries, he heard someone coming closer to him. He turned to find Behas walking towards him.

He tried to move or say something, but the brisk pain constrained him. He wouldn't be able to fight or protect the child now. *Oh no!* He placed an arm over the child to cover him. He could offer nothing else in defense.

Behas leaned over Yam, pulled his arm away, and kicked him aggressively. "Are you the one who killed my jinni?"

Yam couldn't open his mouth.

Behas then lifted the child in his arms and stared peacefully at him as he pulled out a dagger. Yam noticed it was bigger than the white one before, and fancier too, made of gold instead of bone.

The child began to cry louder.

"No, Behas!" Yam finally got out. "Please, don't kill him!"

Behas whispered in the child's ear an ancient language only the jinn spoke. The boy ceased to cry and instantly went motionless and silent.

Yam, helpless and speechless under the dark shadow of Behas, opened his eyes wide in disbelief. He had failed to save the boy.

6

The High Palace of Erum was situated at the highest point on the upper part of the wadi.

Geographically, Wadi Erum was a large, complex city, rooted in a chain of interconnected valleys that veined a rocky terrain. The walls of the valleys formed the lower parts of the city. Homes were caves, carved on both sides of each valley wall, up to a height of three levels and connected with a series of carved stairs. They were dug elegantly, with neat, ornamented doors and windows. Above, the valleys were roofed with another level of stone houses, these ones roofed with dry palm leaves and simple tents and connected with hanging bridges that shaded the ground below.

The land around Wadi Erum was flat. Some of it was desert, but there were also plenty of green farm fields on the banks of two rivers that snaked around and through the city. One river crossed through the valley, and the other turned around its northern side, forming a crescent shape. Both flowed from the mountains far to the south and eventually turned around Wadi Erum to the east, where they merged. The two rivers fed the city through natural and manmade channels. Low streams of water ran in the middle of the valley floors and streets.

And from every corner of the wadi, people could see the High Palace. Its name may have come from its high raised pillars from its position at the top of the valley, or from the high sheikhs who occupied it. They were high in both power and in physical size, being the largest men to ever walk and rule over Arabia.

Gazing out one of the windows of the High Palace was Prince Zufar, one of the many sons of Aad, the Prime Sheikh of Erum at that time. He too was a giant of a man, at almost eleven feet tall. The whole royal family was like that, almost twice the height of an average man. Their size was the main reason why they had ruled the land for such a long time. Ever since they had inhabited the Wadi of Erum, they had claimed their right to rule over Arabia. They had built magnificent raised pillars to guide pilgrims from all over Arabia, which gave the famous city the name Erum of Lofty Pillars.

Prince Zufar had been assigned by his father to deal with a request that had come from Erum's allies, the Noorians, who had asked for the Prime Sheikh's help in saving a child from the outlaw warlock Behas. Zufar did not sleep that night, as he and the Noorians were trying to identify who the calamitous child was and where Behas would strike. As soon as they knew which farm was being targeted, the young prince had given the orders to send only one rider with Yam, in hopes that they would be faster and could snatch the child before Behas did. But now, as time passed, he was worried that he would fail his father, the Prime Sheikh. That feeling pinched his heart at the exact moment when the horse carrying his men tripped and threw them to the ground. But he, seated far away in his comfortable abode, couldn't be sure of his feelings; he could only wait and hope and worry.

Prince Zufar turned his face inside to the *majlis*, or sitting room, where he, the Chief Guardian of Erum, and an old occultist from the Noorian Guild were waiting for the child to be rescued.

"It has taken them long," said the giant prince, looking down at the Chief Guardian. "I sense that they might face some trouble."

The young prince was huge, yet he wasn't the largest man in the palace. His father and older brothers were slightly bigger than he was. He was rather known for being the most handsome prince in the palace, with the blackest hair, the largest eyes, a gentle nose, thin lips, and a little beard that did not fill all his face. His skin tone was a bit lighter than his brothers'—the reason for which, he thought, was that he remained in the palace most of his time and traveled less outside the city of Erum. That also left him with the weakest body out of all the brothers, but his muscles were still neatly sculpted and strong.

"Relax, my sheikh; we have sent our finest horseman and our fastest horse. If my predictions are correct, they should arrive in less than half an hour," the Chief Guardian, Bessel, reassured his impatient prince. He knew how far the farms were and could predict how long it would take two thin men to travel there. Their light weights on a horse meant they would make it to the farms and back faster than any others. That was the only reason the Chief Guardian had picked them for the mission, and that was a big mistake. Though he did not know it yet, he had underestimated Behas and should have suggested to his prince that they send more men.

Zufar was not fully convinced. He stared at a large, elegant hourglass made of wood and edged in bronze. The sand particles dropped through it, measuring time precisely. Less than a quarter of the sand remained in the upper bulb, and the prince felt more worried after his Chief Guardian's words.

Bessel looked like he was in his early thirties, with a warm skin tone and a strong body, but he was in fact more than fifty years old. He was an experienced Chief Guardian and important advisor who rarely gave the wrong advice, but when he did make an error, it was disastrous.

"One rider alone was not enough. If they have encountered Behas…" murmured the old Noorian in attempt to alert the prince and indirectly object to his orders to send only one horseman.

Bessel heard him and went through his reasons again. "One horseman is faster, and he and your student are thin and will travel faster than any of us. Besides, our strong Guardians are protected and can't be *touched* by Behas's jinn. I am sure they have reached the child before him and are now approaching." He was right, to a point—the Guardians of Erum were protected from the jinn, but unfortunately, their horses weren't!

It was Bessel's advice to the prince to send only one rider, but the prince heard the murmuring of his father's guest. He did not want to be blamed if the rescue failed, nor to lose the trust of the Noorians and be seen as a young prince who could not make decisions of his own. He remembered a time when one of his older brothers failed their father, and it was not a position he wanted to see himself in.

"Send more horsemen," he ordered his Chief Guardian, Bessel. "And prepare my horse now. I sense Behas and his jinn are after them. Dawn is near, but I cannot risk him delaying the rescue." He took another glance at the hourglass. He thought his decision would have been best if it had been earlier, but it wasn't too late, he hoped. He switched his gaze back to Bessel. "The child must be here before my father is awake."

Bessel nodded and left swiftly to arrange for their departure.

...

Earlier that night, the Prime Sheikh, Aad, had been finishing his supper in his large majlis with all the high men and sheikhs of all other tribes allied with the Sheikhdom of Erum. There were highly respected tradesmen as well, along with councilors, respected scientists, poets, and many friends and relatives, including his sons, who had come to feast. Every night, guests filled his majlis, and the activities held were as the sheikhs desired. Sometimes they would compete in poetry, or compare the quality of each other's harvests, or discuss religious philosophies and so on.

That night was a regular gathering night for Aad, until his Chief Guardian, Bessel, stood beside him, waiting for him to finish washing his hands. Aad sensed Bessel's shadow. Although Aad sat on the ground, he was large and tall enough that a regular-height man like Bessel would still be shorter even if he were standing. Aad did not look away from the water in the fancy bowl of silver in front of him, and once he finished washing his hands, the servant holding the bowl of water walked away and another reached closer to hand the Prime Sheikh a dry cloth.

Aad knew that Bessel would most likely come to him during the time of the gathering, when new guests were outside and asked to meet the Prime Sheikh. He never minded offering his generosity, but as all his guests were just finishing their meals, these new guests had come at an unpleasant time.

Bessel felt he shouldn't rush with it. He waited for the Prime Sheikh to finish drying his hands and raise his head to gaze on the vast hall before him. His endlessly talkative guests were all busy washing and drying their hands but never took a break from talking. *A hornet's nest, and the loudest buzzer is always the strongest,* thought Bessel every time he walked through this majlis or observed it from the sidelines.

Positioning himself near Aad's right shoulder, where he should stand when bringing good news or non-urgent matters to his sheikh, Bessel began to speak. He did not need to whisper, as the noise in the majlis would cover the sound of his voice. "A request from the Mountain Queen," he said. Bessel did not dare mention her name before his sheikh but referred to her by her common title, given to her because the lands she ruled were high above the tallest mountain in the southern lands.

As Bessel spoke with the Prime Sheikh, Yam and his old Noorian master, Arkin, were left standing before the main entrance of the majlis, waiting for the guards to allow them in. The guards in Wadi Erum wore blue, which differentiated them from the chosen Guardians, who wore white. Arkin was upset at having to wait while he held an urgent letter from his queen, but Yam felt dazzled and excited to be in the magnificent City of Erum. And now he was about to enter the High Palace. *This is a dream! No one would believe me,* he thought. Raised among orphan kids by his poor mother, he had never imagined that one day he would meet with the Prime Sheikh of Erum. He thought that agreeing to serve an old occultist, who had promised him a rich reward of silver and offered him knowledge and food in exchange for his service as a porter, had not been a bad idea.

...

He remembered the day he had first met Arkin.

"Why did you steal the sack?" asked an old man covered in thick gray clothing who was seated on the ground behind a wall near the port where Yam had stopped for breath after managing to escape the angry shipmen.

He looked down at the source of the voice in disbelief. The old man sat with his back against a brown wall of stacked flat rocks and dry mud, enjoying the shade and sea breeze. All Yam could see under the gray cloth was an old humble face with a wide white beard. *Was he watching me?* But the man could not have seen what had happened from where he sat. *A mystic fortune teller, or maybe a wizard.* Both creeped Yam out, and the question now made him feel guilty for what he had done.

"The cheap tradesman gave me only six grape seeds after I helped him carry his dry fruit onto the ship," Yam protested in defense of his actions. "And he had plenty of fruit. I took only a few."

The old man, still staring away from Yam, opened his mouth to speak again. "And did you take the seeds?" he asked, revealing a grin.

"Yes. Here they are." Yam opened his palm to show the stranger the dry seeds. "You can have them if you want," he offered in an attempt to befriend the wizard judging him.

"No, thank you! Why would I want to have six useless seeds?" His face expressed his lack of interest as he turned his head aside to look back at Yam. "I am not even a farmer."

Yam felt ridiculous. At first, the old man's question about why he stole the fruit had felt like an interrogation, but now the man appeared to be mocking him.

"If you had refused the seeds the man offered you after your hard work, he might have given you something else. But you unwillingly accepted them and then decided to punish the tradesman, who thought he was offering you a great reward," the old man continued, "if you had happened to be a farmer. Treated grape seeds are *not* easily found in these lands. I think you should plant them somewhere near water, a place you can remember later.

"Please excuse my intrusion. My name is Arkin, son of Rakin, and I am here only for a day's rest before I continue my journey to Samhan Mountain. I am also looking to hire a young man who would help me in my travel."

Yam didn't resent the intrusion at all, yet he wondered what the man was that he would be traveling to Samhan Mountain. *Must be an occultist, an old man of knowledge, not a sinister saher, I suppose,* he thought.

"My name is Yam, and I am honored to meet you, Master Arkin," Yam greeted him in return. "May I ask how long your journey would be?" He thought he should accept whatever work would take him far from the port, at least until the men looking for him would have forgotten about him.

"Days, or maybe weeks, but nothing more than a month."

"Short! And what would you offer me, Master Arkin?"

"A generous amount of silver, the kind of sum that can buy you a horse. I serve great masters in these lands, and I know that you would not accept dry seeds. Do we have an agreement? Or do you still have more questions?"

Silver? Who is this man? The port never ceased to amaze Yam with the variety of men he encountered who came and left every day. Yam had been born far from here and moved to Sumhuram only for an opportunity to succeed and change his poor life. *I don't need a horse, but I am finally building myself a fishing boat with his reward.* Yam didn't hesitate to take the job; he wouldn't be one who would let such an opportunity pass by. "Of course we have an agreement. I'm in your service as long as you want." Yam saw Arkin smile and felt the reward was already his, an easy take, until another thought occurred to him. He thought he had the right to know for sure if his client was a simple man of knowledge or a warlock of any wicked sort that might lurk in the mountains of the Noorians. Yam didn't want to be involved in dark magic. "I do have one question: How did you know that I stole the sack of raisins from a boat far away from where you sit? Are you a sorcerer?"

The old man laughed. "I am no saher; I am a man of knowledge. A Noorian occultist, nothing else. I only heard the cries that disturbed my nap: 'Thief!' 'My fruit! He stole my fruit!' Then I heard the men running on the pier until one stopped and called to the others, 'The sack is in the water; he threw it away.' Seconds later, a young man barely catching his breath was standing above me, peeking from behind the wall to see if he succeeded in evading his pursuers."

Yam smiled in admiration. The weird old man looked more interesting than he had thought at first. "Another question." Yam now felt that Arkin would be an enthusiastic companion to journey with. *I will enjoy this journey,* he thought.

"I hope I can answer," Arkin said humbly.

A wide and enthusiastic smile spread across Yam's face as he asked, "When shall we leave?"

...

"Behold, Yam. We have finally arrived."

Yam did not reply; he was too busy being tired. He paused to breathe, relieved to hear that the walk had finally ended.

Arkin had finally announced the end of the journey after they had hiked up a foggy range of green plains and hills, then farther up to reach this pale rocky terrain they had been in for almost four hours. They had hiked so high that the port they left from was no longer visible from above the clouds and thick fog. The sun felt hotter than below, and they were not even at the top yet; they had only reached an empty opening, a circle at the foot of a higher mountain peak, bald and formed of brown and gray rocks.

They talked little as they climbed—just regular discussions about the path and how to get to their destination, or where they should stop to rest. Yam, being a porter, had been taught not to annoy his clients with unnecessary questions. Though he had many of those in his mind, such as what Arkin was traveling for, what the Noorians did, and where their secret hideout was and what it looked like, he kept all those questions to himself. *Deliver, take the reward, and go back,* he kept reminding himself. And when they reached their destination, he decided to remain silent, never imagining that all his questions were just about to be answered. His whole life was about to be changed, and forever.

"Is this place a beauty or not?" asked Arkin. He stood a few steps ahead of Yam and appeared to be asking himself. He even wondered what beauty Arkin was referring to—the open round cave entrance before them or the higher tip above, which was known as the Samhan Mountain.

Yam eyed the same mountaintop his master was gazing at. It hadn't been fully visible from below, but now, when they had climbed higher and passed the thick fog, they were able to see it. He shifted his gaze to Arkin, then back again to the mountain. *More mountains to climb,* he feared. There was nothing special to see here. After a long journey climbing the mountain range, he thought they had passed by scenes that were more beautiful for them to stop and wonder at, places such as Wadi Darbat or Tawi Atyar.

"So," Yam finally spoke. "How much farther will we need to walk to reach the Gray Palace?"

Arkin laughed. But Yam sighed, keeping his face blank and staring off in frustration. "We have arrived, my son," the old man said, repeating his initial announcement, then explained, "This *is* the palace of our queen. It is *here* where the Noorians hide."

Yam raised his eyebrows, faking his surprise. He had heard the first announcement and was aware that this *was* probably their destination, but he didn't want to look ridiculous and ask where the palace was. *Is he referring to the mountain itself?* The mountain was enormous, but there were no signs of any manmade structures to be seen, though the opening did have smooth, flat, straight walls. He fixed his gaze on the opening below, two times his height.

You could have just said "cave." Yam thought the so-called palace of the queen was probably much smaller and less dazzling than what he had in mind. He had heard that many men came wandering these mountains, in search of the famous palace where all the occultists and great minds of the Noorians claimed to have come from. All the adventurers came back with nothing, and the tales of the Gray Palace of knowledge and wisdom were thought to be fake. *They should have been looking for a cave,* thought Yam.

"Before we enter, you must understand that you are no longer a porter." Arkin lowered his voice. "You are now my student, a novice occultist. And if anyone asks, you are serving me of your own will in exchange for knowledge and wisdom."

Yam took a moment to sort it out; he was in fact learning from the old wise man, and he portered willingly, but in exchange for silver, not knowledge! "You promised my reward would be in silver," Yam reminded his master.

"I will keep my promise," Arkin reassured the young man, "when our purpose is fully achieved."

Our purpose? Yam thought to himself. "I thought *my* purpose was only to carry your bags."

"You are no longer a porter; you are my student, remember! And our purpose is to save a child from being killed."

"What child?"

"I will explain it all to you inside, after we feast properly and rest. Now let me introduce you to the Gray Palace," he continued with a broad smile. "A place no ordinary man can see." Arkin walked near the opening and then pulled a flute-like instrument from one of his sacks and blew into it, producing a rich and brilliant musical tone.

The tones caught Yam's attention and made him curious, but deep inside, he was afraid of what would happen next.

Arkin stopped and lowered his flute. They heard the echoes of the musical notes fade away into the opening until there was nothing but the familiar slight breeze blowing gently in their ears. Then, after a long, awkward moment of silence, a large rock on the right wall of the opening began to move slowly, revealing the doorway to a cave. The insides were illuminated with a yellow glow of strange lights, neither sunlight nor fire. Yam couldn't comprehend what it was that caused the illumination. The walls were carved geometrically to present an elegant gateway into mystery. *The hidden gate of the Gray Palace,* thought Yam. *Couldn't we have just knocked on the door?*

"Follow me. Let us meet with the Noorians, and let us find proper food to eat," said Arkin.

As they walked inside, Yam felt the cave, or "palace," as they liked to call it, was empty! At least, the entrance was. No one came to welcome them in. And the entrance led to a narrow tunnel dug into the heart of the mountain. One could see the end of the tunnel far away, and Yam did notice gray cloaks moving inside from far.

"You can leave the bags there." Arkin pointed towards a wooden trolley for Yam to place their bags on. Yam carried three bags. One was his, and two were Arkin's. And as Yam deposited them, a strange, loud mechanical noise broke the dead silence. At first Yam thought he had broken something, but then he realized it was just the gate shutting behind them. *What kind of sorcery is this?*

"We can bring them in later." Arkin stopped him from pushing the trolley in with them.

"Who's opening and closing the door?" he asked Arkin as he followed him inside through the yellow lit cave. "Is your flute like a key or something? Does every Noorian carry one?" He hadn't asked anything at all for the whole journey—frankly, he hadn't seen the need—but now, he seemed to embrace the idea of being a student and of learning.

"My flute is much more than a key. And yes, every Noorian has one."

"What else can you do with your flute?"

"Later, Yam. We can talk later." Arkin silenced him as they neared the end of the tunnel.

They reached a wider open space dug within the mountain. The grounds were clean, the walls were so elegantly carved that Yam wondered if the Noorians were men of knowledge or artists, and the ceiling—or rather, the roof of the cave—was high and brightly lit with what Yam later learned was not magic but rather a sort of chemical invention the Noorians had learned from Babylon.

Ancient Babylonian lightbulbs!

There were about six people in the hall. Some sat, some were walking by, and some were standing to talk with one another. Only one, a short, chubby man with a friendly old face, smiled at the newcomers.

"Arkin, is that you?" He hugged the old occultist hard as if he hadn't seen him for a long time. "Where have you been all this time? It's been years since we last met, old man."

Years? Yam kept that thought to himself.

"Meet my student, Yam," said Arkin. "Yam, this is Kareem. We call him Bader. How can I put this? He is the Noorian responsible for all the food in the palace. We met the right person; we are starving after a long journey from the port."

Bader laughed and leaned his head backwards as he did. When Yam saw him laugh, he noticed his round belly and he knew why the Noorians called him that. *Bader* is Arabic for "full moon"! And he, with his round shape, did look like a full moon.

"Follow me, then, Arkin, Yam. I will take you to the supper room."

The supper "room" was rather a huge hall that could fit all the tens of Noorians who occupied the palace in times of ceremonies. The supper room was also lit by ancient lightbulbs, but the walls weren't decorated as much as those in the center hall. The eating tables and benches were mainly made out of short, but well-cut and elegantly shaped, stones.

Kareem seated his guests near the entrance, and then he came back with plates and a pot of cooked food. Like the benches, the plates and pot were made of gray stone.

"Is Hadaus here today?" Arkin asked as they sat and feasted.

"I did see him this morning, but he might have left for his usual hunt for healing herbs around the mountain," Kareem replied. "You seem worried, Arkin. I don't remember seeing you so lost in your thoughts. Is everything all right?"

"Everything is, yes. But I have come on important business. I need to speak with the queen."

Yam stopped eating and started listening. Before they entered, Arkin had spoken of some purpose, but he never explained what it was to Yam. He now remembered and was more eager to know what *did* bother the old man. He hadn't spoken much the whole journey, so Yam had thought he was usually like that. But his old friend Kareem, here in the palace, sensed something else.

"The world outside the Gray Palace has troubled you," said Kareem. "Have no worries, Arkin. Everything will be fine."

"Everything will, Kareem." Arkin turned to face Kareem and bit his lips, forcing a smile. "I hope."

As he said it, a man with red hair entered. He looked to be in his mid-forties. Yam noticed that he looked surprised when his eyes fell on Arkin. "Arkin?" He furrowed his brow. "What brings you here to the Gray Palace?" he questioned.

"El Sarabi!" Arkin stood and greeted him with a smile. "I could ask you the same thing!"

Yam, too, stood. "Hello, master." He bowed.

Kareem came to greet him as well, thinking El Sarabi might have passed by the supper room for a drink.

Arkin introduced Yam, and then he introduced El Sarabi. "Meet El Sarabi, Yam. He is an occultist from the southern island, Socotra. Like me, he leads his own guild of occultists in his hometown. They call themselves the Noorians of the Dragon."

"You *lead* a guild of occultists?" Yam asked Arkin. He forgot he was supposed to act as the man's student, and as soon as he saw the look on Arkin's face, he remembered. "Oh, yeah, right. *Our* guild." He tried to laugh and cover his mistake. *A porter should never ask questions,* he thought, reminded of the advice his mentor back at the port would always give him and the other young porters.

"How long are you staying, Arkin?" asked El Sarabi.

"Not long. The spy Hadaus assigned to watch Behas sent me a letter. I had asked him to do so earlier." Arkin spoke openly. "Behas is coming after a child. I plan to save it this time."

Behas? Yam thought. His mother had told him a tale or two about Behas, an envious and evil jinn master who once released a powerful jinni on a poor village and turned them all into goats for the sake of pleasing his evil jinnic lords!

"I see," said El Sarabi. "Good luck with that, Arkin."

El Sarabi wished them luck and disappeared.

The three went back to their stone seats.

"Again with the child, Arkin? You seem to be determined as always about this *child*," said Kareem.

"No one believes me now, but they will."

Kareem sighed. "Oh, well, then I too shall wish you luck, as I always have."

"Thank you."

Kareem left Arkin and Yam alone in the supper room to finish their meal in peace.

Yam began: "I am sorry about the question I asked; I shouldn't have. But I do have many questions, master. And I shall ask only if you allow it."

"I don't tend to blame you. I have placed you in this sudden position. And do ask; this is a good time."

"Well, you said you led a guild! Then why is it that you are traveling alone? And why are you here? After what I had sensed, a very long time ago? What child are you here to save from—" Yam paused, as he wasn't sure of the name he had heard Arkin say before. "Behas? The jinn master, Behas?"

Arkin laughed. "That's a lot of questions, but I shall answer them. You have the right to know. I come from Ibri, a small village far in the east. As to my guild, well, we are only three: me and my two daughters. And this mission is dangerous for them. It was best that they stayed behind to take care of their mother."

"And what do you call your guild?" Yam interrupted. "Or *our* guild, I mean. I should try to remember that."

Arkin laughed. "We call ourselves Noorians as well. Occultists choose special names, but not us. After all, we all serve the same queen."

"Will I meet her?"

"Very unlikely," Arkin replied. "I will take you around the palace later and show you some of its rooms, but you will not be allowed to see the whole thing. The Noorians here are secretive. Now what were your other questions?"

Yam asked again. "What purpose did we come for? The child. *Behas*."

"Right! The reason I am here, Yam. Well, how can I explain it all in simple words? A special child is born under a special star. No man can tell what this child is, nor does anyone understand the potential power the star it is born under has, but Behas. He seems to be the only one to know about them, and every time a child is born under that star, he kills it."

"Is he afraid of an omen?" Yam asked. "Does he think the child will grow up to kill him?"

"Nothing like that, Yam. This is not a fairy tale your mother tells you before you sleep! It is way beyond that. Behas explained some of it to me before, and he is always determined to kill such an infant. He claims the child can be used to summon great evil."

Arkin continued to explain what he could to Yam, even as they passed through the Gray Palace or met with other Noorians. They spent the whole day talking about it. Yam agreed to help Arkin save the child, although he felt that only the old man cared about it. All the Noorians seemed to ignore Arkin's ideas. To them, children being killed by jinn masters was a common evil that occurred every now and then. It should be stopped, all of it, the Noorians agreed on that, but they did not agree that a particular child was special just because Behas targeted it.

...

At the end of that day, Arkin left Yam in the room given to them and went alone to finally meet in private with the highest-ranked Noorian, Hadaus, who was an African-Arabian occultist in his late forties.

Arkin wanted to convince the queen to help him in his quest to save the child. But to get to her, he needed to convince Hadaus first.

Hadaus got upset at first when he learned that his spy had contacted Arkin, but Arkin pleaded that he needed the man for a greater cause.

"Fine, he can help you, but do not involve him in any fight. I do not want him to get exposed and be caught by Behas."

"He won't get involved with Behas; you have my word."

"Then what do you need from us? You can save the child on your own."

"I seek only her forgiveness. I need her blessing."

"She will not see you. Why would she trust you again, Arkin?"

"Hadaus, if it weren't for me, you would have been an outcast as well. I hope you have never forgotten that. You know how much it hurt me; I cannot live as an outcast forever. It has been twenty years now since—since the incident. I need her forgiveness. And I will save the child this time, trust me."

Hadaus paused for a long time. "Fine, I will talk to her in the morning. But if she refuses to see you, accept it and leave."

Arkin nodded.

7

The next morning, Arkin had told Yam to wait in the hallway while he went to meet with the queen in private. As he sat in the well-decorated cave outside Her Majesty's main hall, two young occultists had passed by. They had stared at him as if they despised him, and one had murmured to his friend in a language Yam did not comprehend.

Queen of no land, but only a cave, and her people are egoistic freaks, he thought to himself. He had not enjoyed his you're-not-allowed-to-see-the-whole-palace tour of the hidden dark caves. He felt he wasn't welcome amongst the Noorians, and no one was friendly to him but Arkin.

Yam got bored while waiting, as the meeting with the queen took hours. He even slept for a while, then decided to walk around a bit. *I'd rather wait in the garden.*

...

The garden of the Gray Palace was one of few chambers where sunlight entered from above. The air in it smelled fresh and clean, and it made Yam feel relaxed every time he explored it.

The concealed garden was not used to harvest food but rather to study the floral world. The room was frequented mostly by the alchemists, and they had discovered many ways to use plants for medicine. They had proven to the world around them that men needn't depend on jinn masters who summoned healing jinn for remedies, which was a huge business at that time.

Yam had entered the garden that day and begun to explore the new shapes of strange short plants. Many he recalled seeing outside, but they looked weirder here. The many bizarre shapes and colors placed in one cave made it feel as if one were walking through the jinnic realm.

That day, walking through the garden, he had noticed someone else crouched and working on the plants. Although she looked pretty, the Noorians' attitude towards Yam had made him despise them all. He had ignored her presence and turned to explore a strange-looking short tree.

It had a smooth trunk, and its branches were bulky, almost as wide as the trunk itself. They looked like creepy heads. A globe of long, spiky, stiff leaves that exploded from the end of each branch and fell like wet green hair formed the crown. He'd seen it a few times on his journey through the mountains with Arkin. It had looked normal back then amongst the rocks, but here it looked out of place. *Like a sad witch,* he thought. Outside, its leaves had not been sad and falling. He had recalled them being sharp and standing straight up, like pointed arrows ready for an archer to pull out and shoot. Here, the leaves looked weak and gloomy. The trunk looked as if it had been injured; on one side of it was a cut that had created a red spot, like an open wound that was still shiny with blood. He had reached with his fingertip to touch it and found that it was wet.

After eyeing the red stain carefully, he had smelled it. It hadn't smelled bad. But before he could think of tasting it, a sharp voice had called from nearby, "Don't eat that!"

He had turned and found the garden lady standing behind him, with a mocking smile on her bright face, and had stood up to face her and apologize. He had assumed she was much older than he was, but as he'd looked closer, he'd found her to be younger than he had originally thought. "I'm sorry for that." He rubbed the stain on his finger with his messy tunic. "I was just waiting here for Master Arkin."

"You can wait as long as you want," she said with a smile, and Yam felt that smile was the nicest thing he'd seen in the past few days. "But do be careful with this tree. Hadaus would punish us both if you injured it. It's his favorite tree." She shot a glance at the tree and then back at Yam. The smile never left her face.

Yam knew who Hadaus was. *The mean alchemist,* he called him. He had known she was right; the man might even punish him just for looking at the tree. But this new mistress he hadn't seen before was nice to Yam, which encouraged him to talk more with her.

"Is it a poisonous tree? Like its owner?" he asked.

She laughed but opened her eyes wide and looked around as if making sure no one had heard. Yam didn't care; he had liked the woman and her laugh.

"Oh, no, it isn't," she said. "It's an Arabian dragon tree. Haven't you seen it before?"

"I have, yes. But I've never seen it bleeding." He looked at the red wound one more time. "Is that what it's called?"

"Indeed, that is its name. Aren't you from these lands?"

"I'm from Port Rori. My name is Yam," he finally found the chance to tell her.

She raised her eyebrows. "From the port! And you've never heard of this tree?"

"No. Should I have?"

"Well! For one thing, ropes are made from its leaves. They make the strongest of the cordage used every day in the port to take the heavy sacks of frankincense on and off the big ships." She then faced the tree and held one of its long leaves. "The strings inside of the leaves are strong and are also used to make slingshots and bowstrings. The center of its crown is food to the mountain folk. Its wood is used to make drums, and the red liquid you've touched is used to make remedies. It is similar to the dragon-blood trees in Socotra, but not of the same size or quality. The ones there are ten times the size of this little tree. A young occultist like you should always wonder and think about how everything around him is made and from what."

Yam had always thought himself to be a curious person and a seeker of knowledge, until he met this beautiful gardener, or alchemist. He never learned her name, but he never forgot her beauty.

"I have thought about many things before in my life, but never to this level of detail. To be honest, I have learned more in these few days with Arkin and you, the Noorians, I mean, than I have ever before. I am truly enlightened."

"Well, that is why we call ourselves the Noorians," she ended with a charming smile. *Noorians* was an Arabic term that meant "enlighteners." Many didn't know.

He had heard familiar sounds of doors closing in the Gray Palace. "I had best go back to Master Arkin," he said and bowed to excuse himself.

"Have a nice day, Yam."

His heart had enjoyed the sound of his name on her lips, but he had only smiled politely and walked away.

Sitting before the closed gate of the queen's hall, he couldn't stop thinking of the beautiful Noorian he'd just met. He felt happy, and everything around him instantly became nicer. If he ever came back to this cave, it would be just to see her again.

...

The white-painted brass door, hinged in the gray walls of the mountain rocks, dazzled him. It looked elegant and fit to lead into a queen's private hall. The door swung open slightly for Arkin to walk out and was shut before Yam could see anything inside, but he noticed the rays of sunlight that illuminated part of the walls inside. *That chamber has windows too!*

"Did it all go well, Master Arkin?" he asked. After waiting two days to finally identify where the child had been born, he knew Arkin had to act faster to save it.

Arkin's face was gloomy as the hall went darker again. "All is well," he said worriedly. "But we have to travel quickly to Erum. We don't have much time to waste; Behas is headed for the child tonight."

Without a word, Yam followed Arkin through the hallway until the old man suddenly stopped and looked at him with fury in his eyes. *It didn't go well, I suppose,* thought Yam.

"I will be honest with you," Arkin whispered. "The Noorians and the queen herself did not fully care to help us; it is only you and me now. But Hadaus convinced the queen to at least write us a letter so we could ask for help from Erum, since the child is expected to be found there. I should say, whatever happens tonight, I will do whatever I can to keep the child safe from Behas's evil grasp."

After his day and a half in the cold caves of the Gray Palace, learning and understanding Behas's profligate nature, Yam had nodded, also enraged. "I will too, Master Arkin."

...

When they reached Wadi Erum later that evening, they were told to wait outside the High Palace. Arkin began to lose his patience. He had explained the urgency of his matter to Bessel and even had a letter written by the Mountain Queen herself to the Prime Sheikh, asking for his help. But he was unfortunate to have arrived at the wrong time. He was aware that the sheikh's majlis was full and busy at this time of the night, and it would be difficult for the Prime Sheikh of Erum to leave his guests for an issue that he might have no great interest in: the child Behas was after.

The gate finally opened, and Bessel walked towards them at a slow pace, showing no sign of urgency or interest.

Relieved to hear the sound of the grand decorated gate of bronze and painted wood finally swinging open, Arkin leaped towards Bessel. He was followed by Yam, whose heart was also pounding in excitement to enter the High Palace, but that excitement faded suddenly when the gate behind Bessel shut again, apparently having opened only to allow his exit.

Bessel witnessed the change in the emotional reactions of his waiting guests. He stopped and explained, "I will escort you inside the palace, but not through the main majlis. The Prime Sheikh will not be seeing you tonight; he has assigned his son, Sheikh Zufar, to handle your urgent request. I have read the letter to the sheikh, and he is waiting for you above in the sage's chamber."

The two guests nodded obediently.

Bessel now turned towards the other side of the gate. "Follow me," he said, waving his hand to direct them ahead as the three walked in silence to enter from another side of the High Palace.

. . .

Prince Zufar left the main majlis after he had spoken with Bessel and asked the oldest sage in Erum to accompany him. The letter from the queen had requested him by name. "We plead urgently for the wisdom and guidance of the respected sage Hammah Bin-Hyem. Save the child of Unuk-Al Hai." Prince Zufar did not comprehend the full urgency or the details of what the Noorians were asking for. His father rarely assigned anything of high importance to him, and he did not sense that this night would end up being as long and complex as it became.

In the sage's work chamber, Zufar asked him calmly but boldly, "What urgent matter would the queen need you for? I do not sense urgency, nor do I see any importance in this letter. If there were, my father would have assigned my brother to handle it." He referred to the Crown Prince, his eldest brother.

Hammah had been the advisor of Zufar's father and grandfather before him; he was the oldest person in the palace or maybe the whole city. Strangely, however, he still looked in his late forties; his gray head still had a few black hairs, his skin was not very wrinkled, and his body was well sculpted. "Do not allow your emotions to take control of your judgments, my sheikh. I do not know what they desire, but they are a close ally to the sheikhdom of your father. Do not dismiss their importance, or your own."

"We shall see," said Zufar, turning to face the doorway when he heard footsteps coming near. Three men walked in: the Chief Guardian, Bessel; Arkin, the old occultist, whom Zufar had seen once or twice before in his father's majlis; and a third, unfamiliar face—Yam.

…

Yam was amazed at the size of the High Palace. He had heard about its raised ceilings and large features that accommodated the giants living in it. Back in Port Rori, people debated whether the name referred to the building's location or to its ceilings. Looking at it now, Yam couldn't tell which tale was right.

While being escorted through the hallways and stairs of the palace, and seeing all the excessively large furniture and decorations, he felt like he had shrunk in size. He also noticed the same Babylonian lightbulbs that he had seen in the Gray Palace were used here as well.

When they first walked in the sage's chamber to meet their hosts, Yam's eyes fell on Prince Zufar. He felt he shouldn't stare for too long, but he couldn't resist the astonishment he felt. He had seen a giant once from afar but had never been this close to one. *Truly, the size of royalty and greatness,* he thought, reminding himself why members of Aad's family were always picked as prime sheikhs of Erum.

Bessel, leading the two guests behind him, bowed before his prince and announced his title to them. They both bowed and greeted him.

The prince greeted them in return and welcomed them; they all sat on the floor around a dining rug that had just been prepared with food and drink for the two guests, and he asked them to feast before they spoke.

Respectfully, Arkin and Yam embraced the hospitality and sat down, but after only one sip from the cup, Arkin began to explain the purpose of their visit at this time of night. "Eight days ago, the spy and jinn master we had assigned to observe any suspicious movements Behas made alerted us to a newborn under the star Unuk-Al Hai." *Serpent-Neck.*

When Arkin had previously told Yam about the jinn master they had hired as a spy back in the Gray Palace, he questioned why they would oppose jinn mastery yet hire them for their service. Arkin had said, "How should I put this? It appears that those who make the rules are most likely the ones who eventually…break them! But to keep a good eye on Behas, we needed someone who knew him best, someone sinister like him, someone who hated him and was willing to help us against him. The enemy of your enemy can be your ally." Yam remembered Arkin's words as the old Noorian continued to explain the situation to the prince, the sage, and the Chief Guardian that night.

"Only yesterday was he able to identify the location. The child was born here in Erum, and Behas is headed here to kill it. We believe, based on where he is coming from, that he will strike tonight. He will reach Erum almost five hours from now."

"That would be an hour away from dawn," interrupted Prince Zufar, who enjoyed the science of measuring time.

Yam remained silent, enjoying the food and drink before him as much as he enjoyed the experience of entering the High Palace and listening to all the important talk. His past few days had completely transformed him from an ignorant young porter to a novice occultist.

The old sage Hammah flipped a large hourglass on his desk, one designed to measure six hours. The sand would all pass through its neck and rest in the lower chamber by dawn. Yam had never seen one that large and elegant before.

"Indeed, my sheikh, time is to our advantage," replied Arkin, assuring that Behas had only one hour of night to martyr the child, while they had four to prepare protection. "He will also be without his jinn once he enters the City of Erum, thanks to the sages of Erum and Bin-Hyem's wisdom in protecting these valleys." What they didn't know at that time was that their spy had made a mistake. The spy had thought that Behas would strike the child *inside* the city, not far out in the farms! It was a diversion created by Behas.

"It has been twenty years since the last time you tried to save a child born under the Serpent-Neck star, and ironically, he is born in our sheikhdom again," said Bessel. Now eyeing the giant young prince, he said, "We will take all measures to keep the child safe, my sheikh. And if he appears, we will do our best to capture the outlaw saher as well. This time, we will make sure he is executed without any interference."

Yam didn't understand what Bessel meant by "interference." Twenty years before, Erum had had the chance to capture Behas but had secretly transported him to the Noorians. Behas had stayed imprisoned in a cell in Erum for more than three years but was never punished with execution like the rest of the outlawed jinn masters who were captured at that time. The interference he referred to was caused by the Noorians themselves.

The prince kept his face blank, trying to comprehend the situation better. "Behas is fully aware of all the protection measures and spells cast upon the Wadi of Erum," said the prince. "He knows his jinnic abilities do not function in the city, and he will not enter it carelessly."

Yam nodded in agreement with the prince. *That's sadly true. I agree.* Arkin had taught Yam all about Behas in the last few days, when they had journeyed together to Wadi Erum, and he knew the prince was right. Behas wouldn't be naive enough to enter Erum and get caught.

"The protection we cast over the city has a major weakness," Hammah declared. "It will prevent most jinn from using their dark powers here, but there is one type of jinn that can circumvent it."

To hear that the famous ban had a secret flaw was unsettling, but Yam saw no surprise in Arkin's eyes. He thought they were all only being reminded of what they knew.

"The transformation jinn can use their dark abilities outside of our borders," the sage continued to explain. "They can transform into deadly beings like snakes, scorpions, and whichever other small creatures are capable of killing a child, and then enter the city. They can then leave and transform back to their original forms outside of it, where the spell is no longer effective." While this would be a fairly simple trick for Behas to perform, it would be much more difficult for them to uncover.

The sage had spent his life studying and understanding the powers of the jinn. He knew jinn were a form of energy, and after long studies and journeys, he had discovered a mysterious ancient metallic stone that could disable their powers. The stone was hidden at the center of the city. It had a radius that covered the whole city and a few places beyond the borders of the city as well. But a transformation jinni could adopt a form that let it harm the child physically and then leave, without the need to use its power.

"We have kept this weakness point a secret so that sorcerers will not perform such a trick," continued Hammah. "But I believe Behas is much smarter than the other jinn masters, and this means his jinni could already be in the city and crawling towards the child."

The sage eyed Arkin, asking, "Do you know where the child is now? Or were you hoping that Behas would lead you to it?"

"I... Our spy is now in the city and is waiting for Behas to arrive so he can find out what Behas's final destination should be," Arkin replied. "Once he discovers where the child is, his plan is to let us know before Behas can reach him. But I am not sure if he would be expecting a crawling jinni instead of the jinn master in person. How could I not have thought of that?"

Yam saw Arkin's face turn red, as if he were choking with disbelief and fear. His plan lacked options and seemed to be falling apart. It was clear that he had forgotten about that weakness and was now lost in his darkest thoughts again. The words coming out of the sage's mouth made him fall silent. He had underestimated his enemy.

How will we ever find this child? Yam wondered. He wanted to shout and advise Arkin to reach out to the spy he had told them about; maybe the man could help them locate Behas and his jinn sooner. But Yam was not fully sure of his abilities, and Wadi Erum was not a city that could be searched easily. *We need a plan, a new plan!*

The prince had heard enough and now ordered Bessel to act. "We shall waste no time. Send out all the guards to look for anything black crawling in the dark—scorpions, snakes, rats, and even black cats or black dogs." He added, "Knock on doors to find the newborn and alert all the families, but do so quietly. Do not confuse and frighten people; I would not want my father to wake up and find the whole city in confusion and turmoil."

Bessel nodded. Before he left, Hammah added this advice: "Bessel, it will most probably be a snake. Tell your men to use rock hammers and smash the heads of any snakes. These are no ordinary reptiles."

Bessel nodded again and disappeared, running out of the chamber.

Now that's a good plan! Yam thought. *And on the bright side, this will also cleanse the valleys of any snakes.* He kept that thought to himself, not wanting to sound less worried than the rest. And he wasn't.

8

Yam stared at the elegant hourglass, which only a quarter of the sand had passed through. He wondered how time had passed so dramatically over the last few days of his life. He'd gone from carrying goods for cheap rewards, to being a novice occultist allowed into a secret palace carved into a high mountain, to finally being seated in a discussion with a prince two times as big as him. He felt like his life to this moment had passed like the sand in the hourglass.

In all his life before, he'd swum with the sand particles in the upper bulb, sinking slowly and without feeling towards the bottleneck in the middle, as if heading towards a critical moment that would quickly change his life. The bottleneck, he feared, would release him to fall freely before he smashed into the bottom and probably lost his life, buried under the rest of the sand piling on him from above. With all the rising tension in the room, he felt like his body was being sucked down like the sands in the upper bulb and dragged towards the bottom.

Bessel returned to the chamber, announcing that he had dispatched his men and given all the necessary instructions to find and kill the transformation jinni. "The men will have started the search for the jinni. Once they find it, they will follow it to its prey before they kill it. Only then will we be able to identify and bring in the child Arkin is searching for." These measures were being taken only as additional safeguards, on the assumption the spy might fail to spot Behas or his jinn or fail to find the exact location of the child.

Searching for black snakes or knocking on doors to find a specific newborn was an extremely difficult task to perform in the complex valleys of Erum, especially at night.

"I fear his jinn will find the child first," Arkin said.

Yam agreed with that. Passing through the complexity of the city's upper parts and bridges that night, and seeing the many lights from the caves in the walls of the valleys below, he had been astonished by its size. It would require every guard to search the city.

Hammah stood up in the midst of the discussion and said, "Well, the time for my sleep is nearing." He sounded calm and careless, as if nothing of what they were taking about worried him. Yam felt it strange but noticed the others were fine with the sage's interruption. "Please excuse my age and tiredness; it has been a long day for me," he said again with a smile as he waved Arkin farewell and wished him luck. He asked permission from his prince to leave, and the prince excused him. "I trust you and Bessel will be able to fulfill this task for your father without me," he said to the prince.

"Do not worry about it," the giant prince replied. "I understand your other obligations, Hammah. See you in the morning."

Yam looked at Arkin with astonishment. The other was clearly faking a smile.

"I wish we had come earlier or that he could stay longer with us," Arkin said after the old sage left them. "But Hammah never skips his rest." Yam noticed him gazing over at the hourglass as he spoke. He wondered now if it had been flipped by the sage to show the time they had before Behas arrived or to know when it would be time for him to go to sleep.

The prince then asked the two guests to join him in a higher majlis where they could watch over the city.

...

Yam felt privileged as the prince walked them through the High Palace. They ascended to the upper floors of the palace and through various halls that were vast enough to fit the members of the royal family.

"Many believe that the valleys of Erum were originally built by jinn," the prince remarked to Yam, or "student of Arkin," as he frequently called him. "They say that my forefathers inherited this palace after defeating the jinnic lords of these valleys," the prince said. "But this palace and the temple of pillars were built by my ancestors' own strength; they wanted to show their strength, righteousness, and fitness to rule over Arabia."

They entered a magnificent hallway of high pillars and open ceilings above the royal residences. Lit by fire below and moonlight from above, the walls and columns were white and bright, and the magnificent size of the structures filled Yam with astonishment. The prince noticed it and allowed Yam to take a step forward, ahead of the rest.

"Situated over the famous rock, the High Valley, as my folk called it, these hallways overlook every corner in Erum. My forefathers built this palace to fit their great sizes, but the smaller sections made for shorter men were added later to help their servants move around," the prince continued to explain as they passed by smaller-sized doorways. "The jinn that originally inhabited these valleys were initially allies to our tribes, not enemies. But due to their betrayals, they were banished, and thus Hammah, my father's sage, had to use all his knowledge to find a way to protect this city and forbid any jinn from using their abilities in it."

...

Bessel entered, carrying the hourglass, and handed it to the prince, who placed it on a raised table made to serve their heights. More than half of the time had now passed. The majlis they entered was divided into two sides, a side that included large furniture and another that had smaller stuff. The prince sat on fat cushions stacked near a small window and faced the smaller side, where his Noorian guests and Chief Guardian settled.

Prince Zufar continued to relate stories about his ancestors and the history of Erum. He told tales about their first ancestor, the great giant Erum, for whom this whole sheikhdom had been named.

Tonight, Zufar was helping the Noorians fight their battle against the dark world of the jinnic realm that Behas represented. The prince knew this was their battle as well, so long as his father ordered, and the Mountain Queen wished. A part of him was following orders and wanted to succeed only to please his father and the Noorians, and a bigger, noble part, deep inside in his heart, wanted to help for the sake of saving an innocent child.

...

Not long after they had settled in the new majlis, a crow flew in from an open window and circled above their heads, as if looking for something or someone.

With all the intense events occurring tonight, Bessel instinctively drew his blade in defense, as the crow's intrusion took them by surprise.

The crow landed neatly in front of Arkin. It placed a few dry palm leaves it had carried in its beak on the floor and then cawed, bouncing backwards and swinging its wings as if it were alerting them to follow it.

"This must be the saher we assigned to spy on Behas," said Arkin. "His jinni is trying to tell us something." In Arabia, jinn are not all evil. A few can be friendly or harmless. The crow did look sinister at first, but when one stared deeper into its eyes, it looked rather friendly and pathetic.

Bessel kept his blade raised. "Well, what is it saying, Noorian?"

Arkin leaned down to investigate the dry palm leaves. "These dry leaves are used as roofs. It probably found the victim's house. It wants us to follow it!"

The crow jumped around, dancing and making a clicking noise. Yam watched it in amazement—it was the first jinni he had ever seen. He tried to make sense of what it did, but it all seemed random to him.

Arkin, though, understood what it was saying, or trying to say. "Behas is not headed here! He's headed to the farms instead. The crow is telling us that Behas is almost an hour away from the child's house; we need to move fast!" Arkin stood on his feet and looked back at Bessel. "Please, lead us out. We need to follow this bird."

He never told me he could speak to crows! Yam thought.

"Bessel, prepare my horse and get the guards to follow this crow," ordered Prince Zufar.

But Bessel raised both his arms over his chest to calm them down. "The eastern farms are far away. We had better use a Guardian messenger to get there faster, but I have only one available at this time of night," he said, reminding them all his men had been sent out to search for black snakes.

"There is no need to create more panic in the city. One of us can go and bring the child back. It will be much quicker that way. The rest can wait here. We still have an hour." He paused in thought for a short moment and then shot a look at Yam. "You are lighter than the rest of us; you will be able to carry the child back." He then suggested sending only one rider with Yam to help him carry the child back. As Arkin was old and the prince was a giant, it would take them longer to follow the crow and reach the child. They would need someone else.

"But Behas is dangerous," Arkin cried. "One rider with Yam is not enough! They won't make it safely back to the city."

"Our horses are faster than Behas. They will reach the child and be back here in the city safely before the jinn master even reaches them," Bessel countered.

The crow cawed, reminding them to follow and not waste time.

"Behas is very far from where we are," Bessel added. "It's all about speed now, not power or numbers."

"I can do it," Yam put in bravely. "I can bring the child back safely before Behas reaches it."

The prince agreed and ordered Bessel to take all suitable measures that would get the child there safely as quickly as he thought possible.

Bessel grabbed Yam and pulled him towards the doorway. "Follow me. Hurry!"

Arkin was forced to take Bessel's word. It all happened quickly. That hadn't been his plan at all. The whole time, he had thought Behas was coming to the city, not the farms. And the jinn master had come earlier than they had anticipated. He had wished there were more Noorians and Guardians of Erum to help in his plan. But his hopes were now in the hands of the only person who seemed to care about his quest to save a child, a porter from Port Rori.

Yam moved fast to follow Bessel. As they neared the doorway, he heard Arkin cry from behind, "Save the child, Yam! Go quickly... Do not be late... Do not fail!"

...

The two men left the majlis, and the crow flew out of the window he had entered from. Those still in the room stuck their heads out the window to observe the action and follow the crow with their eyes.

Bessel ran quickly through the hall, followed by Yam. They descended through a small stairway that was built to their size.

They were still on a higher floor when Bessel opened a large wooden door. On the other side was a small stable that had only two horses tied in it. They had leather belts strapped around their bellies for riders' feet, but no other gear, and were ready to go. There was also a man in full gear seated on the other side.

Yam was surprised to find horses in a room high above the ground, a sight he'd never imagined. *How did they get them up here?* He looked around the stable and saw a narrow stairway at the far end of the room. Hoof marks showed that was where the horses came in and out.

The man in the room jumped in surprise to see the Chief Guardian burst into the stable. He stood to cover a small clay bottle behind him; apparently he had, shamefully, been drinking while on duty, not expecting a mission during this time of peace.

The small stable room was part of the royal couriers' division: the Guardian messengers. They were in full gear and ready to hustle away at any time of the day. They were different than regular messengers; they had access to faster horses, and they had access to several stables scattered around the dominion. Whenever a horse got tired, the rider would change the horse and continue to gallop, not stopping for a rest until the message was delivered. This stable was placed on the second floor because the Guardians wanted to keep the better breeds higher than the rest. This was for the psychological benefit of the horses; it gave them pride to be kept separate from the rest. The faster the horse, the higher it was kept. This stable even had a small opening for the horses to look out and be aware that they were staying high above land. The animals they befriended at this height were birds, and that too made the horses feel special. But there were benefits for the Guardians in the High Palace as well. The floors in the High Palace were far apart, and so the stairways the men used to convey whatever orders they received from their sheikhs on the top floors were long. Most of these quick orders were verbal, not written in sealed letters, which required secrecy. Having only the stable high in the royal wings would ensure that.

"Baaz," Bessel called, "carry this man quickly to the eastern farms. He needs to rescue a child from the grasp of the outlaw, Behas." He gave his orders and summarized the task. "Once you leave the palace, follow the large crow outside. It should lead you directly to the victim's farm." Bessel glanced at the two horses available. "Take Hurr; he's a faster horse."

Baaz was a rider well trained for these types of missions as well; messages that could not wait to be sent in the morning were usually warning letters in times of war, which required speed as well as stealth.

Without wasting time, he swiftly moved towards the black horse, freed it, and climbed on its back. He then guided the horse closer to Yam and lowered his arm to help him climb up behind him. "Let's go," he said.

Without a word, Yam climbed behind Baaz and the horse took off, descending the narrow stairway at full speed. Yam felt uncomfortable and scared, Baaz looked serious and determined, and the horse seemed to be enjoying it all.

As Bessel watched the horse disappear down the stairs, the jar Baaz had hidden behind him caught his attention. The Guardian messenger was probably a little drunk. *Great,* Bessel thought, with slight fear and sarcasm.

He decided to take additional precautions and descended to the Guardians chamber. There he ordered his horse and the prince's horse to be saddled and ready. "Call back some of the Guardians and guards you've sent out to find the jinni. And stay prepared. I fear this night will be more complicated than we originally thought."

Bessel had initially planned to capture the saher, but only when they had thought he was coming inside the Wadi of Erum and would be without his jinn. Now that he was in the farms, it would be useless and dangerous to send men after him. The jinn master would have all his jinn powers to help him escape or harm the guards.

Bessel now focused on the primary objective: saving the child. And he intended to do so by getting him into the city, where he would be safe, before Behas could get to him.

9

The horse descended down the long stairway, which had short, wide steps that let him go down easily. Yam, on his back, pictured the hourglass in his head again. He felt he was now sinking towards the neck, being quickly and viciously shifted from the upper bulb to the lower one.

The gate at the bottom end of the stairway was always kept open, and the guards on the other side made sure the path was always clear of obstacles. Anticipating their arrival from the growing echoes made by the hoofs clapping hard on the stony stair slabs, the guards glanced one last time at the pathway to ensure it was clear.

As soon as they got out into open air and past the guards, Baaz saw the large crow ahead of him, flying low for them to follow.

Baaz gently kicked Hurr to gallop faster, but the horse was struggling to trot. Baaz quickly remembered the horse was carrying two adults, and it seemed Yam's legs were hindering it from moving freely.

It was dangerous for a horse to gallop with two men on its back. The weight could injure its spine, though this was less of a problem for an Arabian horse like Hurr, as his back was shorter and stronger than those of other breeds.

Baaz knew the young horse could run, but not for their whole journey. He shifted his body forward a bit, allowing the leather belt around Hurr to be in between him and Yam. "Hold on to the belt and hang your feet forward," he yelled.

Yam struggled to position himself correctly at first, but as soon as he did what Baaz directed him to do, he felt more comfortable, and so did the horse. Now it could gallop at full speed with two men on its back. The crow led the way through the upper part of the city. The roadways and stone bridges were wide so the giants could pass through them easily on the way into and out of their palace.

While Yam was holding on tight and staring at the crow gliding ahead of them, he remembered an incident that had happened early that morning, when he had been in the concealed Gray Palace and had agreed with Arkin that they would do whatever it took to stop Behas. Now, headed to rescue the child, Yam felt the same rage coming back to him. He remembered Arkin's words, and he wasn't going to let Behas succeed either.

The crow had them follow him from the High Palace and gallop down through the rocky terrain and past the plains and farms east of the wadi. It was difficult to follow it through the night, but the crow made sure it was always flying near and within sight.

When the crow neared the palm farms, it continued gliding low between the palms through a narrow path, but Baaz slowed his horse down until it came to a full stop at the edge of the first line of palms. The path was too narrow for a horse to fit. He looked at Yam from over his shoulder. "Follow it. Quick. I can't ride further in there."

Yam jumped off in a hurry and almost tripped to the ground but managed to maintain balance on his feet and ran behind the crow.

He continued to follow the crow under the shade of the palm leaves to a mud wall at the end of the path, then jumped over the wall and found the bird was no longer in the air. Instead, it was standing on a block of rock that had fallen from the wall and was trying to lift it towards Yam, but the rock was too heavy.

Yam did not understand but picked it up in an effort to help the crow. Then he remembered what Hammah had told Bessel about smashing the heads of snakes with stone hammers. He continued to run behind the crow. As they reached the farm hut, the crow, which had remained silent for the whole journey, pointed with its wings at the hut.

Yam continued to run at full speed, with the rock in his hand. Then, as I have told you before, he broke into the hut, smashed the snake's head, stole the crying child in the midst of the fight between Fad and Behas, and ran back towards the horse.

...

And now, crumbled at Behas's feet, Yam felt his *own* head was about to be crushed.

He killed the child without the slightest thought of mercy! thought Yam as he stared at Behas above him, carrying the silenced child in his arms. *Soon the saher will end me as well.*

"Tell me, young man, before I end your short life," Behas said without looking at Yam, "how were you able to reach this child before me this time? I thought I had succeeded in misleading you all. Yet you reached the hut before me."

Yam remained silent. He thought it was Bessel's idea that had helped them reach the farms faster.

"I understand your fear, but trust me, death can be...relaxing," Behas continued with a sinister grin. "I have just come back from death. You will feel...nothing." He then shot a creepy smile at him.

Yam felt helpless and pathetic, until he noticed the child was still moving. *It's not dead!* Hope shone into Yam's heart. He had to do something to save it and himself, but he had no strength to fight the beast before him; the only muscle he had now was his tongue.

The light of dawn began to grow slowly from behind the horizon, but the sun had not yet appeared. Behas's grin became a frown as he continued. "Fine, you choose not to speak. Arkin shall grieve again in sorrow. Not only will I kill his child of the Serpent-Neck star but also his student."

"Please! Don't kill the child. And I'm not a student of Arkin's. I..." Yam spoke without knowing what exactly he should say. He paused for thought before his next words. "I'm only a porter from Port Rori, and I'm serving Arkin only for a promised reward. I'm nothing more, believe me," Yam said, quivering. "I'm begging you, Master Behas, spare me and the child I've been burdened to deliver safely." Yam sensed his words were disoriented or even useless.

Behas remembered when Zuhal, his all-knowing jinni, was not able to identify who had stolen the child. This boy looked too young to be an occultist who could hide his identity. *Maybe he is just what he says,* thought Behas.

An all-knowing jinni can see all your history unless you have no knowledge of it yourself. Behas was curious to hear what this young porter would say next.

"Whatever you may be, I will spare you if you tell me how Arkin was able to send you here to the farms."

"I'm not so sure myself, but I'd only heard them speak." Yam made his choice to lie in an effort to rescue himself from death. "Arkin has an eye on you. I'm not sure what it means. I heard him mention it to a sage in Erum."

"I know about the *spy*. I misled him into thinking I would go to the wadi. Did he find me here as well?" Behas had figured it all out by himself. "I might have underestimated his abilities. But you will be punished for trying to stop me and for killing my jinni."

Yam had to improvise, as it seemed that Behas already knew about the spy. "No, it's not the spy you know. Arkin told me that one of your own jinn helped him know what your next moves would be." Yam looked pathetic, but inside he felt smart. He had been taught by his mother before that jinn are traitorous in nature and can be disloyal. But he had feared that Behas would be too smart to be deceived by a simple lie. Yet, surprisingly, he was!

Behas took a long moment to digest Yam's words. He knew it could be true; he was familiar with the deceptive nature of jinn and had faced many problems with their loyalties. He had punished some of his jinn who had betrayed him before. At first, he did not want to believe it, but then he thought again, *He is telling the truth.* From the look on the man's innocent, young, and fearful face, Behas could not think of any other explanation for how Arkin had found out where his prey would be.

Behas felt bewildered but could think of no other jinni but Zuhal. His all-knowing jinni was the only one capable of traveling to Arkin and back without Behas's awareness. *I will make him suffer, the unfaithful efreet.*

Efreet is the term for a wild jinni without a master, or a disobedient jinni, or even a rebelling jinni.

"Jinn are betrayers. I will spare you because of your honesty and because you are not an occultist, but only a porter," Behas declared. "But the child will not be spared. I am sorry, but the reward that you will lose will mean a greater gain for all men. This child will only be used for evil."

Yam was speechless. He wanted to save the child as well but also feared that whatever he might say would make Behas change his mind about sparing his life. Yam hesitated before he spoke his thoughts. "Do you really *believe* a harmless child can be evil? Or are you afraid of the omens that it will grow up and end you?" He related the thought he had asked Arkin about before.

Behas was about to kill the wounded child but paused at Yam's question.

"What else did Arkin and the Noorians tell you about me? That I kill these children out of obligation to *please* 'my jinnic lords'? I have witnessed the evil powers the star of Unuk-Al Hai brings, and it cannot be tolerated. Believe that I am a savior of men, not the enemy."

...

While Yam was conversing with Behas, Fad had continued to run until Behas's tall figure came within his range. He tried to ease his run so he would not be noticed, but he also did not intend to slow down and reach them late.

Although he was a farmer, his father had taught him how to throw a spear. Fad tried to carefully approach a position where he would be able to throw his spear-like tool at Behas. He didn't want to risk harming his own child, so he aimed for Behas's legs.

...

"I've heard so much about you, but I didn't believe it all," Yam continued. "But I'm sure that jinn are not worthy of your trust; they'll only lead you astray. Why is this child to be punished for an evil he didn't choose to have?"

Behas bit his lip with a slight smirk and said, "Clearly, you have no knowledge of me or anything about the jinnic realm." He then lowered his eyes, looking at the child.

Yam sensed he was not helping the child as Behas covered the child's bruised forehead with his palm. "Even if you kill this child, another will be born. The Serpent-Neck star will always reappear, and you can't stop it forever. You can't stop the source of it." Repeating the words of his master, Arkin, Yam shouted in an effort to distract Behas from his rituals.

Behas ignored the tremulous ignorant below his feet and whispered words that Yam did not understand.

Yam cursed Behas and his rituals. He crawled with difficulty and grabbed Behas's tight robe from below, trying to pull him down.

Behas kicked Yam's hand away, took a step or two backwards, and continued to pronounce his incomprehensible words, with his golden dagger pointed at the child's chest. While he was stepping backwards, Fad threw his spear from afar. It arced high up in the air, then fell straight down towards Behas, gaining speed and piercing the air with a whipping sound.

The spear missed Behas by a hair. A small bit of the spear's tip pierced a rock in the ground, and there was a loud noise as the rock cracked. Like a bolt of thunder, it stood upright between him and Yam for a mere second before the sharp tip failed to hold in the crack, and the spear leaned slowly and fell to the side under its own weight.

Both Behas and Yam were stunned, looking with wide eyes at the spear that had cut the air between them in half. Behas realized that if he had not stepped back a bit, the spear would have punctured his foot, while Yam too thought that if he had continued to crawl forward, the spear would have pierced his hand.

Fad saw the spear miss Behas and began to run towards him fast.

Behas turned around to face whoever had thrown the spear. He was surprised to find Fad running towards him. Behind Fad, the sun was about to rise. Behas regretted the time he had wasted before striking the child dead and achieving his goal.

He had completely forgotten about the father who had already succeeded in beating him to the ground and stabbing his neck with a blade. Now the sun was rising, and Gaddar wouldn't be able to protect him from death, as the jinni's skills were limited during the day.

However, he could still finish what he had come for. He had the child in one hand and his golden Mystic Dagger in the other, and the father was still far from stopping him. He smiled wickedly and raised his blade to stab the child. But suddenly, his whole body cramped in pain, forcing him to lean forward. Unwillingly, he dropped to his knees and screamed in pain.

He dropped the child unceremoniously and grabbed the source of the sudden pain, slightly above his right heel. He turned his head to find the spear's broken tip stuck between his heel and calf. Yam, on the other end of the spear, was hanging on to it with both hands. His grip and forceful pushing caused a series of continuous spikes of pain.

Behas tried to push the pole out or pull his leg away, but with no result. Yam had jammed it in deep and was pushing it deeper with all the strength he had left. Behas's warm blood was streaming out vigorously, without stopping; the sight of it caused him to feel faint. He dropped to his shoulder. The pain was unbearable, and he felt he was falling unconscious. He could see that the glare of sunrise had now lit the skies. He was powerless without his jinn. *Defeated again*, he thought, before surrendering to darkness.

Fad witnessed everything as he was running towards them. He could not see clearly what had gone on, but he was able see Behas's form collapsing to the ground.

As he neared them, he scanned the site with his eyes, looking for his child. In order, he saw the sad whinnying horse, which lay on its side, exhaling viciously from the pain of its broken knee. Not far from the horse, the rider, Baaz, lay motionless. Fad stopped short above Behas and Yam. One was conscious, the other unconscious and bleeding. He looked again from where he stood, but there was no sign of his child.

Yam was staring at the man above him, perplexed by his unpredictable moves. He didn't know whether to thank him for the spear he had thrown or apologize for failing to keep his child safe. Either way, he decided to wait for the farmer to speak first, but the other appeared busy looking for his son. His long hair swung quickly as he turned his head wildly here and there, not making any eye contact with Yam.

Fad dropped to his knee near Behas and began to search the saher with both his hands, but the child was no longer in his grasp. There was no sign of him around or near Behas either. Fad paused and locked gazes with Yam. "Where is my son?" he asked with both fury and fear in his tone.

Yam remained silent in disbelief; he opened his eyes wide and raised his eyebrows high. He had thought the child was safe after all the action, but the last he had seen him was when Behas had turned around to face Fad.

"*Where is he?*!" Fad exploded again, only louder this time.

"I…I don't know!" were the only words Yam found at the tip of his tongue. "I had your son, but he…he was holding him before I stuck him with…the spear."

Fad, hearing his words, remembered the sight of Behas holding his child, Dileel, preparing to stab him, and then collapsing and throwing the boy away. But Dileel was nowhere to be seen now. There was no trace of his child at all. Nothing. It was as if the boy had just…vanished!

10

Yam pushed at the ground with his hands, trying to lift his head and shoulders higher and get a better view of the area. No sign of the child.

The skies turned light orange as half the sun rose above the horizon. The promising colors of a new dawn seemed less optimistic and gloomier for both Fad and Yam.

Yam had gotten familiar earlier with the child's crying, but now even his voice was absent. He then remembered that Behas had silenced the child after whispering a sort of spell. "Behas must've done something. I saw him whisper in the child's ear while he was crying, and it made him silent. Maybe his jinn are hiding the child from us."

Fad felt a slight touch of hope. *That must be it.* "Do you know how to break his illusion spell?" he asked, tucking his hair behind his ear. "You are a Noorian, are you not?"

"No, but my master is," Yam replied, trying to push himself closer. "If I can reach my master in Wadi Erum… I don't really know; I'm only assuming." He wished he could find the child again. He felt guilty for letting the child out of his grip, but he also knew there wasn't much he could have done. He flipped Behas on his back and pressed on his chest to feel his heartbeats. *He's alive.* "Behas is alive," he said to Fad. "Maybe we should restrain him and then force him to reveal your child."

"I would prefer killing him again for what he has brought upon my wife and son." After the thrill of the chase faded, Fad began to remember his wife, whom he had left unconscious back at his farm. But he had to agree with

Yam for now. He started with tying the saher's hands before removing the spear and bandaging his bleeding leg.

...

The sun had now risen a spear's length or more above the horizon, illuminating the earth and driving darkness away.

Fad had bandaged Behas's wound, laid Yam on his back to relax near Behas, and carried the unconscious rider, Baaz, to lie near them. He had also tried to ease the horse's pain but didn't have enough knowledge to aid a horse, so he only bandaged its bleeding as well, rubbed on its neck, and wiped away its tears.

Fad remembered when everyone he knew was happy to know that his wife had given birth to a boy. He had felt he was the luckiest man in Erum. Not that Fad would have been sad or hurt if it had been a girl, but having a son just made him more proud and happier. Fad and Nada had both wished for a boy first. She, too, had been proud that her first child was a boy. Dileel had stolen their hearts in the last eight days they had spent with him, enjoying the presence of a child in their lives. They had thought they were living their "happily ever after," until this dreadful night had come and bestowed evil upon them.

He then stood above Yam and Behas. "Is he still unconscious?" he asked, looking west towards Wadi Erum. In the morning light, the shining white stones of the High Palace were visible from afar, standing above the hills, but the path to it couldn't be seen clearly.

"I do not see any sign of your masters," Fad noted. "Are you certain they are coming?"

"I'm sure they will; don't worry," answered Yam. "They'll come because we're late."

The moment Yam finished his sentence, they began to hear the sound of many horses galloping towards them. Fad turned his head towards the source of the noise and saw a troop of cavalrymen riding their way.

Yam, lying on his back, leaned forward a bit and turned his head towards the sounds as well. He did not see anything but smiled with the certainty that Arkin and the giant prince, Zufar, were on their way.

"We're fortunate; help has finally arrived."

"The only fortune I had, I lost," Fad said with a sigh, reminding Yam, and probably himself, of his dead wife and lost child. He spoke while his gaze was fixed on the horses coming their way. He would do anything to bring back his wife and son, but with little knowledge of jinn, he knew he needed all the help he could get, and from anyone who might offer.

As the beating of hoofs got nearer, Behas began to move. Still in his sleep, he was shaking his head as if he were being strangled in a disturbing nightmare.

Yam noticed, and although he knew that Behas was restrained, he pushed himself up on his elbows and opened his eyes wide. "Oh, he's moving! Master Fad?" he called out. "Behas is moving."

Fad was standing on a rock, making sure the cavalry saw where he and the rest of the group were. Responding to Yam's call, Fad moved swiftly to stand above Behas. He was indeed moving, but Fad had no patience and kicked his shoulders twice to wake him up.

Behas struggled to open his eyes; he felt his eyelids were trying to stay shut. Losing that much blood at his age made him feel hazy and dazed.

"Where is my son?" Fad addressed him.

Behas was trying to match what he heard to what he remembered. *My son?* He now remembered why he had traveled to Erum.

Fad, impatient, continued to shake him awake and repeatedly asked him to give back his child.

Behas, still half awake, unconsciously spat out his first words. "I killed your son; he's dead," he answered in a whisper.

Fad bit his lips and inhaled before punching the old wizard hard, almost breaking a tooth or two. He grabbed the man's tight robe and pulled him to sit upright. His hair fell into his face again as he exploded, shouting loudly enough that even the men on the horses nearing them might have heard him. "Where is my son?"

While Behas's wrists were still tied together, his fingers were free. He grabbed both of Fad's arms, trying to pull the man away from his chest, and spat words that neither Fad nor Yam understood. Clearly, he did not enjoy being banged around and smacked in the face.

Fad, without hesitation, punched him again. "Speak in *Arabic*. Where is my son?" he demanded.

Behas frowned, placing the tips of his fingers on his cheek to feel the pain; he now remembered well what had happened. "What do you mean, 'Where is my son?' He's right there…" He turned his head to see the spot where he had thrown the boy. Nothing! "I threw him right there after I got stabbed," he said. "I do not *have* your child," Behas continued to explain. "I did, but I fainted and then I dropped him…and I do not remember seeing what happened to your son."

"No more lies and deceptions," Fad interrupted him. "Your jinn are hiding my son. I know what you stinking sorcerers are capable of. I saw you die in my hands and now you're still alive, and it will not tire me to kill you again…and again…until you bring me my son back."

"I came here to *kill* your son. If I had him, he would be dead, not hidden!" Behas simplified. "It is the occultists who kidnapped him from you, not I!"

Fad looked at Yam, who stared back at him with denial in his eyes. Before the porter could offer his defense, the noise from the galloping horses got so loud that no one could hear himself speak.

All three of them observed the cavalry surrounding them. Some halted farther off, others went to the injured horse and killed it to end its misery, and the rest stood above them with weapons drawn, pointing at them.

All three of them froze in surrender. Their attention was caught by the sight of Prince Zufar riding his gigantic horse nearer to them. The other cavalry moved aside, making way for him.

Fad tucked his hair behind his ears again as his eyes fell on the giant.

"Where is the child?" asked the prince, looking at Yam, who was the only familiar face.

Arkin approached from behind him. "Where is the boy, Yam? Did you save him?"

"We saved him, yes," he said, addressing the two. Yam then looked at Behas. "But—"

Fad interrupted, pulling Behas up by his shoulder and saying, "His jinn are hiding my boy. Can you reveal him?" He reckoned Arkin to be Yam's master.

Behas and Arkin exchanged looks. Behas started with a smile: "Is this not a beautiful morning for you and me to meet again? I am truly impressed by how an outcast like you could drag all of Erum out to help him—but then send only a young porter and a single Guardian messenger to take the child from me. That is truly irresponsible, is it not? I wonder if the child *was* important to you, Arkin."

He has a point, thought Fad. And that point might have also reminded the prince and Bessel of their "irresponsible" decision to send Yam alone with Baaz. But they had all been led by Arkin and the spy he trusted to prepare in the wrong ways and look in the wrong place. Behas had tricked them, and now he was mocking them for it.

Bessel remained silent, probably blaming himself. The two young men were now injured as a result of his wrong advice to the prince.

With disgust in his eyes, Arkin frowned and lowered his chin. "This time, you will be executed for your wicked acts against the innocent people of Erum. Tell us where the child is."

Where is the child? He does not know! Poor Fad had expected the Noorian to be able to reveal his son, which was what Yam had promised him. But it seemed clear that even Arkin didn't know where he was! Fad felt his hair stand on end, thinking in horror, *Where is my son?* Behas told him he had not hidden the child, and Arkin was now asking where Dil was as well. Maybe Yam's assumptions were all wrong.

Behas remained silent until Fad nudged his shoulder to force him to speak. Behas smiled at Arkin again and said laughingly, "I thought you had spies watching me. Should they not be able to tell you *where* the child is? As I have said before, I do not have the child and I do not know where he is. If I did, he would be dead."

"Then where is my son? He cannot simply disappear. Explain it, saher. My child was in your arms!" Fad became irritated with Behas's laughing and looking all relaxed, not caring at all. "Speak!"

The giant prince standing above them realized that the Noorian had no control over the outlaw Behas. He stepped closer and interrupted them. "You will give us the child you stole, and you *will* be executed for all your wrongdoing." The prince spoke clearly and went straight to the point. "Speak, saher, since everyone here is accusing you. If you do not have the boy, where else would he be?"

"Believe me, my sheikh, for I should speak only truthfully in your presence," Behas pleaded, sounding polite and humble all of a sudden. "It is true that I came here to kill the child, not hide him. But I have failed to do any of that. I lost the boy when I became unconscious. And if I had known that *you*, my sheikh, wanted the boy, I would have spared him and brought him to you myself."

You might think that because he was an outlaw jinn master and a wicked saher, Behas would naturally lie. But although he was sinister and deceptive, he would never dare lie to a prince of Erum. It was partly his ethical obligation as an Arab and partly Zufar's intimidating size which made him speak the truth. He did not know where the child had gone.

"I truly speak in all my reason and repeat that I did not kill the child, nor am I hiding him, and I do not know where the child is," he continued. "But I can only think of an explanation. There is only one way a child would disappear in the blink of an eye."

"Disappear?" asked the prince.

"He was kidnapped."

"Kidnapped! How? By whom? And where is the child now?" The prince shot all his questions at once.

"The 'how' is simple, and no sage or jinn master in all of Erum will disagree with my explanation of it. An air jinni was used to kidnap the child. But by whom and to where, I cannot answer, for my all-knowing jinni has betrayed me and left me. I cannot sense his presence now," Behas continued to explain. He believed the lie that Yam had made up about his all-knowing jinni. "An all-knowing jinni might be able to find the child, but I doubt it. I sense those who kidnapped the child can hide well."

Behas's all-knowing jinni, Zuhal, would find the child, but he wasn't there now. He hadn't betrayed Behas, but he could not speak to his master at all times. Behas's mind had to be clear and focused on listening to him. Behas knew that, but Yam had influenced his mind to the extent that he accused his most loyal jinni of betrayal. Such things were common between jinn masters and their jinn; their relationships were always filled with distrust and insecurity.

"The air jinni must have a jinn master who directs it," Behas continued. "Whoever has the child now is more dangerous than anything you can imagine. They must be planning to use him to summon great evil; otherwise they wouldn't have gone through the trouble of summoning an air jinni."

That was the conclusion they reached, but no one there knew who had used the jinni or where they would have taken the child. Zufar, Arkin, and Bessel agreed to go back and inform the sage, Hammah. He would be able to give better insight and advice.

The prince ordered Bessel to take Behas to prison, aid the injured novice occultist, Yam, and offer the grieving father whatever he needed. Fad asked for nothing, and deep inside he only wept in sorrow.

Zufar then galloped away with a few of his guards, back to Erum. He expected his father was now waiting for him; he needed a proper explanation to justify his failure to deliver the Noorians' urgent request from the night before.

...

Fad did not easily accept what he had heard. The guards took Behas from his grasp. *Good riddance,* he thought. He followed Arkin hastily. Being told that his child had been kidnapped lightened his heart somewhat. *He's still alive!*

"Is my son safe?" he asked the old occultist. "They will not kill him for offerings to any jinnic lords, will they?" They both stood next to Arkin's horse now. "Please, I need to find my son; he is the only thing I have in this world. I need to know where he is."

"If your son is alive, I would like to find him too and keep him safe as well." Arkin mounted his horse and looked down at Fad. He smiled but looked less optimistic. "I do not know if Behas is telling the truth or not. Find me in Wadi Erum. The great sage, Hammah, might help us learn something, and I will pass my best knowledge to you as well. We hope to find your son."

Bessel then came by them and offered Fad reassurance as well. "I have just spoken with our Guardian messenger. I am sorry for the loss of your wife. And if Arkin is right, I will also offer everything I can to help find you your child. The Guardian's dagger you have will get you into the High Palace," he said, pointing to the dagger at Fad's waist, the one Baaz had given him earlier near the farms. "At any gate, ask for Bessel, son of Mahi." These were his last words before he galloped away to catch up with his prince.

11

After everyone left, Fad looked over the empty plains one last time before he left. There was still no sign of his child, only a handful of Guardians and regular guards who had stayed behind to bury the horse they had killed when they came. He stared for a long moment at that horse. With an awkward feeling, he thought the air jinni Behas had told them had kidnapped his son might be hiding in the horse!

He stood before the corpse, facing its belly. Flies and other bugs had just started to explore it as well. He kicked its belly gently and slowly. "Come out if you are there," he said to the dead horse, or whoever might be in it. "Please," he whispered.

No response.

The Guardians stared blankly at him, without interfering. They did pity Fad, but they were trained not to express their soft feelings.

He waited until every echo from the galloping horses disappeared completely and there were no sounds but the morning winds and the buzz of flies.

No sign of anything he had hoped for.

He slowly walked away, heading back to his farm with his thoughts filled with agony and sorrow for his wife. Among all the memories, he remembered a talk he had that warned him to watch for this night.

...

The night Dileel was born, Fad had just met his new heir, kissed him asleep, and walked out to leave his sleeping boy with his mother, Nada. He needed to sit for a rest after a long walk to the upper streets of Wadi Erum.

Outside the house of his parents-in-law, he found Nada's father sitting on a rug near the front door. Fad's smile never left his face as he crossed to reach him.

The new grandfather had looked back at the new father. "So! How does it feel to finally be a father?" he asked, with joy in his face as well.

Fad had laughed while sliding down to sit near him. "Well. It feels—" He had paused, searching for a proper word to describe his feeling towards Dileel. He hadn't been able to find one. "It feels...different!"

"What? Different? I am not sure that is the right feeling!" His father-in-law had replied, smiling in confusion.

Fad had laughed again. "I don't know how it should feel to be a father or not, but I am feeling happy for certain to see the little boy. I am happy, Master Badde. Nada, too, is happy. Dileel is a blessing."

Badde had smiled again, brightly this time. "Are you planning to go back to your farm soon?"

"No. I think we'll stay here for two days. Nada will need the rest."

"Then we should celebrate, you and me. We should spend a night in Ubar."

Fad had smiled back, but with less assurance. "I do not think we should. I—"

"I am not asking you if you want to come or not," Badde had interrupted. "We *are* going. Tomorrow after sunset, we head to Ubar and we enjoy and celebrate the birth of your new heir, Dileel." He had ended with a loud laugh.

Fad had laughed and looked away. "Okay, old man. One night will be harmless, I guess."

He had gazed at the tree near the cliff, the same tree he had seen earlier that evening, when a large owl had been hiding in it, and had noticed the dark shadow of the owl still there. He had tried to sharpen his focus to see well. "That strange owl is still there," he had thought out loud.

Badde had leaned forward and tightened the wrinkles around his eyes to sharpen his vision in the dark as well. Then he had suddenly leaned back and opened his eyes wide in rage. He'd stood with difficulty and walked quickly towards the tree, then picked up a stone and thrown it at the owl.

The big owl had barely moved. After Badde had shouted and thrown several more stones to scare it away, it had gently glided off, not scared of him but rather annoyed. He had kept staring at it with a grimace until it flew deeper into the dark.

"Calm down, Master Badde. It is only a bird!"

"That is no bird, my son. *She* is probably a transformation jinni and could be a scout for a saher or a witch. She could be searching for newborns," Badde had said as he turned to face Fad. "Be careful going back to your farm; they could be stalking your child."

Fad had given a fond sigh and placed his hands on the old man's back, leading him towards the rug to sit. "The times of jinn and dark sorcery have passed, Master Badde. Aad has made it all forbidden. Now Erum is safer. There is no safer place where one can live and raise a child. Jinn masters and jinn will not dare lurk in these lands anymore. It is only an owl."

"I know, I know Erum is safer now than it was before, my son. Times are changing fast, but one still needs to be careful. There are jinn masters who are outlaws in and around Erum. And there are still harmful jinn out there."

. . .

And Badde had been right, Fad thought, as he reached the farms.

His hut was not far now. The farms were brighter during daytime, and the night before now seemed like a nightmare. Fad began to wonder if perhaps he had been wrong about his wife being killed.

Coming near the farmhouse, Fad sensed someone, or something, moving inside. *She is awake!* he thought, and rushed in. He opened the door, but to his surprise, he found his neighbor, Faseela, instead. She had cleaned the house and had covered his wife, Nada.

Faseela was about their age, a long-time friend and neighbor of Fad's family. And she passed by every morning to check on and help her new friend, Nada, the new mother.

But this morning didn't seem usual.

She turned to face the newcomer. "Where have you been?" she questioned as she walked over to stand near her unconscious friend, who lay between her and Fad. "What happened? Where is Dil?"

"Behas," he said, and then paused to search the room. The snake was no longer in sight, and the room was tidier than he last remembered. He started again. "Dil has been kidnapped."

Faseela's tiny eyes opened wide, her round face turned yellow, and her brown palm covered her open mouth. She remained silent as Fad continued to talk.

"We were attacked last night by the outlaw saher, Behas. There was a snake here. And I tried saving them, I tried saving Dil, but I was too late." He then bent to sit on his knees beside his wife and stroked his fingertips across the bite marks on her neck. He continued: "And Nada, she's been killed by a jinni snake. I failed to save them both. I lost everything I cared about." His voice broke, and he tried to hold back the tears in his eyes.

"No, Fad! She's not dead," Faseela said abruptly. "I know someone who was bitten by a jinni before. Everyone thought he was dead, and his family was going to bury him, but a healer in Wadi Erum helped him." In Arabia, that mistake was common. Many were buried after being unconscious for a day or two from snake bites.

Fad looked at her with raised eyebrows, then looked down at his wife and back at Faseela again. "Erum? Where in the city? I will take her there. Tell me where I can find this healer."

"She lives near the well of Sada. I will take you there."

"We shall go *now!*"

Faseela felt deeply sorry for Fad. She felt obligated to help him and save his wife. She told him what she knew could be done to save Nada! But she had no knowledge of how to save the kidnapped child, although she searched deep in her mind, trying to remember a similar incident, as she knew a lot of stories about jinn. Unfortunately, all the kidnapping stories she knew that involved jinn had ended in tragedy.

"I will pray to the gods of Erum that we find Dil. We can ask the healer about the jinn who kidnapped him as well. She is a wise one."

Fad nodded, jumping up and reaching the door in three big steps. Before leaving, he grabbed his sand-colored head scarf, which hung beside the door, and said, "Wait here; I will bring a mule to carry Nada. Thank you, Faseela. You are a blessing," he added. "I will be back in a minute."

...

Prince Zufar and his company were nearing the city. *Returning with nothing but failure,* he thought.

Zufar had remained silent throughout the whole journey back, rehearsing his excuse speech, or speeches, repeatedly. But in his hopeless mind, his father's reaction to all his excuses would always be unpleasant. He could not imagine a positive reaction at all, not even to the fact that they had finally caught the most sinister outlaw wizard and conjurer, Behas.

From a distance, he noticed a Guardian messenger galloping at full speed through the upper streets that led to the High Palace. He sensed that other bad news was on its way to his father's morning council. *This sunrise seems less promising for the Prime Sheikh of Erum.*

12

Every morning, as the sun rose behind the horizon, the Prime Sheikh of Erum, Aad, would wake in his chamber to repeat his morning prayer and express his devotion and submission to the source of light and life.

Once the yellow circle was completely above the horizon, Aad would conclude his prayers and head to his *hammam*, his bath, to wash his sins away. He would then, with the help of his servants, dress in his rich, heavy single-colored *thawb*, or garment, which was matched with a pair of elegant Indian scarves. One wrapped his waist to hold his decorated *khanjar*, a curved Arabian dagger, and the other scarf wrapped his head to form a symmetrical Arabian turban. The lines of his turban were parallel to his white eyebrows and the wrinkles on his forehead.

He stood before his mirror between two of his servants, who were half his height. He felt proud every time he compared his size with that of others around him. Along with their size, the royal tribe had longer lives than normal men. They could live twice as long as the average Erumian. Some of his ancestors had lived even longer than that. Aad was a proud ruler, and he had every right to be proud: His rule had brought only more prosperity and greater power to Erum. The sheikhdom had grown three times larger during his reign. And that reign was the longest ever. Unlike the prime sheikhs before him, he had ruled from a young age.

Once he was fully dressed, he would unsheathe half of his *khanjar*. I wouldn't call the one made for him a dagger, as it was made larger to match his size. It was almost the size of three swords! The handle was made from the horn of an African rhino, and the sheath was a mixture of silver and gold.

The *khanjar* had been the pride of free men in Erum, but younger generations did not care about carrying it these days. Fad didn't own one, but his father did. The common ones Guardians used were made of strong steel, sheathed in goats' leather, with a handle made of camel bone.

...

After getting dressed, Aad would be escorted to his feasting chamber. Every morning he broke his fast alone and used the time to meditate in solitude. He thought of all the conversations that had occurred the day before and all the issues that required his attention. He used this time to organize in his mind the matters that would be discussed in his morning council, the *sabla*. The morning sabla discussed politics and rulings. As a sheikh, he needed to choose his words carefully and ensure his judgments were right, for whatever he decided could never be argued with unless he allowed it.

...

He would then enter the rectangular hall where the sabla met. All its members—his sons, his Chief Guardians, his religious advisors, his sages, and the sheikhs of allied tribes or their representatives—would be waiting for him to arrive. They would all stand for the giant sheikh.

He was fast for a man who was more than a hundred years old. Today, as on all days, he walked quickly across the sabla's hall, which barely fit his height but appeared massive to the other shorter men. The colorful patterns on the carpet below him were reflected in the designs on the hall's wooden roof. There were rectangular windows on one side of the hall that divided the eastern sunlight into an array of parallel columns laid across the floor. The similarly organized pattern of shadows formed a suspension bridge on the ground.

The guests sat opposite each other on both sides of the hall, and at the far end, his seat on the floor was empty, waiting for him to occupy it. His two servants stood on his left, willingly waiting to serve him with whatever he desired.

Coming in, he noticed two seats were still vacant. One was on the left side, where Bessel, the Chief Guardian of Palace Affairs, should be. The other empty place was three spaces away from the Prime Prince's, where his son, Zufar, should be. He did not show any sign of missing them to any of the attendees. He sat quietly in his place, and everyone else did as well. Respecting the tradition, he gestured for the eldest person in the sabla to speak. And so the morning council began.

The old sage, Bin-Hyem, began by welcoming everyone and stating his daily predictions about the weather and daily and seasonal fortunes, which he said were promised by the stars. He was the sheikh's ancient daily horoscope, as some might say, but he knew much more than that. He spoke more than everyone else and usually had no issues to relate or problems that required attention; his speech seemed of low priority, but due to his age, he always had the privilege of going first, even before the Prime Sheikh himself. In Arabia, precedence in everything was calculated according to age rather than rank.

As the sabla went on as usual, and others now spoke of issues in and around the valleys of Erum, a Guardian messenger walked in unnoticed. He leaped swiftly between the panels on the bridge of shadows and sunlight to reach Bessel's seat, but the Chief Guardian of Palace Affairs was not there. The urgency of his message gave him the right to move ahead to the Prime Chief Guardian in all of Erum, Qassas.

Qassas was Arabic for "cutter." Qassas had a long face, a long nose, and a long stare. A clear scar below his left eye defined his intimidating features. His family had given him the name because they were traditional cutters of camel wool in Erum. They were proud of their history, and he was the pride of their family for holding the highest rank under the sheikhs of Erum.

Chief Guardians wore rings to differentiate themselves from the lower-ranked Guardians, messengers, and other guards and soldiers in Erum. There was only one Prime Ring that signified command over them all, and for the last fifteen years, that ring had been worn by Qassas.

The skinny Guardian messenger stood by Qassas's left shoulder to speak. "A word from the east." His whispers were heard only by Qassas.

Qassas always showed an angry expression, but after the messenger finished, his face became angrier. He conveyed the message to the Prime Sheikh at once.

Aad recognized the urgency of the message. He raised a hand to pause the current speaker. Once the sabla went silent, he lowered his hand and gave his attention to the Guardian messenger. Qassas bowed his chin, permitting the messenger to speak.

The messenger did not delay his words. He moved backwards to stand near Bessel's empty seat, focusing his gaze on the Prime Sheikh, not the sabla. This time he spoke aloud for everyone to hear.

"A word from my sheikh, Shadeed, son of Aad. There has been a series of attacks on the eastern dams. Men have been slaughtered, women and children were taken as spoils, many farms have been set on fire in Akersad, and all dams have been destroyed. The raiders have fled deep into the eastern mountains beyond our borders. We seek your wisdom, my sheikh, for our men are now fewer in number. My sheikh believes the raiders are from Bahla, and he desires to send a stronger warning." He spoke the words exactly as his sheikh had sent him to say, then went silent, allowing the sabla to digest the news.

Aad's son Shadeed was assigned to rule an eastern border settlement called Akersad, meaning "the last dam." It was a small farming settlement in the east, positioned on the bank of the main river that streamed from Erum, the Sada River.

In the last century, the population of Erum had grown rapidly, but rain levels had decreased dramatically as well. The water levels in the rivers around Erum were low, and therefore, the Prime Sheikh, Aad, had ordered the construction of dams in several settlements to preserve the water.

The dams served the people of Erum well, and they were able to survive the droughts. But the dams caused the river to dry completely beyond the eastern border of Erum, and the cities on the other side of that border, which depended on the same river, were negatively affected. The dams created conflict during drought years, and for the past three years, rain had been scarce in Arabia.

"They continue to insult. They continue to blame," said Aad. "We shall destroy their homes. We will rebuild our dams." His words were clear orders to all the sabla. Aad had had enough of the invaders coming into his lands, blaming him for the drought, and insulting his sheikhdom. He had decided that they should be destroyed to set an example.

"Sheikh Shaddad will deliver my blow to the east," Aad continued, assigning this task to his eldest son, the crown prince. He knew his son was a merciless warrior; he had been tested by his father many times before and had always achieved what was desired and more. Shaddad and Shadeed were twins, and they were the eldest brothers, but because of his constant practice of dark sorcery and jinnism, Shadeed had been sent away to rule over Akersad, leaving it clear for Shaddad to be the crown prince and heir to Aad.

"Qassas, you have two days to prepare as many men as Sheikh Shaddad desires."

The Guardian messenger had heard enough. He bowed before the Prime Sheikh and left, promising that the council's response would reach his sheikh in the east without delay.

Walking out through the same hallway he had come from, he saw a giant figure approaching from the other end. It was Prince Zufar, with Bessel walking behind him. The messenger bowed and greeted his sheikh and smiled at Bessel, but the two ignored him, racing down the hallway to reach the sabla before it ended.

13

Below, in the Guardians' dungeons, three guards were roughly dragging Behas to his cell. Two held the stick that restrained his shoulder and back, and one led the way. His mouth was tightly covered so he wouldn't use it to speak or call his jinn to escape—not that his jinn could do anything in Erum anyway.

They threw him in the center of the tiny cell as if they were throwing a sack of grain. He tried to switch his position to ease the pain from his injured leg, but before he could, Arkin walked in and bent low before him. Behas froze in position, staring back at Arkin.

"This is where you end," Arkin said. "Behas, 'the greatest jinn master,' will finally be executed, in Erum, the city he once served. You knew we were spying on you to get that child. You tricked us once again. But this time, you *will* be executed. Your name is fading. You have gone weak. No one ever dared stand between you and your victims before. But now, they dare kidnap a child from your own hands! How pathetic."

Behas felt sorry for himself; Arkin was right. No one had ever dared to face Behas before, but now, someone had stepped up and dared to spy on him, and someone else had stolen the child from his grasp. It seemed his name *was* fading; jinn masters were no longer afraid of him. Even the younger generation of regular men who lived under Aad's rule had no fear of him anymore! He had almost been killed twice in one night, first by a farmer and then by a porter.

Arkin stood up but kept his eyes fixed on Behas, saying, "All my life, I have been curious to understand the powers of the Serpent-Neck star and its effects on those who are born under it, but you forbade me that knowledge." He walked slowly to the door, turning to see his enemy one last time. Arkin held out Behas's Mystic Dagger and said, "After your execution, this and your dead body will be sent to the queen. I don't imagine this was ever the ending you wished for your legacy."

Behas's mouth was sealed, but his eyes spoke of fear and regret. He looked as if he was trying to say something, but Arkin didn't want to listen to him anymore.

"Your soul will suffer deeply in *Barhoot*," said Arkin. Barhoot was a wicked hole in the earth where sahers' souls were trapped.

As the door shut, Behas shouted through the cloth in his mouth, trying to call Arkin back. Too late. The cell was dark and silent, and he was left alone to wait for his execution.

14

Prince Zufar and Bessel entered the hall of the sabla while a conversation about a cursed well was taking place. They walked to their places calmly, trying to avoid drawing attention or creating a disturbance. They then remained silent until all conversations had ended.

After the end of the last discussion, all heads turned to the Prime Sheikh, and Aad turned his towards Zufar, who was now seated between his brothers.

"Zufar," he called.

"Yes, my sheikh," answered the prince.

"Do you wish to speak?"

"I have nothing to relate to the sabla, my sheikh. But I do wish to receive your judgment and wisdom privately."

The Prime Sheikh nodded his acceptance.

Coming late to the sabla without an excuse was disrespectful. Once given the chance to speak, the member who was late should have apologized. But Zufar believed that he had his excuse, and he did not want to share it with everyone; he preferred to offer it only to the Prime Sheikh. This was another protocol of the sabla: When one believed that his issue needed to be kept private for Aad to decide alone, he could request that, but if Aad refused the request, the member would be obligated to speak for the whole council to hear.

When the sabla had finished, Aad stood tall, full of ego and pride. His large figure reminded everyone before him of his superiority and power. He nodded to all, ending the meeting. When he stood, everyone else did as well, and they remained standing motionless like statues, waiting for him to walk out.

After Aad had passed, the last of his sons, Prince Leith, who was only seventeen, turned to look at Zufar and waited for Zufar to look back. Zufar only turned his eyes in his brother's direction. The younger prince furrowed his brow and mouthed, *Where were you?* He made no sound, but Zufar read his gestures.

He was upset with Zufar's actions: coming in late and then not apologizing for being late. He resumed his statue-like position after getting no reply from Zufar. *Late! And not sorry! How could he not apologize?* he thought to himself.

Once the Prime Sheikh and his servants disappeared beyond the doorway, the silence was broken and the majlis split into side conversations. A few members walked towards the doorway; Zufar was one.

He rushed through the crowd, trying to leave as soon as he could and avoid everyone in the sabla. He had to report his failure of the night before to his father in private. But when he was halfway through the hall, his younger brother suddenly pulled his shoulder, forcing him to turn around.

Leith stared at Zufar in perplexity. They exchanged looks for a moment, as if they were both out of words. Leith was expecting an explanation for his brother's weird actions, but at that moment, Zufar had no intention of explaining himself to anyone before he saw his father.

"Where have you been?" Leith finally asked.

"I have no time to talk now; I will come to see you later today," Zufar spoke hastily, and his voice was low. He tried to walk away, but Leith pulled him back again.

He put his head close to Zufar's and matched his volume. "Stop making unwise mistakes! You will get yourself ousted." His words were a warning from a loving brother. They were close, and Leith did not wish to lose his favorite brother. "Be more careful, Zufar." Those who waited for a prince like Zufar to fail were many and would take any advantage they could.

"I will. Do not worry yourself," Zufar said, smiling and winking before leaving his younger brother and heading to where his father would be waiting.

...

He reached the upper floors, where his father resided, and a servant began walking him to the Prime Sheikh's private majlis, but before he reached it, Bessel stopped him. "My sheikh, what is wrong? We should have announced the capture of Behas. That would have justified us being late. Why did you choose to remain silent?" he asked.

Bessel feared for Zufar. The prince would be in trouble for taking the wrong advice from him.

"I will ask for more time for us to accomplish the quest. I still want to find the child, and I believe Behas knows where the child is," the prince tried to explain. His intentions were different than what Bessel had thought. "Tell no one about Behas; I want to ask him again. I want to save the child," he concluded and continued to walk away.

Bessel liked the new idea, and admired the courage his prince had, but he knew that the word of Behas's capture had already spread. The saher had been brought in through the streets of Erum with only a gag, and whatever word had spread in the street had surely spread in the High Palace. He was sure that by now, all the sabla members had heard about their captive, and if the Prime Sheikh did not hear the word from Zufar and was left to be the last to know, he would definitely send Zufar into exile!

15

Faseela led Fad, who had now covered his long hair and put on his proper green tunic, through the lower streets of the wadi to the largest open space in the city. A market was set up in the middle, and at the center of the market was the largest well in the city, the well of Sada. The well had once been the primary source of water in Erum. During the rainy days, the water would pour out of it and create a large pond. But that had not happened since this most recent drought had begun.

Surrounding the live busy marketplace were the walls of the valley. These walls were elegantly carved in order to form doors and windows for the caves in which people of Wadi Erum lived. The healer Faseela and Fad were there to see lived in one of these house-caves.

The pair managed to push the mule and his wagon through the crowd, circling around the edge of the market. Faseela stopped at a carved cave. The rectangular arch of the doorway looked old, with many cracks, and the curtains, dropped from above as a barrier to keep people from seeing in, were rotten. Small strings of smoke escaped from an upper opening on the wall. Something was cooking inside, but it smelled nothing like food.

"Lady Burmiah, are you there?" Faseela called.

"Who is calling for Lady Burmiah?" a quavering old voice answered from behind the curtains.

"It is I, Faseela from the palm groves."

For a long moment, there was no reply. The old woman did not recognize her; she had too many customers and patients to remember them all. However, she called upon them to come in.

Fad tied the mule to a pole outside and carried his wife into the cave-house behind Faseela.

The old healer, Lady Burmiah, was sitting next to a closed fireplace full of hot coals. Although the cave had ventilation holes above the door, her house was still filled with a haze of smoke, and she could barely see their faces through it. They were two adults standing there, and one was carrying a third. *Another sick patient,* she told herself.

Faseela sat before her, and Fad placed his wife on the dry floor between him and the healer. "My dear friend has been bitten by a snake," started Faseela without any prior greetings or introductions. She looked at Fad and he nodded for her to continue. "Please, help her, Lady Burmiah. We seek your wisdom and healing."

Lady Burmiah leaned forward to examine the patient with her eyes as Fad tilted his wife's head to reveal the bite marks.

Lady Burmiah was considered an occultist who used special ingredients and spiritual practices to break a jinni's harmful powers. These occultists didn't follow any guilds and preferred to work alone. They were called healers, as the practice of healing was their sole interest as occultists.

She pulled out a big rounded sack made of palm leaves from a corner and removed its cover. From the sack, she pulled out a rope that had the heads of different dead snakes knotted along its length. She stretched the rope in Fad's face to show him all the heads clearly.

There were seven or maybe eight heads, each different than the others. Fad examined them one by one. They were of all different colors, but none of them was black. He went to examine them again to make sure he remembered correctly, but Faseela interfered.

"It was a black snake," she explained. She knew because she was the one who had cleaned the hut and buried the snake that morning. "A jinni snake, we believe. One of Behas's snakes."

Lady Burmiah opened her eyes wide and threw her collection of heads back in the sack. She blurted out strange words in an ancient language and waved with her hands for the two to carry Behas's victim and leave.

Fad looked at her and at Faseela, waiting for his neighbor to explain, but Faseela hung in shock like a motionless cloud of smoke. He looked back at the healer and begged her, "Please! You have to help me. My child was kidnapped by jinn. I need to save my wife. I want to find my son!"

He held both her hands and locked his gaze on her frightened eyes in hopes of calming her fears. But her expression slid quickly from fear to fury, and she began to yell, "Out! Out!"

Faseela pulled Fad's shoulder, and he, submissive but frustrated, carried his wife out.

...

Fad and Faseela took their dear Nada to the upper city of Erum, where her parents lived. After a couple of knocks on the wooden door and a wait, her father rushed to answer the persistent and unexpected guests.

"Fada? Nada? What happened? Where is Dil?" His reaction was a mixture of confusion and fear as he flooded them with questions and reached to help Fad bring his unconscious daughter inside the house.

The house had only two rooms, a wide one at the front and a narrow one at the back, where they slept. The bathing-room and toilets were outside, where the water was usually stored. Fad placed Nada on a flat mattress in the wider room, which was used for all the daily functions like cooking, dining, and entertaining guests.

"Terrible, very terrible, Master Badde," Faseela answered. She pronounced his name properly, extending the *a* and pausing before the *e* at the end. "Nada has been cursed."

Nada's mother, Nadia, heard everything from the other room and rushed in. She cried out when she saw her daughter, thinking she was dead. They calmed her down by telling her that Nada wasn't dead but rather unconscious, poisoned by a jinni. She cried even louder and asked in concern about Dileel. She would have fainted from the shock if it hadn't been for Faseela, who repeatedly reminded her to stay strong and pray to the gods.

Fad told them about the tragic morning in detail. He was thankful that Nada was still alive and could still be healed, but he was upset by the way the healer had behaved. "I don't understand why she yelled at us to get out. She seemed frightened."

"She should be," said Badde. "No one dares to stand in Behas's way; they believe it is bad luck. But if you say that he is caught and will be executed, then we are finally about to be rid of him. I never thought I would live to see the day that Behas's head got cut off."

"If Lady Burmiah fears to heal her, we should take her to Ubar. We'll find other jinn masters and healers who will be willing to help in exchange for silver or gold," Nadia said.

"I would rather not, my lady!" Faseela interrupted. "I trust no other healer in Erum. I once heard of a girl who was taken to Ubar to be healed by 'a wise and trustful jinn master,' they told her parents. And they took their daughter to him. He did heal her, but she was never the same. Her voice, her eyes, her memory were all different from what their daughter had been before. But the poor parents took her home, although she didn't recognize them as her parents. Then one night, she escaped with the same jinn master who had healed her. It is believed that his jinni possessed her body. The jinn master *stole* her body instead of healing her, and she was never found. The parents were forever saddened."

Jinn masters can be healers as well, but their methods can be darker and more dangerous. Most would rather trust an occultist than a jinn master, unless they were extremely desperate.

"If Behas will be executed tomorrow morning," Faseela continued, "I will take Burmiah to witness it myself. Then I'll bring her here to heal Nada. It is the best thing to do. Trust my words. Nada is a strong woman; she will not surrender easily to Behas's curse."

Faseela had heard about Behas's curse and that it was the most powerful. A bite from any snake jinni was considered a curse. It could leave a person unconscious or paralyzed for several hours. If a healer tried to help a victim of Behas's jinni, it was believed the same curse would pass on to them.

"I, myself, trust Faseela and her plan," Fad assured his in-laws.

Badde was convinced. His wife, Nadia, was not, but she kept her thoughts to herself. The story she had just heard sounded scarier.

"And Dil? What are you going to do about him?" asked Nadia.

"There is nothing he can do; children kidnapped by jinn masters are never found," Badde answered her.

Faseela nodded at Fad. She, like many in Arabia, was interested in hearing about jinn and would believe whatever story was told about them.

"Oh, my dear Nada. We should pray to Somood and make sacrifices so that Dil is returned safely." Her mother reminded them to turn to religion.

Fad thought about Nadia's question thoroughly. *What should I do?* He remembered the master occultist he had met earlier that morning, Arkin. He had been told to come and see him in the High Palace. *Maybe that is where I should start.* He had found the answer to his mother-in-law's question. "I will bring back my child," he said before standing up to leave.

"Where are you going?" Nadia called.

"To the High Palace."

As he left, they all stared at each other in thought and prayed that he succeeded.

...

On his way to the High Palace, he passed by the largest roofless temple in Erum, the shrine of Somood. He froze to stare at the magnificent height of the rectangular pillars, which appeared to support the sky above Erum.

There were pillars of all different shapes and heights in the temple. The largest and tallest were twelve erected columns, higher than the High Palace of Erum. Their placing appeared random and irregular, but each pillar was positioned purposely to resemble one of the twelve constellations that the sun passed through. At the capital of each pillar, a face was carved that resembled the lord of the constellation. Below the faces, some pillars had ancient writings carved on them, while on others, the carvings were of things like animals and tools.

Around the bottom of each gigantic pillar were placed many shorter cylindrical pillars, which recalled the main stars in the relevant constellation.

Fad entered the temple grounds. At their center were a few spherical rocks of different sizes. These represented the known planets, including the sun and the moon. He walked to the center of the spherical shapes, and only one of them was carved to form a face. The carved face resembled Somood, one of three main deities worshipped in Erum.

The expression on the carved face of Somood was vague. It was known that the expression you would see was a reflection of Somood's feelings towards you. Fad saw a gloomy face in that rock and felt more depressed at the sight of it. He fell to his knees and, in ritual, kissed a raised bronze tablet nearby. The tablet had ancient South Arabian writing on it, like many of the others that were spread around the temple grounds and on some of the pillars.

Fad sank into deep sorrow. He wept before his lord, pleading for help to bring back his only child.

16

Being the Chief Guardian of Palace Affairs, Bessel was diplomatic, or rather careful, one would say. The envious and tense atmosphere between the sons of Aad would sometimes become deadly.

Aad had eight wives, who had given him twenty-four sons and twenty-five daughters. Prince Zufar was the fifth son, while Prince Leith was the seventeenth. Bessel knew that many princes in the High Palace did not favor Zufar. Ever since he had lost his mother, they sensed their father's sympathy towards him; he was her only son. But most of them had no sympathy for that, and they would take advantage of any failure to see him as an outcast.

Many times before, Erum had witnessed the Prime Sheikh sending his flawed sons away to take charge of one of the far-off settlements in the sheikhdom. Punishment or lesson—either way, it was unofficially known as exile from power. Those who underwent it were no longer favored to rule in Erum after Aad.

Bessel was the one who had caused the exile of Shadeed by exposing his secret practice of sorcery and jinn summoning in the palace after it was forbidden by Aad. Many heirs who were waiting for their time had thanked Bessel for it. But ever since then, he had been hated by Prince Shadeed, and he didn't want to be hated by Zufar as well.

Bessel feared for his prince that day. He feared their failure the night before would be taken by the other princes as a chance to finally force the Prime Sheikh to send Zufar away.

Now, he waited anxiously for Zufar to emerge from his father's closed majlis. He thought Zufar's decision to seek the child was a good one, but one that needed to be executed carefully. It would either compensate for their failure or extend it.

. . .

Zufar entered the private majlis, and the servant closed the thick door behind him, leaving him alone with his father.

Zufar walked a short distance and sat next to his father in the small white chamber. It got some sunlight, which came from behind a thin curtain hung from a little opening in the high roof above, but had no windows on the walls. The walls were almost six feet thick, not allowing any sounds to be heard by eavesdroppers outside.

Zufar went for a bottle of date wine beside him. Next to it were six cups made of carved stone. Six was apparently the maximum number of giants that could fit in this chamber. He poured wine in two and placed a cup before his father first.

"I apologize for being late to the sabla this morning," Zufar said. He drank a bit from his cup of wine to wet his dry mouth, and then he told his father, beginning with his order to the guards to search Erum, continuing through his decision to send two men to fetch the child, and ending with the capture of Behas.

Zufar was smarter than to give misleading information or to hide anything from the Prime Sheikh. His father had many servants around him who were his personal spies as well, seeing and hearing everything that happened in and out of the High Palace. He even had the feeling that his father had already heard some or all of what he had just said and was only testing him to see if he would tell the tale himself, wholly and truthfully.

After justifying his reasons for failing to complete the Noorians' request, he explained his plans to force the jinn master, Behas, to help them find the child for the Noorians.

"The child is not my concern," his father interrupted. "He is not the first victim of the outlaw jinn master. You have succeeded in capturing him. Because of that, many children will be saved. The Noorians do not care much about the loss of this child; if it were important, they would have sent us their higher-ranked occultists to get it.

"Thirty years ago, when you were about five years old, jinn mastery was still allowed in Erum. People lived in constant fear. Behas served us then; he played an important role in taming evil jinn, and he helped us in our hunt for outlaws and sahers who created fear. He was pledged to serve the great Wadi of Erum. But when we decided to ban witchcraft in our lands, he rebelled. His actions encouraged many to follow in his steps.

"Today, you brought him back to face punishment before all of Erum. I have sent out your older brothers to find him many times before, but last night, I decided to test your wisdom. And you have done well. Tomorrow morning, you will announce to the sabla that it was you who finally caught the most famous outlaw. His execution shall not be delayed after that; it will be made public by noon tomorrow for all of Erum to witness.

"Then no one can question your abilities and maturity or, most importantly, your loyalty to me. You will join your brothers and journey east," he continued. "The time has come for you to lead in battle."

...

Zufar was well aware that some people in high positions in Erum distrusted him because his mother had come from an enemy tribe. But now he realized what his father was doing. He was giving Zufar the chance to prove everyone wrong and finally entrusting him with an army.

He had first come in thinking that he needed to save the child to please his father, but it seemed his father was more pleased with how the events had ended than he had ever imagined. Of all the scenarios he had predicted while riding back that morning, this was the most unexpected of all. He had gone from fearing banishment to gaining in reputation and trust.

...

Bessel was still waiting outside the private chambers. After a long time, the Prime Sheikh's large African servants finally opened the door for Zufar to exit the chamber.

"My sheikh, did it all go well?"

"It all went well." The prince was lost in thought. Although his father's decisions were all positive, a part of him still wanted to find the child first. But now that he had to join his brothers to war, he wouldn't be able to save the boy.

Bessel continued to walk beside him while the prince headed to his room, which was not far away from his father's hall. Bessel wanted to ask him again if everything was all right or not, but he continued to walk in silence.

"My father seemed not to care about the child," Prince Zufar finally said. "He is sending me to join my brothers in Akersad."

Bessel was sharp; he quickly figured out that Zufar was being rewarded rather than punished. The capture of Behas had helped them. Pleased to hear the cheer in his prince's voice, he smiled all his own fears away. But the prince still seemed lost in thought. It felt like he wasn't actually addressing Bessel but rather was thinking out loud and talking to himself. Bessel continued to walk in silence.

They stopped when they reached Zufar's chamber. "About the child," Zufar said. "Last night, I cared only about saving him for my father to be pleased, but then, riding back to Erum, I felt there was something missing from Behas's and Arkin's tales."

Bessel was now sure that the giant was talking to him. "What is it?"

"I do not know, but I want to," Zufar said and bit his lips tightly. He inhaled through his nose, holding his breath for a moment while he thought, then sighed and looked down at Bessel with slight worry in his eyes. "We should rest for now; meet me at the dungeons right after the sunset horn."

A horn was always blown in the temple of Somood an hour before sunset. It was a ritual call that also allowed the people of Erum to tell the time. One would ask to meet an hour before the sunset horn or three hours after the sunset horn. As for the prince, he was planning to rest until then, and then head down with Bessel to see Behas.

Bessel nodded, staring at the raised door of the prince's chamber as it shut in front of him.

...

Zufar woke up late; he hadn't heard the horn, and it was dark outside by the time he descended to the dungeons. "This way." Qassas, the Prime Chief Guardian, was leading him through the dungeons to where Behas was kept. The prince felt lost and in need of being guided; the Guardians' dungeons were a dark maze.

He found Behas near the furthest wall of his cell, under deep darkness. His back was arched, and he appeared to be busy with something in his hands. It wasn't immediately clear what the thing was. Zufar crept nearer to see. It was a child!

Fear rushed up through his guts. He forced the child from Behas's grasp and held it high and close, trying to see it well, but it was too dark. The child exploded into a repeated pattern of loud, strange cries. The noises were familiar to Zufar but sounded awkward coming from a child. A terrible form of fear conquered his heart, one filled with dusk and darkness. He then found himself staring out his window, looking over the valley. The Great City of Erum lay before him in ruins.

He came awake suddenly from what appeared to have been a bad dream. The familiar noise was coming from the temple of Somood—the horn of sunset, not a child's cry.

He stood up from his bed and rushed to reach the dungeons below, where he had promised to meet Bessel. He couldn't shake the dream from his head; it felt real!

He reached the dungeons below, not needing a guide, and found Bessel there before him. The guards were pulling Behas out of his cell and setting him on his knees before the prince.

"Let him stand," Bessel ordered.

The guards lifted Behas to his feet so his head would be closer to the tall prince, but Behas couldn't stand straight because of the injury to his ankle.

"Know that your answers will not spare you from execution," declared Bessel. "We can promise you nothing in return, but we seek your knowledge before it is wasted." He nodded for his guards to remove the gag from Behas's mouth.

The two guards exchanged looks and their hesitant stares shifted towards the prince, but his face was blank, and they had to fulfill the orders. They did fear Behas's jinn and his tricks, but they were in Erum. *No jinn can help him here,* they thought.

Once his mouth was uncovered, Behas inhaled strongly and exhaled his pain so loudly that everyone around him felt it. He coughed and breathed in again before he spoke. "I am honored, my sheikh, to share with you all that you seek," he said, ending with a creepy grin. He seemed to care nothing at all for the fact that he would soon be without a head.

"Why did you want to kill the child? What evil did you speak of?" the prince began.

"The star he was born under has condemned him. He can be used to release great evil—the type of evil that can end us all. I beg you, my sheikh, find the child. Whoever took it must be stopped before it is too late. Trust my words, and many lives will be saved."

"He's bluffing, my sheikh," Bessel interrupted.

"Explain it further, Behas." The prince ignored Bessel's warnings. "Tell me everything you know."

And Behas did. He told the giant prince everything he believed would happen if the child, or whoever stole the child, was not stopped.

"Thank you for your words. I will ensure that you are treated well on your last night. Any other wishes?"

Behas laughed. "I am at your service, my sheikh. Your generosity exceeds my demands." His smile suddenly turned to a grimace. "Save Erum!" He waited for the prince to nod and turn away.

After the prince had left the dungeons. Behas locked gazes with Bessel, who had waited for his prince to leave in order to have a word with the jinn master in private. "You can lie to the prince, but not to me. You will be executed tomorrow."

"I have told nothing but the truth."

Bessel did not respond to that. He walked away, telling the dungeon guards, "We are done with him."

At the doorway, he found a guard from the gate waiting for him. "Chief Guardian Bessel," the man said, "there is a man at the gate of the palace asking for you. He claims you have promised to help him." He showed Bessel the dagger given to Fad by the Guardian messenger.

The farmer, he remembered. "Send him to Hammah's chamber; that is where we will be."

17

Bessel followed the prince as they headed to the chamber of the oldest sage. They climbed the stairs and moved through the hallways above in silence.

As they neared the sage's chamber, the prince thought aloud. "Such strange events, such a strange child. The Noorians' queen sends a letter asking us to save it, while Behas claims it is evil and must be killed. I will never understand both their worlds or their conflicts, occultists or sahers, but I know which cause drives our actions. We're sworn to keep Erum safe."

Bessel remained silent, sincerely doubting what his sheikh's true intentions were.

The giant then stopped. He changed his mind, deciding not to be involved anymore, as he had other work to do.

"Since I have to leave with my brothers to go east, I will have you sent out to seek the child, Bessel," the prince said. "When I am back from the eastern borders, I will be expecting to hear that the child has been found for the Noorians. You will journey with Arkin and *find* the child."

"I will, my sheikh. I will," Bessel assured him.

"I do not expect to see you in my father's majlis tonight. Your quest begins now. You must excuse me, for I have other matters to arrange and prepare. I want to see my sisters before leaving for the east as well." He then locked eyes with Bessel. "I trust the child will be found, since you will be in charge of finding him."

And that was the last time that Zufar and Bessel ever saw each other.

...

Bessel entered the sage's chamber and found Hammah, Arkin, and Yam discussing the events of the night before. They all welcomed him as the two old wise men continued to listen to Yam, who told them all what he had witnessed that night.

"One moment, the child was in Behas's hands, and then a second later, there was no sign of him at all!" Yam concluded.

"I wonder, then—even if we find the child, how can we be sure they will not take him again?" Arkin expressed his concerns. And he was right: Finding him was one thing but keeping him safe was another.

"I don't think Behas's tale was true," Hammah said. "It is extremely difficult, almost impossible, to summon an air jinni. But so far, I too cannot find another explanation. An air jinni moves like a breeze, and they can teleport any physical matter or being, small or large, alive or dead. If they are well trained and at their full potential, they can move something as big as this whole palace from Erum and place it far away in Africa if their masters wish. But they have their weaknesses..." He continued to explain about the rarity of an air jinni and its powers.

Not late after Bessel walked in, a guard knocked at the door to allow himself in and introduce Fad. They welcomed him and expressed their willingness to help him find his son. They also expressed their condolences for the loss of his wife, whom he explained was not dead, and asked if they could heal her after the healer Burmiah had refused to do so. Hammah agreed with what Faseela had told Fad: After Behas was executed the next day, Lady Burmiah would heal her. He also tried to lessen his worries.

"The jinni poison is not deadly for an adult," Hammah said. "And she will be healed, trust me. It will be like waking up from a long sleep."

...

"We shall not waste any more of the night, since we are all here," Bessel said, eager to begin his quest. "How can we find the child?"

"We now know a parent, and that will make it easy for any all-knowing jinni to find the child," Hammah explained. "In Erum, they will not see where he is. You must reach Ubar tonight, and there you can find some of the seers who will tell you where the child is." Then he pointed at Fad. "He is needed by the seers to find the child, and I recommend he ask them alone; it will help the seers focus on his thoughts and find his child."

Bessel nodded. Both Bessel and Arkin exchanged looks, then turned their eyes towards Fad. He was now their key for any all-knowing jinni to find the child, his child.

"I don't trust the seers from Ubar. They're deceitful liars and tell nothing right," said Fad, disagreeing with the idea. He thought right, as many seers, though not all of them, lied for personal gain.

"You are right," Hammah said. "But that is because their jinn can see only the present; whatever they tell you about the future is a mere guess. But they are now your only hope."

"That is why you shall ask where the child is at present, and nothing more," Arkin added.

"And what if they ask for difficult tasks to be performed, something time-consuming, like they usually do?" Fad argued.

The sage continued addressing Fad as if he were the only one in the room. "They can be elusive and cunning, I know. Tempt them with silver, for you have no time to waste on performing their endless tasks."

Fad switched his gaze from Hammah to Bessel and Arkin. *Silver?* He thought. A farmer had nothing to offer but dry dates for now.

"I will provide you with all the silver you'll need," Bessel said, as if he had sensed Fad's worries.

"Outsmart them when you speak," Hammah added. "Convince them, and they shall tell you the truth. They are not all wise and can be beaten easily."

...

And that, if you have not yet figured out, was the only difference between Behas and any other seers and jinn masters in Erum. Behas could find the child without knowing either of its parents.

Fortunately for them, tonight, Behas had led them to the child and its parents but failed to kill any of them, and he himself would soon be executed. But unfortunately, the child was lost, and they had to trust other jinn masters to find the boy.

...

"We should head to Ubar now. We must learn where the child is before dawn. From there, we shall begin our journey to wherever the child may be." Bessel spoke in a commanding voice to Fad and Arkin.

"I... How can I put this?" Arkin hesitated. "I was planning to join you, but only an hour ago I received an urgent letter from Hadaus. The queen has requested to see me. I had first arranged that Behas's corpse would be sent to the queen after his execution, but now I am being asked to bring it there myself. The journey won't be long, I hope. Once I am finished meeting with the queen, I will come to find you, Bessel, wherever you are. I will also look for our spy and bring him along. He should be able to help us find the child as well."

Bessel did not argue. His mission now was clear, and he needed only the parent to perform it. The Noorian could help them after he found his own saher. Fad, too, agreed to it all and urged Bessel to begin the journey to Ubar without delay.

"Can I join them?" Yam asked Arkin. On their way from the mountain, Yam had asked him if he could join his guild and be an occultist, saying that he did not want to be a porter anymore. Arkin was now officially his master occultist. But it seemed that he didn't want to go back to the mountain with him for now; he wanted to help find the child with Bessel and Fad.

"Can you walk?" Bessel asked first, before Arkin decided.

"I sure can," Yam said. But he stood with difficulty, using a stick to get nearer. "The pain is almost gone."

"I cannot take you with us; you will slow us down." Bessel rejected Yam's offer with a strong Guardian's tone.

Yam frowned.

"You should find rest, Yam," Arkin said. "I don't think I can bear to place you in any more danger. I will come to see you here when we're all done."

Yam nodded, but he didn't seem to be in full agreement.

Fad didn't care who came; all he cared about was finding Dil. But he didn't enjoy Arkin's thought. He hoped they could find Dil as soon as possible, perhaps even before dawn. He thought deeply about his wife as well and prayed for her to be healed sooner.

18

Bessel and Fad left the High Palace on two fine Arabian horses, racing through the night to reach Ubar, the third biggest city in the dominion of Erum. They reached it after riding for less than an hour and without stopping.

Ubar was a hub for traders who traveled to and from the Wadi of Erum. The walls of Ubar provided protection, and its wells were filled with water, making it a suitable place for traders to find lodging. It was also cheaper and more flexible in its applications of the law than Wadi Erum.

The City of Wood Pillars, it was called—tent pillars, to be more specific. The name did refer to the many poles erected to hold the numerous and colorful tents, which could be spotted from far above, in the hills.

Traders visiting Ubar preferred to settle in their own tents. There were many tents set up and taken down every day in Ubar, as traders came and left occasionally. They exceeded the number of stone structures, although those were present.

The biggest stone structure was the palace of the sheikh, Zahi, son of Ubar, a young nephew of the Prime Sheikh, Aad. Next to his palace were huge barracks, which also housed a special division that served the Guardians of Erum. A wall of stone circled the city. Outside the wall, the valley was filled with several farms and barns, and inside the walls, every space was occupied with a tent.

...

Bessel and Fad tied their horses at the gate nearest the barracks. Bessel left orders for their horses to be fed, washed, and made ready for them to leave at any time.

He entered the House of Guardians, followed by Fad, and, knowing exactly whom he wanted, he maneuvered through the rooms to reach another Chief Guardian. This division of Guardians was more responsible for dealing with jinnism, dark magic, and sahers. They had been founded long ago to tame evil jinn, and since Aad's new laws had come into effect, they were the ones who made sure the laws were followed. They were called the jinn tamers.

Aad's rules for jinn summoning and jinn mastery were simple. The practice of summoning harmful jinn was forbidden, but the practice of summoning jinn to help others was allowed. Limited, yet allowed.

"Bessel! What brings you from the High Palace at this late time?" a jinn tamer said with a smile on his face as he walked towards Bessel to embrace him.

"Harf, my old friend," Bessel replied. After a hug and a pat on the shoulder, Bessel began with a short explanation intended to prevent any delays or unnecessary conversation.

"We've been sent by Sheikh Zufar to find a kidnapped child. Kidnapped by jinn, as you should know." Bessel then pointed at Fad. "Behas attacked this man, Fad, and his family last night. The saher has been caught, but the child has not been found. The child is very important to the sheikh, and he must be found, and soon."

"So the rumors are true—you *have* captured Behas!" Harf seemed unsurprised. "I knew it, although the only major updates we received from the sabla this morning were regarding the attacks in Akersad. I've always said you were a great jinn tamer yourself, Bessel."

"It will be announced tomorrow morning, and he will be executed in Erum before noon." Although Prince Zufar had told him to keep that a secret, Bessel trusted his old friend Harf. "We can leave that discussion for a later time. We need a seer. We need to help this farmer find his son." He spoke the last sentence while gently pulling Fad to stand nearer to them. "We have no time to waste."

"A seer," Harf repeated to himself, staring at the roof in thought. "There are many illegal soothsayers currently in Ubar. They do come and go every day," he said and turned his head as if disappointed. "I do not recall any of the great seers being at Ubar right now. You can try your luck, but I doubt they could be helpful."

Bessel pulled out a pouch of coins and waved it before the Chief Guardian. Fad gave a slight grin of trust and relief. "With silver, they will speak. Show us where to find them," said Bessel.

They followed Harf a long way through the roads of Ubar until they reached a dark passage between many tents. "This is where they gather, mostly," Harf said. Being an experienced jinn tamer in Ubar, he knew where the seers settled or hid. They hid not from people but from Guardians and jinn tamers like Bessel and himself. "This way," he said, and pointed Fad to a narrow path between dark tents.

Bessel gave him the pouch of coins. "Twenty silver coins," he told the farmer. "You have to go without us now. I will wait nearby."

"Most seers hang camel bones outside their tents if they're available," Harf added. "Do not waste time. Ask them where the child is and be done."

And so Fad turned away from the two Chief Guardians and stepped onto the dark path, illuminated only by a dim glow of some light from each tent. He had never been through these parts of Ubar, only heard of them. Now he was alone and focused on one thing, his son.

That night, he wished he were being guided rather than left alone. Ironically, his son's name, Dileel, meant "guidance" or "clue" in Arabic as well. *I was searching for Dileel without a dileel,* he would later say, describing his quest.

His eyes caught the light of the moon reflected on the white bones hung outside of some tents, like eyes staring back at him, calling him to get near but creepy enough to keep anyone sane away. There were many tents with bones. He also heard voices from some of them, which meant they were busy. Fad was picky, and he despised seers, but now he needed them. After he passed three or four big tents, his eyes fell on an open one, not far, illuminated by a dim red glow—not fire red but rather a dying-coal red. A welcoming necklace of camel bones hung at its entrance, and there, Fad turned to see inside.

A giant brown man with white hair and a white beard sat at the far end of the tent, behind a cloud of frankincense. He had his legs crossed and was staring blankly back at Fad. *An African seer,* thought Fad. One could easily tell from the bizarre animal furs on the ground, the lined brown and black fur of Africa's wild deer. His uniform was a long white garment, and he also wore a gigantic white East African turban, which was almost three times the size of the head it covered.

"May I enter?"

"Of course you may, brother Fada."

His jinni must have told him my name, Fad thought, and walked completely normally to reflect confidence. *My name is a fact in the present, nothing more,* he thought, calming himself. Fad knew well that all-knowing jinn couldn't read inner thoughts. They could tell only facts from the stars above, but not secrets.

The curtains behind him closed as he entered. No one was there to close them, Fad was certain!

"How can we serve you? What knowledge do you seek this night?" the African seer asked in a monotone.

I thought a seer like you would have seen my question coming! thought Fad with a laugh, but he did not dare reveal it and kept his face straight and dull. "My child has been kidnapped. I need to know who took him and where he is kept." Straight to the point, and all easy for an all-knowing jinni. But Fad shouldn't have been that specific; it made him look desperate and vulnerable. The seer would not provide such valuable information without asking an equally or more valuable price in return.

The jinn master closed his eyes, raised his chin, and hummed loud. This was a bit of exaggeration to fool his customers, but he did in fact hear his jinni whisper through his mind. Fad heard nothing but the awkward humming, so he waited for answers.

A seer, or any soothsayer, acts as an interpreter for the all-knowing jinn lord he serves. Sometimes an all-knowing jinni asks for tasks to be performed in return that even the jinn master has no control over. It's a strange relationship; the jinn master can be the dominant one, like Behas, or it can be the other way around.

The round-faced African slowly opened his dark eyes. Silence filled the tent again. "Difficult to find an eight-day-old child. We need a lock of hair from his parent."

Fad unsheathed the Guardian's dagger and held his long hair, preparing to cut it.

"No!" The fat seer stopped him from cutting anything. "Not you. The mother."

"You said a parent. You can use my hair."

"Not I who decides," said the seer. "We wants mother hair only, or we cannot know."

Fad found it hard to understand his foreign tongue. "My wife is an hour away from here! If I went to Wadi Erum and came back to you, I would lose the whole night. Please. Just use my hair instead."

"With no mother hair, we cannot find the child."

Perhaps Fad's negotiation skills were poor, or it might have been that since he lost his child he had become impatient, which was not the habit of a farmer who raised motionless palms and harvested ripened dates that never rotted if they were properly dried and stored. Or maybe he was just tired from a long and unusual day. "I will give you silver. Use my hair."

"For mother hair, we wants four silver coins. For father hair, we wants fifty gold coins."

In Arabia, a *fils* was a bronze coin, a *dirham* was a silver coin, and a *dinar* was a gold coin.

And poor Fad, even if he had sold all his year's harvest and his father's, and both their farms with all their tall palms, would get barely fifty gold coins. All he had received from Bessel that night was twenty coins of silver.

You must understand an important thing about seers. They do it for a living, and it's all about the money. But they are not all poor and desperate. If you cannot afford to pay a seer what he asks for in Ubar, it is best you find another.

After trying to convince the African seer to lower his price, Fad left the smoky red tent, bristling with rage and frustration.

He stood at the start of the path again and looked back and forth to find another open tent with camel bones. Some tents were dark, and some were illuminated from inside but were closed. Farther down the path, there were three open tents, and two had white bones hanging on their doors. They flashed like beacons for Fad to follow.

He walked to the one nearest to him, and as he reached it and stood before the two poles that held its drapes open, he realized that this small tent was only an entrance to a larger complex of tents behind it. There were four other poles at the entrance that held up a single large drape of light red, blue, and gold. As Fad came through the small entrance, he discovered the interior was larger than the East African's tent from before. Inside, there was another closed entrance, and the noise coming from it was loud and live, a mixture of laughter, music, and joyful cries. In the entrance tent, two men sat on three-legged round chairs. Chairs were not at all popular in Erum, where people preferred to sit on the ground. The travelers had definitely brought these small foreign chairs with them. They both wore white pants, white tunics, and long, open pink skirts. One was decorated with a pattern of black squares, while the other was decorated with black flowers. They were both bald, which meant they were servants from Babylon. Most Babylonian traders kept their servants bald to distinguish them from others. And although Fad was a poor farmer from Erum, he could tell from which part of the world people came from. He had traveled with his father to Port Rori many times, and he had met many traders there.

When Fad entered, he interrupted their whispering laughter. One of the two opened his palm to Fad like a beggar, and, eyeing the farmer's cheap green tunic scornfully, he said, "Three coins of silver, and no weapons allowed."

Only three coins of silver. Fad thought this was a much cheaper price than the African's. He paid the fee and handed them his dagger. The two pale boys considered the Guardian's dagger for a long moment, probably having second thoughts about letting him in. After long inspecting stares at Fad and his weapon, they allowed him to enter. There were, in fact, many other reasons a regular Erumian might own such a blade. He could, for example, simply have bought it from a blacksmith in Erum.

Inside the large tent, which had many decorated wooden pillars and torches, there was a crowd made up of all sorts of people: women and men dressed in many colors, dancing and singing and drinking. Fad gazed upon the party before him. There was no obvious leader in the group, and most certainly no seers at all. He knew well what sort of tent this was—a tent of sin and lust. He had been to some before he was married, but tonight he had no time to dance and sing. He had to know where his child was. He thought the bones outside had led him to a seer's tent, but the large cheerful tent led to many others, and he might spend the whole night searching them to find a seer. So he turned back to the small entrance tent where the two young pale servants were.

"I am looking for a seer," he whispered, embarrassed to be interrupting their laughter and private talk for the second time.

One stood, looking as if Fad had not been the first to make such a request. "The seer? Follow me." The servant held Fad's hands and pulled him back inside. They dodged their way through the drunken crowd to reach the far end of the sea of interconnected tents. He opened one of many curtains, and they both walked inside another smaller tent, which was still larger than the first seer's tent Fad had entered earlier that night.

In that tent, there was no crowd. The servant released Fad's hand, and from beyond the still mist in the tent's air, a sonorous voice cried, "Welcome, Fada. We have been expecting you." A seer's bluff, or maybe it wasn't, but that was what Fad felt, at least. He saw the source of the call coming from another fat man with a thick black beard and a broad smile that revealed his set of white teeth. He was rubbing his palms together rapidly and tenderly, warming them up, with his chin lowered to his chest as he smiled eagerly.

"There they are," said the servant, pointing at a lit incense burner in front of the fat seer. The servant wished Fad some luck and left him alone.

They? thought Fad, when he saw only one, but he was not too surprised, as the African seer before had repeatedly used "we" to refer to himself and his jinni.

The tent was blue, and with the red coal in the incense burner, a purple glow reflected on the clouds of smoke that hung below the roof of the tent. Fad walked with care towards the only source of light. This tent, I can assure you, was a lot fancier than the African's tent, and the many goods laid out in it also made Fad feel he had entered a dark cave of many treasures. He saw the shadows of decorated chests stacked one over the other and many small shiny statues of owls and lions. Even the chubby seer who sat behind the incense burner looked like a rich king. He was dressed in expensive thick blue and gold fabrics, and his face was filled with a long beard. Floating beside him was the sad face of a very old man, whose body was all wrapped in blue as well, as if he were bound there. Fad had not noticed him at first, but now, being close, he could not help staring at him. The old man did not stare back, for his eyes were shut.

Once Fad had sat on the large pillow across from them, the large man began. "Welcome, Fada. My name is Mair-Batlo, and I am a traveler from Akkadia, in Babylonia. I travel the world to trade in—you might have noticed as you walked in—everything," he said, and burst into laughter. "I enjoy money the most, but I also enjoy seeing the future. That is why I always travel with my brother, Shar-Shar, everywhere I go. He's a seer." The old man lifted his head, as if alerted by hearing his name. The large man leaned forward towards Fad to whisper a secret.

"Shar-Shar has helped me trade right and become mighty and rich, as you can see," he continued and exploded into more loud laughter. Then his laughter suddenly shrank and ended with a tiny, sly giggle.

Fad felt the pouch in his pocket, remembering that he had paid three silver coins to enter and now had only seventeen left. He now became aware that the three coins were only the entrance fee, and he feared this seer would be more expensive than the first seer; he certainly looked more expensive.

"What's wrong?" asked Mair-Batlo. "You don't have enough coins, farmer?" As he asked the second question, he giggled again. He was a cheerful man who loved to laugh, even if he was the only one who did.

What Fad had feared most was not how much money he had in his pocket, but the time he had wasted to reach this seer. He needed to know where his son, Dil, had been taken, and he needed to know fast.

"Have no worry, farmer, I will take little from you. I do this for fun and joy as well, not *only* for money."

"Then let us begin, for I do not have all night."

The seer was so surprised by Fad's words that his watermelon-sized open mouth shrank to the size of a grape.

"Fine," said the Babylonian. "But first, let me amuse you with the strange story of Shar-Shar." Every time he mentioned the name Shar-Shar, the old man raised his head as if searching or listening, thinking his brother was calling him. "We call him that because he had two unfortunate incidents befall him that made him what he is today," Mair-Batlo began to relate. "One day, when Shar-Shar was a boy of seven years old, his wicked neighbor popped his ears so he wouldn't hear anymore. He can't hear anything at all."

He did seem to hear his name, but Fad now wondered if the old man heard his name, Shar-Shar, called through his ears or by a jinni.

Mair-Batlo continued: "But no one blamed his wicked neighbor for popping his ears, for it was his jealous mother's fault. She was uglier than her neighbor. His mother forced him to eavesdrop on the wicked neighbor every day and then went and told everyone what bad things the wicked neighbor said about them. And for this pointless act of envy, poor Shar-Shar lost his ears when he was a boy of seven!" The old man again moved his head, as if the only thing his disabled ears could hear was his name.

"That was the first *Shar,* which has the literal meaning of 'an unfortunate event.' The second time such an event befell him, he was a boy of only nine years old. He lost his sight. No one popped his eyes out, for after the first incident, you might have guessed that he learned his lesson and became more polite and kind. But poor Shar-Shar."

The old man jumped, hearing his name.

"For his eyes, he inherited from his father. His father had not always been blind, and he was a potter, a hard-working potter. Using his clay wheel, he made all kinds of plates and cups for people to eat and drink from. But one day, while moving his finished pottery, he carried so many that he could not manage to control them, and the poor old potter tripped and fell. The dry pottery he carried scattered, and sharp shards of clay flew straight into his eyes and made him blind. He continued to work with clay, but his work was never as good as it had been when he had his sight." He laughed again, but Fad didn't find that funny but rather horrible. Fad didn't find any of the man's previous laughter justified. And he was there to learn where his son was, not to laugh.

"People warned the blind potter that he shouldn't have more children," said Mair-Batlo. "They told him if he had another child, he would meet the same unfortunate fate. He did not listen to them and added one more boy to his family. That boy was Shar-Shar, and one day, when he was only nine years old, his blind father, who could not move pottery anymore, made his children do it. Shar-Shar carried more than he could as well, and he tripped and lost his sight, like his father before him.

"All this is only the story of why we called him Shar-Shar. It is not yet his strange story that I wanted to tell you about, for this old man you see is my little brother!"

Fad was shocked. The old man looked about twenty decades old, while the fat bearded one, Mair-Batlo, looked to be in his early fifties.

"I was fortunate to be a disobedient son who never listened to his jealous mother and was born before my father lost his sight, and I never helped him with the pottery. And that is why I can still see and hear like a normal man, and my little brother has only his tongue," he continued to relate, wasting Fad's time, although the farmer was slightly curious to hear more.

"But the reason why he looks fifty years older than I do is his all-knowing jinni. No one knows when or how he met his jinni, who took away his youth but blessed him with better insight into the future and whispered in his mind knowledge that Shar-Shar shares only with me. This virtue we were blessed with has changed us from being the children of a poor and blind potter to being the richest two brothers from the village we came from.

"So tell us, what is it you would like to know? But know!" He laughed at that as well. "Our jinni has its own rules. You can ask only two questions: one question about a fact you know but think we don't know, so it can prove to you that it knows everything, and one question that must be about a future that has not happened yet, which you would like for it to tell you about." He smiled wide, waiting for Fad to ask. "I hope you excite us with a brilliant question."

He rubbed his hands again and lowered his chin to his chest as he always did. Every time he did that, Fad felt less trusting, but also less superior to his deception, as if there were nothing one could do to defy him. "Usually farmers are boring, with lame questions. But our jinni told us an extraordinary farmer named Fada would visit tonight! And here you are." His eyes opened wide, two bright stars of excitement and anticipation.

"I—I am interested only in the present. I lost my…"

"Rules. Are. Rules!" Mair-Batlo exploded in rage. His cheerful eyes became larger, reddened, and filled with anger. "Two questions, two secrets for us to reveal, one from the present and another about the future you want to know. And the price will be fifteen dirhams."

Poor Fad leaned away in fear while seated in his place. *Fifteen!* The price was high, but after the big greedy tradesman exploded, he did not seem like one he would want to bargain with. Fad also remembered that he had left his dagger at the entrance, and he was now unarmed as well. *There is no escaping from Mair-Batlo,* he thought. The man knew his name and claimed he had been waiting for him that night. Fad did have an exciting, if unfortunate, tale to tell. The previous night had not been boring at all, and that it had led him to this tent was unlucky in itself, thought Fad. He considered leaving, but he also thought about Bessel, who was probably now worried that Fad had been gone for too long.

As for the cost, he could afford it, but it would leave him with nothing but two coins.

He made up his mind. He could afford the price and had no time to waste looking for another seer. He needed to find his son. *Outsmart them when you speak,* he remembered. But how could he? He was only a poor palm farmer.

"Speak, farmer. Let us not wait any longer." The man's voice softened. The broad smile and hand rubbing reflected more anticipation. Fad sensed it, and it made him nervous.

Fad did not think long about what to ask. He knew what he *wanted* to ask, but the seer before had asked for a hair lock from the mother, and he couldn't afford any difficult requests, not now, so he needed to play by the rules, or seem to. He needed to outsmart the seers. A plan revealed itself in his mind, and he smiled.

"Fine, let us start with the secret," Fad began, and Mair-Batlo drew nearer with eyes open wider and a broader smile. "I have one child; he is now eight days old. But he is hidden. Can you tell where he is hidden now, as we speak?"

Mair-Batlo leaned backwards, and his smile disappeared. "I hope you didn't hide your child in your farm hut, in a basket under a palm tree, or in a well bucket. Let us begin."

Shar-Shar Arr Yar Nar
Tar Far Lar, Oh Shar-Shar
Ayn Al' Tifl Ya Shar
Ya Ramz Al Hikma Wal Shar

Ramz Al Hikma Wal Shar? The symbol of wisdom and evil? Fad interpreted the words of the poem. They were unpleasant, but he kept his thoughts to himself for now.

With that poem, the older-looking younger brother became alert and began to whisper strange words to his jinni. He hummed and grimaced and turned upset, and Fad could tell he wasn't happy. Then Shar-Shar spoke in Mair-Batlo's ears, and the other also grimaced.

"I misjudged your intelligence, farmer. For it seems that you have hidden the child so well that even you do not know where he is! That, I must say, is challenging." He rubbed his hands again joyfully as he lowered his smiling chin. "We need his mother's hair."

Fad bit his lip. He had to act quickly, and he did. He played the perfect act. He switched his gaze back to them with a taunting laugh and said, "You have failed to find my child, and you have no knowledge at all. The only thing right you knew about me was my name and farm, which is what every seer here in Ubar already knows." He stood up in his place and took a pose that suggested he was about to leave. "I enjoyed your tale about Shar-Shar, and I must thank you for that. But I feel my time is wasted. I came looking for the best seer, and it seems you are not at all what I wanted."

"Wait, that is not fair. We can find your child, I promise. And we *are* the best in Ubar." Mair-Batlo didn't want Fad to leave; he shook in rage and his whole tent shook with him. Fad felt the rumble of anger in the Babylonian elephant before him. His brother had in fact failed him, but he tried to convince Fad to stay. "With his mother's hair, we can find him easily."

"If you are the best, you should have known that his mother is dead."

The big tradesman rolled his eyes in panic and raised his palms to his chest like a frightened fat hare. He turned to his brother and scolded him in their language, which Fad did not comprehend. Then he turned back to Fad. The seer mumbled to himself, or to his jinni, revising his words carefully. Then the floating old head turned to his brother and explained what the jinni had told him.

"The mother is not dead! She is only unconscious, bitten by a snake."

"And whose snake was it? Did you not see that as well?" Fad asked.

Mair-Batlo asked his brother again, and then they both turned and faced Fad with shock in their eyes. As they did, the fat tradesman cried, "Behas!" Fad felt that even their all-knowing jinni was shocked by it.

He smiled and sat back before them. "Have you ever heard of anyone surviving the treachery of Behas? I think not." He held a lock of his hair from behind his ear. "Use mine. Then you may be able to find the answer to my secret."

Mair-Batlo nodded submissively, undone by Fad's confidence and his misfortune. The farmer before him had been a victim of Behas. Mair-Batlo pulled out a bone dagger and, not trusting Fad with it, cut a lock of the farmer's hair and threw it into the red coals in the incense burner.

Fad was disturbed by the smell of his burnt hair, but it wasn't worse than the frankincense smell that had already conquered the blue tent.

Shar-Shar Arr Yar Nar
Tar Far Lar, Oh Shar-Shar
Ayn Al' Tifl Ya Shar
Ya Ramz Al Hikma Wal Shar

After hearing his brother, Mair-Batlo jumped in his place with laughter and joy.

"We found it! We found it!" He giggled. "He is hidden well, but we can feel him! He's being nursed by another woman, not his mother."

Nursed? thought Fad. Whoever had kidnapped Dil seemed to be taking care of him. *At least he's not dead. He's even being kept alive,* he thought, and felt greatly relieved. It was as if someone had poured cold water over him to cool the heat in his heart and soul.

"Is it not true?" The fat tradesman leaned forward and rubbed his hands together.

Fad could not tell if it was right or wrong, but they hadn't answered his question about where his child was!

"But *where* is my child?" Fad asked again.

"Well, whatever power you are using to hide him is greater than ours. We cannot tell where he is or how he looks. But our jinni sensed his presence; he's feeding now. That is what he told us!"

What power? Well, the kind that challenged Behas himself, I assume. Fad convinced himself that they were useless. He needed to report back to Bessel what he had heard here. Dil was being fed, which was good news, at least.

"Shar-Shar was right; you are a bizarre farmer!" Mair-Batlo said with more excitement. "Now, your next question. What future do you want us to see and tell you all about?"

Fad remained silent. The first answer had not pleased him completely, and it was broad, like the time when Arkin and Yam had been told only that the child was in Wadi Erum. If it hadn't been for their spy, and the help of a crow, Behas would have succeeded. On the other hand, whatever information could bring him closer to his child would help. He thought he should ask for another hint.

"Where will my son be tomorrow?" Simple and smart. He needed to know the next move of his opponent.

Mair-Batlo stared back, puzzled, and quickly started his ritual. "The stars show nothing for your son," he said, after listening to Shar-Shar. "It's as if he's dead!"

19

Fad drowned in his gloomiest thoughts as he walked out of the Babylonian's tent, thoughts of oppression and cruelty. What sort of evil had been cast upon his child? What wrong had he or his child done to deserve all this? Why was it *his* child who had been driven to such a devastating, dark fate? Did any of them deserve it?

In all his life, he had never expected to be in such a situation. He was a good person and had never intended or wished that harm would fall upon anyone. A humble farmer, raised by kind and loving parents, whom he loved equally and took good care of. He wondered how his old parents would receive the news of his tragedy and was sure that it would break their hearts. He wouldn't want to tell them, not now at least. His father, Turab, was away, busy trading dates by the sea. And his mother, Ruba, traveled to her home village during trade month. As sad as he felt that day, he knew they would be sadder.

"Now pay us, farmer, and be gone. There is nothing you can do to help your child, a victim of Behas." The last words Mair-Batlo had said rang in his mind as he walked back along the path he had taken, heading to meet Bessel.

It was painful enough that his child had been kidnapped, but finding himself unable to do anything to save him and bring him back to their loving home was even more depressing. Sad and unfair. He wondered who could help him now. The Noorian, Arkin, who feared his queen and had said that her call was more of a priority for him than saving the child? The sheikhdom, or the Guardians of Erum, who had suggested he ask a seer in Ubar? Seers who feared Behas, or could not be trusted, for it was most likely another saher who had stolen his child? Somood, Sada, or Haba, or all the holy deities worshiped in the realm of Erum? He didn't know whom to turn to.

But it was still too early for him to give up. Fad did feel hopeless and depressed, but the seer had told him that his child was being nursed. *My son is still alive,* he reminded himself, and that thought added a feeling of outrageous anger to his sadness. *I will find him. It's not over yet!*

For now, he needed to find Bessel. But before he reached the end of the dark path of barely illuminated shut tents, he met with another seer.

...

Just before the end of the path, two women, covered from head to toe, came out of a tiny ragged tent. Free women usually covered themselves in Ubar so they were not mistaken for escorts or were not recognized during wrongful activities like visiting a seer. After them, an old man walked out of the tent, tying its drape to keep it open, and hung his small collection of camel bones over the entrance. He noticed Fad passing by and asked, "Seeking knowledge, brother?"

Fad had heard enough from seers. *I have already spoken with two seers, and they were useless,* he thought to himself, ignoring the seer and continuing on his path.

"That is because their answers did not please you."

Fad slowed down and looked over his shoulder to see if the old man had spoken to him, not anyone else. He had answered Fad's thoughts. *But a seer couldn't hear them.* Fad knew that. *He might be guessing.* Fad thought that with his sad expression, and the fact that he had ignored him, the old man had just made a lucky guess.

"You still do not know who has your son."

Fada stopped at that and turned to face him.

"Nor do you know what they will do to him."

Fad slowly walked towards the seer, with his brows furrowed in confusion.

Standing before the darkness of the path behind him was a short, skinny old man with a fairly long white goatee. One might mistake his figure for a goat standing on its hind legs in the dark. He wore a dark red turban on his head, and by the shape of the large, rusted bronze *khanjar* at his waist, Fad knew where he was from. *Magan,* thought Fad. Magan was a famous city by the northern sea, far beyond the borders of Erum, and it was famous for two common practices: bronze mining and jinn mastering.

"Do not worry. I will not ask for more than the two last silver coins you have. That will be enough, for I will only explain further what the last jinni told you. Please come inside."

"I do not have time to sit and talk. Speak here, and quickly."

"And be seen by others?" The seer meant Guardians of Erum. Whatever jinnic business they did inside their tents was theirs, but outside the tents, it could be considered a crime. Fad agreed to go in, but he pleaded with the seer to be quick.

The man spoke less than Mair-Batlo, but Fad felt he spoke more.

His name, he said, was Ba'en. He told Fad about the company of bronze miners he had come with and about his day job. Seers usually talked to their clients to make them feel safe. The meanings of this one's name and his jinni's were related to clarity and truth.

I don't think a miner will know a thing about my son, thought Fad to himself while Ba'en was still telling his tale.

The seer paused, as if listening to Fad's thoughts again!

"You heard enough about me as a miner, I guess," he said. "But as a seer, I do have a skilled all-knowing jinni that can tell me everything about your son."

"Can you hear my thoughts?" Fad wondered aloud.

"Well, I *can* sense your angry feeling towards those who kidnapped your son, Dileel." The seer switched the subject back to Dil. "Your child was born under a rare star, a star beyond any of the constellations above. It is rare that people are born under it. You might remember seeing one last night: Behas. The famous jinn master was born under it as well. That one star is the most hated star in the jinnic realm. It is rare to find such people, and whoever has your son plans to offer his soul for a reward or, shall I say, to gain evil powers."

"But where are they? How can I stop them?"

"I cannot see where they are or who they are," the seer continued. "For one, I might be wrong about it all. It seems only right to me because it would be the only type of child old Behas would be trying to kill. He plans to prevent that soul from being used for evil, as he usually does."

Fad had heard from many that Behas was glorified in Magan. He was considered a savior amongst its people for having once saved them by killing an evil and powerful jinni that had haunted them for years. Fad began to question this seer's words, which sounded similar to Behas's. "You too believe my child is evil?"

"Your child is not," answered the seer. "But those who have him now *are*."

Fad felt more anger rising in his heart, the kind of anger a disobedient camel being dragged against his will would have. He wanted to find the kidnappers and crush them where they stood. But where were they? He was wasting his time in Ubar, searching for words rather than his son.

"I hope my knowledge has helped you understand."

Fad stood up as the conversation came to an end, and the seer did as well. He pulled out the pouch, which had only two silver coins in it, and asked the seer one last question before handing it to him.

"Do you know if there is anyone who might help me find my son?" After asking, he thought he knew what the seer would reply.

"Behas. No one else can find him but Behas," said the old seer from Magan.

Fad bit his lips in frustration. It was not the answer he had hoped for. He passed the pouch to the old seer, but the seer pushed his hands away. "Keep the coins," he said. "I sense they will be useful to you tonight."

...

And that was all Fad learned from the seers that night. The words from the last seer might not have answered his main questions better, but they gave him more reason to be angry. Fad had never gotten an answer when he asked the seer if he was able to hear his thoughts, but deep in his heart, he didn't doubt it. *That seer did hear my thoughts!*

For now, he hoped the two Chief Guardians who'd sent him to this alley would know what to do next. He had spent nearly an hour back there in the dark smoky tents, and he needed to find Bessel. The night was only getting shorter.

Whoever had kidnapped his newborn was not planning to keep him but rather to kill him, and soon! This was a sign the jinni had seen, which Fad wanted to relate to Bessel, and fast. When he reached the spot where Bessel had promised to be waiting, no one was there. He worried a bit. Ubar was not small or easy to search.

He decided to head back to the Guardians' house where he and Bessel had left their mares and belongings, but on his way back, the echo of a drumbeat dragged him. It was coming from the marketplace, which was on his way. He felt the drumbeats were dragging him there. The closer he got, the more the musical instruments began to interfere with those beats. He remembered the song now.

It was a song that praised the Guardians of Erum, and like every child in Erum, he had once dreamed of being one. When he got older and more mature, his interests changed completely. The thought of becoming a Guardian wasn't as interesting as it had been when he was a little boy. But the song still reminded him of his childhood.

Now, he wasn't being driven by joy or celebration but rather by need. Something in him wanted to pass by and listen to the singing, and the closer he got to it, the stronger that feeling became. It was strange. He felt he was being dragged to listen. He was starting to become curious about why this song was pulling him now, when it hadn't done so the many other times he'd heard it after he'd grown up. *I should be looking for Bessel! For Dil! Why am I stopping here?*

The main market in Ubar was near the center of the walled city. It was busy during the day and busier at night, as travelers and traders who came from Yemen, East Africa, Egypt, and even India gathered to offer their sinful products to those who sought the pleasure of indulging their shameful lusts. It was a place of intoxications of all sorts, prostitution, and loud, joyous all-night music and celebration.

The open space in the center of the market, where the music came from, was not too large. If you stood to one side, you could see the whole area, surrounded by small tents and empty stalls. At night, that center space was lit and packed with musicians, who sang and danced by turn.

Fad stayed a fair distance away, in the dark, like the rest of the shy crowds that remained standing on the edges. He stood still and gazed across the small celebrations lit by fire and moonlight. Around the fire in the center sat many men and women, clapping and singing with a band of musicians from Erum who played and sang a part of the famous Erumian song. The instruments they used created a soothing rhythm for the male dancers to move like one in an organized pattern. There were drums and a *rababa,* a single-stringed violin-like instrument played by the singer himself. He sang the famous poem about Erum, just as Fad remembered it:

O Guardian of Erum, keeper of our lands

Keep us safe from all the evil bands
The greatest stars have blessed your hands
And Erum shall rule all seas and lands

Fad didn't enjoy listening to song that night. The more he heard, the more he was saddened. His mind flashed to memories of Nada and Dil and all the terrible events of the night before. He felt fear crawling up on him again, from his back to his neck, like a spider, or many spiders. His feelings unnerved him, and he wanted to leave so badly, but something strange and powerful forced him to stay. Was it depression or fear of failure? He couldn't tell. The sound of music was starting to annoy him, as was the fact that everyone before him danced and laughed. He fell victim to his envious thoughts, which stung the back of his head like venomous spiders. He felt them, but his inner voice did its best to avoid them.

Once the music stopped and the cheering faded, his dark feelings vanished. He felt normal again. *What is happening to me?!* His sleep deprivation might have been to blame, but he didn't think of it then.

He turned towards the path that led towards the Guardians' house, just before another gang of drummers prepared their instruments.

An old mendicant neared him and broke his train of thought. "Would you want-t to buy one?" he said. He held two rababas in his hand. "My daughter makes these, and I need to feed her." The beggar's accent marked him as being from the deserts of the far north.

Fad stared for a long time at the rababas the beggar carried. They looked small and new, and he remembered a time when his wife had enjoyed the music the instrument made. Buying one would keep him reminded of her, he thought.

He stopped and pulled his pouch out. The old mendicant opened his hands for whatever came out from the pouch. To his surprise, there were two silver coins from Erum, an amount that would keep him from having to beg for a whole week.

"Thank you for your kindness. Please, t-take this gift." The old mendicant revealed a third rababa, one different from the other two. It was probably the smallest and oldest Fad had ever seen, almost ancient. If the first two new-looking rababas had been made by the man's daughter, this one must have been made by his grandmother. Fad took it with a smile in his face, not wanting to object. He didn't care much if it was old or new. He rather considered it an act of charity towards the old man.

The old man then nodded thankfully, a cheerful smile creasing his face. "It's a special rababa; it can bring you good fortune and joy when it's used right. But I must-t warn you about-t it-t," he said. "Never use it-t if there is any sadness in your heart-t. Even a lit-ttle of it-t will be bad. It-t will hurt-t you."

"Thank you?" Fad thought aloud. "I don't even know how to use it."

The old mendicant ignored him and simply walked away with his silver, disappearing on the darker side of the market.

Shortly afterwards, Bessel approached from behind. "Farmer!" he called. "I grew worried about you; where have you been all night?" He paused when he noticed the rababa in Fad's hand, but then ignored it and asked again. "Have you spoke with a seer? Do you know where the child is?"

Fad was surprised and relieved to see him. "I spoke with a seer, yes. More than one, but they can't see where my son is. Whoever has him hid him well. And they did warn me, those who have him are going to kill him!"

"Nonsense. Whatever they tell you about tomorrow is a lie."

"It's not a lie, it's not a vision. It's a fact. My son was born under—"

"Enough." Bessel silenced him and pulled him along. "We've wasted the night. Follow me to the barracks. Harf will know what to do."

. . .

"The child was born under the Serpent-Neck star. We are well aware of it," Bessel said, interrupting Harf as he was explaining what Fad had heard from the last seer. "What we want is to find the boy, not know what his star is. Where is the boy?"

Straight to the point, thought Fad. *I wish you had joined me with the seers.*

"Behas found him, and so did another jinn master the Noorians hired!" Bessel shouted at Harf, losing his patience. Since the night before, he had just gone from one wrong decision to another. "Give me a name, Harf. You've been a jinn tamer for many years; you must know an expert jinn master like Behas. I need someone who can help us find the child."

"I do know a number of good jinn masters. The nearest one to us now, if I remember, is in Qairon Heriti. If you leave now, you might reach him near dawn time."

"Dawn? We lost the whole night, Harf! You should have directed us there from the start." He then said to Fad, "Let's go."

"His name is Atian," Harf went on. "And he is a great jinn master. In truth, he is the only seer in Qairon Heriti. I suppose he should be able to help you. I would like to come with you or send my men, but the orders from Qassas are that we gather all the men tomorrow for war."

Bessel slapped the dagger at his waist. "I won't need a jinn tamer to get a jinn master to speak. I have my own methods."

Harf smiled, holding in a laugh. "He's a good man. Tell him I sent you to him for help. You won't need your dagger."

. . .

And so Bessel and Fad galloped away that night in hopes of reaching the new jinn master, Atian, soon. But they met with a terrible fate on their journey south. In fact, they never made it together to Qairon Heriti!

20

The next day, around noon in Erum, Faseela ran through the crowds to reach the healer's cavern again. "Lady Burmiah!" she shouted from behind the curtains.

No one answered her.

She let herself in and found the old lady napping. "Wake up, my lady. Behas…" She paused to catch her breath. "Behas will be beheaded; his end is near. You must come to witness. Come!"

Lady Burmiah widened her eyes. She had heard the rumors the day before but had chosen not to believe them, and now they appeared to be true. "They should not! We will all be doomed!" Lady Burmiah didn't say that out of warm feelings for Behas but rather out of fear. She believed in evil curses, and there was an old curse associated with Behas: If a city killed him, that city would face calamity.

"Doomed? We won't be doomed, Lady Burmiah! We are saved." Frustrated, Faseela exploded in her face. "The saher you fear is the one who is to be doomed. And you will come with me to witness it, and then you will heal my friend, or I will behead you myself."

Lady Burmiah stared back at her, remaining motionless on the floor. She felt it was the first time, in all her life, that anyone had shouted and threatened her; she had gotten used to being the one doing the shouting and threatening.

Faseela had no patience to spare; she wanted the old woman to witness the beheading herself. She offered a hand to pull Burmiah up on her feet, then did so abruptly. "Ugh, get up, Lady Burmiah. We will miss the sword."

...

Four guards walked Behas to the platform that had been temporarily raised near the market for the special occasion.

Behas's head was covered, and he was brought to his knees beside his executioner. The crowd gathered and the announcement was made. Many praised their lord, Somood, and many others chanted glory in the name of Zufar, son of Aad, who stood high above to witness the execution before leaving for the east and for war.

Behas appeared calm and submissive, as if he knew his time had come. The guard removed his head cover and revealed his face to the restless crowd. Behas lowered his head to shade his eyes from the sharp glare of sunlight.

The crowd cursed and insulted the saher. That day, they witnessed the end of an era. No more would they worry about and fear these traitorous conjurers and warlocks.

Lady Burmiah stared at the famous jinn master, deep in thought. *Since Behas is about to be dead, his powerful jinn will be free and without a master. I wonder who the jinnic lords will choose to succeed Behas now?*

The executioner did not delay his sheikh's triumph. He raised the sharpened, curved sword high above Behas's neck, and without hesitation, he swung it down in the blink of an eye, slicing Behas's head away from his body.

Burmiah witnessed the execution from close up, thinking in confusion, *It is over; he is dead. The master is dead.* She then murmured to herself what everyone else was chanting aloud, "Al majdu le Aad, fal majdu Aad." *Glory to Aad, for glory has been revived.*

Glory has been revived? She thought not. *Erum will face a calamity for killing Behas! We are doomed.*

PART TWO

SALALAH

21

The night before the execution of Behas, Fad and Bessel galloped from Erum, the northern province of the sheikhdom, and reached its southern province, Salalah, almost an hour before dawn.

Unlike Erum, which was landlocked and surrounded by desert, Salalah had a green range of misty mountains that crossed the province from east to west and formed a wall between land and water. Farther south, behind the mountains, Salalah faced the Arabian Sea. Sumhuram was the capital city of the southern province. And our heroes, Fad and Bessel, had just arrived near the mountains, which they planned to enter to find a jinn master who could help them find Dil.

...

"We shall rest here near Wadi Dawkah till the sun rises," Bessel told him. "The fog is heavy in Salalah; we won't be able to find our path in the dark."

Fad agreed. He and the horses too needed a rest after riding all night from Ubar to Wadi Dawkah. Beyond the wadi, the shadows of the Qara Mountains were floating above low, thick fog.

Their rest shouldn't be long, for dawn was almost an hour away. They tied their horses to a lone dead tree trunk. "We wouldn't want to be close to these trees. These are the sacred frankincense trees. The mountain folks would surely not welcome our presence for long, not since we're setting a fire."

Wadi Dawkah was home to the most sacred tree in the south, the *luban* tree, or frankincense tree. The inhabitants of these valleys owned their trees, producing frankincense and selling it in every corner of the world through Port Rori. Wadi Dawkah and Port Rori were the heart of the sacred frankincense trade route. Wherever white frankincense was used, it was most likely produced from the trees of Wadi Dawkah. And because it was a vital source of the sheikhdom's wealth, the sheikhs of Erum made sure no one else produced the sacred incense. Once upon a time, East Africans had claimed their frankincense was sacred as well, which harmed the reputation of traders from Wadi Dawkah, but not for long. An incident occurred, and many of the Africans' trees were burned to ashes. They accused Erum of setting the fires, but it was taken as a sign that African frankincense was not at all blessed, and Wadi Dawkah remained as the only source for sacred frankincense.

Although the two wore Guardians' tunics, they were careful not to disturb the frankincense farmers in Wadi Dawkah. Before they left Ubar, Bessel had given Fad a full uniform, from boots to a tunic and headband. An Arabian man always covered his head and long hair behind a scarf or a headband. The uniform helped reveal where they had come from and keep bandits away.

That night, Fad removed his headband and lay on his rug for a rest as Bessel walked back and forth, collecting wood to set up a fire. It was cold, and they needed to get warm and dry themselves and their uniforms before entering the mountains, as it would be cooler there, and wetter as well.

"We'll miss the execution," said Bessel, starting a conversation after a long and tiring gallop that had kept them silent through the whole journey. They had finally found a moment for a rest, or a talk.

"I don't care to see it," Fad bit out. "I had only hoped it would happen earlier. My wife would have been healed when I was next to her. I thought I had killed him last night. It felt good killing him, now that I remember." Fad related the tale back to Bessel.

"Well," said Bessel with a sigh, "we are finally rid of him now. He should have been executed twenty years ago, the first time I caught him after he had killed a newborn in Wadi Erum."

"That is a very long time." Fad realized that Bessel was much older than he looked. "Do you think we will find my son?"

"That I do not think, but I must achieve. My sheikh, Zufar, has ordered that I return the child *safely*. Do not worry much about finding your child. We will find him. I must find him, and I will."

Bessel now finished setting up the fire pit. He stuffed a handful of straw and dry weeds between the logs, then held a block of flint rock in one hand, with his thumb pressing a piece of Indian cotton flat on the flint, and with the other hand, he held his dagger, striking the flint hard to produce sparks and burn the cotton. Once it caught the spark, it lit red, and he threw it in the straw. Finally, he flapped a fan of dry palm leaves to blow air into the straw, feeding the fire to make it grow. It was a quick trick to produce light. The glare of fire slowly increased, revealing the two travelers and their horses.

Our uniforms should keep them away, Fad thought of the mountain folk. Ever since Bessel had warned him, he had felt there were hidden eyes watching them, stalking them. He could feel their presence like the unseen jinn around us, those who can see us while we cannot see them.

The fire kept them warm and dried their uniforms. It also made them both drowsy.

Bessel asked Fad to sleep and gain some strength before they continued. "I'll stay awake for watch," offered the Chief Guardian, but he too couldn't resist and closed his eyes for a rest after he sensed that Wadi Dawkah was calm. He too needed to rest.

Fad wanted to rest; he hadn't slept since the night before, when Yam had woken him up and taken his child. He lay on his back and closed his eyes, but he couldn't find rest. He was lost in thoughts of his wife and child. The last thing he saw before closing his eyes was the rababa he had gotten in Ubar.

He remembered the time when he had asked his Uncle Badde for his daughter's hand. His uncle had been playing a rababa in Ubar, where the two occasionally met. Fad's father had been there as well.

"Uncle Badde, what did Nada say?"

He stopped playing and grimaced. "I forgot to ask her, still." He then turned to resume.

"It has been two weeks, Uncle Badde. Please, don't forget this time."

"I will not forget. But stop asking me; I will tell you when...when I tell you. Do not mention this to me again, or I'll break the rababa on your head!" said Badde. Fad had frowned in submission, but his father, Turab, had laughed, knowing his old friend Badde better.

Fad questioned his decision to leave Erum before healing Nada. But he couldn't have stayed while Dil was in greater danger. If she healed and woke to find him without Dil, they would both be in greater sorrow. He hoped to find Dil as soon as he could and bring things back to how they were. Him, Nada, and their beloved Dil safe in their arms.

Finally, he slept.

...

He opened his eyes only seconds later to find himself standing under a burning tree. One of the sacred trees was on fire!

"What have you done?" cried Bessel, who stood next to him, holding his hands. "Help me put the fire out!"

Too late. The tree had burned completely. And before the two moved, a spearman appeared from behind the firelit mists, running towards them. Once in sight, he threw his spear towards them, but it missed them both.

Behind him, another spearman appeared.

"Run!" Bessel cried.

Fad and the Chief Guardian ran towards their horses.

The second spearman behind threw another at them from behind the mists, and it pierced Bessel's leg.

"Bessel!" Fad returned to help him up. The first spearman picked his spear up again and aimed at them once more, but he missed them both again. Fad saw the second spearman sprinting towards them.

They were half naked, and their bodies were covered with black mud. They looked more like wild jinn than men.

"Run, Fad!"

"Not without you," he replied.

Without hesitation, Fad picked up the spear that had fallen near them and threw it back at the second spearman when he got nearer to them, but he missed.

The second spearman had dodged the spear and continued to run at them. As he reached Fad, he shoved him and knocked him off his feet.

Bessel had managed to pull the tip of the spear out of his leg. He stood on one leg and swung the spear at the attacker's head, but the other dodged it.

The second spearman pulled his spear from Bessel's hands as the Chief Guardian lost his balance and fell on the ground again. Fad, seeing that the second spearman had turned towards Bessel, picked up a sharp, heavy rock and smacked the spearman on the back of the head with all his strength, knocking him down. His skull must have been crushed!

Another group of spearmen appeared in the distance.

Fad rushed and helped Bessel walk towards the horses. But the first spearman picked up his spear for the third time and aimed it at them.

Fad kept his eyes on the two horses, but Bessel had one eye looking back as they moved, and he noticed the first spearman had attacked again. This time, the spear flew directly at Fad.

"Watch out!" Bessel pushed Fad away and fell to his side. The spear missed them both.

Seeing him on the ground, Fad rushed to reach for Bessel and help him up again, but before he could, a third spearman had already thrown his spear through Bessel's back, leaving him motionless.

Fad fell next to him, stunned. "Bessel!" he cried several times, but Bessel seemed dead. The man had been a brave Guardian who had died defending a citizen of Erum.

Fad heard the cries of the other spearmen getting louder and louder. They were nearer now and wouldn't think twice before killing him too. His survivor's instinct prompted him to run.

Both horses were tied together. He freed them, climbed the nearest mare, and galloped away. He couldn't direct it anymore; the mare seemed to be running out of fear. It galloped deeper and deeper into the fog. The other mare followed them as they all entered the thick fog of the Qara Mountains.

...

The spearmen continued to run behind Fad before their leader stopped them. "Halt!" he wailed. "He entered the fog; we'll follow his tracks during the day; the sun will rise soon. Now, let us bury our brother and the dead Guardian. But first, let us put out the burning tree before it burns the whole of Wadi Dawkah."

Seven of them had come when they had first seen their tree burning, and only one of them was dead, the one Fad had killed with a rock.

"Wadi Erum will come after us!" said one of the spearmen to his leader. "We killed a Guardian!"

"A Guardian who burned our tree and killed our brother!" cried the leader in his face. "A soul for a soul."

The leader then paused, thinking. His brother was right. "Unless it wasn't us who killed the Guardian." He then looked at the shortest one, the first spearman to arrive and the youngest one, who had missed all his throws. "You will head to the nearest Guardians' post, but tell them exactly what I will say to you. Then you can go back home to your mother. We will find that Guardian who burned our tree and killed our brother. He won't go far."

22

Fad woke in fright. He was in pain, and his head felt as if it had been severely injured. He opened his eyes and checked his forehead. There was no blood, just a bump. He was alone. It wasn't dark anymore—the sun had lit the misty atmosphere around him—but he couldn't tell what time it was.

He found himself lying on a green carpet of tiny plants. *The misty green fields of Salalah*, he figured. He knew the place. The surrounding white mist covered his sight with tiny dewdrops floating close to each other. He felt cold and wet as well. He couldn't remember anything of what had happened.

The dew drops he saw in the air reminded him of his wife. He loved the morning dew as much as he loved his wife; the dew had always reminded him of Nada, and he described himself to her as a desert plant that thrived on morning dew. Her name even meant "dew" in Arabic. Now, though the dew filled the air, his heart felt thirsty for her.

They were relatives, but he had rarely seen her when they were growing up. One time, when they were teenagers, his eyes saw her differently, and ever since then he had been fascinated by her beauty. Her dark brown hair, dark eyes, and fair features had stolen his heart.

He remembered a time when they were still young, and he had sat beside her outside their house, where her father had always sat.

"Stay with your mother, Nada," her father had told her. "Your uncle and I have to go for a little work."

She had sat outside, grumpy and upset.

Fad had known that their fathers were headed for Ubar and that he was too young to join them as well, so he also had to stay in Wadi Erum. He had sat near her on the rug outside and had felt heartbroken to see her upset. He would have given anything to see her smile again.

He had stared at her face for a long time, and especially at her nose, which looked crooked from its top between her eyes. Surely no one is flawless, but he had found even that flaw perfect and attractive in her. He had tried to cheer her that day, saying, "What is so special about Ubar, anyway, that makes you want to go so badly? It is a boring place!" He would have taken her there if his father had not told him to stay at his uncle's house as well, but he had been a rather obedient child.

"I don't care about Ubar," she had said. "I just want to leave the house."

"And go where?" Fad had asked.

Nada had ignored him, seeming not to have an answer.

They had both looked away in silence. He had wanted to say more to break the awkwardness but hadn't been able to think of anything.

"It's the fact that I have to stay at home like my mother that bothers me."

He had been glad she had broken the silence. "Why can your mother not leave the house?"

"It's because of me."

He had hummed in wonder.

"When she gave birth to me, she almost died of it; she can't move a lot," Nada had explained. "She also can't give birth anymore; I am the reason why I don't have brothers or sisters."

"It's okay if you have no brothers. I too am an only child to my mother. I think that makes you a special gift."

"It doesn't make me anything. I am never getting married, so I won't have any children or stay in the house like my mother. I want to travel and be a trader or a sailor, have my own stalls in markets and sell my own handcrafts and jewels." She had looked up and pictured her intended future with a smile.

Secretly, he had not enjoyed her idea about marriage, but felt his heart skip a beat when she smiled.

"We can journey together," he had blurted out, then wished he could pull his words back into his mouth. She had only smiled back, with no clear indication of how she had felt about his proposal.

"Let's go to the bridge and watch the market from above." She had stood up with a broader smile.

"Hmm, we are not allowed to leave the house!" Fad had not agreed to the idea of disobedience.

"I thought you said we can journey together."

Fad had realized that she was not suggesting but had already decided. The bridge she meant had been close, so he had worried less. It would be all right, he had thought, as long as he was with her.

...

Now he sat alone in a green field and felt lost in the mist. He couldn't recall how he had gotten there. He held his head and closed his eyes to remember. *We rode south.*

The spearmen, he remembered, and opened his eyes. *They killed him! Who are they?* No sign of them.

He had woken under a leafless tree. Its wood was black and soaked, and a branch dangled over his head, half broken. It must have been what his head had collided with before he was knocked off the scared mare he had ridden through the night when escaping the spearmen. He then noticed the hoof marks below his feet. The mares had left him. And if the spearmen followed the tracks, it wouldn't be long before they spotted him. He searched for his waist-belt; he must have hung his dagger on his horse before he slept. If they found him, he'd be killed for sure, and he had nothing to defend himself with.

Qairon Heriti was his and Bessel's eventual destination, and it had to be close now that he had entered deep into the Qara Mountains of Salalah.

Bessel died after he pushed me out of harm's way. He remembered the brave act. He blamed himself, yet he couldn't recall everything. His memory was still blurred, like the fog in the air around him. *Why was the tree on fire? Did we burn it accidentally?* Then he remembered he had found himself standing near to it. *Was I sleepwalking?!* He had never had an incident like that in his life that he could recall or that anyone else had talked about. It was unlike him. *It cannot be; something else must have happened.*

He needed to find the jinn master they had been looking for. *I should find the mares first,* he thought as well. He also thought he should move quickly before the spearmen found him or the mares! If they had followed him after the mares had sped away the night before, it was likely that they had missed him under the tree and continued to follow the hoof marks. They might have already found the mares, and he might follow the tracks to them. He eyed the ground again: no sign of any other footsteps. No man had followed the mares that night. *Good!* The spearmen were still behind.

His Guardian's tunic was now soaked and dirty, but he kept it on. He had to; he had left his green tunic in the saddlebag on his mare, and if he took this one off, the bugs would bite every bit of his bare skin and leave him scratching to death. They had already bitten him in some places. His shoulder and neck felt sore on the side he had fallen or slept on. The danger behind him would soon catch up; he needed to move on, and with haste. The last thing he wanted was to get caught or killed; he needed to find his son. *Whatever it takes.*

He felt devastated by what had happened to Bessel and thought he should find a post of Guardians and report what he had witnessed. He hoped he'd find Guardians nearby. It would be a lot safer than traveling alone, even if he rode a horse or wore a uniform like theirs.

He walked for hours that morning, passing through thick fog in vast moorlands and hills. It was a land rich in one type of green, the wet leafy verdant color. All the hill grass, scattered trees, and bushes reflected the same shade, while all the tree branches and wood were dark black, fully soaked, and mostly leafless. It was a place untouched by sunlight for two months every year and protected by layers of haze and thick low-hanging clouds. Salalah resembled paradise, a green sanctuary, rich in water and life at the southern tip of the Arabian Desert.

The hoof marks he followed through the misty moors went a long way, leading him up hills, below dales, and near creeks. He needed to find the two mares before he could start searching for the jinn master. He observed the tracks and knew where the mares had run, trotted, stopped, drank, or ate. He felt unbothered by the tranquil chasing after lost mares. *Such a journey they've had,* he thought. But then he would remember with terror the spearmen who had killed Bessel and who were probably chasing him now, and he sped up his steps.

He reached a creek, which he decided to follow, like the mares had. It began to rain, the silent, soft rain that is unheard and unseen but only felt on the cheeks. Fad's long black hair filled with shiny white dew. He continued to follow the mares, feeling he was getting closer to them.

...

The leader of the spearmen called himself Daheen, meaning "smart." He was short but taller than his men were. Their skins were dark, and they all had short, curly black hair. Four of his men from the night before had followed him; the youngest one had left to inform Erum, and Daheen had

had to bury one of his cousins, the one Fad had unintentionally killed. That left five spearmen running after him, seeking revenge.

Daheen stood above the markings that showed where Fad had woken up. He pulled the dangling branch from the tree, and by reading the traces below, he figured Fad had been knocked off his mare and followed it later, on foot.

"He's not far," said Daheen to his four men. "We will make him sorry for killing our brother."

Daheen began to run quickly along Fad's tracks, and the rest followed at an equal pace.

...

After following a running stream for a while, Fad reached a huge pond at its end. Beside the pond, he noticed two black huts and the smell of smoke. The aroma of cooked food made his stomach growl. He noticed his mare's tracks went straight to the huts. As he neared, the huts became more clearly visible: wet, dark rocks had been stacked to form walls, and climbing plants had covered parts of the walls and rested above the wooden roofs of the huts. As he got closer and closer, slow sharp tones broke the silence in the air near where the fire was lit. He reckoned it was a rababa.

Whoever played the rababa played it gently and well, but the sharp tune filled Fad's heart with agonizing fear and gloom. His face crumpled in pain, his eyelids squeezed shut, and he clutched his heart, pressing it inward. The feeling of sharp needles poking through his saddened heart and chest was unbearable. He forced his eyes open and dragged himself towards the sound, feeling heavier with every step. The feel of needle-pinches now spread in all his body, and the blood streamed through his veins painfully, as if it were mixed with glass dust.

An old man with long white hair and a long beard sat on the ground with his legs crossed near the fire, playing the rababa. He paused as he noticed Fad getting closer towards him. The peaceful silence around the pond resumed, and Fad was relieved that the rababa had stopped.

"Greetings, Guardian of Erum. Please join me and accept my humble hospitality." The old man shivered as he waved his hands for Fad to join him.

The name made Fad look down at his tunic, which must have earned him the glorious title. He had forgotten about it after the long walk. Under that disguise, only he knew he was just a farmer. The name also reminded him of Bessel and the spearmen who had killed him.

He saw two mares tied outside the huts, and he recognized them as the horses he and Bessel had ridden. *How did they get here? Did they follow the smell of food?* His eyes caught the rababa the old man had played. It was his, the one he had gotten in Ubar. He remembered the mendicant's advice not to play it when the heart was in pain.

The old man must have found it in the bags hung on the mare and decided to play it.

Fad walked towards him in complete silence. He was annoyed but also thankful for the greeting and welcome. After all, he was also hungry. He might swallow whatever was being cooked before riding away with the horses, or one of them, at least. There seemed to be no sign of the spearmen, but he still needed to be quick.

"I have been expecting your arrival. I prepared food for three; where is your companion? Are you alone?"

Companion? How did he know? "Are you the jinn master?" Fad asked.

"I am a master to nobody. Why would I be a jinn master?"

How would he be expecting us, then? But Fad remembered the mares, tied near one of the huts. They must have been why the old man was expecting him and his companion. The two mares neighed to Fad and tried to pull the ropes towards him but couldn't set themselves free. It was obvious they were happy to see him. At one point, one mare appeared to be scolding the other. They both settled back and turned silent again.

"Did you find any trouble on the road?"

Fad stood in his place, remaining silent and grieving.

"Sit down, Guardian," the man offered again. Fad stepped closer but still remained silent and repeatedly looked back over his shoulder.

"Have you lost your friend?"

"How would you know if I had lost a friend?" Fad finally asked, still suspecting the old man was a jinn master or a seer.

The old man turned his bearded chin towards the two mares tied near his hut. "I believe it is uncommon for a Guardian to wander around with two fine and fully outfitted horses. Therefore, I assume the other rider must have faced trouble, since only one of you has appeared."

Just as Fad had suspected. He then checked the surroundings behind him again, wondering how they had not yet found him; the tracks were clear. He now decided to leave as soon as he got the right direction to where his son might be, or to a Guardians' post so he could report Bessel's murder.

"Are you expecting anyone?"

He turned his eyes back to the old man and said, "Spearmen. They killed a Chief Guardian from Erum who traveled with me, and now I think they'll be looking for me. I followed the horses' tracks, and I fear they'll do the same."

"Which spearmen?"

"I would assume them to be the frankincense farmers from Wadi Dawkah."

The old man stood up. "I am sorry for the loss of your friend. These barbaric mountain folk. They should not have killed a Guardian from—"

Fad noticed his shocked expression and turned to see what had surprised him: the shadows of five spearmen running towards them through the mist.

They had found him!

"Qamaria!" the old man called. A young and beautiful woman appeared from one of the huts. She wore a ragged dark blue dress that somehow covered her from shoulder to foot.

"Take the Guardian to Alma, and hide him there until it is safe. It seems our friends from Wadi Dawkah are angered again."

"Yes, Father," Qamaria replied.

Fad froze in place, staring back at the young girl and the spearmen.

She waved her hands. "Follow me," she said to Fad.

Fad had no idea what he should do. He wasn't certain if he could trust them, but he'd seen what the spearmen had done to Bessel, and he had no choice. He walked towards her hesitantly, his eyes rolling back and forth between the horses and the spearmen.

"Hurry! Before they see us." She ran towards the mares, but before Fad reached her, she had freed one of them and slapped it so it would gallop away. A decoy! *Smart,* thought Fad. He and Qamaria ran in the opposite direction.

As Fad ran, the same pinch from the rababa's sound earlier came back. The old man was playing it again, but the farther away he ran, the less painful it became. *Is the old man playing it to fight them?* Fad wondered. He didn't know where the young woman was pulling him to, but he knew he had to run, regardless.

23

Fad continued to run behind Qamaria. The spearmen were no longer visible behind the fog, but still the two kept moving, until Fad began to feel tired.

"Where are we headed?" he asked as he tried to catch up with her, worried and in definite need of a rest. He thought of his child as well. He needed to find him; he needed to know the way.

Qamaria remained silent, running ahead of him.

"Where are you taking me?" he asked again. He had heard the old man say, "Take the Guardian to Alma," but he didn't know where that was.

Qamaria slowed her pace to answer him. "We're not far."

She wanted to explain more, but before she could, they heard some loud cries coming from behind, which they immediately recognized were those of the spearmen.

"Run," snapped Qamaria.

The two ran faster and deeper through the thick fog. The wet air soaked Fad from top to bottom; his black hair, his bare skin, his Guardian's tunic, and his boots all felt as if he had just come out of water. He wished he had taken his green tunic when he saw the mare back near the huts so he could change.

Fad saw nothing but the shadow of Qamaria running ahead of him in the fog. How she knew where to go, he couldn't tell. She ended their long run into a small cave behind a few bushes. "In here, quick!" They were both out of breath, and Fad welcomed the idea of hiding, as his legs were sore from running. The water dripping off him could have formed three lakes, but to his surprise, Qamaria was dry! *Have I been chasing a female jinni this whole time?* He was scared to ask, as it did creep him out. *Who are they?* He thought of her and her father, the rababa player.

Then he thought about the fact that the old man had stayed behind, but the spearmen were still following them. *Have they killed him as well?*

The cave was not very deep; they could barely stand in it. Not ideal for a hiding place, and particularly not during daytime, when their footsteps outside were clear for anyone to track. "It's a dead end; they will find us here!" Fad tried to pull her out and get her to continue running before the spearmen got closer. *Her idea of a cave is suicide,* he thought.

She ignored Fad's warnings and began to search the floor at the end of the cave.

"What are you doing? They are getting close!" Fad knew that from where he'd seen them last and how fast they had run behind him. He'd have to fight five spearmen now. He picked up a rock, ready for a fight, but he knew he wouldn't stand a chance. He wondered if he would be able to speak with them, reason with them, and explain his motives. He wanted to save his child; he was not looking for trouble.

"Found it! Come here." Qamaria pushed a few small rocks, the size of hens, aside. Fad dropped beside her to help.

After they moved some of the rocks, a hole below the wall became big enough for them to crawl in. They closed the hole securely behind them after getting in. There was a very narrow and dark opening below that appeared to be a hidden path, barely wide enough for a man, under the cave.

Qamaria led him through that path, or hole.

The hole had sharp edges on both its sides. If one was not careful, he would end up with many cuts and might even bleed to death in there. Fad felt uncomfortable, his head close to the floor as he crawled like a rat. The path below him was barely wide enough for one foot at a time, and he could feel the many holes on the walls, which were probably home to many crawling creatures that he wouldn't want to disturb. An unpleasant crawl, but one he welcomed even so; the five spearmen were now above them, and they had probably reached the cave where their tracks led. He agreed with hiding, but this hole could be their tomb as well if they weren't careful while passing through it.

The hole was deep, Fad felt it, and they crawled for a long while. He asked her many times if they would ever get out, while she urged him to follow her and be patient and silent.

"Why did your father stay behind? I am worried about him; I fear they will harm him," Fad said.

"They will not touch us; there is a truce between our tribes."

"Truce? Ouch!" He touched a sharp edge as he asked.

She ignored him and continued to crawl ahead.

Fad noticed a growing green glare ahead of them. They finally reached the end, and it felt like an hour-long crawl until they walked into a small garden under the earth. Fad was amazed that they had reached an underground garden. The plants must have been planted there by Qamaria; they looked unnatural, although some light did enter from a side opening. The walls had many dark holes, both small and large; any tiny, vulnerable creature could inhabit this safe sanctuary away from predators and find a source of food and water. The grounds were lush and looked a bit wet for them to sit on, but the tranquility in the air gave Fad a safe feeling. He leaned on a rock and looked at the rest of the small green chamber in astonishment; he'd never have thought such a place existed. It was as if they'd just entered the jinnic realm, a world he had heard of but never seen.

. . .

Daheen and his spearmen stormed into the smaller cave Fad and Qamaria had first entered but found no sign of them.

"Where did they go?"

They stopped short once they realized that the cave ended with a wall only four steps from the opening.

"I saw them enter here!" another spearman added.

"That witch must have tricked our eyes," Daheen postulated. "We shall spread out around the fields. They will reappear. If you find them, cry out for the rest."

They all nodded as they walked out of the small cave.

I will gut that Guardian! Daheen thought.

. . .

"You can stay here, as my father asked." Qamaria took a folded rug from one of the many holes and laid it in the center of the green ground. "They will never find us here." Once she faced him, she scanned him with her eyes. "You're very wet!"

"We both ran through the wet air!" He was surprised she'd even made the comment first. "How are *you* still dry?"

"We cover ourselves with the witch-plant's sap; it helps protect us from the water in the air and the bug bites. I'll give you some of it." From another hole, she took a plant leaf in which was wrapped a bit of floral sap.

Fad rubbed his arms and some parts of his Guardian's tunic. It wouldn't dry him now but would help later if they went out again.

"I wonder what you have done that has angered the farmers from Wadi Dawkah. I would like to hear your story."

Fad hesitated, deciding whether he should tell her everything or only a part of it.

"Why are they running after a Guardian from Erum?"

"It is a long and complicated story. And I honestly do not remember how we angered them."

"We?" She seemed to think he was referring to her as well.

"A Chief Guardian from Erum and I. They killed him just before dawn."

She looked shocked and placed a hand over her mouth.

His eyes turned wet as he remembered how Bessel had died trying to save him.

"I am sorry about your friend."

"In truth, he was not a friend. I had met him only a day before. He traveled with me in search of my kidnapped son."

The soft and peaceful young woman remained silent as she realized that his story was in fact complicated, as he'd said.

"We came looking for a jinn master in Qairon Heriti; he was supposed to know where my son is. But now, I do not even know if I will ever find my son. Those who kidnapped him are planning to kill him, a seer told me in Ubar."

"Huh?!" She was frightened. "Why would they kill your child?"

Fad had no answer to that. He'd been told many things—a special star, a great evil. But he believed none of it. "I don't know why, but they do possess great power. They used an air jinni to kidnap my son."

She seemed to find his story hard to believe. "Sit down, Guardian."

And they both did.

"There is no such thing; air jinn are a legend," she began. "Let me tell you a story. It's a short story about a lovely couple I've known who lived near this place, in Arkut. They were married for more than twenty years but had never had a child. They met with a healer who told them that they were cursed. And they were. A witch lived in their village; she had loved the man once when he was younger, and out of envy, she had cursed them so they wouldn't ever be blessed with children.

"But they got healed, and finally his wife did give birth to a beautiful little boy. They named him Atya, meaning "a gift." I saw him when he was six years of age, a playful little boy. Blessed and kind, he loved his old parents just as much as they loved him.

"Until one day, the witch became aware that the couple she had cursed were blessed with a boy. And, again out of envy, she decided to end their happiness. That one day, the child played and sang outside his house, when suddenly he went silent. The old couple went out to see if he was all right, but they found him dead! They wept in sorrow, and so did everyone in Arkut. The whole village loved Atya, and they all grieved his death. They buried him, and the old couple decided to leave that village for good, in hopes they could find a place to settle away from Arkut, a place where everything reminded them of little Atya.

"They traveled for months until they reached Wadi Tiwi, and there, to their surprise, they found Atya, walking by the running creek with a mountain sheep. They stopped him, and they were happy to have found him. He, too, was happy to reunite with them. But they had been sure he was dead; the whole village had been there when they buried him. He told them that the day they were separated, he was kidnapped by a witch, and she had sold him for a cheap price. He had traveled by sea to this wadi with his new masters, and here he had worked and lived for months. The couple took him back to the village, and everyone in Arkut celebrated his return but also questioned it! They decided to dig up his grave, and there they found a dead log of wood. What they had all thought was Atya's body was just an illusion created by the witch. They searched for her, and when they found her, they killed her.

"If your son was kidnapped, he might have been hidden by an illusion spell, not an air jinni."

"Where do you suggest I search, then?"

"Think of those who hold a grudge against you or your wife."

"It…" Fad hesitated before explaining what had actually happened. "It is more complicated than what you think."

"I wish I could help you," Qamaria concluded.

"You can help me find the jinn master I came looking for." He searched his head for his name. "I cannot remember his name. I was told he was the only seer in Qairon Heriti."

"Atian?" she asked him.

"Yes, Atian."

"You just met him. He is my father. He probably didn't trust you when you appeared. He usually hides his identity, as any jinn master would do before they trusted in you."

"I thought it was him! Especially when he played my rababa."

"That enchanted rababa is yours? I saw him play it earlier, before you came. I asked him where he had got it from, but he never told me."

"Enchanted?" Fad had undervalued it.

"Where did you get such a rare instrument?"

"From the markets in Ubar. An old man offered it for a cheap price."

"Hmm."

"What makes it so special?"

"It's an ancient instrument. My father never told me about it, but my late mother did a very long time ago. She told me that not many such instruments exist, and they can be used to summon a strong type of jinn."

"What type of jinn?" Fad wondered.

"Any type. If I remember correctly, it depends on the person using it. Several factors are involved: how you feel when you use it, your thoughts, your true intentions, and the most important factor, the star you are born under."

"An item of this significance!" Fad laughed. "I don't think the beggar who gave it to me would have done so for such a small amount. I got it for two silver coins!"

"A beggar, you say?" Qamaria grinned back. "I don't think the beggar who gave it to you was actually human!"

The amusement on Fad's face disappeared. He tried to remember how the old beggar had looked. He had looked human to Fad, who thought the daughter of a jinn master before him must be exaggerating! All he knew was that it did pinch his heart, and it must have been enchanted like she said, nothing more. He kept that thought to himself. But he regretted the fact that he had never tried using it when he had it. Now the enchanted rababa was back with her father.

"Have no fear; it will be safe with my father."

"I don't care about having it that much. But would the rababa help me save my child? That I wonder about now."

"My father would know," she replied.

"I hope they don't harm him."

"They won't." She reassured him again about the truce. "They can't even harm me. I should go and inspect the area now."

She walked to the opening where light came from and climbed a rock to reach it. "I'll be back; you can rest as long as you want in here," she said and began to ascend.

"No, wait. I cannot rest long," he begged her, reminding her that he needed to find his kidnapped son.

"I won't be gone long. I'll be watching from afar until the frankincense farmers are out of sight."

Fad nodded and stayed. *Who are you?* he thought as he watched her climb the hole above. He carefully moved back towards the rug and stood on it as he eyed his surroundings in amazement. The peacefulness in the place made him feel sound. *A perfect hideout.* He then cocked his head and eyed the brown rug below his feet. Qamaria must have come there often to meditate alone and be away from every human soul. He sat on the rug, not minding a rest after a long and stressful run and crawl through the hole.

The calmness in the air made him feel drowsy. Tired and exhausted and without second thoughts, he lay on his back and closed his eyes, at least until she came back and woke him up, he thought.

And that was the exact moment when the execution of Behas was taking place back in Erum.

. . .

Fad drifted deep in his sleep, dreaming, but they were no regular dreams. They were like visions—they felt real, as if he were there, as if he had traveled back in time to when he was as little as six or seven, a moment when his mother, Ruba, had placed both her hands on his shoulders with love as she tried to explain to him why he had no brothers or sisters. "Children are gifts," she said. "And I am blessed with one dear and special to me: you!"

He suddenly turned fourteen; he was seeing a moment when he had become frustrated with the fact of being a farmer's son, and his father, Turab, had, for the first time, taught him how to throw a spear. "In times of peace, we are farmers. But in times of war, we shall be called to fight with our spears and daggers. I will teach you how to aim and throw." And to cheer him more, his father had also promised him that when Fad got older, he would take him south to the ports for the trade season.

Again he aged in his dream, to the time when he first began to have feelings for his relative, Nada, and then the visions showed him his child, Dil, safe in his arms.

His whole life flashed back in his dream. But when he entered his farm hut, his sweet dreams and memories started to turn into nightmares. His hut was filled with black snakes and blood. He called out to his wife, but no one was there. A snake began to chase after him, and he ran wildly in the dark between the palms. He found a tent, and in it the African seer sat staring at him with a strange creature behind him, half man, half hyena, and Fad felt he knew it was the all-knowing jinni the African had. The jinni hissed and said in a sharp whisper, "We know not where your son is. He is lost. And so are you."

He scrambled to his feet to get out and fell into Mair-Batlo's tent. This time, Shar-Shar was younger and seated in the middle, but still blind, and the fat brother laughed and sang their song. It felt safe in their tent, but odd, and then the snake appeared from below him again and he ran away in fear. This time he found the old seer from Magan. "Your child is calamitous; you must save him alone!" cried the seer with burning rage and red eyes. "Anyone who helps you will be harmed. Your child will bring calamity and doom."

He then saw Yam holding his child on the horse. "We are here to save your child as well. We are here to help." Then he saw the horse fall, neighing in pain and bleeding; he also saw the Guardian messenger, Baaz, injured and staring at him with anger. "You can't kill the *saher*," he said. Yam lay injured as well and reached his hands out to Fad so the farmer could help him stand. He then saw Lady Burmiah, then the giant prince, and Arkin. He remembered Arkin's words from that nightmare well: "You must save us! Save us all."

"You!" Fad called Arkin. "Help me find my son!"

And then, again suddenly, his dream shifted and he saw Bessel, who had also promised to find his child. "You must leave me alone!" howled Fad in his nightmare. "Stay away, Guardian," he begged Bessel and pushed him away. He then saw himself grabbing a burnt log in Wadi Dawkah. He threw the log into the crown of the sacred frankincense tree. It lit on fire in seconds. Bessel pulled at him to stop him, but Fad also had a dagger in his other hand.

This time it was he who killed Bessel by stabbing him to death with his dagger under the burning tree; there were no spearmen. His blade still dripped blood as he wandered through the green plains and reached the hut where an old man played his rababa. Once he entered the hut, the music stopped, and he found the old man dead with the rababa in his hands.

He then found himself sitting near the fire outside the huts, where he met Qamaria. She came from behind a wall and whispered. "Follow me. I will help you."

He shook his head in denial and begged her to stay away so she wouldn't be harmed as well. "I need no help from anyone!"

Alone again, but lying on his back at his farm in the dusk, he heard his child cry. He saw him near and tried to get to him, but his back was paralyzed. "Dil!" he cried repeatedly, but the child suddenly disappeared. And instead, he found Behas running towards him with the bone dagger in his hand. He cried aloud in fear, but knowing Behas had been executed, his mind realized finally it was all a bad dream. He woke with a start, inhaling sharply, but then exhaled with relief.

He tried to raise his head but felt his back attached to the rug in the green cave. And this time it was darker than he remembered. Qamaria had left him there till nightfall! He feared something had happened to her. He decided to go after her. But before he could get up, a dark figure jumped on his chest, and a bluish glow of moonlight shone on his face. It was Behas, holding his bone dagger in Fad's face, in the same position they had been in outside his farm that night when he lost his child. Only this time, it was Behas holding the dagger against him. He held Behas's arms and tried to push them away. "Let me go!" he cried. "Please!"

"The child is evil. It must be killed." Then Behas stabbed him in the neck, the same way Fad had done with him. Fad, choking to death, tried hard to yell out for help, but his throat was jammed with the dagger.

He cried out, waking from another nightmare—or was he still in the first one? Filled with fear, he lifted his head to sit up straight, and this time the cave was lit green again, but the tranquility had all been replaced with terror in his heart. He felt himself being haunted by something in this enchanted hole. Quivering, he tried to stand and head to the opening where Qamaria had climbed. But a sharp, creepy wailing sound blew from behind. His heart jumped out of its place, and he turned in an instant of shock and fear.

He found, there at the end of the cave, a large brown owl standing still on a rock and staring back at him with shiny green eyes. Fad's body went cold at the sight. He grabbed a sharp rock from the ground and pointed it towards the owl in defense. Without moving his head, he turned his eyes right and left to search the place again. The owl must have entered from the only opening in the chamber and flown over him to stand there. The tension in his muscles receded, but he remained still and prepared for any sudden movements the owl would make. Her motionless figure creeped him out more. The owl didn't even blink but stood still like a wooden sculpture.

Locking his gaze on the big bird and clutching the razor-sharp rock hard in his hand, he crept slowly backwards to reach the hole and climb out of the green cave. Then, unexpectedly, something grabbed his shoulder from behind and cried his name. He swung the sharp rock in defense. But he was sleepwalking, and it was Qamaria waking him up! She tried to dodge his strike, but Fad swung quicker and slashed her skin. Her blood splashed from her left arm, and she pressed on the open cut hard with her hand.

"It's me! Calm down," she cried. Light filled the place again; it was still daytime.

"I am terribly sorry! The owl, it scared me." He turned, pointing at it. But it wasn't there anymore. He froze in shock.

Qamaria looked down at the cut. It wasn't deep, but she was streaming with blood. "It wasn't an owl," she said. "It's—" She squeezed her lips together in pain.

"We need to stop your bleeding. I am sorry!"

"Hold this." She had a leather bag in her hand—water she had brought for him. She then pulled a handful of wet plant leaves from the earth and rubbed them together, frowning with pain as she placed the green mashed leaves on the cut and wrapped her veil around her waist to press on it.

"I am sorry." He tried to mention her name. "Qamaria, I owe you for helping me, and now I owe you more."

"I'll be fine." She forced a smile and said, "And I believe you have met my friend, Alma."

"Your friend?"

"Your dreams. They weren't dreams. It was Alma; she was trying to tell you something." She placed her hand on her wound with a grimace. "I must go back to my father; he can stop the bleeding."

Was I sleepwalking? Was it I who burned the tree in Wadi Dawkah? He now felt a strong pinch of guilt. Bessel must have been killed because of him. He had angered the farmers. And now he looked at the bleeding woman before him, thinking, *What if I had cut her neck?* That thought creeped him out. His visions suggested he should be alone!

Fad snapped at her. "What have I seen here?" he asked. "I have understood nothing from it. Why did my dreams, or whatever her name was, show me all of this? It felt real, like I was there!"

"My father asked me to bring you here. Only he can explain, but it won't be safe to take you back to him. The frankincense farmers have spread around looking for you. They will find you. I saw a platoon of Guardians of Erum from a distance. If you can reach them, you'll be safe from the frankincense farmers. They were on the path towards Samhan Mountain. If you leave now and run without stopping, you'll reach them before the spearmen find you. I saw a gray cloak traveling with them as well. They must be headed to the Gray Palace."

"The Noorian!" *Arkin,* Fad thought. *He'll help me find Dil. He should.* He remembered that the old occultist had told them the queen requested that he take Behas's corpse to her himself, and after that, his spy jinn master would help them find Fad's son. *The execution must have taken place,* he realized. *Nada should be healed by now!*

"Show me the way to the platoon you saw; the Noorian can help me find my kidnapped son." Now he thought of nothing other than saving Dil.

They climbed out of the cave and stood on the green land under the bright white cover of mist again. Daylight still shone brightly above, but Fad was unclear as to where the sun was and what time of day it was.

Since Behas has been executed, and Arkin has reached the Qara Mountains, it must be at least four hours after noon. How long did I sleep in that cave?

"The spearmen are far away now. And if I wasn't feeling pain, I would lead you myself. But I'll only slow you down. Follow my directions well and you shan't be lost. We place stone piles on the paths for when the fog is thick. The black stones shall take you towards Jibjat. A red flag on that path will mark the way towards the Samhan Mountain. And trust in Alma; she knows."

Fad remembered the words of the seer from Alma's visions. "No! I do not want you to follow me. Go back and stay with your father. I believe Alma wants me to be alone."

"She spoke to you?"

"It is true, I promise."

She then smiled and said, "I believe you. Good luck and farewell. I will pray that you find your son."

"Thank your father for his help. I hope I can thank him in person someday."

"I will," she said with a smile.

"Thank you. And I am sorry, again, for your wound. I owe you." And he left at a quick pace on the path she'd taught him. He needed to be quick before the sun set, and he had to reach the Guardians before the spearmen could spot him. Arkin was now his only hope.

24

A soul for a soul, thought Daheen as he remembered the Guardian who had killed his younger cousin.

Daheen and the other spearmen had gathered again after a long and disappointing lookout. At their agreed meeting point, they shook their heads with disappointment to signal the failure of their search, using phrases in their language that translate to "No sign of them" and "Found nothing."

...

I have told you only their leader's name, Daheen, but not the rest, which I think you should know so you don't misjudge them for having lost their prey and being tricked into an empty cave; for all their names were synonyms derived from the words "smart" and "wise" in Arabic. Daheen and his two brothers, Fateen and Faheem, were the sons of the wisest, and the sheikh of their tribe, Hakeem. Their cousins were Haseef, Thareef, and Areeb, whom Fad had killed the night before. And the youngest of them all was Labeeb, who left with Bessel's ring to reach the Guardians of Erum and declare himself a witness to all the events that had caused the death of a Chief Guardian. These last four were the children of Najeeb, the younger brother of Sheikh Hakeem.

...

"What do you mean, no sign of them? Did you expect them to fly away like *sahers*?" Daheen exploded. "That witch is hiding him nearby."

Daheen was more determined than the others to kill Fad, as he claimed to have seen him killing their cousin.

"We should head back," said Fateen to his stubborn brother. "This is going too far."

"We are not going back. Not until we take his soul." Daheen reminded them that he was their leader.

"And how do you plan to cover his death as well, another Guardian from Erum?" Fateen objected again.

"I will worry about it later. Let us find him before it is dark."

He noticed his cousin Haseef had not appeared yet. Daheen asked the others where he'd be, for they had all agreed to meet at the same time, but they all shook their heads again to say they hadn't seen him. The fog was thick that morning.

A cry caught their attention. The absent spearman, Haseef, stood some distance away and signaled for them to come to him. Daheen ran towards him, and the other three followed.

"I found their tracks," he said aloud before they reached him. "They look fresh; the two can't be far." He took them to where he had found the new tracks. "They went different ways; it could be another trick," he said.

"No, this is no trick," said Daheen, switching his gaze between the tracks. "You two follow the Guardian," he told his two cousins. He knew the two were as determined as he was to find the Guardian who had killed their brother. "But don't do anything till I come. We will find the witch and follow you at once."

Not adding anymore words, they all sprang to their duties. The three brothers, Daheen, Fateen, and Faheem, ran after Qamaria's tracks, and the other two, Haseef and Thareef, departed the other way, following Fad's. Daheen had warned them not to do anything, as he feared they would be motivated to try to kill the farmer who had killed their brother; Fad was more dangerous, he thought, and he didn't want to lose more cousins.

"These tracks look unbalanced; she might be injured. She's not far." They found her tracks heading back to the huts, and they raced after her, hoping to get to her before she reached them or hid again in another hole.

Daheen slowed down the moment he noticed her. She had reached the huts and was about to enter one. "Go around her; if she runs, we'll circle her." He directed his brothers to move around the huts and make sure they caught her if she tried to run away.

Daheen waited for her to enter the hut to make his move. He reached it silently, pointed his spear at it, and called to her, "Come out, woman. Do not try to run this time."

There was nothing but silence coming out of the hut. Only the buzz of flies was heard. The other mare, which had escaped, had returned to near the hut and was tied as well; he found that strange but ignored it. Daheen slowly stepped closer to the open door, but he could hear no sound from inside that could be produced by her presence. He began to doubt if she was there. He moved near the door to where he was able to glance inside.

He thought she might be hiding beside the door with a weapon in her hand, preparing to strike back in defense. "We will not harm you," he said, trying to lure the trapped prey out of her hole. He waited and waited, but without result. His primary target was the Guardian, and he didn't want to delay his chase after him, so he decided to enter, but cautiously.

He thrust his spear in first, and he slowly followed till he was able to see the whole inside of the hut. *She's not here!* He thought. He searched the small hut like a mad hound sniffing for food. There was not a sign of her, nothing but the body of her father, a man he had killed by mistake.

When they first came, the old jinn master had assumed the rababa could reduce their anger and intensity, and so he had played it and hoped for that, but it had only made them angrier. Daheen only remembered his consciousness coming back to him when the enchanted instrument went silent, and to his surprise, he found his spear had stabbed the rababa player, breaking a truce between two tribes. He shouldn't have killed him. He had never intended to do so.

Now, searching for Qamaria before she discovered his crime, he stood at the center of the hut and lowered the weapon in his hand. There was no place for a young woman her size to hide in, there were no windows for her to leave from either, and there was only a single door. *It can't be a phantom or jinni that I saw,* he thought, doubting what he had seen when he followed her. *I must have missed her movements with all the mist.* Not wanting to waste any more time, he decided to abandon this side chase and return to his main prey, the outlaw who had killed his cousin.

Before he left the hut, he stood and took one last glance at the dead body. There was something different than when he had left it the first time, but he couldn't think what it was. Then he figured it out: the rababa was gone! Adding that to the fact that one of the horses that had run away when they first came had been returned and tied again next to the other, someone else might be there, he feared. But they had not seen anyone else. No one lived near this lake but the jinn master and his daughter, he knew; the rest of the tribe lived far behind the hill. *Had someone else seen the dead body?*

He was confused, as there was clearly no one else in the hut. *Where is that witch?* He cursed.

. . .

Qamaria had used the fog to her advantage. She knew they were following her and pretended to be unaware. She did enter the hut, as Daheen had seen, and there she saw her father lying slain and became aware of their hostility. With rage, she pulled out her father's bone dagger and a green blanket. She then covered herself with the blanket and, like an unseen jinni, slid outside the hut and hid behind the green leafy wall. When she saw Daheen enter, she silently walked near the entrance. She could have run, but her injury would slow her. She also knew there were many others spread out and searching, and she wanted to avenge her father as well.

Once she saw Daheen coming out, she swung, aiming for his neck, but he was quicker.

He dodged the blade and smacked her hand with his spear. The shaft struck her hard and knocked her off her feet. She turned, trying to get up, but another smack from Daheen forced her to drop the blade. The pain from her bleeding wound kept her down and powerless. She turned and stared back at Daheen with hate-filled eyes. Not the kind of woman who'd beg for mercy.

"Witch," he called her, and turned his spear around to touch her wound with its butt. "You're hurt."

He cried for his men to come.

"You killed my father," she said. "We had a truce."

"The Guardian you and your father helped, he burned my tree and killed my cousin. You two broke the truce first. Where is he?"

"That is no excuse to kill my father; he was an old man!" She cursed him. "You will be killed for this, I promise." She wouldn't be the one to kill him; she knew he'd kill her like he had killed her father. But the tribe would always take revenge for them. Daheen could cover his crime for now, but eventually, the tribe would learn who had killed their jinn master and his daughter, and they would hunt Daheen and his men. This would start a tribal war in the mountains between the people of Qairon Heriti and the farmers of Wadi Dawkah.

"I was not intending to kill your father, but he started it. He tried to kill us first, with his jinn. We were defending ourselves," Daheen countered. "And we will spare you. I was intending to take you with me to force the Guardian to surrender, but you have enough pain and grief, as I can see."

His brothers now stood behind him. "Help her bury her father," he commanded them. "And allow me to heal your wound," he then offered.

"I don't need your help," she said to him. "And leave my father alone; I will bury him myself," she yelled to Fateen and Faheem, stopping them from entering the hut.

They stopped and waited for Daheen to sort it out with her.

"Do you think I would forgive you for killing my father?" she spat and raised her head and chest closer to the butt of the spear. "We will hunt you down, Daheen. You started this war, and everyone will know it. You will never be a sheikh like your father. You are nothing but a killer; you are a dirty hyena, and I pray you will be killed by one." Her eyes began to fill with tears. "May you and your souls sink in Barhoot."

Daheen raised his spear away from Qamaria and smirked. "I offered you my peace." He then turned the spear to point the sharp tip at her. "Barhoot is where jinn masters and witches like you and your father are thrown. Not us." He punched his spear at once into the center of her chest. She anticipated the pain, but it was more painful than the wound Fad made on her. It was more painful than she could have imagined, though she tried not to show it; she tried to look strong. She tried to open her mouth to have the last word. She wanted to remind him that he and his cousins would suffer in this world and the next, but she couldn't. Her jaw was clenched tight. Her soul then left her body; her eyelids dropped, and darkness fell around her.

"Let's bury them both," Daheen commanded after he pulled his spear from her dead body. "And be quick. That Guardian shall not be spared."

25

Fad continued on the road Qamaria had described to him without stopping for a rest, not knowing that he was being followed by two of the spearmen. He did worry about leaving her and her father behind with the brutal spearmen who had killed his companion before his eyes, but she had mentioned a truce between them, and maybe she and her father, unlike him, wouldn't be targets for the half-naked scavengers of Wadi Dawkah. That thought kept his mind at peace. And he thought, too, of the many flashbacks he had seen in his dreams, or whatever it was that Alma had shown him.

What he thought of the most from the visions was the time when he had burned the tree. The feeling of guilt haunted him again.

Fad continued his trot up and down and up again through the plains below the Qara Mountains, following the black stone markers that Qamaria had described. He ignored the few villages and settlements on the sides of the paths and stopped only two or three times for a sip of water from the water skin Qamaria had given him. By the time he reached the open field of Jibjat, the sun had begun to set. It would be difficult to find his path or the Guardians if the sky lost its light. Qamaria had described the paths well, and the stone piles marked the routes around the mountains clearly. Fad had never wandered these plains alone; the only times he and his father left their farms for trade, they had been guided by a caravan with other tradesmen, and Fad had never cared to know how the caravan found its paths.

With difficulty and after searching carefully, he found the flag Qamaria had described. Now all he needed to do was see if the path had fresh tracks or not. If not, he could just wait for the Guardians and Arkin to pass by, as it was the route to Samhan Mountain. He hoped to find them before it got dark, and he did. The tracks were clear, and they looked fresh. *They must be near, behind the hill,* he thought, and he ran.

The two spearmen continued to follow him from afar. He hadn't noticed their presence the whole time.

Fad reached a crest, and from above, his eyes caught the traveling group. They were setting their camp for the night, as the sun had just set, and they weren't far from where he stood. *Great! There they are,* he thought at first, but when he got there, he wished he had traveled the other way.

...

The Guardians noticed him coming down the hill, and they all drew their weapons as he neared. He reached them and saluted them all with a sense of relief and security.

Three Guardians faced him with upset looks and weapons drawn.

But he thought it was normal for them to be alert when a stranger with a Guardian's tunic appeared from over a hill. "Pleased to have found you!" Fad said.

"Are you the farmer, Fada?" one asked.

"Yes, it is me." He sighed calmly, not yet realizing what had happened. Not many knew how fast a Guardian messenger would spread news and alerts.

"Tie him up!"

The Guardians did as their chief asked, as Fad remained still and utterly confused.

"Where is the Noorian, Arkin?" Fad asked. "I need to talk to him."

"I do not think talking to anyone will help you now. You will be executed for the crime you committed against the Chief Guardian, Bessel."

Bessel? They must think I killed him! he feared, in shock and out of words.

Arkin and two other Guardians approached to witness the event. Fad cried and begged desperately in his defense, telling them his party had been attacked by spearmen, but the orders they had received from Erum were strict.

"Arkin, it is I! I have not betrayed Bessel," Fad pleaded with him, but he saw no reaction from Arkin. The occultist stood by silently. And he would, for he had known Fad for only the length of a day or less. "Please believe me! Why would I kill him?! I need to find my child, and...and Bessel was helping me!" Fad tried to explain as much as he could, but the Guardians had no patience for him and dragged him to one of three enclosed areas they had prepared. "Arkin, I need to know where my son is. Please. Help me find him." And as he said this, he saw flashes of the dreams he had had in Alma's cave, when Arkin had pleaded to him the same way he did that night. It was as if the dream had been inverted.

...

Seeing it all from afar, the two spearmen hid farther away in the darkness and decided to wait for their cousin Daheen to arrive.

...

The enclosed area Fad was kept in was a set of fabric walls without a roof; it was set up to protect the chests and crates and keep wild animals away or thieves from stealing easily. In it, there were several small chests which probably had food or other treasures being moved from Wadi Erum to the Gray Palace, and there was also a coffin. Fad figured it had to contain Behas's corpse.

Fad was tied to a leafless tree at the center of the temporary room. After he had been there a while, Arkin came to visit him.

"Arkin!" Fad called. He was sitting down, with his hands tied behind the tree trunk. "I did not kill Bessel. I would not."

"How should I say this?" Arkin said and bit his lips. "There is nothing I can do for you. The orders are to take you back to Wadi Erum," he said. "But you mentioned spearmen; what happened to you? What we heard before we left the city was that you had killed Bessel to steal his horse and that you had burned a tree in Wadi Dawkah."

"That is not true!" Fad went on and explained all that had happened to him and Bessel.

"I will try to explain it to the Guardians. But they will have no power to set you free. That all must be explained in Wadi Erum; you are wanted for murder now. I am sure it is all just a misunderstanding."

"It is!" Fad interrupted. "Help me, Arkin. I can't rest until I find my son. He is in danger."

"I will," Arkin said. "I have more important things to deliver to the mountain now, but after I am done with them, I will do my best and find your son."

"What things are more important than finding a kidnapped child? The longer that is delayed, the farther away he's gone. I have to find my son, Arkin. You are my only hope! I thought you came to save him last night!"

"I still want to save him. But he is not the first child I have failed to save from Behas."

Fad found Arkin's motives somewhat strange and frustrating.

The occultist did not help Fad that night. Fad lost all hope in the Noorian. The Guardians told him they would be taking him back to Wadi Erum for trial first thing in the morning.

26

That night, after the execution of Behas, Yam rested on a large bed, the largest he had ever slept in in his life. He enjoyed the comfortable and generous hospitality of Erum. He didn't want to leave the High Palace even though he had recovered enough that he was able to walk. He wished he could serve there and live in Erum rather than going back to Sumhuram.

The healer of the palace walked in with a pot in his hand; he'd come to check on the patient who remained in a small guest room on the ground floors. These were the rooms where the important guests rested, not where injured Guardians would be. "I asked them to make you soup," said the healer. "It is beef broth, mixed with turmeric and salt. I also brought some of the turmeric in water mixed with olive oil for you to rub on your injured leg. It will soften your bones and help affix them back to your flesh."

"Thank you, master. I am forever grateful to you and to all of Wadi Erum," Yam said as he forced himself out of bed and onto the rug on the floor, his face twisting and stiffening from the pain. His healer had directed him to move as much as he could. After the painful journey from his low bed to the floor, he finally settled before the soup. "When I was in Port Rori, we had dining tables and chairs made of wood. I expected Erum to be more advanced in that sense, you know. Why is it that you still dine on the floor?"

The healer laughed. "We are advanced in some respects, but unlike you folk who live by the sea, we prefer tradition."

Yam opened his eyes in wonder at the healer's words, then shifted his gaze to a Babylonian lightbulb. The healer followed his gaze to see it as well.

They looked back at each other, and the healer laughed again. Yam gave a sly smile. "I assume tradition has a variety of meanings, master," said Yam. He began drinking his soup from a small pottery bowl.

"Tell me, Yam, is it true what they say? Is Behas your real father?" asked the healer.

Yam almost spat the soup from his mouth but chokingly swallowed it and coughed. "What?"

"I heard them say it in the palace. I did not believe that, and I had to ask you."

"Who would say such slander?" Yam shouted in both rage and confusion.

"Your mother. She came to the palace this afternoon. She wanted to see you, but the guards would not allow her in, so she left."

My mother? How'd she know I was here? His mother was a poor old woman; she would never have the resources or strength to travel to Wadi Erum. He hadn't seen her for three months, ever since he had left her and traveled to Sumhuram. He could not imagine how she would know where he was, but he wouldn't be surprised if she had turned to seers to find him. And Yam had never known his father; his mother had always told him that his father chose to leave her. *She must have thought her son had become what he'd promised! She came all the way to see me in the High Palace of Erum!*

"I will not stay with you, Mother," he told her once. "I have to leave; I have to find my destiny. One day, I will become rich, and I will free you from this tiring exertion you are in."

He knew she had never wanted him to leave, but now she had come looking for him, he thought. "She told someone Behas was my father?" he asked again quietly.

"That is what I heard."

She had many times cursed his father in front of him when he was younger, and she might have referred to the man as an outlaw, but he couldn't think why she would claim that. *Could she be referring to him?* he worried. *Could she have heard about the execution as well and traveled across the desert to reach Wadi Erum?* Yam had witnessed the execution from the High Palace that day and now thought his mother must have spotted him from below. He couldn't imagine his poor old mother all alone and lost in the big valley. He had to find her.

He forced himself up again. "Where is my cane? I must go and find her."

"You sure? At this time of night?"

Yam's eyes shone with terror and delight all at the same time. "Yes, she's my mother! And I must know why she claims Behas is my father!"

...

Earlier that afternoon, and after witnessing the execution, Burmiah and Faseela walked straight to the healer's cave. The old woman took her sack of medicines and climbed behind Faseela up the long stairs of the valley-wall to the upper parts of Erum. They walked on swift feet to Nada's parents' house, where she lay unconscious from the snakebite.

Only Nada and her mother were there. Badde had left earlier to see the execution as well but had not yet returned.

Without further delay, Burmiah placed her sack next to the unconscious Nada. She revealed a stony mortar and a wooden pestle, and she threw in it a mix of Indian dry pepper, dry garlic, date stones, and a sprinkle of salt. She gently crushed all the ingredients and repeatedly, in Arabic, whispered in the mortar as she did the names of the three main gods worshipped in Erum. "By Somood, by Sada, by Haba."

When all the crushed ingredients became one bit of powder, she added a few drops of a dense red liquid to the mortar and mixed it all again using the pestle. She then used two of her fingers and placed the final product, a bit of wet black substance, on the bite marks. "Bring me the incense burner," she instantly requested.

Faseela sprang up to reach for an incense burner and placed two burning coals on top. She handed the incense burner to the healer, who placed it near Nada's neck. She threw in a few small stones of frankincense, a smell the harmful jinn despised and the healing jinn enjoyed. Or so it was believed.

"The curse will soon be out. We must wait."

"Thank you, Lady Burmiah," said Nadia. "Let us serve you with something to eat." She offered the food she originally had cooked for her husband, Badde, who had not yet returned.

After an hour, Badde reached his house. He entered to find three women clustered around his unconscious daughter and staring back at him. "Is my dear Nada healed?" he asked.

"Not yet," answered Faseela.

"Father!" murmured Nada at the sound of her father's voice. The other three women all turned their heads to her at once.

"She has awakened! Nada!" called Faseela.

"My dear daughter. Praised be the gods."

"Praised they be," said Badde with a broader smile.

Burmiah wiped Nada's neck with a cloth soaked in water; nothing remained on her neck but the bite mark. The two black dots became darker and clearer on her white neck.

"Father!" she said again and slowly opened her eyes. A blurred image of her father's shadow stood above her, covering the light from the doorway. "Where am I?" she was finally conscious, but the last she remembered, she had been sleeping at the farm, not her parents' place. She placed her fingers on her bruised neck; there was no pain but rather an odd feeling.

"You are home, my dear. You are okay," said her mother in an effort to calm her. She held both her arms to help Nada sit up.

She remembered now; her child had been sleeping near her, and not far from her, her husband had slept as well. "Where is Dil? Where is Fad?" she asked smoothly.

The rest exchanged looks, not knowing where to start nor what to say. Nada looked at her mother, waiting for an answer.

"You were bitten by a snake, my dear child, while you were asleep. Fada carried you here to Erum, and Lady Burmiah healed you from your long sleep." Her mother tried her best to explain everything else. "And Dil is…" She did not know how to mention what happened to him.

"Snake? And where is Dil? Is he okay? Has he been bitten as well?"

They all remained silent until Burmiah spoke the truth. "Your child has been kidnapped by jinn. The jinn master Behas attacked you in your sleep and stole your child." She narrated the tale as she had heard it from Fad when he had first begged her to help him.

Nada swallowed the air in disbelief.

"It is a blessing that you are now conscious," her mother said. "And Fada is safe as well; he has left to bring Dileel back."

"Do not worry, Nada. Fad will be back soon with Dil," said Faseela.

"Everything will be fine, my dear. Calm down and rest." Her mother soothed her as well. "Come with me," she said as she helped Nada to the bathing room outside the house. Her mother cleaned her in warm water to refresh her soul.

"How long have I slept?" she asked her mother.

"It has been more than a day, my daughter. Fada brought you here yesterday morning," her mother replied.

They finished bathing and went back to the house, where her mother fed her well.

Faseela began to explain everything she knew to her. "Fad should be here by now. It has been a long time since he left us to go to the High Palace yesterday!" Faseela wondered, sharing her thoughts with everyone. "I fear for him now; I will go to the High Palace and ask about him."

Since the day before, when Fad had left them for the High Palace, they had all been worried about him and Dil. He had never told them he was headed to Ubar that night, and they decided to wait for morning and hoped to hear from him then. When morning came, they all got busy with the execution and Nada's healing. And now that she was healed, Faseela reminded them of Fad again.

"I will come with you," said Nada.

"No, you need to rest, daughter," her mother insisted.

"I feel well; I don't need more rest, Mother."

"I shall come with you as well," added Badde. He then faced his wife. "We will be back before sunset. Do not worry."

The three, Faseela, Nada, and Badde, left for the High Palace.

Burmiah carried her sack and prepared herself to leave as well. "Thank you for the food. I hope she finds her husband. And her child." The healer left after telling the mother goodbye.

. . .

The three crossed a bridge to reach the High Palace. On their way, they passed by the temple of Somood but decided to go to the palace and ask about Fad first. They reached the palace and stood still below the high raised gate, without a clue what they should do next.

A guard observed their arrival from the guards' observation room, which was placed straight above the gate. This room had hidden holes that allowed him to observe the gate entrance without being noticed himself. He waited for their next move, but they didn't make one.

After a while of waiting and walking back and forth around the gate, Nada called for her husband. "Fad!" she shouted. "Fad, are you there?"

The guard above observing them asked his companion to check the records for that name. The other shook his head. "That name is not on the list." The guard nodded to his companion and left the dark observation room, descending to meet them.

"Who are you?" he said at the exact moment he appeared from a hidden opening in the wall. "What brings you here to the High Palace of Aad?" He spoke to them in a strong, wrathful voice. Judging from the way they dressed, they weren't guests of the sheikh.

"I am looking for my husband. He came to the palace yesterday but has not yet returned."

The guard had not been on duty the night before, and so he had not seen who had entered. "And for what reason did he come?"

"He came looking for my son. My son has been kidnapped."

"There are no husbands looking for their lost sons here," said the guard. "The army is busy preparing to journey east. You may not remain here longer, for it is a time of war. Please be gone."

Nada gazed back at her father and Faseela, silently asking support.

"My son-in-law, Fad, came here yesterday," said Badde. "If you have not seen him, then where is he?"

"I think you must look elsewhere," the guard replied. "We observe the gates and record everyone who enters or leaves through them. The guards before us report who has remained and who is no longer here. There are no men with that name on our list. I will ask the other guards if they have seen anything, but you need to search for him elsewhere. Now be gone."

His name *was* on the list, as when he had come in the night before, he had told them his name was Fada, son of Turab. The other guard would surely have missed his name in the lengthy list of guests entering the palace every night. And mispronouncing one letter in Arabic can change the whole shape of the written name.

Nada squeezed her empty fists tight, and Faseela noticed it. "Let us go, Nada. I am sure he is fine and is on his way back," she said. "Let us thank Somood for your health and ask for him to guard your beloved child and husband, wherever they may be."

...

The three had left the gate and stood now before the rounded rock in the center of the roofless sacred temple. They gestured their tribute and offered their prayers separately before the head of Somood.

Badde saw a proud face staring back at him. He asked for strength and support to help find his son-in-law and grandson.

Faseela tried not to stare long, as she saw an angry and fearful face every time she peeked at it. It made her feel guilty for the tiniest of sins she might have ever committed in her life. Her feelings were not related to her friend's situation, but she remembered a horrible mistake haunting her as usual. She looked away and tried to concentrate her prayers on her friend Nada and not herself.

Nada prayed to find her child and husband. The anger she had felt at the gate still dominated her thoughts. She looked at Somood from below, and the rock appeared to be smiling.

Why is it smiling? she thought. *Has he answered my prayers?* She felt less worried and less angry now. She felt Somood trying to calm her down. She felt the rock was now whispering to her, "You ask for them to be safe? Yet they are safe and well."

Then I should pray for you to help me find them! she thought again. And the face still smiled back. She felt eased and thankful.

"It will be dark soon. Shall we head back home?"

"Yes. I feel better now, Father, thank you. We will find Fad and Dil. I am sure we will. I feel confident," said Nada. And the three left the temple.

. . .

After sunset, the gate guard who had forced them to leave ended his shift. He left his post to meet with his lover, a servant who worked in the High Palace. He hugged her, kissed her, and told her how tiring his day had been. "Just before sunset, a crazy woman came by the gate. She believes her husband is looking for her lost son here in the palace!" he said.

"Maybe she is right; why would you call her crazy?" his lover replied.

After that, the servant walked to the chamber where she and her friends lived. She told them about a woman who had lost her son and that her husband had gone to the palace looking for her son before her, asking them if they thought the woman was right. Another said, "Maybe her son *is* here. I saw a teenaged outlander boy being treated near the healer's chamber." She was referring to Yam, who did look like a teenager.

Then, another muttered, "If that would be the son, then who would her husband be? Who entered yesterday and is not here today? Behas?" They squeaked a laugh that only they heard. But before the laugh, another nosy servant had overheard them as she passed by them on her way to the kitchen.

She met with an old cook and told the tale as her ears had picked it up, but she did add a couple more words. "Behas had a wife! She claimed that her son is being held in the palace and that he is the same young man you are cooking this soup for."

The cook opened his eyes and added to the tale as well. "I had heard before that Behas had a son; it could be him. Maybe he is why Behas came to Wadi Erum. The saher wanted to find him, but it all went badly for both. The young man up there, they say, was raised by the Noorians. He is a young occultist, too, and that is why he helped Erum capture the outlaw saher, his father." The cook finished preparing the pot of soup and handed it to the nosy servant. "Take this to the healer, and send our thankful regards to that young man for being righteously brave."

...

And as you and I know well, none of that gossip was true! Fate, destiny, God's will, or coincidence—call it what you want. Whatever it was, it worked in the most mysterious ways. If the guard had known Fad, he might have just sent his wife away, telling her that the man had gone to Ubar. And if the tale had reached Yam as it was, he might have not cared much about meeting her. But the tale reached him in such a convoluted way that he became eager to meet the woman he thought was his own mother!

27

Yam forced himself up again. "Where is my stick? I must go and find her."

"Are you sure? At this time of night?"

Yam's eyes shone with terror and delight all at the same time. "Yes, she's my mother! And I must know why she claims Behas is my father!"

"It will take you forever to search in the wadi! Let the guards who banned her bring her here; it will be faster if they do," the healer suggested.

Yam paused, standing at the doorway, looking back at the healer. "I assume you're right, master."

"Rest, Yam. I will ask if the guards can help and bring her here to you," he said, then stood to leave.

"Master, please tell them to find her quickly. I fear she has no place to stay in this city."

The healer nodded. "I will be sure to tell them that."

...

The chief of guards heard the healer and gave orders to his men to bring back the woman they had banned earlier from entering. After a few hours of investigating the upper parts of Erum while two of his companions searched the inns below, the gate guard who had formerly banned Nada found her father seated at his usual spot in front of his house.

"You! You came with a woman at the gate this afternoon. Where is that woman who came looking for her child?"

"My daughter, you mean? What happened?"

"I apologize for not believing her at first." His voice softened. "Her son is well and resting in the palace. He could not walk far; he sent us to bring her back to him."

"Her son? Wait here. I will get her." *Her son? The fool, I think he meant her husband.* He walked in to get his daughter. "Nada, the guard from the gate is here, asking for you. He says your husband is well in the palace but is unable to walk!"

"My prayers are answered! I will follow him at once."

"I will join you there." Faseela followed her.

"I cannot leave your mother alone in the house at night. But I trust you to be safe with the guard, and back with Fad."

"I know, Father, and trust we will be safely guarded by Somood."

The two friends, Nada and Faseela, left at will, escorted by the guard. While she and her friend expected to meet with Fad, the guard, who had never seen Yam, thought he was escorting a mother to her son. And Yam waited with anxiety back in the palace, expecting to meet his helpless old mother.

Nada and Faseela followed the guard at a distance behind, trying to catch up with his fast steps. They continued to walk in silence, pleased to hear her husband was well, but Nada also wondered about his condition. *Why can't Fad move?*

Once the two women arrived at the room where Yam was resting, they were all struck with confusion.

Yam was the first to break the awkward silence. "Who are you?"

Both Nada and Faseela frowned and stared at their escort.

"Is this not your mother?" the guard asked.

When Nada turned her head, Yam noticed the two black spots on her white neck, partly hidden behind her loose veil and long, silky brown hair. He ignored the guard and stared at the marks. He did not relate them to the snake he had killed at first, but they caught his attention, for they were neither small nor normal.

"Whose mother am I? Where is my husband?" Nada yelled angrily, in a temper and impatient after walking to the palace and expecting to reunite with her family. Now she sensed her hopes had been shattered in an instant. "You brought me from my home to see my husband. Where is he? Where is Fad?"

Fad? Could this be? Thought Yam. He exchanged puzzled looks with the guard, trying to comprehend the scene before his eyes.

"How dare you drag two respected women out late at night for nothing? We did not expect our time to be wasted." Faseela joined her friend in her protest against the two strange men.

"Where is my mother? You said my mother came to the gate earlier; where is she?" Yam questioned both the guard and the healer.

"My ladies, please, calm down. We mean you no disrespect." The healer tried to calm them all down. When he spoke, they all listened. "Who are these two women that you have upset? Clearly, neither of them is Yam's mother." The healer now questioned the guard.

"But this *is* the woman who came this afternoon, asking us about her husband." The guard pointed at Nada. "You asked me to bring her, and there she is! We did not see any other woman at the gate."

"I...I came this afternoon asking about my husband and child. You told me my husband was well. Where is he?" Nada cried at the guard again.

"My lady, I think I know your husband," Yam interrupted her. "Master Fad. Are you his wife?"

"Yes, he came here yesterday. Have you seen him?"

"Praised be the moon! You have been healed. Is that the snake's bite on you neck? Behas's snake?"

She went calm and touched the mark. "I've been told it is, yes."

"I see it all clearly now! You came looking for your child and husband, Fad, and the guards thought I was your son, so they led you to me. Is she the woman you told me was my mother, who claimed Behas was my father?"

Addressed with the last question, both the guard and the healer agreed that Nada was the only mother who had come earlier asking for her child.

"But I made no such claim regarding Behas or any of you," Nada clarified. "I know neither of you. I only asked for my husband, Fad, and my only child, Dil, who is now only nine days old."

"That, I am a witness of," added Faseela.

"She tells the truth; Behas was not mentioned by them at all," the guard confirmed.

Yam shot a perplexed look at the healer, his source of information tonight.

The healer raised his eyebrows in wonder, then smiled slightly, with a shy laugh, as he realized what seemed to be a misunderstanding. "My honest apology for all the confusion tonight," he said. "I have completely forgotten the way gossip and rumors pass around these high walls between servants. Here, like ingredients in a soup, words change a lot from their origins, like clear water when it is mixed with a variety of ingredients, creating a different taste, a taste far from that of water. I carried the soup in my hand and the servants' gossip in my ear and passed it all to you. Please forgive me."

Yam smiled in relief and shifted his eyes back to Nada. His mother was still far away in his hometown. He hoped she was well and safe. "Please forgive us all. It's a grace to see you well. I killed the snake that bit you, and it was me who carried your son away from Behas, but I am sorry I lost him then. I am deeply sorry. It was out of my control, and we had no choice." Yam carried on explaining to Nada, in detail, what had happened. What everyone had told her was that her child was well, and Fad had left to get him back. Yam told her the whole, and opposite, bare truth.

"As you can see, I haven't been allowed to join them. I don't know where they might be now," Yam concluded.

At the mention of Bessel, the gate guard raised his eyebrow as if he'd remembered something. He leaned his head backwards and eyed the roof for a thought before he spoke. "Last night! I remember now. The guards before me told me that they saw Bessel exiting the palace with a man I did not know." He detailed his main features, including long black hair that covered his ears, and Nada confirmed those features to be Fad's.

"Rest assured, he left traveling with a Chief Guardian," Yam said. "I am sure they are safe. I will ask the Guardians of Erum in the morning if they have heard anything about them and where they might be. Go back to your home, and tomorrow, I will send you word about your husband."

"Thank you, for everything."

"My lady, it is the least I could do. Not only did I fail to keep your child safe, but your husband saved my life from Behas as well." Yam concluded, "I will pray to the moon to keep him safe, and may he be guided to find your child."

The women left the palace and went back straight to Nada's parents' house. Nada rested her head against her pillow but could not rest her mind, as she wept in worry for her child's fate.

28

Nada woke in an instant from a terrible nightmare. She strongly felt that Fad was in terrible danger. She tried to remember what exactly she had seen, but her memory betrayed her. She woke at sunrise, but it felt dark in her parents' house.

Faseela had just arrived at their house after a long walk from the farms. She had woken up earlier and had prepared and brought bread with her for Nada and her parents. "Good morning!" Faseela started with a smile. "Are you all right?"

"I saw a terrible dream. I can't remember anything, but I feel that Fad is in trouble."

Before Faseela spoke, the door opened and Badde entered with eyebrows raised in fear, as if he had seen death. He and his daughter stared eye to eye; one looked frightened and the other confused. "Nada, come outside. Men here have word of your husband."

Nada jumped up and rushed to the door, while Faseela followed. Yam stood there, looking worried. Beside him was the guard from the night before, who had led him to their house.

"My lady, I have terrible news." Yam began relating to her what he had told her father. "I am not sure how to explain it all. After you left last night, I slept for only a few hours. I woke up early this morning, before dawn, and I went on trying to meet with any of the Guardians. They were all busy, and almost none of them looked at me. But one did." That one had been Baaz.

"I asked him if he would know where Bessel and your husband, Fad, might be. And to my surprise, he told me that Bessel had been killed."

Nada covered her mouth, with tears of worry starting in her eyes.

"At first, I hoped they were only palace rumors. But he confirmed to me that his division of royal couriers had received orders to go and spread the description of their first suspect, Fad!"

At the mention of Fad's name, Nada opened her terrified eyes at once, as if something had stabbed her heart.

"Fad is a relative of mine and my son-in-law," Badde said in a quivering voice. "He would never betray the Sheikhs of Erum, and he would never murder anyone, let alone a Chief Guardian."

"It's true!" Nada wiped her face but continued weeping as she defended Fad. "Fad is innocent. I am certain of it."

"I am sure that the orders have been issued by men who know nothing about him," said Yam. "I have decided to travel to the mountains to tell it all to my master occultist, Arkin. He can help us find Fad, and he has the connections to issue orders from the Mountain Queen. The Noorians could help us through their influence on the High Palace and save Fad from any trial. I am sure if they knew that Fad had helped in the capture of the outlaw Behas, they would spare him."

In the High Palace, all the credit for capturing the famous Behas had gone to Prince Zufar, Bessel, and the occultists Arkin and Yam. Fad remained an unknown hero, although some of the credit should go to him. Yam, being one of the few who had witnessed Fad's heroic actions, felt that he should help him. He couldn't trust the tales that spread in the palace about the death of Bessel or Fad's betrayal. He decided to help Fad and find out for himself whether what he had heard was true.

"I will come with you to see the Noorians. I can't stay here!" Nada said.

"We should leave soon," Yam said.

"We can hire a convoy," Nada suggested. "I will pay for it."

"Great. I will wait for you here, and we can leave once you are ready."

Faseela offered to join them as well, and both the women went inside the house to prepare.

Badde thanked Yam and the guard. He then entered his house to find his daughter. "Nada, I cannot allow you to leave."

"Why not? Fad is in trouble. I must reach for help, any of it."

"It is not safe outside the city. The Noorians' mountain is far away, and the journey is dangerous. I cannot join you, though I wish I could, and I cannot leave your mother alone. She would be sad if you left. That man has offered to go and help Fad by himself. I am sorry, but I will be forcing you to stay."

"Fad is in danger! And I will not wait here for him to get killed," she said in a lower tone. "You have no right to force me to stay here; you lost that right the day I married Fad." She spun around, ignoring him, and continued to pack with Faseela. Her eyes filled with tears, and she couldn't see anything but a blur, but she continued to keep her hands busy so her father wouldn't notice it.

He walked his rage out and sat on the rug outside his house to calm down. She was right, he thought.

. . .

He remembered when he and Turab had once returned from Ubar at night and found only his wife in the house. They had both told Nada and Fad to stay at the house. But to no surprise, he found that his daughter hadn't stayed like he had ordered her to.

"Where did she go?" he asked his wife, Nadia.

"Calm down, Badde; our daughter will be safe. She went out for a walk with Fad."

"A walk! It is nighttime, Nadia. That stubborn girl. I told her not to leave. They must have lost their way. We will go and find them."

Turab, too, had seemed upset that Fad had disobeyed him. He thought he should have left Fad at the farm with his mother. "Did they say where they were headed?" he had asked Nadia.

"She told me they were headed to the nearby bridge." She had sighed. "Don't yell at her, Badde. She is only a child."

"She is fifteen years old, Nadia. A woman of her age should never disobey her father."

. . .

He knew the type his daughter was, difficult and stubborn. He would eventually be forced to back down. *They are leaving to go to the Noorians and ask the occultists to help Fad.* He tried to calm himself as he sat outside and observed the sunrise, then went back in and gave his daughter enough silver to hire a convoy. Then he began to think of what he should tell her mother. He also thought about whether there was anything he could do to help Fad. He couldn't join his daughter, but for now, he would pray for their safe departure and return.

29

The Gray Palace: hidden from plain sight, far from regular reach, high in the clouds, above all ignorant minds, deep in the mountains, deeply secretive, and divine.

The guild of occultists that lived in these dark caves called it a palace, and it had the necessary luxuries to be so, but it had once been a fortress, a safe hideout for minds that sought refuge from the reckless and powerful enemy that haunted all beings on earth: ignorance. They had chosen to color it gray to represent ambiguity, which constantly reminded them of all the hidden mysteries of the world that they sought to unravel.

Amongst those who had chosen to leave the world behind and turn to the hidden beacon of wisdom in that palace was Hadaus, one of the most devoted Noorians to serve the purpose of the guild.

His facial features were more Arabic, but his hair and skin tone suggested his African origins. His beard had a mixture of white and brown hair. It grew in ant-sized hair circles, scattered sparsely across his cheeks. One could count his facial hairs and barely find more than ten. Hadaus was already skilled in medicine when he first joined the guild, and he enjoyed the wisdom of mixing herbs and other ingredients to create diverse remedies. He also quickly gained more knowledge in every field, becoming the most skilled occultist among the Noorians. And his loyalty passed every test in the eyes of she whom the Noorians considered the most divine and wisest creature to ever walk the earth, the Mountain Queen.

He entered the queen's chamber every afternoon before she or anyone else did. It was usually cold; the slight streak of sunlight coming in from above offered no warmth at all. He bore the chill of the chamber by wrapping himself in many layers of white African linen and wearing a goatskin around his shoulders.

He entered that day holding a block of carved white limestone that formed a *mubkhar*, an incense burner. The lit coal in it emitted heat that warmed his fingertips. He placed the incense burner on a stone table on the side of the chamber. On it, there was a human skull, a bottle filled with blood, and a pile of writings and drawings burned onto wild rabbit parchments.

He opened a brass container that was also on the table. It was filled with colorful stones. Hadaus pulled out a transparent one, snapped a bit of it off, and placed the rest back in the container. He then positioned the tiny bit of crystal-clear stone above the charcoal, and it suddenly hissed, creating instant black bubbles that evaporated to white smoke. He walked in circles around the chamber, spreading the smoke and cleansing the room from any unwanted jinnic harm before his queen entered.

Hadaus, unlike the other Noorians, performed special tasks that the queen desired. After the incense burner had gone cold and the incense turned to ashes, he cleaned it and went to sit alone, waiting for her.

When she entered, she moved slowly towards her throne. She saw Hadaus standing and lowering his head to prevent any eye contact with her, although she always hid her pale white and wrinkled face behind a transparent red veil. He could still see the many jewels she wore around her neck, especially the one necklace she wore all the time. No one could ever miss that. The pendant was a silver plate the size of an open palm, with an engraving of a six-sided flower on it. But many did not know that behind that silver plate hid an engraved image of a woman's head, the head of the goddess she and all the Noorians believed in. Sen, the goddess of the moon.

Hadaus waited for the old lady to settle on her chair, which barely fit her big legs. Then he walked slowly to stand before her, head lowered.

"That old fool failed to save his child again, didn't he?" she said in a tired monotone.

"Indeed, but the child was kidnapped, not killed."

She revealed no expression. In truth, she never cared if the child was killed, kidnapped, or saved. Many children were killed or kidnapped by wicked jinn masters every year. To her, Behas's capture was a bigger gain.

"And as I informed you the day before," Hadaus added. "The execution of Behas took place yesterday. Arkin should be reaching us soon."

"Yesterday morning, you say?"

"Indeed."

"Then Arkin should be here by now," she said. "Why is he delayed? Did I not ask you to write him an urgent note?" She was a wise woman. She rarely left her palace, but she knew how long a journey should take.

"Indeed, I did. He must have stopped for a rest."

"The Mystic Dagger is not safe out there. Whoever kidnapped the child might be looking for it as well."

Hadaus nodded.

"Get out there and make sure the dagger is here, and safe."

"Indeed I will."

She paused for so long Hadaus thought she was finished. "Arkin is no longer needed here," she added suddenly. "I cannot stand his presence. But we cannot lose the dagger again, Hadaus. You have one hour to bring it here."

Hadaus nodded, frowning. His eyes remained trained on the floor below him. "*Siratukym*," he muttered, a word only the Noorians' guild used, and walked away. *Your path is the righteous one.*

He left her chamber fully aware of her intentions. She cared about only one thing: Behas's Mystic Dagger, a tool for summoning jinn, which he had received from the Council of Jinn.

Hadaus had the dagger on his mind. He needed to bring it to her faster. But he also thought of her other directive. *Arkin is no longer needed!* Hadaus had wanted to kill Arkin once or twice a long time before, but she, the Mountain Queen, had told him not to do so. He was known to be the most obedient Noorian, but he had his secrets.

He disliked the old man's presence in the palace as well, and he would be more than glad to tell him that their queen had asked that he never show up there again.

He grabbed a steel dagger, a bow, and a few herb pouches from his room. He feared he might need the ingredients in those pouches for his next mission. Weapons and medicines, agony and remedy.

He pulled out a small stone of white frankincense from one of the small pouches. He threw it in his mouth and bit on it, breaking it into pieces. He ate frankincense stones regularly, ten or more stones every day. He believed it made him stronger every time.

Siratukym, he reminded himself before leaving the Gray Palace.

30

"He's ten days old today," said Nada with wet eyes as she noticed the morning glare behind the curtains of the *howdah*.

"I pray to Somood that our Dil is kept safe," Faseela thought aloud.

After a long journey from Wadi Erum, Nada and Faseela waited to reach their destination in silence, riding on the howdah, a carriage without wheels. Howdahs varied in size and use based on where they originated or the functions they served. They could be open, decorated beds carried on the back of an elephant or on a camel's hump, or they could be fully covered carriages, carried on front and back poles by two working animals such as large donkeys or mules.

Nada and her friend hid behind light curtains in their howdah, which was carried by two large creatures—two very bizarre creatures. Yam didn't dare question the convoy and its escorting guard, which Nada had hired cheaply, about the creatures carrying the howdah. He tried to hide his surprise, as if they were commonly known animals, but they weren't.

They looked completely mesmerizing in a hideous or an uncomfortable way that left a strange awkward feeling in the mind of whoever stared at them for long. Besides their appearances, their loud growls also pinched Yam's heart every time they released air through their nasal channels. Yam could not dismiss the idea that the two could actually be jinnic creatures, something beyond the common forms of the animal kingdom.

The creature carrying the front of the *howdah* had the body of a rusty brown horse and the head of a zebra. Only his left back leg was brown; the other legs had zebra stripes all over. The creature carrying the back side was taller and had darker and more hostile features. It had the full, round belly of a fat, hairy mule and the large head of a tired gray donkey. Its dark mane grew tall and straight above its head, but not taller than the hair that stood on its ears like giant antennas of an ant. Although the two were just African mules, the cheapest breeds in the market, used for transporting goods and people, Yam felt the howdah was carried by a creepy horse-like zebra and a giant, sinister gray spider with a donkey's head.

Yam, a hired pathfinder, and a hired guard from Wadi Erum all rode on separate horses. It was the first time he had ever ridden a horse all by himself, and he found it to be easier than he had thought. He had told them that he never had before, so they gave him the oldest horse in their stables, the most obedient and laziest horse, which would never escape or throw Yam from its back. In fact, they all rode old horses; the better ones had been requisitioned for the war. Yam did bond with his old horse, and he did find it calm and not at all aggressive, but he also felt that the old horse did not obey him at all. It followed its own will! But he did not mind that.

Since they had left that morning, their journey to the mountains took almost six hours of eventless time. Yam even noticed his old horse yawning from time to time.

The gray-haired, brown-clad pathfinder, Saad, who had marched ahead to lead the way, found Arkin's camp, but everyone in it was unconscious. He came back to alert them. The cheaply hired chubby guard, Murr, remained with the howdah while Yam and Saad cantered ahead to reach the camp first.

"Most probably the work of bandits. But these are Guardians from Erum," Saad said to Yam, pointing at a group of men lying near one another. "It seems they encountered them in their sleep, and judging from the gray cloak over there, this could be the Noorian you were looking for. Whoever did this seems to be far away now. And they did not steal much." He pointed at closed crates. Only the largest one, a coffin, had been left open and empty.

After a long, tiring journey, that scene was the last thing Yam had expected.

"Take my horse," said Yam as he dismounted and walked towards the gray cloak. He feared the body under the cloak belonged to Arkin. All Noorians wore the same thick gray, the color of their sacred palace. Yam lifted the cloak to find that it was Arkin—still breathing, but unconscious. "Master Arkin!" he called aloud in disbelief and shock.

The old occultist barely opened his eyes, breathing with extreme difficulty and trying hard to speak. "Be—"

"It's me, Master Arkin. It's Yam."

"Behas," murmured Arkin. "Behas."

Arkin had told Yam that he was taking Behas's corpse to the Gray Palace, and now, it seemed to Yam that someone had stolen it!

...

The howdah was placed on the ground, and the bizarre cheap mules, still tied to it, were allowed to rest and feast. Yam sat near the howdah's open curtain. He and the women stared in frustration at Arkin.

The old occultist had not spoken to them since becoming fully conscious. Completely ignoring their presence, he continued to search in his chests and thought loudly as he searched back and forth for what he repeatedly called "the dagger."

Arkin had never told Yam about it, although Yam had seen that golden dagger in Behas's hand when he had tried to save Dil from it, just before the child had vanished before his eyes. But he did not remember it that day as he observed Arkin's strange actions.

The other Guardians, who had been found unconscious, had all woken up and began to tidy up the mess. Some helped Arkin search. They had no clue what had happened to them the night before. None of them recalled anything. The last thing they said they remembered was the capture of Fad.

"What is he doing?" asked Faseela.

"It seems he lost something," Nada replied.

Yam remained silent, lost in thought. He had never told Nada that Fad had been caught by them before they mysteriously lost consciousness. After accompanying Arkin for several days, he had never seen him in this nervous state, not even when they had found out that the child was lost or kidnapped. And the old man had murmured Behas's name while unconscious. Yam asked him what he had meant, but Arkin didn't answer. Nor did he ask Yam to help him search.

"Where is it?" cried Arkin and cursed. He collapsed to the ground with frustration. His face was gloomy and filled with fear.

Yam hovered above Arkin while the old occultist covered his face with his hand. "What is it?" Yam asked.

He took a deep breath. "What can I say, Yam? It's Behas's Mystic Dagger. I lost it again. The queen will kill me this time. The dagger is what the dark saher uses to summon his jinn; with it, he controls the jinnic realm. And we have been seeking it for more than twenty years."

Yam finally recalled the golden dagger from that dreadful night!

"Oh, I see." *Is that why he called Behas when he woke?* thought Yam to himself. But the corpse, too, was missing! He wanted to ask him again what had happened with Behas's dead body and who had taken it. But he chose to wait for Arkin to stop his whimpering first.

"Well," Arkin said finally, "we should reach the Gray Palace and ask for help. Whoever took it shouldn't be far."

"Who took it? Did they take Behas's body as well?"

"I have no idea of what happened here. Even Fad disappeared. It might be the same jinn masters who stole the child that day," Arkin replied. "They seem to possess a collection of powerful jinn. They are the only reason I can think of why the Guardians here and I lost consciousness and never felt or heard anything. They stole the child first, and last night, they came back to steal the Mystic Dagger."

"And what about Fad and Behas's dead body?" Yam asked about Behas again.

Arkin seemed to be frightened by the question. "I have no idea!"

"That's...Fad's wife over there," said Yam, changing the subject and pausing between his words. "Should I tell her that her husband was here?"

"His wife? I am not sure if you should. They are accusing him of killing Bessel!"

"That is why we left the city. We came here hoping you could help." Yam hoped for an answer that would help him confirm Fad's innocence. He did not know him well, but he felt sorry for him. The man had lost his child, and the fact was that it had been Yam who had failed to save the child.

"Then let us not waste any more time," Arkin said. "We need to reach the Gray Palace for help. Things seem to have gone way beyond what I had planned for or ever imagined would happen."

Staring at the path that led towards the Samhan Mountain, they noticed a gray rider galloping towards them. When he came closer, Yam saw it was Hadaus, from the Gray Palace before. Yam hated his serious attitude.

"Oh, great, the Noorians are here!" said one of the Guardians to Arkin.

"It's Hadaus," Yam added.

"Greetings, Arkin, Yam," hailed Hadaus in his heavy African-Arabic dialect before dismounting his horse. "I see you have met a terrible encounter with some…" He paused a long time, looking around, and then stared back at them, not knowing which word to use to describe the awkwardness of the scene before him.

"Bandits," one of the youngest Guardians supplied.

"Indeed!" Hadaus replied in confusion.

"They stole the dagger," Arkin said. "We need to find them before they get farther away."

Yam looked around at the open chests and scattered belongings. Not the work of bandits, he thought as he remembered Arkin's assumption. *The unknown jinn masters stole a dead body. Why is Arkin not mentioning it?*

"Indeed." Hadaus reached for a white stone of frankincense from his pouch. "May I speak with you privately?" he asked Arkin, and then he crushed the frankincense stone in his mouth.

…

Yam left them to have their private conversation and continued to wonder about the jinn masters who had kidnapped the child. Nothing made sense to him. *Why did they steal Behas's dead body as well? Will they resurrect him from the dead? Can they reattach his head to his body? Is that even possible?* Yam freaked out at his creepiest assumptions as he walked back to where the women sat. They too probably had many questions for him. About Arkin, the African Noorian, the bandits, and Fad for sure. They first asked what had caused all the mess. He had no idea how to start or what to say to them.

"Did you ask him about Fad and Dil?" Nada asked.

That question, Yam preferred not to answer. *Unfortunately, I didn't ask him about Fad,* he thought to lie. "Well, he seemed to be too busy. But don't worry. Hadaus is highly ranked among the Noorians. If he will help us, be sure that we'll find Fad and Dil," he reassured her with the unconfident smile of a liar.

She had only just met him the night before, but she sensed he was acting strangely. "Is everything all right?" she asked him.

"Well. I hope everything *is*," he replied. "The Noorians will help us." He forced another smile over his worried face and turned his eyes towards Arkin, only to open them wide in shock at what he witnessed then.

Hadaus had stabbed Arkin deep in his stomach and released him to fall on his back. He stared at him until he was sure that Arkin had breathed his last. He mounted his horse with the bloodied dagger in his hand. He eyed Yam for a long time.

Yam saw fear in Hadaus's eyes rather than the usual angry stare!

The hired guard, Murr, and the Guardians who had escorted Arkin all unsheathed their swords and stood between Hadaus and the women, but they seemed to be no match for the highly ranked Noorian.

"I strongly recommend you go back to Erum," said Hadaus. He tried to express anger, but Yam sensed nervousness. "Arkin betrayed our queen and deserved this, but you are no trouble to us. For now." He spoke only to Yam.

They all stared in disbelief as he rode off, disappearing behind the green hills of Jibjat. He did not travel to the mountain but went in another direction completely.

Yam rushed to see his teacher and master.

"He killed him!" cried one of the young Guardians as he approached Yam.

Yam remained silent and in shock. Arkin was indeed dead. Losing a master he had had for a week brought sorrow to his heart.

Yam had been in the Gray Palace with him and had seen how the Noorians treated Arkin with hostility and disdain, but he also knew how much Arkin loved the guild. He loved the Mountain Queen, too, and was very loyal to her. Now his master had been killed in cold blood, but the reason was vague.

'Arkin betrayed our queen'? What did Hadaus mean? thought Yam. *Is it because we lost the child? Or Behas's dagger and his corpse? Who are those unknown jinn masters, and where in the world is Fad now?* He stared at his dead friend and drifted away in his thoughts until the escorting guard interrupted.

"We have to go back to Wadi Erum!" said Murr in a quavering voice.

The pathfinder, Saad, nodded.

"I agree," said one of the Guardians who had come with Arkin. "We have sent one of our men back to report our situation and get help from the High Palace. We do not recommend that you stay here. It seems that there is a perplexing war between jinn masters and occultists right now. Last night, we must have been affected by some sort of jinnic spell, and it won't be safe to get in the middle of this conflict."

"I can't go back, not until I find Fad." Nada had finally walked out of the howdah and was standing beside Yam, looking at Arkin's dead body.

Yam wept and remained silent. He was in deep sorrow.

Faseela stood beside her friend. Nada wasn't happy with how it had ended up for them. "You can go back yourselves; I won't return until I find my husband and my son," said Nada.

Yam closed Arkin's eyes and left him to rest in peace. He turned to the others, asking them all to be calm, and said, "The guards and the Guardians are right; it's not safe to wander these lands anymore. Besides that, we have no idea where to look for Fad now! We journeyed here to get Arkin's help, and as you all have witnessed, Arkin is dead."

"If you will not help either, you can head back to Erum," Nada said to Yam. She had seemed suspicious of his actions ever since he had met and spoken with Arkin. "Faseela and I will find them ourselves."

"Where?" Yam yelled. He didn't make the point that her husband had been caught, but he felt he should just blurt it out. As stubborn as she was, he was convinced that even that wouldn't stop her. *Where?* he asked himself as well. Like her, he wanted to know where Fad was, and he wanted, too, to save Dil. He was also curious to learn what had happened here.

This whole journey with Arkin had begun with a promised reward. He had gotten his reward from the old man, and he welcomed the adventure, but given what he had seen and heard so far, he wouldn't want to risk more lives in it. A child had almost been killed because of him, and now Arkin. He wasn't the man to protect Nada and Faseela from the Noorians or the unknown jinn masters, and nor were any of the men they had hired. That, he was sure about.

Nada searched for a reply. She had no idea where her husband or child might be. "I will find them! Wherever they might be," she cried, walking away to the howdah again.

"Somood will guide us," added Faseela in hopes of calming Yam and convincing him to help them rather than take them back. She then returned to her friend, and they both hid behind the curtains of the howdah.

"We have to go back," Murr whispered to Yam.

"We'll wait for help to return." Yam reminded him of the other Guardian who had left earlier to get help.

Yam did agree with sending the women back, but he didn't want to return himself. "We'll bury Arkin first, and then we can discuss heading back to Erum."

While they buried him, Yam noticed the man's flute was still in his cloak, the flute he had used to open the secret gate to the Gray Palace. He remembered Arkin had told him that he came from Ibri. He decided to take his instrument himself and return it to his daughters there. Yam chose to believe nothing of what Hadaus had said; he had seen nothing to justify calling Arkin a traitor, and he felt the same way about Fad.

31

In the howdah, Nada lay on her side and cried.

She remembered the day almost fifteen years ago when she and Fad had decided to observe the market from over the bridge.

"Let us go down there, Fad."

"We shouldn't, Nada. We should go back to your house!"

"Are you afraid, Fad?"

"I am not afraid, but I do not want to see you in trouble with your father! Besides, even my father told me that I should stay and not wander around."

"Fine, then you can go back. I will go down to the lower streets of Wadi Erum on my own."

"Nada, you shouldn't. You'll be in trouble for it."

"I will be back before sunset." She had ignored him and walked away, towards the staircase. She had felt him hesitate behind her, but it had taken no longer than a minute for him to start following her.

"Fine, we can descend to the lower streets, but we have to return before sunset. Before my father and Uncle Badde return," he had said, repeating her plan as if it were his.

Nada had hidden her smile from him as she led the way down the stairs.

. . .

"I cannot be at ease seeing you in this state," said Faseela. "Please stop crying."

"How can I? I lost my child and my husband," wept Nada. "Fad is in danger; I can feel it. I can't go back and sit and do nothing. I need to find them."

"We will. Somood will keep them safe and lead us to them."

"But where are they?"

A loud bark outside, not far from them, disturbed the tense silence that morning. The black shadow of a hound approached from behind the curtains. The ladies opened the curtain to find that an Arabian hound was in fact barking at their howdah. The hound remained in its place, continuing to bark.

Yam, Saad, Murr, and the Guardians who had just finished burying Arkin ran towards the other side of the howdah, where the barks were coming from. They all drew their swords, but the Guardians lowered their arms when they saw the dog; they recognized her. A whistle from afar made her stop her barking and sit, and they all sighed in relief.

That black hound was called Kashefa, and it was because of her master's whistle that she stopped barking.

The tall figure of a Guardian riding a white stallion got nearer to them. He wore the same uniform the other Guardians of Erum did, though his looked older and more worn than of those younger Guardians. It looked more charismatic. He too looked old, like his uniform, but not too old. His long hair still had a few black streaks, and his beard was still full enough that it hid half of his long neck. Many tools, weapons, and travel essentials, from food and drink to clothing, hung from his horse's saddle.

"Help has arrived," said one of the young Guardians, pleased to see an equipped and experienced Chief Guardian from Erum. He recognized the face from the High Palace, as did all the Guardians.

The Chief Guardian, or Hound-Master, dismounted from his horse and handed the reins to one of them, then gave his hound a piece of dried cow meat. He remained silent the whole time. Then he pulled a dark green tunic and a rababa from one of his saddlebags. He held them both in his right hand and brought them near his hound for her to take another sniff. She barked twice at the howdah, as she had done before.

He then raised both the green tunic and the rababa high over his head for the women in the howdah to see. "Have any of you seen a farmer with long hair? He is more likely wearing a Guardian's tunic."

Nada recognized her husband's green tunic but remained silent.

"We caught him last night," answered one of the Guardians. "But we have no recollection of the events that happened afterwards. We woke up and found our camp was a mess."

"Fad was here?" Nada cried, looking between the Guardians, her husband's tunic…and Yam.

The Hound-Master noticed her strange reaction, and the fact that she knew the farmer's name. "Do you know the man, Fad?"

"I am his wife," Nada replied cautiously, fearing that the Hound-Master had caught him.

"Where is he?" he asked.

Nada didn't reply. She had come here asking the same thing!

"We're looking for him as well," Yam put in. "We think he might have passed through here."

Nada stared angrily at Yam.

The Hound-Master seemed not to like the answers he got. He lowered the tunic and the rababa and whistled to his hound, Kashefa. She sniffed the tunic again for a long while, then barked and ran off. He took his horse's reins back from the Guardian holding them, preparing to follow his black hound.

But it was then when Nada stopped him, and their journey together began.

"Wait!" she called. "Where is my husband? Can you find him?"

"I aim to find him, yes. But first I need to investigate what has occurred here, and I have no time to waste."

"We will follow you. But please know that my husband is innocent."

He paused, considering her words.

"Please, I need to know if you will harm him or not," she begged. "He's innocent."

"Well," he sighed, "allow me to search the area for answers first. Later, I would love to ride in the howdah." He then noticed the two cheap mules that carried it, a brown horse with a zebra's head and a horse-sized bushy gray donkey. They did look strange. He hesitated for a moment, but his legs were tired from the long horse ride, and he preferred to sit and travel in the howdah. "I will tell you all everything I know about your husband, and maybe you could help me prove his innocence."

The ladies eyed each other with hope and agreed.

"The howdah will not carry us all," said the Hound-Master.

Everyone stared at Faseela; it was clear he referred to her.

Faseela, being a fat woman, saved herself the embarrassment of anyone asking her to get off. She offered to ride a horse so the Hound-Master could sit with Nada.

"I will need a moment of time to check the wrecked area here. Did you witness what happened?" he asked the Guardians, and they explained all that they had witnessed the night before, when Fad had shown up in their camp and they had tied him to a tree. They did not remember what had happened after that.

"We've also witnessed one murder," Yam added. He felt justice should be served for his friend, and he wanted to see Hadaus punished. Yam showed the Hound-Master everything and explained the mess around the chests. He told him about the dagger Arkin had been looking for, and about Arkin's assumption that jinn masters had attacked them.

The Hound-Master investigated the tree where Fad had been tied longer than anything else around. He sensed that whatever had attacked the camp the night before was far from usual. When Yam finished, the Hound-Master asked for the howdah to be prepared.

All the men helped raise the howdah up and tie it on the mules again. This time they left all its curtains fully open at the Hound-Master's request.

"Now let us follow Kashefa; she will lead us to Fad," said the Hound-Master, directing Yam, Murr, and Saad.

The rest of the Guardians stayed with the treasure and waited for help from Erum.

And so their journey began.

Yam, Faseela, Murr, and Saad all rode ahead on four separate horses. Faseela rode the Hound-Master's horse, and Yam noticed it suffering under her weight.

The ropes pulled the mules behind them as they all followed the black hound, Kashefa, at a gentle pace.

32

The Hound-Master sat in the howdah, facing the path ahead. He sat upright with his left leg crossed, and his crippled right leg stretched straight out. He had injured it once before in battle, and the injury had kept him from ever joining in battle again.

Nada faced him, sitting on the other end of the howdah.

He closed his eyes and took a deep breath to fill his lungs with clean air. He fixed his gaze on Nada, trying to show her a friendly smile below his long black mustache. He noticed her staring in wonder at his stretching activities and settling rituals, but he hoped his smile would encourage her to trust in him and get her to speak truthfully about her husband. Many people had been charmed by his charismatic smile. Except for his wife.

"First, allow me to introduce myself to you properly," he started. "My name is Rasheed, son of Masc, but I am also called El Kashef, for I am a man who tends to 'reveal' the truth. I speak nothing but the truth and prefer to hear nothing but the truth. I even call my hound Kashefa, 'revealer,' as she also enjoys revealing the truth.

"I believe in details. They are important when one seeks the truth. Therefore, I will tell you everything from start to finish. Please stop me at any time if you need me to clarify something. I will try not to judge what I have witnessed, for it could also upset the thoroughness of *your* judgments and might lead you from the truth. For the time being, I have more questions than answers. But I hope to get closer to the bare truth. Allow me to relate what I have investigated so far."

El Kashef told Nada that moments after the execution of Behas took place, he, being the Justice Division's Chief Guardian, had been summoned by the Prime Chief, Qassas.

The High Palace had received the news of Bessel's death from a Guardian messenger who had arrived that morning from Wadi Dawkah, and so El Kashef had been assigned to travel south, investigate, and speak with the witnesses. Crimes that were complicated, like this one, required his skills to reveal the truth.

"I thought our division would be taking a rest from mysterious crimes, since the most wanted outlaw had been executed," he told Nada. "But that peace did not last long for us.

"To tell you the truth," El Kashef continued, "I was shocked and grieved when I heard. Bessel was a friend of mine. I forced my injured leg to take me to Qassas faster. The Prime Chief spoke quickly, as he was busy preparing to leave for the east with the rest of the army that day. 'The guards last saw Bessel on a journey south with a farmer named Fada,' Qassas said. 'He is our only suspect for now. Find the witnesses at the murder scene, and if it is true the farmer killed Bessel, find him and force him to confess. I give you the right to execute him on the spot if needed.' He then gave me a ring like his, the Prime Chief Guardian's ring. It will allow me to act on his behalf in every city in the sheikhdom."

He went on telling Nada how he had reached the site of the crime. He met with one of the witnesses from Wadi Dawkah, Labeeb. Labeeb had been assigned by his tribe to watch over the farms. He had told El Kashef that two Guardians rested near their farms just an hour before dawn: Bessel and Fad.

Labeeb told El Kashef that he had observed them carefully until one of them, the victim, slept, while the other Guardian, the killer, woke up. He had grabbed a burning log from the fireplace and then thrown the log at one of their sacred trees, lighting it on fire.

El Kashef had seen the burned tree, but he had never understood why Fad would have needed to do that. Labeeb had also claimed that after he went to call his brothers and cousins, they ran to stop the fire.

"'The Guardian who burned our tree stabbed his friend and went for the horses,' the witness said. 'My brother, Areeb, was the fastest of us all, and he threw his spear to stop the killer from escaping, but he missed. The killer then took his spear and threw it back at him. Areeb, my brother, was killed as well.'" El Kashef included every detail he had seen or heard in his investigations.

"That's impossible. My husband would never do such a thing!" Nada interrupted him.

El Kashef nodded with a sly smile.

"What do you find funny in my words?" Nada snapped. "My husband is innocent."

El Kashef apologized for laughing. "I am not laughing at you. But your words reminded me of my wife. If I were ever accused of murder, I believe she would claim to have witnessed it, even if she hadn't, just to send me away or see me punished," he said and laughed again. "I respect the love you have for Fad. And as my investigation carries on, I hope your husband is found innocent."

The crime scene and the witness had left El Kashef with more questions than answers. But he never shared his inner thoughts or the questions he had in mind with Nada. The ride on the howdah was unbalanced as they rode along, up and down through the green hills of Jibjat and under the misty air. But El Kashef enjoyed the ride, the rest, and the scenes around him. El Kashef was known for his calmness and ease in life. He continued to relate his journey of the day before to Nada.

He told her that he had continued to ride through the green hills, following the tracks of two horses. After some distance, Kashefa had barked repeatedly, sensing a horse running wild. This was the horse Qamaria had set free.

The two had followed it, and El Kashef had lured the hungry mare with some food. The mare must have noticed his tunic and responded, being familiar with Guardians of Erum. He had taken the horse and continued to search, following fresh tracks, until Kashefa had found the other mare tied up near old rocky huts beside a pond. The place had felt as quiet as a graveyard.

El Kashef tied the mare he found next to the other one and went on to investigate the place, but he had been left with more questions than answers.

First, he had searched the saddlebags on the two mares, and one had held a dark green tunic, while the other held only Guardians' uniforms, so he had figured it to be Bessel's mare. The green tunic must have belonged to Fad.

"It's true; the green tunic is his," Nada confirmed.

"I had Kashefa sniff the tunic," continued El Kashef. "But she then led me to one of the huts. An old man lay dead, stabbed with a spear. Kashefa, to my surprise, did not point me towards the dead man; she pointed me to an old rababa in his hands, the same one I showed you earlier. The old man must have been killed while playing it. When I turned to leave the hut, Kashefa barked and pulled me back to the rababa again. I took it with me, hoping to find another clue, but the more I searched, the more questions I had.

"Outside, near a fireplace," he continued, "I found food that had been cooked and served but had not been touched by anything other than flies and crawling bugs. Nobody else was there in the other hut. I had to keep moving. I tried my best to search for tracks, and Kashefa did find Fad's. It was clear that he had been running, and there were other tracks close to his: five or six barefooted men who I assumed were the frankincense farmers from Wadi Dawkah. I also found a woman's tracks. The woman had been running close beside Fad too."

"A woman?" asked Nada with confusion.

"The tracks told me," he answered. "She must have helped him escape."

Nada seemed jealous when she heard, but she knew her husband well. Fad was faithful. And he was in trouble; he needed any help he could get out there.

"But I questioned the witness's tale," El Kashef went on. "If Fad had intended to steal the mares, why did he leave them and all his belongings? He could have used them to escape from the mountain folk! And why had they not used the mares to follow him faster? Second, why did Kashefa bark at the rababa the dead old man had been playing, unless she sensed Fad's scent on it? Was it his?"

"Please tell me my husband will be safe," Nada wept. "I haven't seen that rababa before. But be assured that Fad would never harm that Chief Guardian, nor would he kill a farmer from Wadi Dawkah! Why are they chasing after him? My husband is a farmer as well; he would never burn a sacred tree. If it weren't for that cursed night that we lost our child, he would never have left his farm."

"I can't know if he'll be safe or not. And I do want to hear it all from you, but allow me to finish first," El Kashef replied, then continued his tale.

El Kashef had followed the tracks to the cave Fad had entered, but there, to his surprise, he found that Fad's footsteps and the lady's went inside, followed by those of the mountain folk, but only the mountain folk had exited the cave. He had feared at first that the two had been killed in there, but he later discovered it to be a hideout, so he had decided to wait for Fad and the lady there, in front of the cave. He had also needed to rest his injured leg, so he tied his white horse next to the opening of the cave and sat inside.

That day, he never spotted any of the spearmen, and they never spotted him. He had waited in the cave until he accidentally fell asleep.

Kashefa had barked and woken him when it was dark. He had cursed his tiredness but decided not to leave the cave and search for Fad at night. He had set a fire in the cave, prepared some food for himself, and thought about the questions in his mind: the burned tree, Bessel's death, the witness's tale, the horses, the old man with the rababa, the woman running with Fad, the cave. The causes of Bessel's death were more complicated than what he had first imagined when he left Wadi Erum.

He slept again after a long night of analyzing the clues and questions he had in his mind.

Kashefa woke him up before dawn; she had found a trail for them to follow. She was well trained, and that was what El Kashef liked about her. She would not rest until she revealed the truth. This time, the tracks were only Fad's and those of the mountain folk, who appeared to have followed him later. After hours of walking, he encountered Yam and the others instead of finding Fad or the mountain folk.

At that point, he concluded the tale he had been telling Nada.

"This place seemed interesting. I sense Fad is near, very near. So do tell me, what happened to your husband that made him act in such a way?"

"To be honest with you, I myself am trying to find out. You see, I woke up from a curse spread by a jinni's bite," she said, pointing at the marks on her neck. "And I have been told that my child has been kidnapped by jinn and my husband has gone away to find him. But it was Yam who witnessed it all. He killed the snake that bit me, he carried my child away from Behas, he saw my child disappear into thin air, and he saw my husband capture Behas. We heard early this morning that Erum was looking for Fad, and we decided to get help from the Noorians, but things got more complicated here."

"Then I should have a talk with Yam. I need to know what happened that morning when Behas took your son," said El Kashef. He then ordered the party to stop and left the howdah so he could ride his horse and talk with Yam.

...

"Hold on!" said El Kashef. Yam had spent the journey telling him the details of all he had witnessed. But El Kashef stopped him right before he reached the part when the child disappeared. "You say you poked Behas with the spear so hard that he fainted?"

"Yes. That's when he fell and the child disappeared!"

He continued to speak, but El Kashef ignored him, trying to remember what he had seen at Behas's execution. When Behas had walked to the scaffold, he had not limped or otherwise struggled. El Kashef had an injured leg himself, and he knew how it felt when a spear pierced a leg. He had experienced it in war before. He noticed in retrospect what Yam had not, and at that moment, he began to suspect something.

If Yam was right, then the execution had been faked!

33

Tied to a tree and left behind a temporary wall of fabric, Fad didn't surrender to his ill luck, which would soon result in him being executed for a crime he had not committed, or so he thought. Instead, he looked around, searching for anything sharp he could use to cut the rope that bound him. There were many chests in the tent, along with some small barrels, a few sacks, and a coffin which contained Behas's corpse. But even if he could spot anything suitable, everything was out of his reach. He had nothing to do but rub the ropes against the tree and hope they broke.

He thought it would take the whole night before the rope was cut. The coffin, he noticed, was locked with a thumb-sized nail. *As if the dead could escape.*

He continued to rub the ropes against the tree. They showed no sign of fraying, but it was the only plan his mind was able to devise.

Fad spent almost half the night that way, to the point that he became drowsy and almost, or might have, shut his eyes to sleep for a few seconds before quickly opening them and trying to break the ties again. He wasn't able to get loose; the only thing that happened was that his skin became irritated because of the friction, and it hurt him so much that he wanted to give up completely.

The firelight that came from outside had completely faded, and he was left alone in complete darkness. He leaned all his weight back on the tree to rest his tired shoulders. He would take a break and continue later. As he stared at the coffin, he remembered the dreams or visions Alma had shown him in Qamaria's cave earlier and the nightmare in which Behas had jumped on top of him and stabbed his neck with the dagger. It had felt real.

Suddenly, he sensed movement behind him, inside the enclosed area. It sounded like something was sliding towards him.

He turned his head towards the source of the sound and was able to see the shadow of a black snake crawling close by. It was similar to the one Yam had killed in his farm hut, but a lot smaller. *Is it looking for food?*

He tried to pull himself away from the tree to escape it, but it was no use at all. The snake continued to close the distance between them.

"Help! Help!" he yelled, but it all was too late. The snake raised its head before his face, prepared to strike. He turned his face away and tried to hide as much of it as he could behind the sides of his tied-up shoulders. But then the snake suddenly shifted, as if it had realized that Fad was not who it was looking for. It opened its eyes further and checked him again, and then it slid away towards the coffin.

"Guardians! Arkin!" he cried, but no one heard him. The camp had fallen into complete silence. *Is this another vision of Alma's?* he wondered fearfully, for by now it was almost morning, and they shouldn't be in deep sleep. They had promised him to take him to Erum near dawn.

The snake rested beside the coffin, hissed, and waited. It was not long until Fad saw a torchlight floating outside the tent. The torch appeared to be held by someone walking outside, who slowly made his way into the tent. It was one of the Guardians, but not one Fad recognized from the night before. He looked younger, and his round face showed him to be a common Arabian man, one who could easily blend into a crowd and be unnoticed.

"Good work, Saefa," he said. The shadow of a smile on his face that the torchlight revealed disappeared when he saw Fad staring back at him. "Saefa! You kept one awake!"

The snake hissed and whispered to its master. Fad understood none of it, but it appeared that the torch-holder did. *Is he a jinn master?* Fad wondered.

"He isn't a Guardian? He is dressed like one!" he said. Then he laughed, remembering that he too wore a Guardian's tunic for disguise. When he walked past Fad, he recognized him. "It's the farmer from the palm groves! We'll leave him be. He won't trouble us; he's troubled enough. Besides, your enemy is our enemy as well," he added, addressing Fad now. Then he turned to his snake. "Where is the old worm?" He grinned after his last words, looking around for Saefa, and snaked his way towards the coffin. But he began by opening all the other chests. He broke the first one open, took a glance, then closed it, doing the same with the second and the third. In the fourth chest, he found what he seemed to be looking for.

"Aha, there it is!" He raised what Fad noticed was a golden dagger. He recognized it from that day when he and Yam had caught Behas. It was the same blade which had been held against his son's throat.

Fad observed his movements silently from under the tree he was tied to, not sure what to say or do. The man and his snake must have paralyzed all the other Guardians in the camp that morning, just as that snake had done to his wife before.

The fake Guardian pulled out the thumb-sized nails that kept the coffin sealed and lifted the top. Fad tried to steal a glance. The naked body of an old man lay inside. A dark cloak covered some of the lower part of it. Fad couldn't see the face well at first, but he knew it was Behas.

"There he is! This is the end of his era. It is time for me to rule the Majlis of the Jinn." His snake hissed with joy as he revealed the golden dagger and threw its sheath under his feet. He raised it slightly, preparing to stab the corpse.

Fad couldn't understand the fake Guardian. Why would anyone want to kill a dead man? From his words and his jinni snake, Fad figured him to be a rival jinn master who had come to take his revenge on Behas. Holding the torch in one hand and the dagger raised in the other, he swung it down to stab Behas. But Behas's hands moved quicker, stopping the attacker before the blade touched his naked chest. Behas then opened his eyes wide and murmured words in a language Fad did not comprehend. The scene left him speechless with confusion.

Behas had promised the jinni that if she chose him as a new master, he would set her free. And as he spoke to her, the snake leaped and bit the hand holding the torch. The torch fell and the fake Guardian, or envious jinn master, jerked backwards, shaking the snake off his hand. Behas let go of him at once, and he almost fell. The torch, though, dropped into the mud near Fad's legs. The jinn master disguised as a Guardian grabbed the snake with his uninjured hand, throwing her to the far side of the tent, where she escaped. He tripped, flipped, and stumbled when he threw her, but he tried his best to stand still as he witnessed Behas rising from his coffin as well. His snake was ten times weaker than Behas's snake, but her poison did have a similar, though lesser, effect.

Behas stood tall before him, grinning widely, and picked up his Mystic Dagger. The blade in his hands shone brightly in the torchlight.

"Thank you for opening the coffin. I felt lonely and bored in there." Behas mocked his failure. He picked up the sheath as well as he moved towards his attacker with a crippled leg.

Fad noticed the injured foot and remembered how the injury had come about. *He's not executed!* It took him a while to digest the scene, but he felt certain it wasn't a vision from Alma. He remained silent the whole time, with his eyes wide. He had been spared by the first saher, who wore a common Guardian's tunic. But Behas wouldn't spare him, he thought as he saw his fearful figure, standing half naked and half covered in his dark cloak, moving slowly in the dimness. The last time he had met with Behas, he had stabbed him in the neck, thrown a spear at him, punched his head twice, and vigorously pushed him around like a sack of rotten dates. Now, being tied to the tree, he feared Behas would notice him and remember him. He was unlikely to show mercy to Fad as the first jinn master had.

"Very smart, Behas," the younger jinn master spat, pressing on the snake's bite. "Turning my own jinni against me. That, I must admit, was clever."

"You led the Noorians to me in Wadi Erum, and for that they killed my jinni. Let us say we are even on that one." Behas then raised his Mystic Dagger. "But trying to kill me?" His grin became a grimace. "That, you must pay for."

The young saher took a finger-sized bottle from his pocket, struggling to open it with his shivering hands. "I am sure you weren't expecting this," he said. Then he swung the arm with the bottle across the tent, allowing its contents, a thick blood-red liquid, to splash on Behas's cheek.

A few drops fell on Fad's long hair and forehead.

Behas wiped a few drops from his cheek and smelled the substance. Fad unconsciously sniffed as well; the smell was strong.

Behas's eyes were suddenly filled with terror. "Where did you get this from?" the old saher demanded.

The young saher laughed and revealed a victorious grin. "Does it matter now? If I were you, I'd start running! Farewell, Behas, for this will be your last night." The young jinn master escaped, leaving both Fad and Behas behind.

Fad began to hear strange, crackling howls from all around the tent. He had never heard such strange noises around the date farms where he came from. The howling began to increase, moving closer. Some of it was mixed with giggles and cracking noises, and all of that was followed by the noise of claws scratching on rocks.

He looked back to where the two sahers had been standing, but both were gone, and the strange, terrifying voices became so near to him that he was able to see the shadows of what made them from behind the fabric wall of the tent: the shadows of a pack of large striped hyenas.

Hyenas had conquered the southern mountains of the Arabian Peninsula and were believed to be possessed by wild and rabid jinn. Now, they were sniffing around outside the tent. They sensed their master's target was inside and began to rip the tent with their claws to get in. Fad stretched his legs out quickly, trying to drag the fading torch towards him. As he dragged it on the hard ground, the fire faded to nothing but three tiny tongues of flame, which were just enough to burn through the ropes that tied his hands. He also burnt a large patch of his irritated skin, but he cared less about that pain once he saw that one of the hyenas had managed to cut through the wall of fabric and was moving towards him at full speed. He flipped himself behind the tree, leaving the striped hyena to drive its teeth into the bare tree trunk. Chunks of wood came away in its jaws.

Two more hyenas entered the tent, and Fad, without a second thought, sprang through the opening Behas and the other jinn master had left from, still holding the torch in one hand. He closed the curtain wall behind him, leaving the thoughtless creatures momentarily confused about where he had gone. But they followed the smell of the red substance and broke out to follow the fading torchlight.

Fad threw whatever was left of the torch at the wild creatures and ran to the horses he had seen when he first came. The Guardians who had sat near them to guard them were unconscious—Saefa's doing, and that of her former jinn master.

Two horses had already been taken by Behas and the other saher. Fad grabbed another and rode blindly, going wherever the horse took him. He thought the animal was probably following behind Behas's horse. The young saher had galloped in another direction, watching and waiting from afar for the hyenas to kill Behas. But instead, the hyenas were chasing Fad. Fad and his terrified animal galloped faster than the mad hyenas behind them, hyenas which were probably driven by wild jinn.

...

From afar, Daheen, his brothers, and his cousins witnessed the young jinn master leave the area first. They couldn't see well from that distance, but they noticed his Guardian's tunic, and so they thought he was Fad, escaping. They ran after him.

He took one of the horses and galloped away. Daheen and his men could have taken the others, but they were no riders. They ran behind him instead, and they were fast runners.

At some point in their chase, Daheen noticed the Guardian they were after fall off his horse. They ran faster to get to him, only to find out that they were following the wrong Guardian! They held their spears against him, ordering him to stop as he tried to stand.

He struggled to stand straight after the fall. The snake bite had not yet taken full effect, but he was feeling some of the poison. It had made him weak, and that was probably why he had fallen off his horse.

The men from Wadi Dawkah didn't care about him; eventually, they'd have let him be. But, fearing their pointed spears and creepy figures, he splashed the last of the liquid in his bottle on them as well.

The jinnic hyenas now had a new target. They turned towards the spearmen. The men, being mountain folk, were well aware of such creatures and stood their ground to fight them. They knew hyenas would usually escape from a fight with a stronger predator. But these weren't regular hyenas, and none of the spearmen from Wadi Dawkah made it through that night. When Daheen saw his cousins falling one by one, he tried to retreat with the only other fighter who remained, his brother Fateen, but the cursed creatures ripped them into pieces. And only Daheen survived, for he was the only one the red cursed liquid had not touched. He fought the hyenas to the end, though they injured him severely. After he succeeded in killing one, the others fled. They knew he wasn't their master's target. Daheen had lost too much blood and died later on that day.

...

Fad stopped his horse when he noticed the hyenas chasing them had moved away in another direction. It had begun to rain, but getting wet or staying dry was the least of his concerns that morning. He now had no destination in mind. He wondered if he should go back to Arkin, but the man had not helped him the night before and had seemed to be less concerned about his child. And the Guardians around him were planning to take him back to Wadi Erum.

Behas is alive! The fact that they had hidden Behas in a coffin and were taking him to the Gray Palace made him doubt that they cared about him or his kidnapped son. Arkin seemed to have other interests.

Still on his horse and under the rain, he tucked his wet hair behind his ears and sat thinking about what he should do next or where he should go. He gazed beyond the green hills in the direction where Behas's tracks led and wondered if he should go after the jinn master again. But this time, he wouldn't hand him over to Erum. This time, he needed to force him and use him to find his child.

The saher found my son the first time, he thought. *He should be able to find him again.* He bit his lips and closed his eyes, inhaling deep before deciding what he should do or where to go. He sighed. It seemed to be the only choice he had. The jinn master who had tried to kill his son would now help Fad find him.

He caught up with Behas after a long gallop. "Halt!" he cried from afar to slow him down. He first needed to find out where the jinn master was headed.

"You!" Behas recognized Fad. He stopped to face him at once and pulled out his golden dagger, though he saw Fad was unarmed.

The sun had appeared from a gap in the clouds and the rains had stopped. Only the black clouds above remained.

"I will not fight you, Behas. Do not be angry with me! I only want to find my son. I thought you were executed in Erum, but I was surprised to see that you were still alive. I will not hand you to Erum anymore, unless..." *Unless you still want to kill my child.* Fad kept his last thoughts to himself.

"I should."

"Should what?"

"I should have been executed. They faked the execution with the help of Sheikh Zufar and Arkin. Arkin told me the Guardians escorting him did not know that I was alive, and if they found out, they would probably take me back or kill us both, me and Arkin. So I remained silent, not revealing myself. I waited for the right moment. And it came. Why were you tied there on that tree? What wrong have you done?" he asked.

Fad sighed. "I am accused of the murder of Bessel. We are now both wanted outlaws, I believe."

"Well, I should thank you for saving my life, and I should forgive you then for all that has passed," Behas said.

That was a lot of "should"! Fad noticed Behas was now smiling, which made him look less terrifying, but he wondered why. "I saved your life?"

"Yes. If you had not spent the whole night making noise, I might have slept and been killed in my sleep."

Fad remembered rubbing his rope against the tree all night.

"You cried for help as well when the snake came in, and I heard the other saher speak to you, which alerted me to his presence."

"Do you know him?"

"No. But I would guess him to be the spy who led the Noorians to your child."

Since he opened the subject, thought Fad. "Where are you headed now?"

Behas tilted his head as if he was about to say something but hesitated and changed his mind. He sheathed his dagger.

"Are you still looking for my child?"

"I am not headed anywhere. I am escaping. It is too late now to look for your child; evil and doom will soon be upon us. I recommend that you leave these lands."

"Why is it late? What evil are you escaping from? You owe me an explanation for all this madness."

"I owe you nothing." Behas turned his horse away. Fad followed at a gentle pace.

It began to rain again. The rain droplets were so tiny they were floating in the air rather than falling. It was such a soft shower, it felt like the cloud had descended to cover them and they were walking in it.

"I want to find my child. Help me. You are the only jinn master who can find him," Fad begged.

Behas stopped his horse. "How many days old is your child now?"

"Why?" Fad did not know the answer to that. He had lost count.

"He is probably ten or eleven days old now." Behas answered his own question angrily. "And on his twelfth sunset, which could be this one, they will kill him. Great evil will be summoned and released, evil that will bring us all to our doom. Wadi Erum will be destroyed, and everyone in it will die. Those who have your child will not be easily stopped. And even if *you* find them, you will not be able to stop them. They are much more powerful than you and I alone."

Behas continued to explain: "The only way to keep their evil powers from being released was to kill every child born under the Serpent-Neck star before they found it." Behas then kicked his horse gently and rode away. "There is your explanation. And if you still choose to search for your child and find those who took it, which I doubt you will—"

"He *is* ten days old," Fad interrupted. He remembered.

"Well, that means you have one more sunset after today. On the second sunset, his blood will be spilled," Behas explained.

He could be right, but whoever they are, they must be stopped, thought Fad. He had no idea who or what enemy he was chasing after, much less where they were, but with his child being the target of it all, failure was not an option he could think of. He knew he needed help, and Behas had the skill and the experience to help him at this stage.

"It sounds to me like you do know where my son is and who took him."

"I do know where he is, and yes, I do know who took him. He is far from where we are now. It will be difficult to reach him, since we are both wanted criminals."

"We *have* to stop them before sunset. I am willing to do whatever it takes to get my son, and I will help you stop them once and for all. Then you will never have to kill innocent newborns again. Please, take me to where he is." Fad stared at the horizon, where the sun had just risen.

Behas was a man who would change his mind if he thought of a plan on the spot. He had given up the search for the child at first, and he had planned to escape the lands of Erum. But now an idea sparked in his evil mind, and he decided to help Fad, or have Fad help him stop his enemies, whichever. They could use one another.

He stopped his horse and turned his eyes to the Guardian's tunic Fad was wearing. "There is one thing we can do! Do you have a Chief Guardian's ring?"

"A ring?"

He looked around, searching for the right direction, and then he smiled. "I do have a plan. Follow me," he said and kicked his horse into a gallop.

...

They cantered uphill for a while until they reached the edge of a cliff that overlooked a huge sinkhole. This was Wadi Teyq, the biggest trench in the Qara Mountains. It looked as if the moon had collided with the earth and bounced back to its position, creating a steep valley. Water streamed from all around the mountains and filled its bottom, creating a huge lake. Water also collected from two main streams in the dales above Wadi Teyq, and during this season, those streams became giant waterfalls dropping into the lake. The rest of the year, Wadi Teyq was dry. If you reached the cliff where the two fugitives stood, you would see a V-shaped opening on the other side, which led into the many caves and holes where people lived. These caves kept them safe, and they drank and ate from the lake at the bottom, which was refilled every year.

"There's Wadi Teyq," Behas told Fad. "I guess we should be able to find a Chief Guardian here. The tribes of this wadi are allied with Erum, so there should be a Guardians' post."

"Aren't we wanted men?" Fad questioned his plan.

"We won't be handing ourselves in to them. Just follow my plan."

Fad had never seen Wadi Teyq before. The sound of waterfalls echoed through the valley, making it too loud to hear anything else, and the afternoon sunlight struck the upper cliffs, while the wadi below hid in its own shade. Fad could see, from the openings on the walls of the wadi, that many men and women populated the caves. But it seemed unclear to him how they could get there. "How do we get to the caves?" he asked. There was no sign of stairs or ropes they could use to climb down the walls of the wadi.

Before Behas could respond, an arrow from behind pierced his back. Its tip, red with blood, jutted from the center of his chest. He fell off his horse, and the animal panicked and fled. Behas lay at the edge of the cliff. The other horse neighed, shying. Fad tried his best to tame it, but another arrow flew towards them and hit the jumping horse. Fad fell besides Behas, injuring his leg. He couldn't see who had shot them. It could not be the men of the wadi while he wore the Guardian's tunic, and the weapon had not been a spear, so that excluded the farmers from Wadi Dawkah. He thought it might be the young jinn master again, still determined to kill Behas.

"Jump into the water!" Behas breathed out. Fad hesitated at first, but after another two arrows barely missed him, he rolled on his injured leg without another thought and dropped off the cliff into the water below.

Behas tried to crawl to the edge to jump behind him, but the pain in his chest slowed him down. He was stopped at the edge of the cliff by the anonymous shooter just before he could jump off.

...

Fad had been warned by Alma that to save his child, he needed to be alone. Everyone who had tried to help him and save the calamitous child had either died or been harmed in the process: Bessel, Qamaria and her father,

Arkin, and before them, Yam, Baaz, and the horse. Now, even Behas had been struck by the child's curse.

...

The arrows were shot at them by Hadaus. After Fad had jumped, he came near and searched Behas. He found what he was looking for: the Mystic Dagger.

"Coward!" Behas spat out.

"Indeed." The arrow still moved with every heartbeat. Behas was still alive, as the arrow had missed his heart, but he wouldn't survive much longer, thought Hadaus. "Here is where you will end, Behas."

34

Every person had his or her own intentions. El Kashef had been assigned by Qassas to investigate a crime. Arkin had wanted to prove himself worthy to his queen and everyone else in the guild. The Mountain Queen found an opportunity when she learned that Behas had finally been caught, and she acted fast to ensure Behas remained alive and captive in her palace so she could try to acquire the Mystic Dagger. When the young jinn master, whose name was Laeem, learned about Behas being kept alive, he tried to steal the Mystic Dagger and kill Behas for his personal gain in the jinnic realm. Behas felt obligated to kill a calamitous child. Fad, being the father of the kidnapped child, certainly had only one intention: finding his child and keeping him safe.

But may I remind you of another man who desired to save the child as well, Prince Zufar? He had assigned Bessel to do so for him, but only hours after Behas's execution, and hours before he and his brothers were to leave for war, he learned that Bessel had been killed.

Prince Zufar left the palace that day with great grief for the loss of Bessel, not knowing what to do next. After almost a day had passed on their journey east, he sent word with a Guardian messenger to someone else he trusted deeply, someone who could complete the quest for him and save the child: his younger brother, Prince Leith, who had remained in the High Palace and had not been given the honor of joining his brothers to war.

It was not that he was incompetent, but some of the sons of Aad had to remain to protect the Prime Sheikh and the Sheikhdom of Erum. Leith, as you may know, means "brave" in Arabic, and brave he was. Leith is also one of the hundreds of Arabic names for a lion.

Leith received word from Zufar on the same morning that El Kashef met with Yam and the others near Jibjat. Because the letter had bade him to keep Zufar's request a secret, he planned to leave Erum alone, but only after he found an excuse for his father to allow him to leave. He tried, but he couldn't conceal everything from his father, so unlike his brother Zufar, he convinced him instead.

"I cared less about the child at first," Aad said calmly. He sat alone with Leith in the private majlis. "But you are right. I should not tolerate those who kidnapped the child playing with dark sorcery in my lands. And I will not allow you to wander the lands outside of Wadi Erum alone. You are a sheikh, a son of Aad, and you must have an escort of strong Guardians as befits your name. Whoever kidnapped the child from us must pay a great price in blood for it. You must set an example for everyone to remember."

Leith nodded in obedience and agreement.

"Your brother, Sheikh Zufar, has asked you to help in saving the child. You shall do nothing more beyond that. Find it. Hand it safely to the Noorians, and return as safely as you left. Be quick. The Noorians have requested help from Bin-Hyem. The old sage should know better than I what they want."

Leith nodded again and excused himself to leave. He became more excited to leave the city for an expedition with as many men as he could gather from among the ones who had stayed behind in Wadi Erum. But he had one major knot he needed to untangle before leaving: He needed to define his destination.

Looking for a seer in Ubar would be a waste of time, as Bin-Hyem had taught him that he would need one of the parents to perform any star-tracking of the child.

"There were only three who left with my advice to find the child," Hammah continued, directing the young prince. "Fad and Bessel left together for Ubar. But, as we have sadly learned, all went badly for them both. The third person was Arkin, and by now he must have reached Samhan Mountain, where the Gray Palace hides. Find him, and he shall help you better than I can."

"What is it that makes the child so special to the occultists and the sahers who kidnapped him?" asked the prince.

"A great evil can be summoned by sacrificing his precious soul, or so the jinn master believes. As to the kidnappers, I do not know who they are or what they know, and I honestly do not know what exactly makes the child so special to them."

Leith thought this hard to believe! What evil could a poor child's soul summon? He didn't understand the war between the occultists and sahers. But he had to find the child for his brother, and he had to teach the kidnappers a lesson for his father. "Fine, I shall find Arkin, then."

"Ensure you are protected. Those who were able to kidnap the child from Behas are surely in possession of fearsome power." By that, the sage meant that the prince should visit the temple of Somood to receive the god's blessings. A spiritual belief among the Erumians was that Somood watched over all Guardians of Erum and kept them safe from any evil jinn.

Leith nodded and forced a smile.

35

The capture of Behas and his Mystic Dagger was a dream come true for the Mountain Queen and the Noorians. Before these events, they had never believed it could happen, as they had spent twenty years trying all the methods they could think of to capture the outlaw again after his first escape. As soon as they learned about his recent capture, the queen had directed Hadaus to send a message to Arkin, asking him to bring Behas in alive, and his Mystic Dagger with him. They had urged him to do so with secrecy and haste.

When Arkin received the letter from the queen, he had felt proud that he could finally do the guild and the queen a great favor. He had no idea of how he could fulfill her request, so he had secretly met with Zufar. The prince had agreed to help the queen, knowing it was a great chance for him to make up for his failure to fulfill her first request, which had been to save the child. The prince had devised the plan to fake the execution by replacing Behas with another condemned outlaw, one the guards had had to sneak in that night from Ubar. The guards who watched over Behas had been forced to keep it a secret, or they would have lost their tongues.

The spy, Laeem, had tried to sneak into the High Palace to kill Behas there first but had then learned about Arkin's plan to transport Behas by chance when he overheard one of the guards. He thought he would have a better chance of accomplishing his goal outside the city. Laeem had always planned to kill Behas, but he had never dared to face the greatest jinn master. And that was the main reason why he had written to Arkin about the child born under the Serpent-Neck star in the first place. He had wanted Behas to either fail or be caught.

When Arkin traveled to Samhan Mountain that day, Laeem had followed him and waited for his chance to strike.

Behas's all-knowing jinni wouldn't have been able to identify Laeem specifically by his plans, because almost every evil jinn master in Arabia wanted the honor of eliminating Behas and then succeeding him, but Zuhal had warned Behas that a well-hidden jinn master was spying on him. And while Behas lay in the coffin, his all-knowing jinni had visited him right after they had walked out from under the protection spell on the wadi. The all-knowing jinni had told Behas everything: who had taken the child, where it was, and the fact that the Noorians' spy was following them and waiting for night to come to kill Behas. Zuhal had turned out to be a more loyal jinni than Behas had thought.

…

The following morning, Hadaus had left the palace in a hurry to make sure the Mystic Dagger would not be stolen from Arkin like the child was.

He never heard the cries of the spearmen or the cackles of the hyenas, as he arrived after the massacre, and so he spotted only their injured spy on the path. It was fortunate for Laeem, because if Hadaus had not shown up, the poison might have taken full effect and left him unconscious for hours.

"Laeem! What has happened to you?"

"I've been bitten by a snake." He wallowed in pain on the ground. "Help me, Hadaus."

"Climb the horse." Hadaus took him away to a dry place where he could set a fire and perform his tricks to extract the venom. He made a cross on each bite mark, then heated them and pressed on Laeem's arm to squeeze out as much venom from the man's blood as he could. Laeem still felt ill and drugged afterwards, but at least he wasn't going to faint.

"Did you know? Arkin failed to save the child from Behas," said Laeem.

"Did he?" Hadaus acted like he was surprised hear it. "Where is Arkin now?" He knew where the path was; he asked only to be sure. "Indeed," he said after taking directions from Laeem. "Rest here for a while," Hadaus advised him, then left.

…

Hadaus's father had been a jinn master from East Africa, who had traveled to Southern Arabia with his family for a better life. Hadaus and his brothers and sisters had learned a lot from their father about jinn and jinn mastery, and their mother had taught them a lot about the arts of mixing herbs and potions. Hadaus had left his family in his twenties when he met a beautiful Noorian and decided to become an occultist instead of a saher.

"Hadaus, you wish to stab me in the back!" His father had objected to his desire to leave with the Noorian woman. "The Noorians are not to be trusted; they are opposed to people like us."

"Father, I do not want to be a jinn master."

"But you will be! It is not a choice," his father had said furiously. "You will not leave us."

"I have made my choice, Father!"

His father had bitten his lips hard. At that moment, he had probably wished that he had never left Africa or that he had watched his sons and the friends they made more closely. "One day, they will ask you to kill jinn masters like me. What if they ask you to kill your own father or brothers?"

"They are not killers, Father. And you are not an outlaw."

"Indeed they are! They are cowards, hiding in caves. I did not raise my children to be cowards," his father had said. Not long afterwards, Hadaus had become an occultist, a servant of the Gray Palace.

...

After his unexpected meeting with Laeem, he traveled quickly to reach Arkin. Laeem hadn't told him the truth about the snake bite and all the details of his failed attempt to kill Behas, and Hadaus had never asked him the reason for his presence.

The queen was right: The dagger would be pursued. In Hadaus's view, the worst scenario would be if Behas were able to escape with it. If Laeem had told Hadaus that it was he who opened the coffin for Behas to get out, he would have slaughtered him for his foolishness instead of healing him. *I cannot allow him to take it again.*

He reached the camp while Arkin, Yam, and the rest of the Guardians were searching for the dagger. They weren't able to find it.

"They stole the dagger," said Arkin. "We need to find them before they get farther away."

"May I speak with you? Privately," Hadaus asked him. After Yam gave them their privacy, he began his interrogation. "Who took the dagger, Arkin?

Be specific." Hadaus wished it had been bandits of some sort, but he knew quite well it was Behas.

"We were unconscious, Hadaus. We cannot know for sure. But since the old jinn master is gone, I can say he must have managed to escape with the dagger again. He shouldn't be far; we can be quick and follow the tracks of the horses he took."

"You have failed us again, Arkin. The queen does not want to see you anymore."

Arkin grimaced. "Well, maybe she should learn the truth, Hadaus. How would she feel about you?"

Hadaus unsheathed his dagger. "Are you threatening me, Arkin?"

"I should tell her what I saw that day. Every Noorian should know."

"Indeed you should!" Hadaus replied, stabbing him.

Arkin had not expected to be killed by another Noorian.

"Arkin," Hadaus whispered to him, "this is for Meleeka."

After he saw Arkin collapse, he felt slight guilt and regret. He had been taught by the Noorians never to kill one of his fellows. But he thought he had no choice.

Then he told Yam and the others that Arkin had betrayed their queen, and he galloped away as fast as he could to find Behas.

Hadaus could cover up for his crime and sort it out with the queen. He had no fear about his crime having been witnessed by so many. He knew how to talk himself out of trouble and how to keep his secrets hidden.

...

As he galloped after Behas, he remembered the first time he and Arkin had met, and why they had hated one another.

"Since when are we accepting sahers into our guild?" Arkin had said sarcastically when an occultist named Meleeka introduced Hadaus to the others for the first time. It had been Hadaus's first day in the Gray Palace.

"We heard from Meleeka that you are good with mixing potions and healing remedies," said one of the other Noorians, who had welcomed him with excitement.

"His father being a saher, he might be using jinn while mixing potions," Arkin had put in.

"Arkin!" Meleeka had scolded.

"I am not a saher," Hadaus had explained. "And I am here to help the Noorians acquire more knowledge and reveal the secrets this world hides."

Meleeka had smiled with pride, and the other Noorians with admiration. Only Arkin had grimaced. Arkin was younger, and later Hadaus had learned that he was only jealous of him for befriending Meleeka, who had refused Arkin when he had asked to marry her before.

Arkin had always felt superior to Hadaus, until Erum had captured Behas.

The queen had requested that Behas be kept alive until he confessed and told them where he had hidden his Mystic Dagger, but the Noorians had failed to get any information from him. The Prime Sheikh had lost his patience with the Noorians, telling them to either take the prisoner to their Gray Palace or let Erum execute him, as his stay had hurt the sheikhdom's reputation. And the queen had agreed to take him.

The saher had been taken to the Gray Palace and secretly tortured to make him talk. And he had finally told them where the dagger was, but only because he was sure that they wouldn't know how to use it. The queen had continued with her torture, trying to get Behas to tell her, until Arkin had told them he had a plan.

"We should befriend him; we can get him to talk."

The queen had never been convinced, and only two were allowed to see the prisoner: her and her secretive new servant, Hadaus.

Arkin had wished he could please her and succeed with his plan. He had wanted to show her that he too was worthy of her trust and had hated the fact that Hadaus had become closer to her and was of higher rank than he was.

One day, he had managed to enter Hadaus's room. He had been desperate to find something to use against his rival, and he had. Hadaus was a jinn master, a man who secretly hid his practice of summoning evil jinn, and Arkin had evidence.

Arkin had threatened to tell everyone unless Hadaus allowed him to secretly meet with Behas at night. Hadaus had had to agree, but he had sworn Arkin to secrecy.

Arkin had spent time visiting Behas and asking him about his wrongful acts and why he did them. Arkin had been young and naive, and he had fallen into Behas's trap. Behas had told him a lot about the Serpent-Neck star and the children born under it, and why he had to kill them. He had promised Arkin that, if he spared one, Arkin could keep it and raise it as his own son. Then he would learn the true powers of the star. He had told Arkin that he himself had been born under that star.

After weeks of regular visits at night, Behas had waited for them to make a mistake, and they had.

Meleeka had noticed her lover leaving her regularly every night. She had followed him one night and had seen him and Arkin enter Behas's prison cell. She had decided to stop them. And then the unexpected had happened.

Behas had found a way to hide a tool to use as a weapon when his chance to escape arose. And that night, when Meleeka had knocked on the door, Hadaus had opened it for her, catching Arkin off guard, and Behas had taken his opportunity and escaped.

Meleeka and other Noorians had died that night as a result, and Behas had been able to locate his Mystic Dagger and escape with it. Hadaus had wanted to kill Arkin ever since, but Arkin had promised to take full blame for the incident in front of the queen, and Arkin told her that he had stolen the keys from Hadaus every night. Ever since then, he had been an outcast.

...

After he had killed Arkin, Hadaus wondered what his life would have been like if Meleeka had still been alive. He had reached such a high rank among the Noorians, advisor to the queen, but he wished she could have been there to share his success. He wished he had never listened to Arkin.

After a long gallop, he reached Behas and Fad on the cliff above Wadi Teyq and shot his arrows at both of them. This time, he finally took his revenge on the jinn master. He reached Behas after he saw Fad jump.

"Coward!" Behas spat out.

That word reminded Hadaus of his father.

"Indeed. Here is where you will end, Behas," Hadaus said after taking the Mystic Dagger from him. He tucked it away and went to unsheathe his own dagger, the one he had killed Arkin with. But as he did so, he made his old mistake again and took his eyes off Behas.

Behas used all the strength he had left to grab a small rock and smack Hadaus with it, pushing him off balance just as he was changing daggers. He tried to take back his Mystic Dagger, but Hadaus shoved him away, and Behas fell off the cliff without having taken his dagger back.

Hadaus took a deep breath to steady himself as he stood up again. He had the Mystic Dagger now, which was most important to him and the queen.

The arrow he shot Behas with had missed his heart, but the old man was bleeding and wouldn't last long, he thought. Hadaus also smirked as he remembered that his arrows were poisonous. No healer in all of Erum could cure Behas of that poison.

"Good riddance!" Hadaus pulled out a frankincense stone and chewed on it to ease his tensions.

He thought they had no need for Behas anymore. *He* did not need Behas anymore, for he was secretly a jinn master himself.

36

Kashefa came from behind a hill, barking to alert her master, El Kashef, to her new findings. She would go far ahead to inspect the path and come back to tell him if there was danger. He had never seen her terrified like that before; she acted strange. She was trying to drive them the other way, not wanting anyone to go farther but her master.

"Wait here," he said to the hired guard, Murr, telling him to stay with the ladies and the howdah while he, Yam, and Saad the pathfinder all followed Kashefa.

What the hound had found was terrifying: a pool of blood and scattered body parts. A pile of dead men.

The mountain folk! thought El Kashef, judging from their uniforms, which were similar to Labeeb's. He noticed one of them who appeared to have at least tried to escape, and still lived, but barely—he had been brutally beaten and was bleeding to death. He galloped over to reach him before he died.

It was Daheen. A hyena lay dead near him, with a spear in its head. A chunk of flesh had been torn from one of Daheen's legs, and he now lay there waiting for death to take him and end both the pain in his body and the pain of regret in his heart.

"What happened here?" El Kashef asked while Yam came up behind him.

"A wicked Guardian from Erum did this to us," answered Daheen with difficulty. "He must be a jinn master; he summoned those beasts to attack us!"

Daheen was referring to Laeem, but El Kashef and Yam both thought he was talking about Fad!

"How did he summon the beasts?"

"He used some form of liquid, and they appeared from nowhere!" Daheen's voice could hardly be heard. Before he breathed his last, he said, "Send my apologies to my father and uncle."

"He's lying!" Yam exclaimed. "Fad is not a jinn master."

"One doesn't need to be a jinn master to summon jinn," El Kashef said calmly, looking around the area.

"What do you mean by that?" Yam had never heard that before. He had always thought that if one needed to summon a jinni, he or she needed to be a jinn master first, which required sacrifices and offerings to the jinnic lords. It wasn't that easy to be accepted by them.

"One can use a tool to summon jinn," answered El Kashef.

"A tool?" Yam asked again, but El Kashef ignored him.

"Go back to the howdah and tell the ladies to rest where they are for now," he commanded. "And bring Murr with you. We shall bury the dead before we move on. Let us be quick; Fad is not far from here."

Yam did not nod or answer him, but he climbed his horse with a frown to follow the Chief Guardian's orders.

"Yam," El Kashef called to him. "You do not need to tell Fad's wife what you have just learned about her husband."

And this time, Yam nodded before he went away.

. . .

After burying the bodies of the spearmen, El Kashef told Yam, Murr, and Saad to take the women back to Erum.

"This path has turned out to be more disturbing and dangerous than I had thought," he told them. "We cannot take the women farther, for we know nothing of what lies ahead."

"They won't want to go back," Murr said. "We tried telling them before."

Yam remained silent. He didn't want to go back either.

"It will not be their choice," El Kashef replied.

"Good luck convincing them," Murr taunted.

"I will continue with you," Yam said.

"Stay with the women, Yam," El Kashef repeated. "You are the one who dragged them to this cursed place; you cannot leave them unprotected. You yourself told me what the Noorian did to your teacher."

Yam nodded, though he wasn't fully convinced. He still wanted to continue and find Fad and help him find his son.

When the four men went back to the howdah, they learned from Faseela that a terrible illness had fallen upon Nada, and because of that, it wasn't difficult at all for El Kashef to convince the women to go back.

Faseela told them that once they were gone, Nada had fallen on the ground and begun to shake oddly and abruptly. Faseela had tried her best to hold her, but the other had lost consciousness. In Southern Arabia, that illness was known to be some sort of harm caused by the attack of an evil jinn on the sick person.

"Take her back to the same healer who helped her before." El Kashef suggested they go back to Wadi Erum.

"No, we need to go back to the village we passed by this morning, Jibjat. It is the nearest to us, and I know of a famous healer there—the most famous one here in Salalah Province." Faseela sounded confident, and El Kashef was astonished by her knowledge of healers and jinn diseases. He did not wish to argue further with her as long as they were not following him in his quest to find Fad.

"Fine. Yam, please escort them back to Jibjat," El Kashef ordered. "I will continue my search for Fad."

"All right." Yam nodded, obliged to agree against his own will.

"Guardian," Faseela called to El Kashef before he could mount his horse. She came closer, whispering to him sadly, "I beg you to help Fad find his child, Dil. It would worry my dear Nada to death if the child were not safe. I am a mother, and I know. I also care for Dil as if he were one of my own children." She then smiled and said, "I helped in his delivery. Fad and Nada deserve none of all the calamity that has been bestowed upon them."

"I will find Fad, and then I will see how things shall go from there," he interrupted her, not wanting to waste any more time. He pulled Fad's green tunic out for Kashefa to sniff again, reminding her that he was looking for Fad.

After a long gallop on his white horse, following his black hound, he remembered that he had left the rababa in the howdah. But he did not care to go back for it now, especially after Nada had told him that it didn't belong to Fad. He disregarded the idea that the rababa might help him in his investigation in any possible way. But as he remembered the scene of dead frankincense farmers, and the fake execution of Behas and the empty coffin, he feared what might lie ahead for him. His search for Bessel's killer was more complicated and dangerous than he had thought.

37

Fad snapped back into consciousness. He found himself lying on a flat rock beside the waters in the sinkhole below. He raised himself up and looked around, trying to figure out where he was. After a moment, he remembered.

He looked up, searching for the sun. It hid behind the clouds above, but he could tell more or less where it had positioned itself. It was two hours or less until sunset. His gaze moved over the steep walls of the wadi to the cliff from where he had jumped, and he remembered the fall, but he knew he wasn't a good swimmer. Someone must have helped him before he drowned. And judging from his half-wet, half-dry tunic, he had been left on the rocks to dry. He even felt his long hair was damp when he combed it backwards with his fingers.

He moved his legs, and a stinging pain made him flinch. His thigh pinched where he had injured himself after falling from the horse. He gently pressed the spot to test the pain in his leg; he grimaced, but it felt better than he thought. He couldn't recall at all what had happened after he jumped.

The noise of music and the echoing splash of waterfalls caused him a slight headache. There were people singing nearby, and the sound created a feeling of serenity that he needed after a long and tiring escape. Soon, however, his mind reminded him of the sole reason he was in this wadi. He needed to find his son, whose name was... *Dil!* As the child's name came back to him, he tried to stand, deciding to start by investigating the source of the music, which was coming from the cave nearest to the water.

Where is Behas? He remembered another name that had led him to this place. Behas had told him he had a plan that could help Fad find his son, but he had been shot with an arrow when they were at the top of the wadi. Fad remembered seeing the arrow come out of the old saher's naked chest, but he had still been alive and talking; he had told Fad to jump into the water. *The arrow must have missed his heart.* He couldn't remember anything of what happened after he touched the water, but he sensed the old jinn master must have jumped after him as well. *Where is he? I have to find him, whatever plan he said he had, it's my only hope now. Dil, in the name of all the sacred stars above, I will find you.*

He stood, bearing the slight pain in his thigh, and walked easily towards the open cave. It was large enough to fit a whole tribe in there! And the opening had a ledge so broad that twenty men could stand next to each other on the edge and still have some space between them.

A band of men and women were dancing around each other in a large circle, with musicians playing around three specific types of drums and a rababa in the middle. The crowd clapped and cheered and cried with joy to add to the music. They were dancing what the people of these lands called the rababa dance.

The dance was usually performed between four men and four women, or sometimes more. The dancing men Fad saw that day wore blue head covers with white tunics and matching long blue Arabian skirts. The women wore all blue as well, from tip to toe, but their dresses were decorated with hand-sewn embroideries of variant colors. They timed their movements around each other to be in sync with the drumbeats and the rababa's tone, so it seemed as if they were playing a skillful game rather than dancing. They were all smiling and happy.

That rababa was surely not enchanted like the one he had gotten in Ubar, as he did not feel the pain he had felt before when Qamaria's father played it.

Despite the noise, Fad wasn't distracted. He looked around for Behas, but there were no signs of him. Everyone else in the cave was dancing or singing. Fad tried to get their attention by just looking at some of them, but no one looked back at him.

He noticed stairs at the far end of the cave and walked behind and around the crowd to reach them. They led to the upper caves where the rest of the cave village was. He was keen to find Behas and Dil instead of celebrating or dancing around. He knew he had little time. Behas had told him he knew who had taken Fad's child and had a plan to stop them, whoever they were. Fad needed to know what the plan was.

As he climbed the stairs, he thought again, *I need to find Dil!* He feared Behas hadn't survived the arrow early that afternoon. He needed to start thinking of another way to search for his child again, but the idea of doing it alone was unappealing. Whoever had shot the arrows at them later did not seem familiar to Fad, but he felt Behas would not be beaten easily. An arrow through the chest could kill a man, for sure, but he doubted if the one who had survived Fad stabbing him in the throat was even a man!

The cavern villages of Wadi Teyq were not dark and gloomy, as you might think; they were lit with enough natural light from above. The cave roofs had many holes that allowed both sunlight and streaming water to drip inside, and the open walls that overlooked the large lake, or sinkhole, let in light and air. Every corner in Wadi Teyq amazed Fad with its beauty that day.

Traveling tribes from the coasts or the deserts inhabited Wadi Teyq during the rainy seasons in the summer and autumn of every year. They gathered there in the shaded halls to enjoy housing that offered better temperatures, fresh water, and food.

Fad passed through the caves, searching eagerly between gatherings of women who sat around for a cheerful chat or men who came around this place once a year to meet their friends from all over the sheikhdom and relate peaceful tales to each other about harvest and weather. He skipped all the celebrating and dancing groups, hoping to find any clue that could lead him to Behas or to his child, but nothing in the caves seemed sinister. He did hear newborns and children crying here and there, and from one cave or another, and he did chase after the cries, thinking or hoping it might be Dil, but none were. And he still couldn't find Behas.

People were welcoming and joyful. They greeted him with offerings of colorful fresh food and drink. He did accept some dates, which reminded him of home, but he never stopped searching for Dil or Behas. His Guardian's tunic helped him look in every corner without being suspected or stopped by anyone. Even the other guards nodded greetings when he passed by. Unlike the previous ones from Arkin's camp, the guards here did not know who he was or what he had done. They did serve the same dominion, but since they were far away in this outer settlement, it appeared that Wadi Erum had not sent them any news or orders to capture a farmer wearing a

Guardian's tunic. He finally asked one of the guards, a friendly-looking man who wore yellow, as all guards in Wadi Teyq did, for some information.

Fad asked the man if he knew who had helped him out of the water. The guard directed him to go back down to where he had first awoken, telling Fad that the men in that cave were the ones who had helped him.

He stood near the edge of the walls of the large sinkhole and glanced at the skies. The sun still hid behind the low clouds, which made Fad lose track of time. The clouds looked darker than before, but there was still a little light, which meant the sun had not yet set. He had time before sunset, but not *enough* time, so he went back down to where he had first awoken.

What he didn't notice as he roamed through Wadi Teyq was that someone was stalking his every move: Laeem. The young saher had disguised his appearance by wearing a regular tunic and a blue turban on his head. He hid behind every corner, acting normally and moving smoothly behind Fad wherever he went, like a distant shadow. He too searched for the sinister jinn master, Behas.

Fad reached the cave nearest to the water, where the blue-clothed tribe was dancing. He had noticed that every tribe in Wadi Teyq distinguished itself by the color of its clothing. There were tribes wearing green, blue, brown, light red, dark red, and yellow, which was worn by the prime tribe. All the guards were from that prime tribe.

No one was singing anymore, but the large open cave was still filled with joy and laughter. On one side, a group of women were sitting in a circle teaching a child how to walk. One helped him stand and directed him to walk to the other women on the other side of the circle. Every time, the child struggled to take his first three steps, but he then laughed and smiled at the women who cheered for him to carry on, and near the finish line his steps got faster and he jumped on the laps of the women dressed in blue. Fad passed them to reach the bank. On its edge, men sat with nets, strings, and poles. Fishing, Fad assumed.

The small fishes in the sinkhole didn't taste good, but they were a staple food for the tribes in the wadi.

Fad turned to the fishermen and opened his mouth to ask if they knew who had saved him from drowning, but he hesitated before interrupting them rudely, as they all faced the water and looked busy chatting and eyeing the fishing lines, anticipating a catch. He tilted his head over the water from beside them, waving in the friendliest manner and showing them his face. He wanted them to see him and greet him first so he could speak.

They all stopped what they were doing and looked back at him, smiling. Before approaching them, he wondered why any of them had not even asked him where he came from or why he had fallen from above—if, of course, they had even seen him. He didn't remember seeing anyone when he was falling from the cliff. The Guardian's tunic he wore was stained and ripped, and he had thought at least one would ask if he was all right or needed help! No one in the whole valley, above or below, cared to ask him that. They did greet him and offer him food, but not help. It might have been that Guardians from Erum were used to being the help around and usually knew what they were doing.

"Greetings. Did anyone see me jump from above?"

"Yes," answered a thin boy who held a fishing line in his hand, while the others nodded in agreement. Apparently, they had all seen Fad jump! "We helped you out," he added, "and the lord." The others nodded again, smiling.

"Lord?" *Behas, no doubt.*

"Hoop!" the boy cried in surprise. The string pulled his fingers. The net had caught something, and they all cheered for him, ignoring Fad and anticipating the catch. "This is a *big* one!"

"Come on," the other men cheered, "you can do it."

"Don't lose it!"

"It's your catch!"

Fad stared blankly at the event before him. A farmer like him had no interest in fishing at all. "Where...where is the lord?" he asked, but either no one heard him, or they ignored him. He grimaced and lowered his eyebrows in frustration. Fad was forced to wait for the catch as well. *Come on! Catch the fish and answer me!*

The little string-holder pulled and pulled as if reeling in a whale. He stood above everyone else on the edge and hauled with all his strength. His face turned red, he held his breath, his eyes popped out, and no one helped him; they only cheered for him. It was his catch alone. When the fish finally appeared from the water, Fad thought it was small. And when the fish was finally forced all the way out of the water, it was actually smaller than it had appeared to be under it. The fish was smaller than his palm!

They all laughed at his catch, but he seemed to be proud, as if it were his first catch ever.

Fad stepped closer to another man in blue and white. "Brother, answer me. You said you helped the lord as well. Where is he?"

"I do not know where he went. After we took you both out of the water, he calmed down after knowing you were alive. You murmured a name repeatedly—Nada. Then you fainted. The lord then asked us to leave you by the bank to dry. He was bleeding as well, with an arrow in his chest!" He then pointed his chin towards an old woman. Also in blue, she sat on a rug with other women at the other end of the cave, far away from the water. "She healed his wounds and stopped the bleeding. Unlike you, the lord was conscious. He talked with her before leaving."

Fad furrowed his brow in worry, glancing above. The skies were becoming darker, with thicker clouds. He felt panic with every heartbeat but forced himself to act calm as he walked towards the woman.

Laeem, still doing his best to blend into the crowd, observed Fad, his only lead to Behas, closely.

"Greetings, sister!"

"Greetings, Guardian of Erum. How are you?"

"Well, I can walk. Thank you for asking me."

"How can we help you, Guardian?"

"Have you seen...the lord? The man who fell with me into the water?" he finally asked, struggling every time he had to call Behas "lord" like they did. Fad did not have much respect for him, but the tribes of Wadi Teyq treated Behas as a savior. He had once saved them from an evil jinni that had lurked in their wadi. They had turned to him for help, and Behas had killed the jinni. Ever since then, they had considered him a blessed man, not an outlaw. "Did he tell you where he was going?"

"He did," she replied.

"Where is he?"

She hesitated before answering. "Yesterday, we heard rumors that the lord would be executed in Erum. We were all surprised to see him here and alive. And you are a Guardian of Erum, so we thought it was your doing that he was injured. But he must be your friend, as he asked us to take good care of you."

Fad eyed his tunic but decided not to reveal his true identity. "Behas *is* my friend," he said. "And he is helping me find my kidnapped child." He wasn't certain he needed to tell her everything, but the woman did look trustworthy.

"I see. He did ask me if I knew of any orphan newborns in these caves, and I did direct him to a sick child in the upper caves who was in need of his blessing."

He's searching for Dil without me! Fad knew he shouldn't have trusted the saher. "Where is he?"

"Why don't you ask the other Guardians above if they have seen him? He might have left Wadi Teyq by now."

"Guardians?"

"You look surprised. Yes, the Guardians' post at the entrance of Wadi Teyq."

After all, these lands *were* under the rule of Erum.

He left her without another word, forgetting about the Guardians, whom he and Behas had actually come for…to use in a plan Behas had not told him about. If the Guardians above had received news of Bessel's death, they would have taken him captive. Fad was afraid of that—and worse, of the possibility that Behas might have abandoned the idea of helping him and continued with what he had first wanted to do: execute Dileel.

The clouds now darkened as the sun began to set, and the caves now began to be lighted with torches and lanterns.

Fad climbed up again, and from a higher point, he looked out to see the caves above, which he hadn't yet reached. He hoped to see something that would lead to Behas, and he did see the man's unique dark cloak near a torch!

The saher was not only standing near the open window of a cave, but he was looking down at a child in his hands. *Dil!* thought Fad. He quickly measured the distance. *Two floors higher.* He began to run towards the stairs.

As soon as he made it to the upper floor, four Guardians surrounded him, with swords and daggers drawn. "There he is, Prime Chief! We found him."

Fad surrendered, revealing his empty hands. A calm voice spoke to him.

"Long hair, tired bearded face, hawk-beak nose, and lips always pressed tight with anger," El Kashef said, making his way over to him.

Fad turned to face him. He noticed the broad smile under the man's shiny mustache. El Kashef was happy to have finally found him, but Fad felt only panic and fear.

"Your wife described you well, Fada. I can assure you from my experience, many wives would fail to describe their husbands as thoroughly as yours has done to me!"

Nada! She has been healed then, he thought with relief. But he was also frustrated by his own misfortune; he had ended up being caught again. "Please help me; they have my son. Behas has my son!"

Although El Kashef had figured earlier that the execution was fake, he still looked surprised to hear it confirmed. "Behas? Where is he?" El Kashef was glad to hear it from Fad, and why would he not be? He had now killed two birds with one stone.

38

Meanwhile, the young prince, Leith, had taken seven Guardians of Erum with him when he left the High Palace. He and his men continued on their quest to find the child and bring it back safe for the Noorians. The old sage directed Leith to find Arkin, and he did, but it was all too late.

They found the disturbed camp and all the Guardians who had been bitten by Laeem's snake. Their help had arrived, and they were about to head back to Wadi Erum.

"We buried him there, my sheikh." They explained everything that had happened there, whom they had seen, and who had killed Arkin.

"Can you tell us which way El Kashef went?"

"He and the others traveled that way, uphill," answered one of the Guardians. "They followed those horse tracks, I would assume."

Leith and his seven Guardians rode ahead to wherever the tracks led them. They came across a marker El Kashef's party had left where they had buried the spearmen. There, they noticed the tracks split, and the pathfinding Guardian picked out El Kashef's from the others. "El Kashef seems to have left alone on this path towards Wadi Teyq; I can tell by his hound's tracks."

They continued to ride uphill on the same path, which led to the great sinkhole. The prince thought about what the Guardians he'd just met had told him, and he mostly thought about the dead body that had been stolen from them. He remembered that his father had told him not to be tolerant of those who practiced dark and evil magic and jinn mastery in his lands, and he became furious with whoever had dared to attack a camp of Guardians in those lands.

And unlike you, neither the prince nor his cavalry was at all aware that Behas was alive!

...

El Kashef and the Guardians from Wadi Teyq all followed after Fad through the caves, seeking to find Behas. El Kashef's injured leg slowed him down, but he was able to see the last Guardian and follow him. The colorfully dressed, joyous folk in the wadi were confused to see a chase of some sort occurring in the caves, which were connected to each other by narrow man-dug tunnels.

As all the Guardians were busy following Fad, and as the tribesmen were busy lighting torches and fires to light and warm their caves as the sun sank below the horizon, El Kashef was the only one to notice the thick black clouds. *A storm is coming,* he thought. *A calamitous storm.*

When the Guardians finally stopped, he began to hop on his injured leg to reach them faster. They had caught Behas with a child in his hands, but it was not Dil, which left Fad frustrated.

El Kashef noticed Behas and Fad having an argument, and so he interfered, for they had created enough panic in the wadi. "Take them both to the dungeons." His voice was loud enough to silence everyone. Both outlaws turned their confused eyes to his.

A Guardian positioned himself near El Kashef and whispered, "Prime Chief, we don't have a dungeon here in Wadi Teyq!"

It took him a moment to decipher the hissing in his ears. He turned his back to the outlaws so they wouldn't hear him. "Then what do you do with wrongdoers here?" he asked the Guardian.

"Each tribe punishes their troublemakers. That is, if there are any."

"Fine." El Kashef kept his voice down. "Take them to the Guardians' cave and tie their hands." The cave was the nearest to the main entrance above ground, and he had a bad feeling about it. The closer the two were to the exit, the better chance they would have to escape. But he needed a private place to interrogate them. He needed to know what had happened to Bessel and what role the two had played in all the madness he had witnessed.

A man in a yellow scarf approached the outlaws and moved towards Behas. The Guardians tried to stop him, but after he clarified his intent by reaching towards the child, they allowed him to pass. He grabbed the child from Behas's hands and murmured some words El Kashef and the four Guardians could not hear.

"The sun has set, and I must find my son or we will all be doomed," Fad began. Only a few in the cave noticed him nod at Behas. "We have to find the child."

"Doomed by what, Master Fada?" El Kashef asked sarcastically. "Does your kidnapped child justify your betrayal of our Chief Guardian, Bessel?"

"Great evil. If we don't stop them, it will not matter what we do," Fad continued to explain, now addressing everyone who could hear his loud cries.

El Kashef noticed the men in the caves begin to increase in number. They came out of every corner and dark tunnel, and they all seemed to be listening to Fad. El Kashef then remembered that this area had only recently been forced into an alliance with Erum, and the tribes were among the few that glorified Behas, not condemned him. But he was more surprised to see that Fad and Behas were helping one another. *Are they trying to turn the men in the caves against the Guardians?* he thought as he noticed the crowds of tribesmen wearing different colors and the yellow-clothed guards begin to gather around him and the Guardians. They weren't getting close just to see what was going on. Their faces revealed different intentions.

"And what is their plan? How do you plan to stop them?" El Kashef cried louder to interrupt Fad. "How did you plan to save your child by killing a Chief Guardian?" El Kashef tried to remind everyone in the cave that the two caught were outlaws accused of murder, but he saw that the men in yellow scarves had slowly begun to position themselves behind the Guardians. There were only four Guardians stationed in this wadi, and with El Kashef, they were five. The tribesmen behind him were more than double that number, and they too had weapons. Maybe the word "dungeons" earlier had sounded wrong, and he needed to reposition himself and remind the allies with stronger words who they were.

"You two have disturbed the peace in this valley. You will be taken back to Erum." In saying that, he hoped the tribesmen would step down and be reminded of the Guardians' supreme authority in these lands. "Guardians! Take them away." But the effect of his statement was the opposite of what he had planned.

"It is you who have disturbed the peace!" came a cry from behind. El Kashef looked but could not find the source of it. Before he could respond, he and all the Guardians found themselves being held by at least two yellow-clothed tribesmen. They stripped the Guardians of their weapons, and one forced the Prime Chief's ring from El Kashef's hand.

The leader of the yellow tribe went to hand the ring to Behas before the saher and Fad ran away.

"Wait!" El Kashef called, but it was too late, and the tribesmen raised their daggers.

. . .

Behas had seen El Kashef enter the caves looking for Fad, and he had taken advantage and devised a perfect plan as things escalated around him.

El Kashef stared helplessly as his captives escaped with Qassas's ring. He also noticed one man in a blue turban running behind them. At the time, he did not know it was Laeem.

Behas had not known El Kashef was coming, but he had had a plan to steal a Chief Guardian's ring from Wadi Teyq, as he knew there were Guardians stationed there. But his plan had changed when he saw a better opportunity arise, for he felt that the deities would always act in his favor. That he always survived and that fate was always on his side was a miracle, not a coincidence.

Behas and Fad had found their way out of the caves. The sky above was dark and gloomy, although the moon lit parts of clouds.

"We are late! We have only a little time to reach and save your son," said Behas as he looked up. They found where the horses were being kept by the Guardians, and they went to steal two. Fad found his green tunic in the saddlebags of a white horse—El Kashef's horse.

Fad was surprised to see his tunic and decided to mount that horse. But the horse resisted Fad's will and tried to kick him. A black hound tied next to it barked aggressively as well.

"Just climb another one!" cried Behas, who was already mounted.

Fad pulled on his green tunic and went near another horse, a gray one. It seemed frightened, but Fad held the reins and tamed it easily.

"We need to find our way to the sea," Behas said. "Follow me."

"The sea?" asked Fad.

"Yes. If we travel through Wadi Darbat, we will reach Sumhuram and find a boat before dawn. We need to reach the island before sunset."

"What island?" Fad had not yet climbed the horse.

"Your child is in Socotra. Mount, and let us ride quickly, or we will end up being late."

"It will be impossible to reach Socotra before sunset tomorrow!"

"We will reach it. I do not have time to explain it all now. Climb a horse and let's go."

Fad went to change from his Guardian's tunic into his green one before mounting the horse, but Behas stopped him.

"What are you doing?"

"I need to take this tunic off."

"No! Keep it on. You will need it; it's the only way my plan will work."

Fad nodded. He hadn't yet heard or figured out the saher's plan, but he didn't want to waste any more time by asking. They both took off in the direction of Wadi Darbat, trying to reach the sea.

. . .

Back in the caves, El Kashef and the Guardians were still being held against their will. The tribesmen wouldn't dare to harm them; they were just slowing them down so their lord could escape execution. El Kashef had never expected anything like this would happen. Why was Behas even alive, and why was the same farmer who had helped Erum capture him now escaping with him? He and the four Guardians who protected this wadi tried to reason with them, but the tribesmen covered their mouths so they wouldn't speak. El Kashef felt that they were treated like thieves or traitors.

The storm he anticipated had arrived. Torches lit the caves, but it was very dark outside, and now there were rain showers. He remembered the doom the two outlaws had spoken of. The only doom he sensed was soon to fall on his head; just when he thought his task was complete, the outlaws had escaped.

The tribesmen forced them to stand and guided them towards the stairs to tie them up in their Guardians' cave, but before they moved up the steps, three men with uniforms similar to theirs descended into the caves. They were Guardians of Erum, and with them was the giant prince himself, Prince Leith, come down to the caves. They must have found El Kashef's white horse and black hound above and come down searching for him.

Leith's head almost touched the roof. He might even have needed to bend in some places to avoid the hanging rocks above. But he stood at his full height on the last step down, gazing upon the situation, which made no sense to him. "What is the meaning of all this?"

The tribesmen all froze in their places. The largest of them, who wore a yellow turban, stepped forward to speak to the tall prince. Although he was huge, he looked tiny compared to the giant.

"We have caught these fake Guardians trying to kill another Guardian of Erum," the leader of the yellow-clothed tribe explained.

What? El Kashef's exclamation of surprise was muffled by the cloth in his mouth. He couldn't believe the man would use that excuse after he had shown him the ring when he first came and had told him that Behas and Fad were outlaws.

"Here, my sheikh," said the large tribesman, handing a ring to the prince. *Qassas's ring,* thought El Kashef. He was relieved that it hadn't been given to Behas, as he had originally assumed. "They killed a Chief Guardian and stole this ring."

The prince held the ring, and after a quick, searching glance at it, he focused on El Kashef. "Let him be free," he said, pointing at him, whose face he had seen many times in his father's majlis.

"My sheikh," El Kashef began. "We had caught both outlaws, Behas and the farmer who killed Bessel, but the men of Wadi Teyq must have been deceived by the jinn master, who turned them against us." El Kashef tried to blame it on Behas, not the tribesmen, for he knew they could end up being punished severely, and he did not wish for that to happen.

"Behas is alive?" Prince Leith wanted to be sure he had heard El Kashef right.

"He escaped with the farmer, my sheikh. It was Behas. He is alive and well," El Kashef tried to explain further.

"Deceived, then. Is that true?" Leith asked the large man in the yellow turban.

"It appears to be a misunderstanding, my sheikh! Please forgive us all."

"I see. It is not at all your fault," the prince said, then swung his head towards El Kashef. "For even I have been deceived by the saher! I saw the old crow executed in Erum two days ago. And now our revealer of truth, El Kashef, claims the saher is alive."

El Kashef remained silent, terrified by his prince's tone, which seemed to suggest blame or doubt.

Not long afterwards, the other five cavalrymen, who had been delayed tying the horses, arrived. They were heavily armed, and when they entered, the prince changed his behavior dramatically.

He walked slowly towards the edge of the cave and stared out at the disturbed water. The noise of waterfalls and showers filled him with rage and a desire for punishment. The reflection of the lit caves and their torches and fires were the only visible light on the water of the sinkhole. It felt completely dark and terrifying, as if one were looking down at the hole of Barhoot.

"It shall not be easily forgotten. Nor will it be forgiven without punishment." He turned and continued: "Without punishment, your acts against Erum will only be a sign of our weakness." He seemed to be addressing the tribesmen.

Everyone remained completely silent, waiting anxiously to hear the next words the giant young prince would say. All the Guardians were untied and their weapons retrieved, except for one thing that hadn't yet returned to its owner—the ring in the prince's hand. Qassas's ring.

"You have obstructed the Prime Chief Guardian of Erum's effort to complete his quest." He held the ring high and walked forward a few steps, placing it in El Kashef's open palm. "There must be punishment."

The big tribesman with the yellow turban fell on his knees and begged forgiveness. "Please spare us, my sheikh; it was all a misunderstanding."

"These four Guardians who reside here and are assigned by Erum to serve in this wadi, how long have you known them?" asked the prince.

"They are here every year, and we treat them like our own. Please, my sheikh, we beg you to spare us. We are forever loyal to your father and the Sheikhdom of Erum."

"All who have drawn their weapons against our Guardians shall step forward near the edge, for I shall hear from each one in person."

The leader yelled to his men to comply. Fourteen men sprang to the edge. They were instructed to kneel at first, but the prince then asked them all to stand instead so their heads would be closer to his. They stood facing the cave, with their backs to the sinkhole.

The open edge on the wall was large enough that they all fit, and there was still space for another twenty men.

Prince Leith approached the first man in line and asked him. "Did you deliberately stand against a Prime Chief Guardian sent from Erum, and help the outlaws escape?"

"No, my sheikh, I did not. But I have been deceived," he answered proudly. The giant prince only raised his tall sword, and with no effort at all, swung it across, slicing the sinner's head off easily as one would slice a weak plant from the ground. The head fell at the prince's feet and stained his pants and leather boots, while the body tumbled into the water.

The other accused men trembled with fear, but they were frozen in place. Their souls seemed to have left their bodies before they were even executed.

El Kashef was shocked, but he dared not stand against his prince and defend them or try to soften him.

The prince stepped over the severed head and stood before the next sinner, looking angrier. The tribesman shrank in fear, expecting the same fate. He answered the prince with the same words, but without the pride of the man before him. "I have been deceived; please spare me," he begged. But it didn't help him, and he too lost his head, which fell near the third man. The prince kicked it, and it flew into the sinkhole. That scene made the third man sob like a child.

"Did you deliberately stand against a Prime Chief Guardian sent from Erum, and help the outlaws escape?" he asked for the third time. El Kashef hoped it would all stop with the third man. He saw from their pathetic looks that they had surely learned their lesson.

"Forgive our wrongfulness and ignorance, my sheikh," begged the third man as he sobbed. "You are the son of Aad, of whom we have heard nothing but kindness and forgiveness."

"True, my sheikh. And we all, be sure, will be forever thankful," added the fourth. The others murmured as well, begging and sobbing for forgiveness.

The prince raised his head to look at the others, and they all went silent again. He switched his gaze back to the third. "Answer my question."

"What you say is true, my sheikh. It was deliberate, but we were deceived."

The prince sliced his head off as he had the first and second man's, without giving him the chance to add another word. This time his swing was better, and both the head and the body flew into the water.

The prince had heard the confession he wanted to hear. He passed his tall, reddened sword to one of his men for cleaning.

El Kashef was relieved to see the end of it all, but it wasn't his first time witnessing or hearing of such acts by sons of Aad. Those acts, however, had been committed in wars and battlefields, not in a peaceful village like this. *Three died, and the rest were spared,* thought El Kashef. But he thought wrong, and so did everyone else.

"Thank you, my sheikh, for your kind forgiveness. We shall hail your name in our wadi forever." Their leader bowed before the prince.

"I have not spared anyone," said the sheikh in a fearsome tone. "I have only grown tired, and I feared my sword would wear on sinners."

Their leader smiled with perplexity and confusion. But El Kashef had heard this sentence before from one of Leith's older brothers. He knew then it wouldn't end pleasantly for the wadi, as he had earlier thought.

The Guardians brought another sword, cleaner but older. This one he did not use; he only gave his new orders. "Execute all the sinners who have deliberately obstructed a Prime Chief Guardian sent from Erum."

His seven escorting Guardians acted accordingly, while the four who had been stationed in this wadi froze in shock; the men being slaughtered had never done them wrong before that night.

The sinners begged and cried, but the executioners had no mercy. Women and children were heard weeping and wailing, but none dared to come close, except one: the healer in blue who had helped Behas and Fad earlier. She weaved her way into the center of it all and stood before the prince.

"Stop this, please," she cried with fear and sadness, but the Guardians ignored her and continued their executions. There were only two men left, so she jumped to stand between them and the Guardians like a mother bird stretching her wings to hide her little ones under their shade. "Enough!"

The Guardians stopped to look back at their prince and wait for his commands.

"How dare you stand in our way?!" cried the prince. "These men have challenged Erum. Stand aside or you will be punished as well."

She ignored his warnings. "You have killed enough. They did not need to be punished for your failures! The outlaws are out there escaping, and you are here, killing loyal men. Men loyal to your father and all of Erum."

Now the prince was faced with a challenge. It was one of those moments where he had to choose between softness or toughness, wisdom or rashness, courage or fear, punishment or forgiveness. The young prince had to decide quickly. If the men were being punished for obstructing the works of a Prime Chief Guardian of Erum, she was doing worse by opposing the prince himself.

El Kashef did not know Prince Leith as well as he knew his older brothers, and he could not predict what he would do to her. Like all other sons of Aad, he was stubborn. But Prince Leith was also wiser.

"Bring me their leader," he said, pointing towards the yellow-turbaned man. The healer had protected two of the fourteen tribesmen, but she had forgotten the prime sinner of them all, the one who ordered them to do what they did, the man behind stopping El Kashef and freeing the outlaws.

He fearfully dragged himself over to stand before the prince, who lowered his head to whisper under the yellow turban. El Kashef couldn't hear what was being said, but he was able to see the man nod, then move towards the healer in blue and whisper in *her* ear. She lowered her arms, beginning to weep again. Then the two stepped aside, and the last two sinners lost their heads and were thrown into the dark waters with the rest!

...

That night was never forgotten. The tribes of Wadi Teyq spent the rest of their season fishing the waters to get the bodies out. It was a difficult task that took them three weeks.

Luckily, the water in this sinkhole was renewed daily, and it rained almost three times a day for the following month, which cleaned their wadi and the lake below before they went back to their villages, bound to return there next summer.

It was fortunate for El Kashef that their leader had been spared, and the healer woman as well. He needed to speak with them if he wanted to understand this calamity that Fad and Behas had brought upon them. He needed to be quick with his discussions and interrogations, for the prince had ordered him to join him that night in pursuit of the outlaws and help find the kidnapped child.

PART THREE

SOCOTRA

39

"Where is the Serpent-Neck Child?" asked a deep voice.

"He is safe," *he* answered.

"What about the dagger? Without it, there will be no ritual!" another voice complained.

"It is with the Noorians for now," *he* answered again.

"You should have taken it from Behas when you snatched the child," a third voice scolded.

"I couldn't take it from Behas; it was too complicated. But I have another plan to get it here, and it will be here before sunset," *he* explained again.

"How do you plan to take it from the Noorians? Without the dagger, all our preparations will be for nothing!" the earlier voice growled again.

"Have no fear, *Protector*. We will have the dagger here today. And tonight, Erum will see the end of its prosperity," *he* reassured.

40

The Mystic Dagger was kept safe in the Gray Palace after Hadaus had retrieved it from Behas on the cliff above Wadi Teyq.

He rode back to their mountain with haste. When he reached the gate, he found that a number of the Noorians were outside and were preparing to depart. The queen herself was out with them.

"You're safe, Hadaus. The moon be praised!" cried one of the Noorians.

"Where are you all going?" asked Hadaus.

The queen had asked him to go out and make sure the Mystic Dagger came to her safely and quickly, but he had been delayed, and she had feared for him. She had asked her guild to follow her in an expedition to find out why Hadaus had been delayed. And just as she and her guild were preparing to go after the dagger, he had come back.

"Have you got the dagger?" she asked him.

"Indeed, I have, my queen."

"And the jinn master?"

"I had to kill him," Hadaus explained.

"Fine; he would never have told us how to use the dagger anyway. We shall learn that ourselves. Follow me inside." She waved, and it was only Hadaus who followed her. He was able to reach her and walk beside her.

"Here it is." He showed her the dagger when no one was watching them. She gave it only a slight glance.

"Did you have to kill the old man?" she whispered. She and the Noorians had learned that he had killed Arkin.

"You told me to…"

She stopped and eyed him angrily. "I would *never* ask you to kill a Noorian. Do you have a mind to think with, or a heart to love with?" And it was true; she never would. She had not liked Arkin, but she had never wished him dead.

"*Siratukym.* I have misunderstood your guidance," Hadaus tried, acting naive.

"Give me the dagger." She grabbed it and pulled it away from him, then unsheathed it to make sure it wasn't fake. She touched a six-petaled flower engraved on the lower end of the blade, which matched the hexagram symbol on her silver-plated necklace. Now she was confident that it *was* the Mystic Dagger of Behas.

"Finally," she said with a sigh. "Keep it in the treasury." She handed it back to Hadaus. "And keep your eyes open; whoever kidnapped the child will try to take the dagger as well, I fear." She walked away through a different pathway.

Hadaus turned to head towards the treasury but paused suddenly, feeling like someone was watching him. He decided to act as though he had not noticed and move on.

After reaching the treasure room, he placed his own dagger in a chest as a decoy and made sure all three of the chest's locks were secure.

He locked the treasure room as well and went to his garden, waiting there for night to come. *If anyone is planning to steal the dagger, they will do so at night,* he thought. *The rat will pay for his treason! I will make sure he suffers thoroughly before he dies. He shall be made an example for anyone who tries to join our guild for their own gains.* No man could enter the Gray Palace unless he were accepted as an occultist. Whoever planned to take the dagger had to be a member of the guild; Hadaus was sure of it.

…

Hadaus fell asleep while waiting for night to come. He remained hidden and out of sight, not too far from the treasure room, in a corner where he would hear if any rat approached near the door. He woke from a bad dream after hearing the locks click. He was like a cat, lurking in the shadows alone while everyone else fell deep into sleep. Not a small cat, though—a big African cheetah. And now his prey was cornered in the treasure room. He slowly moved towards the sound coming from the treasury.

The thief tried his best to pick the locks quietly, but the clicking echoed through the silence. Hiding behind the unlit walls, Hadaus remained silent and pictured the spot where the traitor stood in his mind. He heard the traitor succeed in picking the door's lock, enter the treasury, and close the thick doors behind him. Hadaus thought of surprising the guilty thief, but that might be risky. He decided to stick with his original plan and lock the treasure room behind him, call everyone else, and then expose the thief to them.

He reached the door and found the lock had been removed from its place. *Smart and cautious!* he thought. He pushed the door gently to peek in. The thief was busy picking the last of three bronze locks.

Hadaus noticed his gray cloak. It was a Noorian, just as he had thought.

Finally, the last lock clicked, and the thief hastily raised his blue lantern and poured its light into the chest but found only silk garments, women's gold ornaments, and a rusty dagger. He did not even bother to search deeper. He stood and stared at the dagger, which he probably knew belonged to Hadaus. He realized he had been fooled!

After the thief stood up, Hadaus noticed he was one of the new young recruits, no match for a strong muscled man like Hadaus. He opened the door fully.

"Looking for this?" Hadaus revealed the decorated golden dagger in his hand.

"Hadaus!" The traitor jumped in panic. "This is not what you think!" The traitor raised his lantern and his free hand in surrender.

Hadaus smiled and unsheathed the Mystic Dagger, marching nearer to his pathetic prey to end his life as he had Arkin's. "It is exactly what I—"

A pinch in his neck forced him to freeze. He pulled a wooden dart from his neck and figured it to be a paralyzing dart, shot from the darkness behind him. He couldn't tell who had done it. The poison spread in an instant; his legs failed him and he collapsed to the ground. He tried to open his eyes to see who had shot him, but he could not.

He wished he had closed the door after cornering the thief. He had left his back exposed and been incautious, which was his usual mistake. And there was another lesson he would never forget from that night: *There could be one, or two, or even more traitors!*

41

The prince and his Guardians were preparing the cavalry to continue their search for the outlaws and the child. Two men had already left to scout the routes and search for their tracks, and El Kashef had little time to interrogate the leader of Wadi Teyq or the healer.

There were still many questions in his mind that needed to be answered. A vital one was this: *Why would the farmer leave with the same saher who tried to kill his child a few days ago?*

El Kashef spoke with the healer woman before she descended deeper into the wadi's caves. He wanted to know what had made her step down from her courageous stand in front of the executioners. Her name was Saeeda, which was Arabic for "happy," but tonight was too gloomy for anyone to smile or even think of happiness in Wadi Teyq.

"May I ask what made you walk away after the whisperings from your leader, Haneef?" he asked, after excusing himself to speak with her alone.

"I understand the sin of our children," Saeeda started. "And the laws of Erum must be forced upon all. One should not stand between a Guardian of Erum and his duties. But I asked for forgiveness, and so I hoped the sinners would be spared. Haneef told me if I did not move aside, the son of Aad would have to execute more men and women. It was better to stand down than to lose more people!" She almost wept after every word, which made it difficult for El Kashef to hear her. Though he doubted the prince would say such a thing, he needed to ask Haneef, and he needed to do so fast.

"Thank you," he said. Interrogating her while she was grieving would only be disrespectful, so he told himself to leave her be and give her no more pain than what she had seen already.

But before he did, she added another word. She told him that Behas had been hit by a poisonous arrow and that she was the one who had healed him. "And if you must know, the lord is dying anyway," she said.

"Behas?"

"Yes. I healed him, but his wound is deep below the heart. I did what I could, and I warned him, but he ignored me. He told me he needed to find a child. His wounds are sewn shut, but not for long; he will bleed again. He won't make it until sunrise. He is now breathing his last."

Her words were music to El Kashef's ears; it would have been catastrophic for Prince Zufar and his reputation in Erum if the execution was later learned to be fake! The people of this wadi had seen Behas and now believed that the execution they had heard about was a rumor.

"Nothing can heal him now," she continued, "unless he could summon an ultimate healing jinni for help. Getting one is not easy, but the lord could, and there is a jinnic lord I tend to visit often nearby, in Wadi Darbat. Behas might be headed to that wadi."

"Thank you, Lady Saeeda, for all the information. May the souls of those you lost tonight find peace from behind the moon." El Kashef thanked her and ran to find Haneef, ignoring his injured leg as he did.

Most of the men and women had descended to honor the bodies from the water and bury them properly, but Haneef remained above with a few of the elders.

El Kashef sat beside him, looking at his grumpy face hidden under his gloomy turban. "Tell me, what was it that the sheikh said to you before you convinced the lady to step aside for the executioners?"

He rolled his sad eyes around, searching to see if anyone was listening, and then turned them keenly on El Kashef. "The sheikh is just and kind and did not punish her for what she did. I convinced her to move aside, and that is all that matters," he whispered, spitting with rage more than speaking. He made it clear that El Kashef wouldn't be learning the truth from him.

"Then tell me, why did you help the outlaws escape?"

"Outlaws? We had not known them to be outlaws, but we should have listened to you carefully rather than be deceived. We were surprised to see him alive and not executed. I asked the lord why he and a Guardian from

Erum had fallen into our wadi, and he told a lie we thought was true. He spoke of a child who would bring us all to our doom and said that he and the new Prime Chief Guardian from Erum were being hunted down. When you entered our cave, he told us you were the traitor who had stolen the Prime Ring from the other Guardian who fell with him. He told us we needed to act quickly. I saw the long-haired Guardian running from you, and when you and the Guardians cornered them, he cried his tale aloud. Many of our men had believed it earlier, as they had heard it from the lord.

"I didn't believe his tale until I saw the ring on your finger. Earlier, he had told me, 'Once your men hold the Guardians for us to escape, fetch the ring and hand it to me.' But he left without it, and I kept it in my hands! They escaped before taking the ring. So when the prince came with his Guardians, I thought I had done the right thing by handing him the Prime Ring. I beg forgiveness for my mistakes tonight, but how could I have known that *you* were the Prime Chief Guardian?"

El Kashef's eyes fell upon the ring every time Haneef mentioned it.

"I am fortunate that they left without taking the ring from me." Haneef continued to fill El Kashef's face with his saliva every time he spoke. "Otherwise, I think my head would be swimming with the fishes in the waters below."

El Kashef questioned the honesty of his words and why they had helped Behas, but he too was thankful that the jinn master had not taken the ring. "Thank you for your time."

"I hope you find them," Haneef added when he saw El Kashef standing to leave. "And cut off their heads for the desolation they brought upon us! We helped them out of the water and healed their wounds. But in return, they turned our waters red with our own blood and have left us with open wounds and grieving hearts." He bit his lips with fury and regret and swung his gaze away. That made El Kashef even more suspicious, but he kept it to himself.

He promised Haneef justice would be served and peace would be restored in all the lands of Erum, as he always did to ease the pain of the victims he interrogated. Haneef thanked El Kashef before he left.

...

Above the caves, in the open fields, the prince and five of his cavalrymen were all set and ready to ride after Fad and Behas. The two horses Fad and Behas had stolen were replaced by two of the four that were kept for the

Guardians stationed in Wadi Teyq. El Kashef found his white horse and his black hound waiting for him, and he noticed that Fad's green tunic, which he had hung from the side of the horse, had been taken. Now he wasn't sure if Kashefa would be able to help him track Fad. His hound did greet him with barks of worry. "I know, Kashefa. I can see. He took his tunic. But we will find them."

"Are we all set?" cried the prince.

"My sheikh." El Kashef approached him before they climbed their horses. "May I ask before we leave, what was it that you whispered in Haneef's ears that he later convinced the woman to move?" Since Haneef had never answered him, he wanted to ask the prince in person and be certain that what Saeeda had been told by Haneef was true.

"I would not be enough of a fool to harm an innocent woman, but he was a sinner for taking away your ring. I told him to convince her to move away quietly, or it would be his head in the waters instead of the sinners."

After hearing his words, El Kashef figured it all out at once—it clicked in the back of his head, though he still hoped he was wrong.

He took off the ring and placed it close to his eyes, trying to see it in the dark. It was so dark that he almost poked his eyes with it.

"What is wrong, El Kashef?" asked the prince.

He looked at the prince with fear in his eyes. "The ring is fake, my sheikh," he said. "We need to find them fast before they use the real one wrongfully!"

Prince Leith jumped onto his horse, and so did the rest. "We shall not stop," he ordered his men. "Ride."

...

Behas had deceived them all, but not the leader of the yellow turbans in the caves! El Kashef figured it all out from what the prince had whispered to Haneef. Although the man was their leader, he had feared death and had preferred to see his men die than lose his own head! When the prince had threatened him with punishment, he had lied to the poor woman that more men would be executed instead. He wouldn't have dared go against Erum and interrupt El Kashef and the Guardians unless Behas had also threatened him with death.

To him, Behas was not a lord to be glorified but rather a lord to be feared, a devil in man's shape. El Kashef had seen Haneef give Behas something before he escaped. How could he have not figured it out before? Amid all the chaos down there, it had not occurred to him to think Behas would even want to have the Prime Ring. He thought his eyes had cheated him.

The fake ring weighed and looked the same in the dark, but if one looked closer, he would find it to be different. A Prime Chief's ring and a Chief's ring were exactly the same in size and shape, but their color and material differed. The Prime Ring was made of gold, while the other was made of bronze. The fake ring was a Chief's ring coated in cheap gold. El Kashef had scratched it and realized Behas's trick.

Now Fad and Behas had the real Prime Chief Guardian's ring, and they were far ahead of El Kashef and Leith. The Erumians had wasted enough time in Wadi Teyq. First, they had been stalled by the tribesmen, and then, when the prince had come and released El Kashef, he had waited for all his Guardians to join him in the cave before announcing the punishment he would mete out. El Kashef had then spent some time speaking with Saeeda and Haneef.

If that added up to be half the night, then Fad and Behas would have reached their destination and used the ring to their advantage already. They could deploy an army and wage war with that ring. Behas had planned it well, very well!

...

The two Guardians the prince had sent in advance waited for the rest on a slope that descended into a narrow valley filled with trees and rocky paths.

"Their tracks lead to Wadi Darbat," stated Abed, one of the Guardians. "It's difficult to ride through it with the horses. The two outlaws must be hiding in there."

"Wait here, my sheikh. We will search for them," Taleel suggested. Taleel was the pathfinding Guardian from Leith's cavalry.

Why would they hide in Wadi Darbat if they have the Prime Ring? El Kashef thought to himself.

"The wadi snakes down to the sea," said the prince. "They might be headed to Sumhuram."

El Kashef agreed.

"If they are headed to Sumhuram, this road will delay them. I doubt it, my sheikh," Taleel clarified.

"The sheikh is right," El Kashef interrupted. "There is no point in hiding, since they have the Prime Ring. They *must* be headed to Sumhuram."

"Then why did they not take the right path, the one above the wadi?" Taleel asked again.

"Behas is dying. He's looking for a healing jinni before he continues to Sumhuram." El Kashef explained what the blue healer had told him. "We shall take the quicker path. If we are lucky, we will reach the end of Wadi Darbat before them, and from there, we can stop them."

The Guardians seemed convinced, and the prince agreed with El Kashef. "We would not question your wisdom. They are hours ahead of us," Prince Leith continued, now addressing everyone else. "We will ride above to reach the end of the wadi faster. If we do not find their tracks there, we will wait at the end of Wadi Darbat."

Behas, Fad, and the Prime Ring were now an hour or more ahead of them! A lot could be done in one hour. But El Kashef deeply hoped they could stop the outlaws before anything worse could happen.

42

"Remind me why we rode through this ditch of flies," Fad said. "We could have reached Sumhuram from above."

"They won't follow us through here easily," sighed Behas. The two outlaws climbed down a small cliff and pulled the horses behind them by the reins with difficulty.

The clouds above them looked like torn blankets of black wool. The moon peeked from behind the holes as it moved or when the clouds allowed. And every time their faces were illuminated, Fad noticed the grimace on Behas's. The saher pressed his hand on his chest from time to time.

"Still in pain?" Fad asked after they had overcome another obstacle.

"Climb your horse." Behas ignored his question. "The path is flatter now. We are almost there."

Fad did so without adding another word and followed the saher. Fad had never in his life known how it felt being a wanted man, but now every Guardian of Erum was looking for him. He was first accused of murdering a Chief Guardian, then of helping an outlaw escape being caught in Wadi Teyq—the most wanted outlaw in the realm. But he had to keep going; his son was in greater danger. To a certain extent, he didn't care if Erum executed him along with Behas, so long as he could save his son, Dil, first.

Wadi Darbat was like a river, a shallow river hidden under trees and bushes at the bottom of a valley that extended south from Wadi Teyq to the edge of the Qara Mountains near the coastline of the Arabian Sea. It was extremely difficult to walk or ride a horse through these narrow woods and soaked rocky lands of stones and long grass. The whole path sloped down from mountain to sea, and after a long descent, the path would end with a small cliff or a waterfall. To reach the flatlands, the two needed to climb down a steep slope. Not to mention it was night, and the clouds of biting insects filled the wadi and stung every bit of bare living skin they could sense, leaving it irritated.

Fad and Behas managed to find their way through during that night, although they had to walk and pull the horses by the reins more than ride smoothly across. They also stopped in six caves throughout the Wadi. Some were small for two men to fit in, and some caves were large enough to fit sixty. At every cave, Fad waited for Behas as he went in, said strange words, and came out angrier, with a disappointed look. Behas was trying to summon a healing jinni, but the jinnic lords in Wadi Darbat refused all his requests. Without his Mystic Dagger, summoning an ultimate jinni was difficult. It required a great sacrifice, and Behas had nothing to offer them that night.

The pair had reached the final lengths of the wadi when Behas began to cough blood. The sound of his cough was disturbing; it was the type of sharp cough that could harm one's ears.

"Do you need to rest?" Fad asked.

"No. Move on."

The path then opened up onto low treeless plains of water and green bushes. Behas galloped and Fad followed. But they did not gallop for long.

Near a long lake at the end of Wadi Darbat, Behas fell off his horse and tossed and flipped on the bank.

"Behas!" Fad glided after him. "Are you all right?" He helped the jinn master turn to lie on his back.

"Do you have a dagger, farmer?" Behas breathed out, and a cough followed, louder than before, and wet with blood.

Fad was worried by his request. "I think there is one in the saddlebags on the horse. Why?"

Behas reached out and gave Fad the ring he had stolen from El Kashef. "Cut your hair, farmer. Shave as much as you can from your beard, and, using the ring, disguise yourself as a Prime Chief Guardian. You will need an army to help you reach Socotra; the island is well protected."

Fad took the ring, and it fit his finger. He helped Behas sit and rest his back on a rock near the water. "Go now, and be quick," the saher added, coughed, then inhaled and tried to speak again. "It is still dark. You must not wait for dawn; the island is far away. Order the Guardians in the port to prepare a battleship and sail at full speed. It's windy now, and the currents will take you there quickly." He coughed after every sentence.

"Speak slowly, old man; you are coming with me to Socotra," said Fad. In his hurry, he had probably heard almost none of what Behas had said to him. He was eager to leave, but with the saher, not without him.

"To tell you the truth, I passed through this wadi in search of an ultimate healing jinni, but I couldn't summon one. My time as a jinn master is over. There isn't much time to spare now," Behas continued. "I cannot join you in Socotra. Besides, if the Guardians see me with you, they will be suspicious. And I am dying." Behas spat as much as he could between the bloody coughs. "You need to reach the island before sunset. Go. Lead an army, find where the summoning ritual is happening, and stop it before sunset. Find your son. And kill all those who kidnapped him."

That was the plan he laid out to Fad. But Fad did know something about sea travels; he knew Socotra was far, and there was little chance of reaching it before sunset. But he kept that thought to himself.

Fad only nodded, doubtful if he had the courage to carry on and wage war. But if that was the only way to save Dil, he would do it.

"If you fail, Erum will be doomed." Behas spoke his last words: "Kill the child if you have to, if it is the only way to save everyone else." His words ended with the heaviest cough of them all, but still he managed to add, "Great evil will be summoned."

Fad didn't enjoy hearing that last advice. He wouldn't be killing his son, never. "I hope you find peace in death, old man!"

Fad left him be.

He climbed the horse and galloped away towards Sumhuram. He thought of the saher's words. *Was this his plan? The Prime Ring! How will I lead an army by sea to Socotra?* Fad doubted himself and the plan, but he had no other choice. He knew he had little time to reach the island and find his child before sunset the next day.

The rain had stopped, and the night sky was now clear. After a short ride away from Wadi Darbat, he could see the lights of Sumhuram from afar. At night, and at this distance, Sumhuram looked like a constellation of yellow stars, hung between sky, land, and water. His eyes were fixed on the Guardians' barracks on the highest cliff in the city as he rode towards it.

43

In his last moments, Behas wondered if he had succeeded in his pathetic life. To him, it seemed to be ending with nothing but failure and regret. He was dying in defeat. His lifelong enemy, the Mountain Queen, had bested him and finally taken his dagger from him.

He wept in agony; he cursed the many names he remembered from the jinnic realm, those who had made him and brought him to this stage in his life. He spoke nonsense, swearing and begging in the ancient jinnic language, hoping they would respond, but they didn't. Even if they heard him, they ignored him, knowing he now had nothing to offer in return. The pain was inevitable. Every soul must taste death, that he knew, but as it approached him, he resisted it. And adding to his misery and pain, his new young rival now appeared from behind a rock.

Laeem wore blue like most of the tribesmen did back in Wadi Teyq. Behas had almost mistaken him for one of them, until he heard his frog-like laugh.

"No one will hear you now," the younger man gloated. He held a dagger in his right hand. "Even my jinn wouldn't listen to you if you tried this time."

"I've been waiting for you. Come and end my misery." Behas was most likely addressing the angel of death, not Laeem.

"Gladly!" He approached Behas and raised his dagger, pointing the sharp tip at Behas's chest.

Behas noticed the blade was much taller and wider than the small arrow Hadaus had struck him with; this weapon wouldn't miss his heart.

Laeem leaned closer, intending to pierce Behas's chest.

Behas grabbed Laeem's wrist but was too weak to stop him. Laeem felt his hands surrender to his movement and drag with the blade, as if Behas held his wrist to pull it faster towards his heart.

"May your soul suffer in Barhoot!" said Laeem with a smile of victory.

Behas then tightened his grip, and with his other hand, which he had been hiding under his leg, he stabbed Laeem's forearm with a Guardian's dagger he'd found in the bag on the stolen horse.

Laeem dropped his own weapon and cried loudly in pain. Behas twisted the dagger and forced Laeem to his knees. Then, with all his strength, he pulled the dagger out of Laeem's flesh, turned him around, jumped over him, and held the dagger to Laeem's throat. "You ignorant fool of a saher. How dare you befriend the Noorians and work against us? How dare you betray another saher for an occultist? How ignorant your generation is!"

Laeem was now held down like a sheep about to be slaughtered. He felt the sharp dagger pressing hard against his defenseless neck. "Spare me, Behas," he croaked. "Spare me, I beg of you!"

"I am a dying old saher now; I will die sooner than you will. But I would rather take an incompetent like you with me than allow you to claim to be my successor!"

"I beg you, spare me in the name of all that is good in you! Spare me."

Behas pulled off and lowered his dagger, allowing Laeem to breath. "I must admit that you have impressed me with your skills, but sometimes, you lack the experience." Behas's voice turned calm. "You spied on me for years without me noticing or knowing your identity, and you beat me to the child born under the Serpent-Neck star. No saher has ever dared to challenge me before like you did. And I lost the child!

"That all hurt my pride, but it will make a better saher of you. You have confidence in yourself, jinn master. I admire that. Stop the sobbing; I will spare you," Behas continued, but he still held the dagger to Laeem's throat. "Killing you will only give another victory to my enemies, the Noorians. I do not blame you for your ignorance, but I shall teach you. History shall repeat itself, and I shall pass my legacy to you. You remind me of my own self when I was young."

Laeem stopped sobbing. He had never thought Behas would be admiring him. "I have always admired your supremacy," he said to Behas. He removed his blue turban and bandaged his bleeding arm. "They told me I could be like you if I helped them. I—"

"Never mind," Behas interrupted him. As a dying saher, he probably felt he should teach the younger jinn master. At least if he died, someone would carry on his vengeance against the Noorians once he had taught his successor who their real enemy was.

They had used the ambitions of a young saher against the all-powerful jinn master, Behas. And they had succeeded, but he now thought he should try to turn their own weapon against them. He pressed the dagger to his opponent's throat slightly harder and said, "I know how cunning they can be. I will spare you if you promise to avenge me. Avenge our jinnic tradition and destroy the Noorians. Destroy the occultists' guild and bring pride to all of us jinn masters."

"I will, my lord." Laeem, having a dagger to his throat, had to agree; he had no other choice but to submit to Behas. He knew well that all jinn masters hated the Noorians. "O Behas the Great!" He used the titles he knew Behas would like to hear. But as he wept and sorrowed, his regret sounded honest to Behas. "I will carry your legacy; I will take revenge."

They appeared to get along, but deep inside, they both knew well that one saher should never trust another.

Upon hearing Laeem's words, Behas did see his younger self in him. Here was a saher who was wildly ambitious but who still needed to be guided well. A saher used by their old enemies, those who claimed to be righteous!

A saher and an occultist never got along. A jinn master followed the rules of the jinnic realm, while an occultist tried to control the jinnic world and claim use of it with knowledge. Ever since first men contacted the jinnic world, these two sides had been opposed. Behas excused Laeem for not knowing it all. He had spent his whole life trying to destroy the Noorians, but what he should have done was recruit younger jinn masters like Laeem instead of working alone. Like the occultist queen had done. He wished he had done so before. It was never too late; they were not yet defeated, and his legacy did not have to end here.

They had turned a young saher against him. Laeem had tried to kill him in his sleep, then set a pack of hyenas to chase after him, leaving him vulnerable and exposed to the arrow shot from Hadaus, a high-ranked Noorian. Now he was left dying because of its poison. All the healing offered to him by Saeeda had only extended the time he would spend in pain. Even the Jinnic Lord of Healing Jinn in Wadi Darbat had ignored him tonight without his Mystic Dagger.

But now he thought it was fate, his chance to finally hand over his legacy to a younger saher. Someone healthier, and a talented jinn master skilled at blending in.

"I will tell you the secret of my power, but you must promise me to use it in the name of my legacy and kill the Noorian queen."

"The secret of your power?" Laeem held his breath to listen.

"The Mystic Dagger," said Behas. "Once when I was young like you, the Council of Jinnic Lords gifted me with that dagger, which I can use to bind any jinni to my will. But without their blessings, the dagger is useless. They blessed me with it."

Laeem knew about the dagger, but not what he heard from Behas. He had not known that a jinn master had to be chosen by a council of jinnic lords. He thought possessing it alone could work.

"To use it, young saher, you needed to be blessed with my approval. And I am willing to pass it over to you."

"Where is the Mystic Dagger?" asked Laeem impatiently, while Behas still held a dagger to his throat.

"The Noorians stole it from me again, but they won't be able to use it, not without my blessing." Behas coughed up more blood and pressed his chest, hoping to hold in his pain and keep his heart beating long enough for him to be able to pass his legacy on to Laeem.

"I will bless you with it, but I must burden you with a task to be fulfilled. You must kill the queen with it. Only then will the dagger be yours to use, and all the jinn you wish will be your slaves."

"But how do I kill her? She hides in a hidden fortress. And the Noorians, they will defend her well."

"You have a great talent for hiding and blending in," Behas reminded him. "Use your skills." His voice began to fade away behind his pain.

Laeem thought his words could be trusted. The dying saher was now desperate for revenge.

"Blend in, find the Mystic Dagger, and kill the queen with it. Only then can you use it, and only then will you become my successor!" Behas could sense the excitement in the young saher. And in his dying moments, he saw an image of his younger self. "Before I die, I will pass you my blessings. Then take my head to them and do as I have told you."

"I will, my lord!" Laeem began to trust Behas's words.

Behas sat straight, and, keeping the dagger pointed at Laeem, he pulled him to sit and face the lake. Behas then cried aloud in the ancient jinnic language with the voice he had left. He spoke sentences that Laeem understood well.

"I have called upon you, lord of this wadi, King Darbat, to be witness to our ceremony and ritual!"

Laeem raised his head, and they both witnessed the waters in the lake ripple after a howling wind blew across them.

"Witness that he, Laeem, has been accepted to be my successor," Behas carried on, "and he will carry out a task I have burdened him with. If he succeeds, he shall be granted all the powers I have been blessed with. He shall carry my Mystic Dagger after I am dead and use all its powers to be able to bind any jinn to his will."

Laeem closed his eyes as the winds blew over his cheeks. He had never expected to find such good fortune. The greatest jinn master, Behas, had not only spared him from death but was now transferring all his powers to him. All he had to do was disguise himself as an occultist and join the Noorians, gain their trust, find the Mystic Dagger, and kill the queen. He could then go on to be the successor to Behas! He hid a smile in his heart. His reign would soon begin, and all the jinn would bow before him.

"O saher, do you accept our legacy and burden?" Behas cried.

Laeem opened his eyes to see Lake Darbat once more and cried excitedly, "I do!"

"I do" became his last words, as Behas plunged the dagger in his back. The blade was wide, and Behas pressed hard, forcing Laeem's ribs to split apart. The dagger pierced his lungs, and his mouth filled with blood, which burst out of it as he exhaled in shock. Behas could bet that Laeem had never tasted blood before in his life. Nor had he tasted the betrayal of the greatest and most cunning jinn master—and nor would he again after that night!

The dagger remained in the younger man's back as he fell forward, flat on his face. His blood streamed down the banks and touched the waters of the lake. It did not matter where a soul went after death, but the sight before Behas made him think that Laeem's soul was not resting in peace at all.

"O lord of this wadi, King Darbat, accept my offering to you: the fresh blood and young soul of one who trusted me," Behas cried. "In my time of need, I used him not to help me but to give to you."

...

When Behas had passed through the wadi with Fad, he had gone through several caves, searching for King Darbat. When he had found Darbat, Behas had asked him for a very powerful healing jinni, one that could better help the saher. But the jinnic lord had his rules that could not be changed, and a jinn master always had to follow the rules of the jinnic realm. Behas had to offer the soul of a man who trusted in him in order to gain an ultimate healing jinni. At first, Behas's plan had been completely different. He had dragged Fad to the wadi with him so he could offer his blood. If he had gained Fad's trust, he would have used him to get the ultimate healing jinni he wanted. After being poisoned by the arrow, he *needed* it.

Behas had originally planned to dress up in the Guardian's tunic after killing Fad and use the Prime Chief's ring to reach Socotra with an army. His plan was never to help Fad save his son. It remained the same: to kill the child born under the Serpent-Neck star.

But his plan had had one main flaw—Fad hadn't trusted him fully! He had sensed it from the younger man's words as they passed through the wadi, which was why he had become frustrated after searching several caves. But then, from behind a distance, he had spotted a blue turban following them. At first, he had thought it was one of those men who praised him as a lord, a soul that trusted him. He had thought he was fortunate, so he had quickly changed his plans again.

He had deliberately fallen off the horse so they wouldn't ride far from the Wadi, nor far from whoever was following them. He had decided to give Fad the ring and had asked him to prepare a battleship and sail towards Socotra. He could still have killed the man, but he thought that if his new plan failed and he did die, at least Fad would be there to stop the summoning in Socotra and save Wadi Erum. After Fad left him, he had sobbed and cried, hoping his follower would come and help him, hiding a dagger under his legs and waiting for the right moment to strike.

But to his unexpected surprise, it hadn't been a tribesman who trusted him but rather someone who was planning to kill him, Laeem!

And again, his cunning tongue had saved him. He had managed to convince his killer to be his successor, gained his trust, and then offered his soul to the jinnic lord, King Darbat.

...

"Devious and sinister, O Behas! For a moment in your speech, I believed that you had decided to die and pass on your legacy. Truly a cunning jinn master, you are," cried the lake, or the lord of the wadi. The voice came from afar, and only Behas was able to hear it. "The offering is accepted—a trustful soul for an ultimate healing jinni."

"I need it now! Let it heal my current pains!"

"Your request will be granted. The jinni will take away all your pains."

The rippling stopped, the winds turned calmer, but there was no silence in the air. Behas cried louder, screamed and howled so much that even Prince Leith and his Guardians heard it from far. The prince galloped faster when he heard the screams.

Behas coughed vigorously, vomiting blood and poison out of his guts.

Saved by a healing jinni, Behas felt his heart now beat faster and stronger. He stood on his legs and felt the pain in the one that Yam had injured disappear as well. He tied a dark scarf he had gotten from Wadi Teyq across his cloak and chest, placing one end of it over the pool of Laeem's blood to soak it up.

"Time to kill!" He spoke his sinister phrase as he usually would before he ran after his prey. He hadn't expected to be far behind Fad, but now he was. It had taken him a while to convince Laeem and gain his trust. Now he ran towards Sumhuram. *Those who challenge me shall be destroyed,* he promised.

...

The prince and his men reached the lake they had heard Behas's cries coming from. They found the stabbed corpse of Laeem bleeding its last drops into the water.

El Kashef did not take much time investigating the new crime before him. It too made no sense to him. Whatever Fad and Behas were up to, he could not understand it. But he guessed that Behas must have found what he had come for and had probably been healed.

They did not stop long. Three Guardians remained behind to bury the corpse and follow the party to Sumhuram once they were done.

44

Find your child before sunset! Fad couldn't stop worrying as he rode downhill from Wadi Darbat to Sumhuram. He galloped as fast as he could, stopping only to cut his hair and shave his chin as Behas had told him to do. The Guardian's tunic disguised him well, and he planned to show the Prime Ring as proof that he was the Prime Chief Guardian of Erum. He would then sail on a battleship to Socotra, and he had to find his child before the day ended.

Sumhuram was a well-protected city. It was built on a cliff overlooking the Arabian Sea. When climbing uphill to reach its center, one needed to pass three walls, with three well-guarded gates.

As the port was usually busy with travelers from land and sea all year round, the whole city was torchlit every night. Of all the lit structures that night, Fad's gaze was fixed upon the one that stood alone, which was slightly larger and looked different from all the other structures in Sumhuram. He remembered it: the Temple of Sen.

...

Fad remembered the first time he had visited the city with his father. He had been sixteen.

They had traveled with a trader's convoy to sell their dried dates in exchange for bronze or silver.

Once they had settled inside the city, Fad went with his father to the temple to pray. The Temple of Sen was the oldest structure in the city, alongside the well and the wooden piers on Port Rori.

256

The temple had first been built two centuries before by sailors from Babylon, who had stopped in the natural creek of Port Rori in hopes of finding fresh water. Besides the well, they had built the temple to bless their travels. It was believed that they had found the well at night, which was why they had dedicated the temple to Sen, the goddess of the moon.

Fad was amazed by the carvings and miniature statues of Babylonian gods, kings and men, lions and unicorns and owls, and many other animals. The roof was decorated with colorful carvings that resembled the stars, and at the center of the galaxy, there was one giant planet that ruled them all, the moon.

Outside the temple, he saw a high wall. The wall was part of a large cubic monument. "Father, what is that?"

"My son, behind these walls lies the well, the source of fresh water in Sumhuram. It is like the well of Sada in Erum, only this one is protected and hidden!"

The whole city was protected and hidden behind the levels of thick walls, Fad thought. The many guards and walls that restricted everyone's movement were something he'd never seen back in Wadi Erum, which was reasonable, as the giants of Erum were strong and had no need to prevent enemies from attacking them.

They had left the yellow maze of walls around the temple and descended down to Port Rori. Fad had seen a rectangular pillar, high above everything else, a pillar with a green flag that signaled Aad's rule over the port. But his eye had been caught by the many vessels scattered on the water. It was the first time he had ever seen ships and sailboats.

These don't look at all like camels! He had just taken a long, tiring journey on a camel's back and remembered that he had heard many call the animals the "ships of the desert." He had wondered back then if riding a sea boat was like riding a desert ship. But when he saw them for the first time, he found them different. People were walking on board those *sea camels.*

"Father, have you ever been on a boat?" he had asked.

"I have, a few times."

"Is riding a boat as tiring as riding a camel?"

His father had laughed and said, "Trust me, Fada. It is a lot worse than riding a camel."

. . .

And now he had reached Sumhuram again, fifteen years since he began visiting it every year, but this time, he came to sail on a wooden sea camel.

"Halt!" yelled the guard at the gate. The guards in Sumhuram wore different uniforms than the guards in Wadi Erum. These ones were dressed in red. But they were all ruled by Aad, and they all recognized a Guardian of Erum.

Fad slowed his horse near the torches to reveal his white tunic. "A Guardian of Erum... Open all gates at once!" cried the gate guard to his comrades at the other two gates higher up the slope. This Guardian, he knew, could be a Guardian messenger, and he needed to be quick.

Fad galloped through the narrow streets, focused and determined to execute the plan Behas had devised for him. He reached the highest point in Sumhuram as he remembered it: the barracks. The soldiers who were stationed there served Erum but never join in any war outside of Sumhuram. Their duty was only to protect the creeks of Port Rori. But that night, Fad intended to use the Prime Ring to fill a battleship and make an attack on Socotra.

His horse was taken away to the stables, and he was guided to the commander's room, which overlooked the sea and the port.

Two young guards were there to greet Fad. "Welcome, Guardian of Erum! What urgent matter has brought you at this hour of night?" They were surprised when he showed them the ring. Not only had the Prime Chief Guardian appeared in their barracks, but he had come alone.

After cutting his long hair and shaving his chin, Fad felt like a new person, and with the ring he wore, he felt more powerful and recognized. "We have no time to waste." Even his voice became deeper as he commanded them. "Prepare a battleship and fill it with as many men as it can carry. War is upon us; we must sail at once to Socotra."

The two guards exchanged worried looks. The one who sat behind the commander's table spoke after a thoughtful stare at the hourglass on the table. "At this time, Prime Chief? Most of the men are asleep, and it will take an hour at least to fill a ship with food and water and men. We won't be able to sail at once. Not before dawn, at least!"

Dawn! I need to be there before sunset tomorrow to find Dil, thought Fad. He was still the highest authority in the room, and he didn't want to reveal his plans. He held back a moment, thinking about what he should say or do. Fad blushed in panic. He managed to hide it, but he did feel a drop of sweat sliding down his neck. He had no other plan.

"Then we'd better start preparing now!" Fad ordered again.

The guard behind the table took another glance at the hourglass and out the window. It was still dark and cloudy, with no sign of dawn. He seemed suspicious of Fad, who had appeared out of nowhere. "But I have no authority to do so. Only the commander, Assar, can place such orders. And he is sleeping at this hour!"

Fad remained silent and nervous. He looked between the two young guards, not knowing what to say or do. "Can we...wake the commander up?"

The guard behind the commander's table hummed and eyed his comrade. He did not want to obey a hesitant Prime Chief Guardian who seemed undecided with his own demands. But his comrade messed up his plan.

"Well, you *are* the Prime Chief Guardian of Erum. Your authority exceeds that of our commander. Does it not?" the second guard asked the first, who now began to tap on the table nervously.

"We..." He couldn't get out of the trouble. His friend had said more than he needed to. "We *can* execute your commands."

After a long pause for thought, Fad spoke with a deep voice again. "Well, wake everyone up, then, and prepare the ships with haste. We need to reach Socotra before sunset tomorrow." Fad stared at the first guard, who appeared to be Assar's deputy commander, and waited for a response.

"Right away," said the deputy. He then faced the other guard in the room and said, "Blow the horns and wake the guards. We are now at war. And send word down to the ports to prepare the ship."

A few moments after the horns were blown, a man with brown hair entered the room. It was Assar. He was fully dressed and prepared for battle. The two guards in the room stood up at once, but he ignored everyone and walked towards the windows to look over the sea. He stopped to face Fad once he noticed him and jumped in shock after seeing the golden ring of the Prime Chief Guardian of Erum.

"Prime Chief," he exclaimed. "What happened? Are we under attack?" He first feared that they had been attacked or were about to be attacked. He knew that when Erum was at war, Sumhuram would be targeted by those who would want to take advantage of the absence of Erum's men. But he fell into the chair after he learned that it was they who were preparing for an attack. He opposed the idea.

"Prime Chief," he tried to explain, "Erum is now at war in the east; we can't leave the creeks and open war with Socotra. In times of war, soldiers are to move only by orders from the Prime Sheikh. Without a sealed letter, I cannot follow your orders. My soldiers must remain stationed in defense of Sumhuram." Not only did he speak the truth, he too felt suspicious of Fad.

Fad couldn't argue with him. Assar knew what was right and wrong, and Fad felt he should ask for directions instead. He had to explain his reasons now. "Well, give me whatever men you can spare to help me in my quest."

"Quest?" Assar became more suspicious. "I thought we were preparing for war?"

Fad had to improvise, and the situation began to slip away from him. He had thought that with the disguise and the ring it would be easier, but it was turning out to be more difficult. "Whichever. I was sent here by the sheikhs and asked to bring a…a wanted man from Socotra. I need to find him before sunset tomorrow." Fad began to sweat even more as he bluffed about his quest. He couldn't simply tell them that he was looking for his child.

The commander still grimaced. He did not want to move his ships or any of his men for whatever mission the Prime Chief Guardian had come for. Every word the Prime Chief said made him more suspicious, but he wouldn't dare question him or the shiny ring in his finger. But the word "sunset" caught his attention. "Sunset? It will be impossible to prepare a battleship and sail across the Arabian Sea to reach Socotra in that little time! Unless…" Assar then turned to face his deputy. "Tamm," he said. "Check the wall. How many ships are leaving for Socotra soon?"

The young guard ran to a wooden wall filled with symbols, names, numbers, and more. The board contained all the information about any ship that entered the port, where it came from, when, who was on it, when it would be heading out, and to where.

"Well, Commander, as I read here," he said, turning his head between the many marks on the board and the hourglasses on the table, "there is one heading to Socotra very soon. A small *abra* from the Khuriya-Muriya Islands. It leaves Port Rori as soon as…now, Commander!"

"Stop that abra!" cried Assar to his deputy and looked out the opening to find it. "There, it still is roped!"

Eager to get rid of the new and suspicious-looking Prime Chief Guardian of Erum before he issued other too-difficult-to-follow orders, he turned to face Fad and said, "You'll need your horse in Socotra; take it with you. And since you're heading to enemy territory, I would advise you to go there in disguise and alone. You will also need to hide the ring and get rid of your tunic, or else you won't be welcomed in Socotra—as you well know, Prime Chief! The boat is leaving. It is small, and it will reach the island before sunset. But you'd better hurry and board it rather than delay it further."

Fad thanked them and rushed down from the highest point in Sumhuram to the water. A guard helped him with the horse. The sun had not yet risen, and many soldiers cursed Fad and the horns for waking them up and sending them back to sleep just before their morning shifts began.

"We cannot take the horse," protested the captain of the sailboat. "We have reduced weight as much as we could to account for the weather; a storm might face us at sea."

And he was right, for it was August, the winds were strong, and the thick clouds one could see below the full moon were moving fast. The sailboat already carried two dozen men onboard—sailors, tradesmen, and others, along with their goods. There were also animals of all shapes and sizes. The sailboat belonged to a transporter, or *abra* in Arabic: a sailor who took a small fee to transport people around to two or three ports. This one traveled between Sumhuram, the Khuriya-Muriya Islands, and Socotra Island. All these three ports were near to one another.

"We'll take you alone, Guardian, and for no fare. You can rent a horse on the island."

"We'll keep it safe for you in the stables," said the guard. "Take what you need from your bags."

Fad took the dagger, and, remembering Assar's words, he pulled out his green tunic as well, then climbed hastily into the sailboat.

His journey had gone beyond what he had imagined, but he was willing to go on—he needed to. His son could still be alive, and he would do whatever it took to find him. He had abandoned Behas's plan, it was true, but he eased his thoughts by convincing himself that he didn't need an army to save his child. He wouldn't want to see more men die because of the boy.

He thought only that Bessel had died because of him in Wadi Dawkah. He had not witnessed all the other calamities that followed him everywhere he passed. The horrible death of Qamaria and her father in Qairon Heriti, Arkin in Jibjat, the fourteen men who had been executed in Wadi Teyq— they all had died helping him. And if he had known about them, he would have felt sorry as well for the men he now rode with to cross the Arabian

Sea. Poor sailors. If they had also known, they would not have carried him along.

...

"How long will it take to reach Socotra?" he asked the captain.

"Twelve hours if we catch the right winds. The full moon will pull us faster as well. If we are on time, we'll reach Socotra in the afternoon."

"Great," he said. "May I find a place to rest? I did not sleep last night."

"Yes, Prime Chief. Follow me."

The boat captain took him to the lower deck, where there was an open space. Men and their goods rested on either side. "You can rest here."

Not all the men were sleeping; most of them had just boarded the vessel as well and were settling in their places. Two men lay near Fad and fell into a deep sleep. They were both covered by their gray cloaks. *Noorians!* Fad thought. Their cloaks looked similar to the one he had seen on Arkin, but the two sleeping beside him were slimmer than the old man. Neither could have been him.

He didn't care much about them now. His identity was all different as well, and that reminded him. He changed into his dark green tunic and folded Bessel's spare uniform into a pillow on which to lay his head.

While he was lying there, thinking of his son, Dil, and how he could actually save him alone and without an army to fight with, another man came to sit near him. This man looked younger than Fad and had long dark hair which reminded Fad of his own, which he'd had to cut. The newcomer wore light red. He began to converse with Fad by introducing himself and kept him awake for some time. Later, the other extraordinary and unfortunate events they encountered would keep Fad sleepless, as well, for almost the whole journey!

45

The poison dart should have kept Hadaus unconscious until morning or later, but the frankincense in his blood worked its spell and killed the poison. He awoke a few hours later that night.

Try sleep-poisoning an alchemist occultist, especially one as experienced as Hadaus, and you surely won't succeed. But the traitors might have thought of that, which might have been why they tied his hands to his back, tied his legs, gagged his mouth with cloth, and locked the thick-walled safe from the outside. Hadaus woke up drowsy from the poison, and as soon as he remembered, his eyes popped out in panic. He tried screaming, but it was no use. With the complete absence of light, it was difficult to tell where he was. But given his last memory, he had to assume he was still in the treasury.

Rolling around, trying to stand and touching objects around his feet, he managed to determine his position and raised his body to lean against the thick door. After several hopeless kicks and bangs on it, he lowered his mouth to the door handle, using it to rip off the gag carefully, without injuring himself. Success. Then, inhaling as much as his lungs would allow, he pressed his face to the space under the door and shouted as loudly as he could.

"Help! Help!" he yelled without pause, waiting for any response. There were no night guards or security in the Gray Palace; they had never needed them. But he continued to yell in the hope his voice could reach the sleeping quarters. Anyone might hear him call and come to help.

After several cries, he felt he needed a new plan. *I have to free my hands and feet.*

He crawled on his back to reach the chests, in search of a sharp object, but as he recalled, there weren't anything but chests of gold, silver, and bronze. *I hope they left my dagger.* He tried to open the large chest where he had left it, but all he felt with his hands were gold, jewels, and silk fabrics.

Sharp, sharp, sharp! He tried to search his memory to remember what other options there were in the treasury. *The chests could break.* He thought if he could drop one of the smaller wooden chests, which were stacked high above the larger crates, the wood might break into sharp pieces he could use to cut the rope. It was hard to move or climb in utter darkness, using bound hands and legs and a blurry memory of where everything was placed.

After moving with great care to stand over the larger chests, he leaned over and pushed all the smaller chests at the top with his shoulders. He heard a bang from the flat rock below, but there was no cracking noise. He feared the chests had not broken. They were strong, and the fall was short. Before climbing down to check, he pushed another column of chests, and from the crashing sounds of wood on rock and the splashing echoes of coins bouncing and tinkling below, he knew some chests must have cracked open. Hadaus slid down in search of broken wood.

He tossed his back from one chest to another, searching for any broken edges until he felt one suitably sharp enough.

As he leaned backwards to cut the rope, he noticed the blue light from below the door turn darker. Someone stood on the other side and had probably pressed his ears to it to hear what was going on inside. The crashing and banging of chests must have woken a Noorian nearby.

A strange feeling of fear traced over his skin at the sight of the silent and motionless shadow. He looked under the door again to see better, but the hole wasn't large enough to reveal anything but hairline shadows.

Are the traitors still here? But they wouldn't kill him; they had had the chance to do so and had not.

"Who's there? Open the door," he called.

"Who are you?" the voice outside cried, and Hadaus could tell it came from one of the young Noorians.

"It's me, Hadaus. Open the door now!"

The young student probably panicked at hearing his name—a high-ranked Noorian, the advisor to the queen.

"It's locked, sir," he said in a quavering voice after trying with a push and a pull on the bronze lock.

Hadaus sighed. "I know! Break the lock and open it." He tried his best to control his temper at the naive observation.

Hadaus could hear him trying to pull it out using his hands. "Master, I... I can't find the keys!"

"Apprentice! I said break it."

"Sure, master, wait here. I'll need to get a hammer."

I'll wait indeed! Hadaus mocked himself.

The lock required five strikes from the stone hammer. The first two hits were soft and slow to prevent loud noises. But after being scolded by Hadaus, the apprentice hit harder and broke the lock. More Noorians might have woken up from the noise.

When the door first opened, Hadaus couldn't see the face of his rescuer clearly.

Shocked to find Hadaus tied and locked up, the young Noorian leaned down to help him up at once. "Master Hadaus! What happened to you?"

Hadaus ignored his question, managing to stand on his feet and lean in the doorway. "Do you have a blade to cut the ropes?"

"No, master, but my room is not far."

"Run, then."

The apprentice returned swiftly, and Hadaus turned to let him cut the ropes and be done. He was finally free.

"The new apprentice, with the red hair, where is he from?"

"You mean Saffron?" replied the apprentice. "He's from Socotra. Do you want me to wake him for you?"

Hadaus rubbed his curly white beard and paused, thinking.

"Has he done this to you?"

"Why would you assume such a thing, apprentice?" Hadaus asked.

"No specific reason, but I do have my suspicions about him."

"What suspicions?"

"I do see him mingling outside of class times with our chemistry teacher, Master Fattir, a lot. They've been acting strange lately."

"Master Fattir!" *It must have been him who darted me,* thought Hadaus. *But why would the two be after the Mystic Dagger?*

"What else do you know about him? Have you been talking to him? Did he ever say he planned to go anywhere?"

"He never spoke when we had lunch together, and he never had his lunch with us when his friend from another guild came to visit."

"Which friend?"

"An occultist from Socotra visited the Gray Palace last week and stayed for few days. I heard he came from a guild named the Noorians of the Dragon. I never got to know his name, but the two did spend a lot of time together. Maybe since they are both from Socotra."

El Sarabi! Hadaus remembered. *El Sarabi did visit the palace few days ago, and he left the Gray Palace on the same night that…* Hadaus opened his eyes wide in shock. *It must have been him who stole the child born under the Serpent-Neck star.*

Hadaus knew El Sarabi as an old servant like him in the Gray Palace. El Sarabi had once told Hadaus about an enchanted instrument that could be used to create an illusion and hide one in plain sight. He had left the Noorians to go in search of it; Hadaus thought now that he must have found it and used it to kidnap the same child Arkin was after. El Sarabi and Arkin must both have been informed about the child by Laeem. Hadaus bit his lips in regret. He should never have trusted Laeem, the traitorous saher. Arkin had always wanted to save the child, but El Sarabi's motives were the complete opposite, and Hadaus had figured that out too late. El Sarabi was from Socotra, an envious enemy of Erum.

El Sarabi, Fattir, and his young student, Saffron, now had the child, along with the most powerful enchanted instrument used to summon jinn, the Mystic Dagger! And they had to be taking both to Socotra. *The traitors,* thought Hadaus. *I will make them regret this.*

"I knew they were up to something," the young apprentice told Hadaus, "and I was right. They were thieves!"

Hadaus ignored the young Noorian's accusations. "Guard this room till dawn. Then wake Harma and ask her to check if anything has been stolen."

"Yes, master!"

He took the dagger from the apprentice. "This is a fine blade; I shall borrow it. And if I learn that you took anything from the treasury…"

"No, master, I won't!"

"Indeed." Hadaus wanted him to keep it a secret, but it was too late. Soon, everyone, including the queen herself, would know of his failure. He had to travel fast and find the Mystic Dagger before it was all too late for him.

He walked quickly to his room. The first thing he did was pick a white frankincense stone and break it in his jaws. He hoped he could find the traitors before the queen woke up and learned that the Mystic Dagger had been stolen! *They will regret not killing me!* His thoughts fueled him with rage, the same rage that had driven him after he had lost his beloved Meleeka as a result of Arkin's ruthless plans.

He picked up his Noorian flute, sheathed the dagger he had borrowed, and grabbed his pouch of medicines. He then opened a secret box he kept behind a broken stone in the wall. From it, he took two finger-sized bottles— the same kind as the one Laeem had used to summon the wild hyenas. In fact, it was Hadaus who had given that one to him a long time before.

He left the Gray Palace at once and galloped at full speed towards the sea. The night was still dark and gloomy under the thick black clouds. There was only one port to depart from if you were heading to Socotra, and Hadaus knew it well: Port Rori.

46

"The sun will soon be rising; you shouldn't sleep now!"

Fad had only just rested his head when he sensed someone had sat near him. He opened his eyes slightly to see the talking intruder, noticing the man's long dark hair first.

"We should pray. I am sorry if I have disturbed you. My name is Shaf'e, son of Shafi. What is yours?"

"Fada."

Shaf'e hummed in thought. "Fada, as in emptiness, or the grand vicinity in the sky above and the whole universe. It's either everything or nothing!" he reflected with a friendly laugh. "Your name, like mine, has many influential meanings. I have suffered many times before because of my name, but I have found my ways to live with it."

His broad, friendly smile made Fad curious. He had preferred a rest at first, but now he thought he might learn something about his own name. "What do you mean?" He lifted his head and sat straight.

"My name, as you know, has two meanings as well. The first meaning is 'a double.' I have always met misfortune when traveling alone or with a group where I make an odd number. But that I solved by always traveling with a group that would total up to be an even number! Before climbing on this boat, I asked the captain how many were on board. He told me they were twenty-three, and with me, we all became a group of twenty-four."

Fad wondered if he had been counted before or after Shaf'e joined. As the last man to join the boat, he thought he was probably the twenty-fifth person! He kept that thought to himself and hoped he was wrong.

"Another burden my name carries is 'mediation.'" He smiled again; a shaf'e, as Fad knew, was a mediator.

"But that is a good thing, is it not?" said Fad.

"It is a good thing, but only if you use the name in the right place and in the right way," he said. "For I have once upon a time misused its meaning, and I was punished for it."

Fad nodded in curiosity, a signal to the speaker to carry on.

"Hear me, then, for I come from the Khuriya-Muriya Islands. And ever since I was a child, I have been a mediator, helping resolve the minor conflicts among my brothers and people around me. I grew in fame among all the seven tribes of the Khuriya-Muriya Islands, and people from all over came to me for help with their conflicts. See, I was born under the Libra constellation, which is a gift that my name's meaning completes, as it made me wiser with my judgments.

"A few years ago, I was called by our beloved queen, Muriya," Shaf'e continued. "Her eldest princess, Zenobia, had just returned after a long time, having eloped with her lover, who was a Greek tradesman. She begged her mother to accept her back into the castle after she had left against her father's will.

"The queen called upon me for help after King Khuriya told her that he was planning to imprison the princess for life. 'Shaf'e, son of Shafi, the mediator of the Khuriya-Muriya Islands,' said our queen, 'help me resolve the conflict in my family, and you shall be rewarded. Fail me, and you shall be punished.'"

Fad raised his chin in anticipation.

"The sun will now be rising. Do you want to join me above to pray and hear the rest of my tale?"

Fad wished to stay and sleep, but he felt he should pray. He also wanted to hear the rest of the story.

There were a few men on the upper decks. The sun could not be seen behind all the black thick clouds, but its shadowy glare could be noticed behind the eastern horizon.

The southern winds blew strongly, and the sails were fully open; the winds came from the gap between Samhan Mountain and the Qara Mountains, directing the boat south to its destination, Socotra. The winds did lift the boat slightly above the waves from time to time, but its weight kept it steady. Fad felt the speed of the winds, and they brushed his shortened hair pleasantly. He was pleased with the strong winds blowing them towards his child.

He and Shaf'e stood on the starboard side and prayed that their journey would be safe.

Our one and only, Somood, Fad prayed, *I turn to you in my time of need as I head towards the unknown. My child is unsafe, and I ask you to keep him safe. I ask for your guidance: Show me the way, lead me to Dil, and help me keep him safe from my enemy.*

"Behind the Samhan Mountains are our beloved seven islands, the Khuriya-Muriya Islands," Shaf'e said. "I should now repeat to you the rest of the tale, and how I learned my lesson and used my name better."

Fad barely heard him with all the wind. "Do tell." He raised his voice and got closer, hoping Shaf'e would raise his voice as well. And he did.

"I spoke first with the king. 'My king. Do not punish your daughter, for her actions were driven by love,' I said. 'She is back now, and it proves that her love for you is greater than her love for any other.'

"'How was she able to go against my will? If I forgive her, her wrongdoing will encourage her younger sisters,' the king said, expressing his worries. 'If she was blinded by an evil love jinni, I will forgive her, but only if she was. If she was not, I will imprison her for the rest of her life.'

"I then met with Princess Zenobia and told her what her father thought of her. She said, 'I am not blinded by any jinni. I loved the man and I chose to marry him; I have no regret about what I have done. If my father wishes to punish me, I shall accept his punishment.' She did not seem to be blinded by any jinn. But if her father punished her, our queen would punish me as well. Both the father and his daughter were stubborn.

"After long thought, I went to the king and I suggested that he only punish her for a period equal to that of her absence, not her whole lifetime. He agreed and ordered that she was to be imprisoned for two years.

"When I told the queen, she did not like what I had suggested to the king. She then ordered that I was to be lashed seven times a day for seven days! On the eighth day, the queen ordered that I be brought before her. And she said again, 'Help me resolve the conflict in my family, and you shall be rewarded. Fail me, and you shall be punished.'

"I went back to the king, and I told him what the princess had told me. 'She said she is willing to accept my punishment?' He was surprised. 'She did, my king. She will no longer oppose you or act against your will,' I explained. And to my surprise, he accepted her apology, and they all lived in peace. The conflict in our royal family was resolved."

"But I do not understand why you were punished the first time," Fad wondered aloud. "You were only a mediator! Why should you be punished when the king was the one who made the decision?"

"All true. But I learned so only after my punishment. For when I acted to my benefit and made a decision for my king, I acted as an arbitrator, not as a mediator. I should have recommended a decision and offered options for him to forgive her, not chosen a way for my king to punish his daughter. And ever since, that has been how I use my name. I am Shaf'e the mediator, not the arbitrator. The names our parents choose for us define our fates, and we are destined to live our lives as best befits what our names mean. Otherwise, we might end up harming ourselves and others around us. That is why, as I've said, I never travel with a group that has an odd number of people."

Fad gave a worried smile and thought to himself, *I hope I am not the odd one out!*

The sails began to stretch further, and the boat flew halfway over every wave, wobbling slightly when it landed again. "We'd better go back down to lower decks before we fall into the water," said Shaf'e. "The waves seem merciless today."

A lightning bolt struck far away, but the roar of thunder was right above them. Before they descended to the lower deck, Fad felt it begin to slightly rain, and he began to worry.

The two wobbled their way to their resting places. "Your neighbors are gone, the Noorians."

Fad noticed it as well. He searched around for gray cloaks, but there was no sign of them. Except for the sailors, everyone else on board the sailboat was now sheltered below.

"The waves and the sound of thunder might have awoken them," said Fad.

"True," Shaf'e agreed.

They found it difficult to settle in their places. Fad became more tired than before and laid his head down. He felt seasick and wanted to sleep, but he couldn't. *My father was right,* he thought. *This is a lot worse than a camel ride.*

He remembered when he was fifteen and Nada had expressed to him her dream to ride on the sea. They had spent a whole day together, wandering around through the markets in the lower parts of Wadi Erum.

"The sun is about to set, Nada," he had told her, concerned. "We have to go back before our fathers return."

"They won't be back until nighttime," Nada had said. "Let's pass by the temple above and watch the sunset."

And before he could stop her, she had already walked towards the path that led to the temple above. He had followed her with worry in his heart.

After they watched the sunset, they had walked back to her parents' house, where they found their fathers had already arrived. And Badde had not hesitated to scold his daughter. All the neighbors heard him.

Turab had smacked Fad hard on the shoulder, but his scolding was a whisper compared to Badde's. "I told you not to leave the house, Fad. You have put the poor girl in big trouble with her father." Turab was more concerned about Nada than his son.

Fad had worried about her as well and had not enjoyed the scene before him. He had regretted letting her stay out until after sunset. He had stared at her face worriedly as she took all the barking from her angry father. But once her father had turned and left her, she had turned her eyes to Fad and winked, giving him a sly smile. Fad's regrets had all vanished when he'd seen her smiling.

Now, remembering her smile, he bit his lips in regret and heartbreak. He wished he could find their son soon and bring him back to Nada and see her smile again. He knew he had to go through all possible dangers for them.

He had difficulties managing to stay in his place as the strong winds took their sailboat up and down, lifting it up to glide in the air and then smash hard on the water. Fad could not rest in it at all. He sat up, opening his eyes, and found the Noorians had not yet returned. Shaf'e was sewing palm leaves to create a small sack. It reminded him of his own palms, which had been left without water for almost four days now; he hoped the rains had reached Erum as well. He did worry, but his farm was now the least of all his concerns.

"Is this all normal?" he asked.

"No," said Shaf'e. "The waters are usually less disturbed. But let us not forget, this is a flood year; once in every decade, the weather is disturbed and unnatural."

Fad could see his smiling face shift up and down with the waves, but neither the man's smile nor his words worked to reduce his worry.

"You seem less worried," said Fad. "I see you are making a basket; do you have a farm of palms back in the Khuriya-Muriya Islands?"

"Oh no," said Shaf'e. "This I received as a gift for helping as a mediator in Sumhuram. Two poor farmers had a long disagreement. I got this as a gift from them, and I thought it would give me something useful to do on the journey." He eyed Fad's Guardian's tunic, which he had used as a pillow, and his weapon. "I see a Guardian's tunic. I have never seen any heading to Socotra in the past years. What business is bringing you to Socotra?"

Fad eyed his tunic as well. He remembered it was Bessel's and wanted to say, "It isn't mine; I'm just a farmer," but he preferred to avoid any unwelcome questions. "I am visiting a friend," he said.

Shaf'e smiled and told Fad why he was traveling to Socotra himself. "I heard that a great healer lives on this island. My mother is sick, and I came here in hopes that I could find the healer and get medicines to help my mother."

At his words, the sailboat flew high above the water. Fad felt his heart had leaped out of his chest and fallen down with the boat, which smashed back down onto the waves, harder this time than ever before. Everyone tumbled over, crates fell and broke to pieces, the animals cried, and Fad saw every face filled with fear. *How far is Socotra?* he wondered. Noon was far off, for they had just repeated the morning prayers on the upper decks. From one of those decks, a sailor now called out a name—a name Fad had heard only in fairy tales!

"Kattaf-Raffay!" *Sail-Reaper.*

"Hold the sails!" cried another. "Hold the sails and tie the ropes!" Everyone on the lower decks heard and raised their heads in anticipation and terror.

"He claimed the sails! It's too late," the first sailor yelled in reply. "He's too strong!"

Fad felt the boat rise high and at full speed. It hovered above the waves and stood a second in mid-air before it glided down fast and smacked the water hard. A loud, howling cry drowned out all other noise. Fad felt they were in the stomach of a flying beast!

"Hold on!" The sailors above were still resisting the abnormal power of Kattaf-Raffay, a mythical Arabian beast of the sea that came in the form of a strong wind which could rip the sails off boats.

The boat hung in the air a second time, then fell freely down into the waters again. This time, the impact broke parts of the hull, and seawater splashed in. They all heard one of the sailors falling off the boat and crying for help, but the cries were getting farther away and were fading quickly. With all the chaos Fad had witnessed below deck, he could sense the upper decks were more dangerous.

The hatch above opened, and all the sailors and their captain descended. They went in search of their spare wood and tools to fix the leaks.

The beast, Kattaf-Raffay, continued to lift the boat up and drop it down, smashing it hard on the water. The loud wind sounded as if a giant man were howling with rage outside.

"Why are you all below? Have you dropped the sails? Who's guiding the boat?" Fad turned his head towards the person asking all the questions. It was one of the two Noorians who had disappeared from his side. They had probably hidden behind some of the crates.

"Kattaf-Raffay has the sail now!" the captain replied. "He is too strong; he will reap it and claim it for himself." With difficulty, he and his men continued working on the leaks, and some passengers helped them.

"We can't give up the sail," cried the red-haired younger Noorian. "We'll never reach Socotra if we lose the sail."

At these words, Fad raised his eyebrows in worry.

"I lost a sailor," cried the captain. Everyone grieved and feared they might meet with the same fate. "I would rather we reach Socotra safely and late than drown us all. The beast will take the sail, and then we can go back to Port Rori to find another."

"Fine! Allow us to go up and hold the sails," said the older Noorian.

"It's too strong; you won't be able to overcome the beast."

"I will help them," Fad put in. He tried to stand on his feet, but he found it difficult to hold still like the sailors did. They made it look easy.

"We'll need more men." Shaf'e stood to join them. "Are any of you willing to join us?"

Four other men stood up. The captain ordered his sailors to stay down and patch the leaks, with the help of those who stayed below. He then led the brave men and climbed with them to the top.

Fad didn't know what to expect or what he would be facing up there. They climbed above to fight Kattaf-Raffay all by themselves: a farmer, a mediator, two occultists, four tradesmen, and the captain of the boat.

The hatch let them out at the front of the upper deck. Fad stared a long time at the shape of the sail. It wasn't the blank white sheet he had seen before; this time it was fully stretched out, with the shadow of a giant's face behind it. It was as if the head of the wind were stuck in the sail and pushing it hard and fast, carrying the boat above the water.

The giant face behind the sail opened its mouth, and a loud howl blew in their ears. There were two end ropes below the sail, and one was flying loose. "Quick," cried the captain, "hold the rope!"

"Hold on," Shaf'e warned them every time the boat reached the tip of the crest.

The men pulled the rope as tight as they could. They worked well together. Fad stood nearest to the sail, and with every loud howl, a strong pull on the sail followed. Both the Noorians and Shaf'e lost their grip and almost fell off, but Fad and the others didn't. After another smash on the water, everyone tripped away from the rope, but they managed to hold on to the wood. Fad, however, was still holding on to the rope.

"Let it go, Guardian!" cried the captain, but it was too late.

The rope pulled Fad high in the air, and while the boat was gliding down, he saw the others far below. They looked like tiny ants. His mind blanked as he fell freely towards them, but luckily, he fell while the boat was going down and he reached the wood before the boat smashed back into the water. He stood up again and jumped to his feet to reach the other men.

The Noorians held the rope again and pulled it hard. "Go away, you wicked beast!" they cried.

Shaf'e and Fad joined them and pulled the rope harder. "Go away!" Shaf'e cried as well. The rest of the men helped, and they pulled and pulled, trying hard to keep the boat steady and straight against the waves.

Kattaf-Raffay was famous for stealing sails in the midst of the open seas. If they lowered the sail to hide it, the waves might topple the boat and flip it upside down. From the words of the captain, it sounded as if he had only one sail. If he lost it, they would have to go back to get another one.

"These sails are not yours to take!" cried the young occultist in an effort to convince the beast to leave them be. But Kattaf-Raffay only replied with a howl and a stronger blow.

"Leave these poor sailors! You have killed one already, and so you will be punished by Sen," cried the elder occultist. This time, the howl sounded more afraid than furious. "Go away," he repeated, "or Sen will punish you for your sins. Leave the poor sailors be! Leave them or I shall call Sen upon you."

The gray clouds still covered the whole sky above them, but the winds began to soften and the waves shivered away. The occultists continued to threaten the beast. "Go away! Go away!"

As soon as the howling disappeared and the winds became calmer, the sailors appeared from the bronze hatch. They were extremely delighted to see their captain and the travelers had succeeded in driving the beast away and were safe. Everyone on the boat was happy and thankful.

Fad was also relieved to learn that they had gained speed and would reach Socotra sooner. After a long chase from Wadi Teyq to Sumhuram through Wadi Darbat, and being tired from little sleep, Fad couldn't tell when the last time he had slept, eaten, or drunk had been. He felt his head spinning, and his eyes were blurring. Unconsciously, he sat on the wet wood and tried to force his eyes to stay open, but they wouldn't. He lay back, trying to breathe, and reached an arm up to press on his head.

"Guardian! Are you okay?" asked the captain.

"He fell from a height. Kattaf-Raffay beat him hard," said Shaf'e. "He needs a rest."

"Bring the healer up!" The captain waved to his men. "Tell him to bring all his remedies. Tell him it's the Prime Chief Guardian from Erum."

...

"Here, eat some dates," offered the healer after he noticed Fad clutching his stomach hard. Everyone called him "the healer"; most of them had never even known or wouldn't remember his real name, and he often called himself that as well.

Fad held one and took a long look at it before biting. As a date producer himself, he would investigate the qualities of the fruit he knew well. The shape and taste were familiar to him. After the third piece, he became aware that the dates the healer offered were from his own farm!

"Where did you get such fine dates?" asked Fad with a proud smile.

"Sumhuram," said the healer. "They said they came from the finest and richest farms from Wadi Erum."

"Did they say so?"

The healer smiled. "That is what they told me. Where do you feel injured?" he asked Fad.

"My head and my stomach," Fad replied. "It might be that I haven't eaten much for the last two days, or that I haven't had much sleep."

"The sailors claim you fell hard on your back."

"Nothing I can't bear."

"Good," the healer said with a sigh. "It must be what you have said, then. Drink this."

Fad grimaced from the bitterness but forced himself to finish his second sip. "What is this thing?"

The healer tucked the bottle away and gave Fad more dates to sweeten the taste on his tongue. "This *thing* will help your stomach crave less food, and it will also reduce your headaches."

"I have never heard of such a remedy!"

"These are boiled beans from Africa. I call them Qahwa beans."

"Qahwa as in 'loss of appetite'?"

Qahwa is the original word for coffee, which means "loss of appetite" in Arabic.

"Exactly," the healer replied. Right after he said it, the boat smashed against a wave, and Fad threw up all the cold coffee he'd been offered into the sea.

"Are you all right?"

"I've certainly lost my appetite now!"

The healer laughed loudly and offered him more dates, but Fad asked for water instead.

"You're probably just seasick." Then he leaned in and whispered, "You fought the winds instead of the naive sailors! Who believes strong winds are a beast wanting to steal their sails?"

"You mean Kattaf-Raffay?"

"Whatever they called it."

"But I saw the beast. We all did!" Fad was confident that he had seen the face of Kattaf-Raffay. He disagreed with the healer. To him, the beast was no longer a fairy tale.

"It was brave of you all, controlling the boat during the strong winds. But I wouldn't be surprised; a Prime Chief Guardian from Erum should be an example of bravery in such times."

Fad rolled his eyes in worry, and the healer noticed it.

"Oh, do not worry, 'Prime Chief.' We know you're trying to hide your identity from Socotra. We will not expose you to our guards."

"Are you from Socotra?" asked Fad.

"Yes, but my mother is Erumian."

"Then—" Fad hesitated for a moment at first, but he knew he had no other chance. He would need help and guidance when they reached Socotra, and he decided to trust this healer who was half Erumian. "I'll need your help."

47

The day before, when Nada had fallen ill, Yam, Faseela, the young guard, Murr, and the unconscious Nada were all led by the pathfinder, Saad, safely back to Jibjat village. Faseela had told them she knew a healer who could help Nada.

When they arrived, they left the horses and all but one of the mules in an outer stable, while Murr and Saad stayed with the animals. Yam carried the ladies' belongings and bags. He noticed the rababa and figured that El Kashef had either left it there or forgotten to take it. Yam too left it there with his own bags and followed Faseela towards the healer she knew. Nada was carried on one of the mules, as the howdah wouldn't fit in the narrow streets.

Jibjat was surrounded by a few scattered farms. The outer edge had two or three barns, and there were no more than ten huts in the center of the village. The largest house had a semi-walled field behind it, on which a *zar* ceremony was being prepared.

As they passed, several old men and women stared at their unfamiliar faces. Yam had heard the term "zar healings" before and had even attended one, but he had never understood what they really were. Now, he learned more about them from Faseela.

A zar was a jinni that had possessed a human. The zar ritual was therefore similar to exorcism, but with one important difference: Those who were sick or ill but not possessed could also participate and ask to be healed.

Zar meant "visitor" in Arabic. When this type of jinn possessed a body, it could be made to leave via the ritual. But there was another type of jinn called *sikin*, which meant "resident." Those jinn simply stayed with a person until he died, and they were more dangerous.

When Faseela explained it all to Yam, she opened his mind to a new sort of fear he had never had before. He had thought the zar ritual was only to heal the ill and disabled, nothing jinn related.

"Can I be possessed by a sikin or a zar?" he asked her.

"They possess only weak souls."

"How do I know if my soul is strong or weak?"

"You can't know. Only they do."

He thought her answer was creepier than having them possess him.

...

Faseela knocked at the door, and a woman dressed in a long turmeric-colored dress answered them. She opened the door with a welcoming smile. "Greetings! Here for the zar rituals?"

They all went silent, and Yam stared at Faseela, waiting for her to speak. "Yes...is Ajlan here now?" Faseela asked. Yam figured the healer she knew was not the lady before them.

"He is here, yes."

"We need him to see our friend now," whispered Faseela.

The lady stared awkwardly at Nada, who lay unconscious on the gray mule, and then demanded they bring her inside.

The healer's house was large enough to fit everyone in the village, but Yam counted only seven people in it, including themselves. Only a small section was roofed—probably the sleeping area, he thought. The rest of the structure was open from above, and the ground was wet from all the rain. Yam laid Nada on a flat wet rock that formed a healing bed, then sat near her on a rug that was under shelter.

"Wait here," the lady said to them and walked to the roofed side to wake a man napping on the ground. This was Ajlan, the zar healer. He awoke and raised himself, and Yam noticed he had wrapped himself in a large piece of animal skin. The man washed his hands and beardless old face before approaching Nada with an L-shaped black rod.

He placed the rod beside Nada and began tilting her head left and right to check behind her ears and neck.

"I can see that she's been bitten by a snake jinni," Ajlan pronounced. "When did this happen to her?"

Again, Yam shifted his eyes towards Faseela, signaling for her to answer.

"Yes. Yesterday, Lady Burmiah in Erum extracted all the poison from her, but she fell ill this morning, and she's still unconscious. This has never happened to her before."

He turned Nada's face to the other side and searched her head again. His wrinkled fingers moved through her hair, and then he stopped and called for the lady in the turmeric-yellow dress. "Kaldah!"

She came quickly, holding a net of brown ropes tied together. She worked it around Nada's head and held it tight as the old healer, Ajlan, carried his rod to the burning fire and began to heat it.

Ajlan returned with the rod, still black but smoking with heat. "Hold her," he said. And as Kaldah did, he pressed the rod to Nada's head just a little to heal her. She woke, panicked and screaming in pain.

Faseela did her best to calm Nada and ease her fear as Kaldah carried on healing her head by applying honey to the burnt skin, and Ajlan returned to his nap.

...

"I will not stay here! I must find my husband and child," Nada argued, trying to excuse herself and convince the others, Yam and Faseela, to leave.

"It will come back to haunt you," said Kaldah. "You must wait with us and attend the zar ritual to complete your cure. The snake jinni that bit you is strong and must have caused extreme damage to your head."

"Listen to her, Nada," Faseela added. "We need to complete your cure. Otherwise we will be less safe out in the mountains with your unpredictable condition."

Yam did not mind staying there at all; he had left Wadi Erum only to help Nada find Fad. He had then seen his master and instructor killed before his eyes, and he knew how hostile the Noorians would be if the group disregarded Hadaus's warning and continued to venture into the mountains. He had also witnessed the massacred spearmen, unlike Nada and Faseela, and he knew his skills would be limited if anything like a pack of striped hyenas found them.

He wished he could help Nada find her husband and child. He wanted to, but for now, all he had to do was observe everything around him and report it back to El Kashef in the hope he could convince the Chief Guardian that Fad was innocent. He also hoped to see Hadaus punished for what he had done to Yam's master. He pulled Arkin's flute from his pocket and looked at it for a long time, tears forming in his eyes.

He sat with the women in the healer's house for a while but very soon found himself outside, walking around the village and mingling with the villagers.

He found a rock by the pathway and sat there for fresh air and silence. The rain was soft, and he was wet already from the journey. He thought of going back to the howdah for his own belongings, to get new clothes and find a place to wash himself. He also craved some food, a good place for a nap, and a little time to rest his head after a long, awkward, and devastating week.

Three boys appeared and stood before him. They were about nine, twelve, and thirteen years old. Each one had a stick in his hand, and the tallest one also held a rock. They greeted Yam with warm smiles and welcomes.

"My name is Yam," he answered them.

"My name is Ras," said the tallest.

"My name is Hadi," said the boy with the blue headband.

"I'm Aswad," said the chubbiest and shortest one.

"And we're the jinn tamers of Jibjat," they said.

"Where are you from?" Ras asked him.

"I'm from Sumhuram," answered Yam.

"Where is that?" asked the shortest, Aswad.

"It's the city near the sea, idiot," answered Hadi.

"Would you like to play a game with us?" asked Ras. He raised the round rock in his hands.

"A game?" asked Yam.

"Yes, the *ahayeel* game."

"Never heard of it," said Yam.

"It's easy; we'll show you how it's played." The three ran to a flat area, and Hadi drew a large circle around them with the stick. They threw the rock in the middle and started hitting it with their sticks. A taller boy, probably sixteen, came and joined them to play. Yam observed them all, but he never understood the rules of the game.

That day, Yam enjoyed Jibjat. The people were friendly, the food was tasty, and the zar rituals at night, which included a lot of music and dancing, were joyful and fun.

When night came, he helped the villagers prepare for the rituals. They placed a tent in the open field behind Ajlan's house, when they noticed it begin to rain a little. Torches were lit in the tent, and three chairs were placed

THE GUARDIANS OF ERUM

at its center for three patients: a little girl, an old disabled lady, and Nada, who was asked to sit on the last one.

In the tent, Yam felt that the whole village had come to witness. He saw Faseela sitting on the far side with other women from Jibjat.

A band of musicians faced the three patients: two drum players, a tall brown clarinet player, and a woman who held a small tambourine. They began playing and singing. Yam tried to listen to the song but couldn't recognize the language. Several other men who had come to witness the zar ritual stood up and danced from time to time.

While sitting and clapping, Yam noticed a silver tray being passed around among the guests. When it reached him, he found tree leaves, white jasmine flowers, and an egg in the center. Everyone took either a green leaf or a flower. Yam found the flower pleasant, grabbed one, and passed the tray, but he was curious why there was only one egg there.

The old woman sitting beside him, who was almost Yam's grandmother's age, noticed his hesitation before he picked the flower. She grabbed a leaf after him and told him with a smile, "You made a good choice." But he never knew what she meant! After the tray, an incense burner was passed around, and the visitors placed their hands over the white smoke coming out of the burning frankincense.

The music never stopped. After the tray and the incense burner had been passed around to everyone else, they reached Ajlan. He took the egg from the tray and ate it, throwing the shells behind the patients.

Nada looked surprised and nervous every time Yam saw her.

Ajlan pointed at the girl first, saying strange words, and the little girl got up and danced happily. Then he pointed at the old disabled lady, and to Yam's surprise, she too got up and jumped and danced like none other would do, as if she had faked her impairment or as if her legs had been supernaturally healed!

The last patient, Nada, seemed worried when it came to be her turn. Yam too was tense, and he held the flower hard, almost crushing it. He feared Nada wouldn't heal like the girl and the old woman before her. But she suddenly smiled and got up and joined the two patients with the dance. The three were healed.

He ate all he could and slept well after the zar ritual was done.

...

The next morning, the same morning on which Fad had climbed into the sailboat, Yam was woken before dawn by the noise from a *guarga'a*. The guarga'a is a child's toy made of dry palm sticks wrapped together at one end and left loose at the other end. The child shakes it to create a clicking noise made by the sticks hitting against each other.

It was dark because of the fog, so Yam thought it was still midnight when he got up. He went outside and walked beyond the village to find a place behind the trees to relieve himself. No one would spot him from behind the thick fog anyway, he thought. But still, he went very far to make sure of it.

Walking back to Jibjat village, he noticed the shadows of three creatures moving together. They were getting closer to him. He wasn't expecting anything weird or creepy, and they weren't. He was able to figure out who they were from their shadows: the three young brothers he had met the day before when he reached Jibjat with Nada and Faseela. The three jinn tamers of Jibjat, as they had called themselves.

"Boys?" he called to them from behind the fog.

When they heard his voice, they sprang towards him. "Yam! It is you. We thought you were the Night Horse Jinni," they said.

"The Night Horse Jinni?" Yam had never heard of it before.

"Yes, the Night Horse Jinni. He comes at night and steals the weaker souls," one said. "We're going to stop him!" added another. "Want to join us, Yam?"

Yam held back his laugh. "No, thank you. Good luck finding him."

"If you see anything, do cry for our help."

"I will." Yam smiled and walked away through the fog.

When he became alone in the fog, he sensed someone—or something—was following him. He turned at once, looking for it. He heard strange hoofbeats, which stopped when he turned, but found nothing was there.

"Boys?" he called. No one replied.

He tried to ignore what he'd heard and continue on his way, but he sensed it again. This time, when he spun to see the source, a wicked thing in the shape of a horse was following him. It stopped and stared back at him. Yam froze in his place with his eyes wide open.

Is this the Night Horse Jinni? It had the figure of a horse but was nothing like one. Its face floated alone above its body; it had no neck. The hair on its back was all sorts of dark colors—some was blue, some purple, and some red. And it stood on only its front legs—the rest of its body was being dragged behind!

Yam took a slow step backwards without looking away from the jinni horse. And the jinni took a similar step towards Yam.

Yam froze again, and so did the Night Horse Jinni. The scene was so weird that Yam had no idea what to do. The kind of thing one would only see in nightmares was staring back at him blankly.

The village wasn't too far, he thought. He tried to move away more slowly, so the jinni wouldn't notice it. But it did, and it followed him. Yam increased his pace, and so did the horse. At this point, Yam turned and began to run fast towards the village. The jinni flew behind him at an equal pace.

Luckily, the village was near, and as he got closer, he saw a man walking by.

"Help! Help!" he cried.

The old man saw him. He ran to rescue Yam with a stick in his hand. "Leave, leave, you wicked soul! Leave, leave!" cried the man, shaking his stick at the jinni.

But before he could reach him, Yam tripped and fell, and the shadow of the Night Horse Jinni covered him.

Among the things Yam had heard about the day before, and now feared the most, were the types of jinn that could possess a weaker soul. This one covered him wholly, but he was not sure if it was a zar or a sikin!

He struggled and slipped, tossing himself around, trying to get out of whatever that thing was. From inside the belly of the evil spirit, Yam could hear the man from the village shouting and scolding it.

"Leave him alone. Leave him alone. Set him free."

He also heard Ras, Hadi, and Aswad. The three boys had come to rescue him as well. He could hear them whipping the jinni with their sticks.

Suddenly, the jinni disappeared from above him. It was as if a blanket had covered him and been suddenly lifted. Yam was able to see the three boys and the old villager standing over him. There was another boy, too—the sixteen-year-old he had seen playing with the three brothers the other day. He was holding a blanket. The blanket had the same red, blue, and purple colors as the Night Horse Jinni.

"Leave him alone, you fools!" the old man said.

"We were just playing a game, Uncle Brak," said the sixteen-year-old, who Yam later learned was called Gafi.

"A game?" Yam repeated.

"Yup, the Night Horse Jinni is a game," Ras added. "Haven't heard of it either?"

Yam stood up, not knowing if he should be angry or laugh. "No! I haven't heard of this game," he hissed with anger. "Thank you for not telling me in advance!"

"Well," Gafi said. He had worn the Night Horse's disguise and chased after Yam. "I caught you. It's your turn to be the Night Horse Jinni."

Yam laughed.

Uncle Brak murmured something and walked away, seeming upset.

Yam took the blankets. "You had better start running, boys!"

After almost ten minutes of chasing the boys through the fog, Yam got tired. He couldn't beat the three younger boys, but he spotted Gafi and decided to get his revenge. He raced him, but Gafi ran quicker. In a desperate effort, he took off the blanket and threw it at Gafi. He succeeded—the blanket and the fake wooden horse head flew over the boy and caught him. But Gafi got up upset.

"You can't throw the horse at me. That's against the rules!"

"Why?" Yam asked.

The three boys arrived.

"You are meant to be the jinni," Gafi protested. "You can't throw it."

"Well, consider me a jinn master then. I summoned it." Yam smirked.

"You can't simply summon a jinni!" Gafi replied.

"You need an instrument to summon a jinni," Aswad, the shortest, added.

"And you don't *have* an instrument," Ras smiled.

"An instrument?" Yam asked.

"Yes, an instrument," Hadi said as he scratched his blue headband. "An enchanted instrument, like our sticks, or a jinni lantern, or a musical instrument like the ones used last night for the zar ritual."

"The musical instruments were used to summon jinn?"

"Yes," Ras answered Yam. "Healing jinn, to be specific."

And according to Aad's laws, healing jinn were allowed.

Yam remembered Arkin's flute. He checked his pockets and pulled it out. "Can this be an enchanted instrument?"

"It can be," Ras replied. And Yam smiled, while Gafi frowned.

...

As they returned. Yam couldn't stop thinking of what the boys had told him. When morning came, he met with the healer, Ajlan, and asked him about Arkin's flute, as he remembered how it had opened the secret door to the Gray Palace.

"Nope," Ajlan said. "This looks like a regular flute, nothing enchanted about it."

"How can you tell?" Yam answered.

Ajlan remained silent for a moment and then answered rudely, "From experience. I know."

Yam then walked back to the howdah to grab his bag and find a place for a bath. When he did, he noticed El Kashef's rababa.

Could this be an enchanted instrument? he thought. He picked it up and went straight to Ajlan again.

"Hmm." Ajlan seemed surprised and in deep thought. "Where did you get this one?"

"It's a long story," Yam replied.

Ajlan flipped it and showed Yam a hidden engraving: a circle with a six-petaled flower in the middle. "If this is what I think it is, it must be extremely rare."

"Does it summon a jinni?" Yam asked.

"It sure can; it summons any sorts of jinn. But that all depends on the one playing it. And trust me, it is complicated."

Yam remembered his mother; she too was a rababa player, but he had never asked her to teach him. He now wished he had. "Can you play it?" Yam asked Ajlan.

"I would like to try." He did, but nothing happened—only musical notes were produced. Ajlan went silent and stared at the instrument again.

"Did it work?" Yam asked.

"It seemed not to be responding to me. As I said, it all depends on the person playing it. It depends on their current feelings, their thoughts, their intentions, and the star they're born under."

"That *is* complicated," Yam thought out loud.

"Keep it safe, Yam," Ajlan said. "It could be dangerous if it fell in the wrong hands."

...

Yam left Ajlan's house with his bag and the enchanted rababa, heading for the bathing house. The door was locked. Someone must have been inside using the bath.

"Give me a few minutes," a man's voice cried from inside. "I just got in here."

"I am sorry for disturbing you," Yam replied. "I will be waiting for you outside."

"Okay; I won't take long," the man assured.

Yam sat on a rug nearby and eyed the rababa for a long moment. He was unsure if he should try it or not. Ajlan had told him it could be dangerous, adding that there was no way to predict which jinni it would summon.

What star was I born under? Yam wondered. He then remembered that when Ajlan had tried it, nothing happened to him. He thought he should try it, at least.

He held the rababa in his left hand and lifted the hair-bow in his right. He tried to rub the string and play it, but he had no clue how to do so.

He closed his eyes and tried to imagine how his mother played it. She too would close her eyes and smile, feeling the tones in her heart. Yam copied her, playing the rababa exactly as she would…and it suddenly worked. Yam summoned a jinni!

48

Behas reached Port Rori after having his internal organs cleansed of all the poisons and having to run from Lake Darbat on foot to reach the sea.

The cliffside city of Sumhuram was walled and heavily protected, but the sea channel was far below, and the docks of Port Rori were outside the walls, visible and accessible to any outsiders. He reached the port just in time to witness the battleships being prepared to sail to Socotra. He could see the soldiers running back and forth, getting them ready. His plan was going right. *Good job, farmer!*

Yet he wanted to be surer. He snuck through the tents in the lower basin to reach the port. Hiding under a dark cloak, that morning on the docks, he looked like a lost trader who had awoken amid all the disturbance the soldiers were creating.

"What happened?" he asked one of the soldiers running by in a panicked voice. "Are we under attack? Should we escape or fight?"

"No, we're not. Go back to your tent, old man." The soldier carried on with his works, and Behas smirked in pride.

He snaked his way to the battleships. He could tell that two were being prepared, but there were no signs of Fad anywhere.

Light struggled to penetrate the thick black clouds, but Behas knew it was morning already. By the time they were finished preparing the ships and setting out, it would be difficult for them to reach Socotra before sunset, he thought with worry.

He stayed hidden, observing the soldiers, and had a sudden flash of inspiration.

"Zuhal!" he called, sensing the all-knowing jinni's presence behind him. "Where have you been?" Behas had told Zuhal to keep watch on the child and report to him when necessary the last time they had met in Behas's coffin near Jibjat, as it was being transported to the Gray Palace.

"I have been above the clouds, observing the stars as you asked. The child is still alive in Socotra, as I told you before."

"You came in time," whispered Behas. "I will need your help to reach Socotra faster."

Jinn are not all loyal, but Zuhal was the most loyal to Behas. He had met Behas before, when he was a child, before he even got the Mystic Dagger. And now Behas needed his help, because Zuhal could help him summon other jinn without the dagger.

After a few moments, he could hear the soldiers calling that the ships were ready, but there was still no sign of Fad. To his surprise, however, there was a giant approaching one of the ships. Behas recognized him: Prince Leith. And among his escorting Guardians, he saw another familiar face, Hadaus! The ships were being prepared for them, not Fad. *How late am I?* He had come to the port right after he was healed, but he had come on foot. Fad had reached it before him by horse. And the galloping cavalry he had seen heading to Sumhuram that night had been the prince and his Guardians from Erum! He had not suspected it was them at all.

. . .

Earlier that morning, before sunrise, Prince Leith, El Kashef, and all the other Guardians had galloped at full speed towards Sumhuram. The guards at the gate had noticed their uniforms and his large figure from a distance and had opened all the gates for them.

They had ridden straight uphill towards the barracks, hoping to find the outlaws who had stolen the Prime Ring. They had still assumed that Fad and Behas were traveling together and were surprised to learn Fad had come alone.

"You let him escape?" the prince had asked Assar, the commander. Prince Leith did not enjoy standing in the commander's room. The roofs were too low for him.

"He ordered us to prepare all battleships and cross the sea to Socotra!" Assar said. "But he left in a hurry on another abra boat."

Socotra? El Kashef thought to himself. *Is that where his child is?*

"Did he need an army to find a child?" the prince asked El Kashef. But he could not find an answer; he had no idea what would be waiting for them in Socotra. But after what had happened to them in Wadi Teyq, he would say *they* needed an army to stop the outlaws.

"Well, we cannot guarantee how cooperative the Socotrians will be and whether they will help us or help the saher. The tribes in Wadi Teyq did help him escape before; he is very manipulative," El Kashef had answered. He had still assumed Behas was with Fad, somehow.

"Are the ships being prepared?" the prince asked the commander.

"No, but they can be, and soon, my sheikh," answered the commander.

"Fill them all with as many soldiers as you can, and right away." He had probably remembered his father's request that he return safely. Lion that he was, he shouldn't hunt alone, even if the prey was as small as the independent island of Socotra.

Assar had feared for Sumhuram more than he did for his head. "But my sheikh," he had protested, "that will leave the ports unguarded. May I suggest you take forty men? The lighter the ships, the faster they will sail. Take two battleships so if one is sunk by any means, the other will still float. Raise white flags to show Socotra that you are not approaching for war, and explain to them that you are only after the outlaw."

"Agreed. We shouldn't take all the soldiers," the prince's advising Guardian, Abed, added.

"Then we shall sail at once, with no delay," the sheikh concluded.

As he turned to leave the low-roofed room, Hadaus entered. The prince recognized his gray cloak. A Noorian. He had been told before that an African Noorian had killed Arkin, and he felt suspicious it was this one.

"My sheikh," Hadaus breathed. "May I request to join you?"

Prince Leith knew that his aim in saving the child was primarily to deliver it safely to the Noorians. "Were you the one who killed Arkin?" Leith confronted him.

"I did," Hadaus replied without hesitation, sounding truthful. "And I am now after three other traitors. They have betrayed our guild and the queen."

The prince did not question his words any further. He needed a Noorian witness to his quest. "We are headed there to save a child for your queen. I will allow you to join us."

Hadaus nodded, but he had been after the Mystic Dagger, not the child.

"How did you learn of our destination?" the giant prince asked.

"We learned recently that the traitors were hiding the child there."

"I see." The prince began to feel more confident with the Noorian, who might help him find the child and keep it safe. "Your advice might be needed to help us find the child."

"Then we must leave at once; it is important to reach the island before sunset!" Hadaus explained.

"That will not be possible!" the commander interjected. "Socotra is far. You will reach it after sunset for sure!"

Hadaus was not knowledgeable about sea travel. "Let us hope we don't," he added as they all followed Prince Leith towards the port.

...

Behas had spotted them when they were climbing on board and thought the farmer might have gotten caught—not that he cared. He just wanted to know. "Where is Fad?" he asked Zuhal.

"The farmer is on a sailboat, moving towards Socotra."

He abandoned my plan! Behas thought. *The farmer did not even know where his son would be.*

Regardless of Fad's situation, Behas still needed to reach Socotra. He had already found a way to sneak onto one of the ships, and it wasn't the ship the prince and his party had boarded.

They did reach Socotra before sunset that day. The currents moved the ships swiftly across the sea. Behas, with help from Zuhal, had summoned sea jinn for it.

49

"There they are," said the healer to Fad. "The creeks of Hadibu, the main port in Socotra. This coast has several waterways and settlements, and all of them are very distant from one another. You will be searching for a needle in a haystack...or several haystacks. But I know where we can start looking for your son."

Fad had told the healer that he had traveled to Socotra in search of his kidnapped son, and the half-Erumian had agreed to help Fad in his search.

The clouds were heavier over Socotra, but the sun did light the overcast skies above. Fad sensed he had some time before it began to set. He also noticed the farms and palm trees that filled the coast and braced the ocean, leaving no sign of beach below. "The palms are standing above sea water," he said calmly. "Where do they get fresh water?"

"This creek has fresh water. Hadibu sits at the end of a river. And wherever you dig along the coast, you will find nothing but clean water below," the healer explained.

"Miraculous!" Fad whispered to himself.

"I know. All the water flows down from the high mountains."

"These are truly high rocks!" exclaimed Fad as he continuously switched his gaze from the coasts to the mountaintops. The difference in greening patterns was notable. The flat plains stretching from the coast deeper into the island were filled with the floating spike-balls of palm trees, while on the slopes of the mountains, strange flat green disks stood on raised branches. And there were plenty of them.

"What are those trees on the mountain?" asked Fad as the boat neared the mouth of the creek.

"Those are our precious sacred trees—the dragon-blood trees. You might have heard about their red frankincense."

"I have never heard of nor seen such a tree!"

"That would be because it is forbidden to trade its extracts in Erum. It has been so for a long time. Erumians do not want it to compete with their sacred white frankincense from Wadi Dawkah."

The name of the wadi reminded Fad of Bessel, and he began to have second thoughts about dragging another person into helping him. He hoped nothing would go wrong here like it had there.

"The trees here on our island are all unique," the healer continued. "I have traveled to many places in search of ingredients and herbs, and nowhere have I ever seen a tree similar to the ones we have in Socotra."

The sailors tied the boat to the docks. Safe and sound in Socotra, Fad felt at ease. Now he needed the healer to help him find his child. He thanked the captain for the free transport, and the mediator Shaf'e for his stories and company throughout the journey. He and the healer left the boat first, as they didn't have any goods to carry or slow them down. He left the Guardian's tunic in the boat and carried on in his green tunic. The Prime Ring he hid in his sash; it wouldn't help him here. But the dagger he hung at his waist, as it was plain it might be needed.

"Follow me. We will start our search in the Red Temple."

And Fad followed. "I never learned your name; everyone seems to call you 'the healer.'"

"My name is Mudawe," he said. "But like everyone, you can just call me 'healer.'"

Fad followed him through the crowds. He was hard to miss by far. He wore a long, colorful skirt and plain light-gold linen. His height was close to Fad's, and his long hair covered the back of his neck. That too made Fad jealous, since he'd had to cut his long hair.

The narrow roads beyond the docks were all white sand. The houses varied from street to street: Some were made of mud, some of dry palms, and a few of stone blocks.

After running through a sandy maze, Mudawe and Fad finally stopped and wiped their footwear at the entrance to the temple.

"Here in our Red Temple, newborns whose mothers cannot feed them are brought to be taken care of and fed by different volunteers—mothers who can feed them. Some of the children here are jinxed children," said Mudawe. "I also help heal the sick and injured in this house. If your child has been kidnapped and brought into Socotra, it is most likely that we will find him here."

As they entered, Fad asked, "What is a jinxed child?" He had heard that word before but had never thought about its true meaning.

"A jinxed child is one whose mother dies giving birth to him. A lot of women here die giving birth, so the jinxed newborns are brought to us. Follow me."

They walked into the Red Temple.

. . .

Meanwhile, back at the dock, the Socotrian troops came to the boat to search and inspect all the transported goods before they were unloaded. All tradesmen and sailors stood waiting outside for the regular inspections to finish.

"Chief, we found this!" One of the inspectors had uncovered Fad's tunic, although Fad had hidden it under the animals' haystacks as Shaf'e had recommended to him.

"Explain this, sailor," the Socotrian guard chief demanded of the boat's captain.

The captain was shocked, for he and his sailors had assumed that Fad would take it with him instead of leaving it behind. The Guardian had helped them reach Socotra; they did not want to betray him by revealing his identity.

"It must have been left there by accident from our previous journey, master. We have not transported any Guardians from Sumhuram to Socotra."

The Socotrian guard chief eyed the tradesmen, who all nodded. Some did so out of their loyalty to Erum, others were loyal to the sailors who regularly transported them, and some or all were probably thankful to the Guardian of Erum, who was among the brave men who had steered the boat and saved them from Kattaf-Raffay.

It was noticed by everyone there that the Socotrian troops did not enjoy the responses. Their chief knew well that the travelers without any goods to be searched had already left and would be difficult to find in the city. And he couldn't prove them to be wrongdoers or liars. Besides, his primary job was to inspect the goods, not the travelers.

"Captain," he asked, "why is your boat two hours ahead of its expected arrival?"

"Hear us, for we nearly met with a terrible fate. We almost lost our sails, and the boat cracked and filled with water." The captain went on to relate everything that had happened when they encountered the greedy sail reaper, Kattaf-Raffay.

"Kattaf-Raffay? We all know he appears only at night," answered the Socotrian chief.

"It was cloudy and dark; it might have been before sunset!" The captain tried to convince the inspectors, but he was silenced again.

"Take them all in for interrogation, and confiscate all their goods," he ordered. "Hold them until one confesses and explains the presence of a Guardian's tunic. There are laws on this island, and Guardians from Erum are not welcome here. Tell us where he is," he continued, now speaking to the crew and passengers, "and we will let you go."

"I saw him," cried one of the tradesmen, who from the start had been eager to expose Fad and save his precious hungry cattle. "He left with the healer earlier, through the streets of Hadibu!"

"The healer?" asked the chief.

"We know him, Chief," interrupted one of the Socotrian troops. "He serves in the Red Temple." The chief then handed him the tunic and asked him to rush and report it to all the Socotrian guards.

"And as for you," he said, addressing the captain of the boat. "You shall pay the tax for breaking the laws and for transporting a Guardian into our island. This is a breaking of the truce. You will be held by us until the guards find him and return. As for the tradesmen," he ordered his inspectors, "delay their goods for three hours. Two for reaching here earlier than they were supposed to, and one for lying."

...

When he entered the Red Temple, Fad's lungs expanded, allowing the strong, pleasant odor of red frankincense to fill him. It gave him a feeling he had never experienced with the regular Arabian white frankincense back in Erum. A pulse of both energy and tranquility moved through him with his every heartbeat.

The healer noticed it and smiled. "This is the dragon-blood incense I told you about."

The temple was a square room made of stacked rocks and stones and roofed with wood. There were three doors to the temple, each set on a different side. On the fourth side, a fire topped with dragon-blood incense had been lit. Its smoke filled the room.

"*Mudawe!* You have returned," said a young woman with a child, two or three years old, in her arms. She came in from a side door. "We have prayed every day for your safe return."

"Hadia." He bowed in greeting. "How are your children?"

"They are all well and have grown older than you last remember."

"Where is Mother Sekina?" he asked.

"She is in the gardens; let me take you to her."

Mudawe and Fad followed her.

The garden was vast and was surrounded by high mudded walls to prevent unwanted intruders—not at a height that would prevent seeing eyes but at one that would prevent animals from crossing over. The walls protected a number of rare trees. Some were small bushes, and some were taller than the walls. They varied in shape, color, and size, and Fad had never seen most of them before. The largest tree sat in the center of the garden, and Fad recognized it from when he had first seen it from the boat. It was a dragon-blood tree.

The grounds below the dragon-blood tree were raised to keep the other plants away. It had a single wide trunk that stood straight as a brown pillar of marble. At the top of the pillar, the branches and twigs spread upwards and sideways, tangled around each other to prevent any chance of sunlight passing through them. Their tips ended in a perfect flat circle. The crown above looked like a green plate turned flat on its face, and the leaves were like long needles poking out of every branch end and pointing up towards the heavens. Standing below it, you would think from the strange branches that it was a tree that had been flipped upside down by a giant who had left its roots to dry under the sun.

When the three came near the tree, Fad saddened at the sight of the bleeding trunk. The red liquid leaking out was like real blood.

An old woman was cutting the tree with a sharp blade.

"She is wounding the tree to get Socotra's blood," whispered the healer to Fad. "The island is named after a great female dragon who used to reside here. She was wounded fighting a fearsome enemy who came to destroy the island and its people. Socotra defeated the enemy but was so severely hurt that she lay at the center of the island and died. The gods turned her into the mountain we saw in the middle of the island. Her blood drained into the land, and these trees provide us with it.

"In Socotra, we do not call our leader a king or a sheikh like you do in Erum. Here, our leader is called a protector, for he vows to the people to protect Socotra's sacred body and sacred blood."

"Welcome back, Mudawe," said the old lady. "Your journey took longer than you promised."

"I found trouble, Mother Sekina, but I brought the stone," he said, showing her the seed of some sort of plant.

"Good," she replied and turned to face Fad. "And who is your guest?"

"His name is Fada; he's a farmer from Erum."

"From Erum," she said with a smile. "And what do you farm, Fada?"

"Palm trees. I harvest plenty of dates every year."

"And they are fine dates, I can assure you," Mudawe added. By coincidence, he had bought some of the ones from Fad's farm when he was in Sumhuram.

"Are you here in search of a remedy?" she asked.

"No," Mudawe answered for Fada. "His child was kidnapped, and he's been told the boy is here in Socotra. He's eleven days old today, and we came to search here first."

"Take him to the nursery," Sekina said. "We have many children here near that age, but I doubt any of them has been kidnapped. I do trust in those who brought them to us."

"We will look there," Mudawe said.

"Follow me," called Hadia, who had stood there the whole time but said nothing. The two thanked Mother Sekina and left her beside the bleeding tree, following Hadia and her quiet child.

She walked them out of the garden and into a small hut with red walls. Inside, it was dim and quiet.

"Make no noise; the children are sleeping," she whispered to them.

There were almost half a dozen newborns inside. "Are any of these your lost child?" she whispered again. In front of Fad, three little newborns had been laid to sleep, and two others were uniquely tattooed on their upper arms so that their mothers could identify them if they were ever lost or kidnapped.

He stared a long time, and, noticing the tattoos, he wondered what sign he would need to remember if he needed to distinguish Dil from others.

He could not recognize any of these children as Dil! Too, he feared that even if his child were here, the greater issue would not be recognizing him but taking him back to Erum.

Hadia noticed him staring pointlessly.

"There is another one there, but he's older than twenty days."

She was right, thought Fad. That child did not look at all like Dil.

"Are any of them yours?" she asked again.

Fad turned around to take another look. He couldn't tell if one was or wasn't, but he shook his head to say no every time. Although he wasn't sure, a feeling told him none of the sleeping children was his Dil.

Hadia looked at the children, then leaned close to whisper, "Wait here." She lowered the older child onto a flat cushion, then walked to the far end of the long hut, where another woman sat in the dark with a child in her arms, nursing it.

Hadia stepped back out of the shadows with another newborn in her arms, and as the child floated nearer and nearer to Fad, he saw a scar on its cheek. He had never seen it before on Dil, but seeing all the other features, he knew it was him—he remembered how his child looked. The sight of the scar, though, triggered a sudden bad memory: He recalled the moment when he had run towards Behas, and his son had vanished while falling.

His heart pounded with both excitement and fear. He reached his arms out to take the baby. All this was unexpected, but it was true: He had found his child. He had found Dileel.

50

At last! As he held his child close to his heart, Fad felt overwhelming relief and joy. He was so excited and thankful to both the healer and Hadia for bringing his worries and fears to an end. The only thing he thought of now was taking his son back to his beloved Nada. *She must be dying for him to return.*

"I need to get back to Erum as soon as possible!" he exclaimed.

"No!" cried the nursemaid from the back, walking quickly towards them. "You shan't take him anywhere. They will kill us all!"

Fad covered his child with his arms. Mudawe stopped her. "Who will kill us?"

"Calm down, all of you! You will awaken the children," whispered Hadia, pushing them out the door. Her honey-eyed child followed her. "Are you sure this is your son?" she asked Fad after everyone was out and the door was shut.

"Yes," Fad replied, "he is my son."

The nursemaid began to act strangely towards his son, as Behas had. She started to weep and cry and curse, pushing her way towards the child.

Unexpectedly, a man burst into the hall where they all stood. It was Shaf'e, from the sailboat. "Fad, there you are. The guards are looking for you," he breathed out. "You need to run. Hurry!"

Fad held his child tight, not knowing whether he should hide or run. Dil was still and quiet, sleeping in his father's arms. The sad nursemaid before him had probably spent the last four days taking good care of him. He thought it would be unjust to simply despise her. She begged only for the child's safety and wellbeing and seemed sad and worried for him—or because of him!

"Who brought my child to you?" asked Fad.

She paused, looking at him worriedly. He sensed her hesitation.

"Speak!" he urged.

"We need to go now!" reminded Shaf'e.

"Run!" The nurse's voice turned deep and serious. They all fell silent and turned their eyes on her. It was as if she had moved from sad to angry. "Run, and don't let them have the child!" She took off the oval-shaped scarf of dry palm leaves she had wrapped around her. It was a *med-ana*, used by nursing women to carry children. "I will stall them, and I will try to meet with you in the port. If you're taking this child, I want to come with you and take care of him."

"Thank you," Fad said to her.

Shaf'e gently pulled Fad towards the exit. "Follow me."

The healer came with them. They all moved down the path at a quick pace, heading back towards the port.

"They found your tunic," Shaf'e explained. "And after questioning, a trader told the guards you had left with the healer. Luckily, I heard him and ran as quickly as I could to get to you. If we take these alleys behind the main road, we'll get there unseen, but sneaking you onto a boat and back to Erum is another issue."

"I know a way," interjected the healer. Both he and Shaf'e walked in front of Fad.

"Thank you both," Fad exclaimed, feeling more than just thankful to the two gentlemen who had offered all their help without his asking. But his words hadn't yet reached their ears when a loud cry erupted from in front of them. A guard who had been not far out of their sight jumped into their path from behind a wall.

"Here he is!" cried the guard. "The healer!"

They all unconsciously turned around and ran back. "Run, run, run," they cried to each other.

"Stop!" Two other guards appeared in their new path. Now they were cornered. Their only chance was to slip out of the alley and find the main road.

"Here," cried Shaf'e, who was not from Socotra but apparently knew the streets well. But before he could step out of the alley, a spear was thrust at his nose, forcing all three men to stop at once.

"No one move," said the guard holding the spear. And with that, Fad knew they were finally caught. All the other guards surrounded them in the alley. One abruptly pulled the healer's shoulder and asked him which one was the Guardian from Erum, but Mudawe remained silent.

"Speak or I'll cut your ears, healer."

"I'm the one you're looking for," Fad interrupted. "Leave these two men; they only helped a father searching for his kidnapped child. I'm not an enemy to Socotra, nor am I a Guardian of Erum. I'm only a farmer, and I came only to find my stolen son. And I will *leave* as soon as you'll allow it."

"Take them back to the ports," cried the guard. But they were shortly stopped again. This time, more Socotrian guards came, and Fad noticed three gray cloaks amongst them. *The Noorians from the boat!* He remembered the two had helped them by scaring Kattaf-Raffay away. *Are they caught too?* But Fad could see that they weren't being forced around like him and his allies, and they approached his group with confidence.

"Take the child," one of the Noorians ordered the guards.

After a struggle, they forced Dil from Fad's hands and struck his head, rendering him unconscious.

"Who are you? What are you doing?" asked Shaf'e, who also recognized the other Noorians from the boat.

The Noorians ignored him, and after the child had been retrieved, they continued to give commands. "Take the Guardian to the port. It's unfortunate we can't kill him as well. But do not hand him over to the battleship until after sunset."

The Socotrian troops nodded.

"Take the healer, too. He might require a caretaker after that blow to the head," added the leader of the troops.

. . .

The three conspirators were taken to the port and thrown in a cell. Mudawe and Shaf'e rushed to inspect Fad's head. Mudawe placed his fingers below Fad's skull. "He'll be fine," he said. "He needs to rest for a bit. But...we need to find a way to rescue his child." He spoke more eagerly now. "Fad told me they were planning to kill his son at sunset. We must do something, for the sun will soon be setting!"

...

Meanwhile, the battleship had reached Socotra only half an hour after Fad did. Its arrival near the port of Hadibu made the Socotrian troops suspicious, so they searched the sailboat thoroughly and found a Guardian's tunic.

"Tell me, El Kashef," said the prince. "Is a father permitted to murder to save a son? How many lives is he allowed to take to save just one child?"

El Kashef sensed in his question a slight reference to his own father, Aad. The Prime Sheikh had once before done more than Fad to save one of his many sons. Leith's late brother, Prince Harb, had waged war against Socotra thirty-nine years before, but he had lost the battle and been taken captive here on this island. Aad had sent more and more men to free him. Many died, including his captive son. After learning of his death, and after many Erumians had been killed, Aad pulled his armies back.

Only those who remain are good, his father had said after Harb's death—a saying that had been interpreted on many occasions. One could argue about whether it was right or wrong, but many times, it was proven right.

The sentence came from an old Erumian story about a sad shepherd who lost a healthy newborn goat but later convinced his grieving soul that if it was truly healthy, it would have lived, and the ones that remained were the good and healthy ones. Many parents who lost their newborns used these words to relieve their grief. "Maybe he would have lived to be trouble," they would say. "Only those who remain are good."

Similarly, only the princes and sheikhs who remained in Erum and were neither dead nor exiled were good in Aad's eyes.

"A father would do anything to save his child, my sheikh. But only those who remain are good," El Kashef answered his prince. He could not answer fully, nor justify or condemn a murder without fully understanding all its causes. He believed every murder had its own story and would justify or condemn itself. For now, the evidence he had only served to condemn Fad for the killing of Bessel and the farmers from Wadi Dawkah.

The ship had reached Socotra, but they were not allowed to dock. Although they had raised white flags, Socotra had not given them clearance to sail into the sea channel, so the prince had sent a small boat with four men to investigate the unwelcoming behavior and explain the reason for their unexpected arrival at the port.

...

"They say a Guardian from Erum snuck into Socotra, and that they are currently keeping him hostage."

"That is no excuse to hold us here," interrupted the prince, upset that his men had returned without getting clearance for the battleships to dock.

"We told them that he was an outlaw and that we wanted him handed over. But they said they will hand him over and allow us to dock only after he is awake and has been interrogated. And only one ship, they said. They will let us know when we can enter the port."

"They are trying to stall us. It will be too late by then!" Hadaus suggested to the giant prince. "Sunset is nearly an hour away. Can we dock elsewhere?"

"Our ships are too large to dock elsewhere," explained the captain of the voyage.

"I know what should be done." The prince eyed the hourglass on the mapping table; he sensed he could wait, but not for long. "Do you know where to find the child?" he asked the Noorian.

"I was once told about a ritual cave in Socotra. They must be taking the child there."

After hearing the prince's plans, Hadaus agreed. He held his dagger and switched his gaze towards the island. "Indeed we should, my sheikh," he said.

The prince walked out of the command room to stand on the deck of his ship and eye the port. It was far from where they were anchored. The sun was still far enough away from the horizon, but the cloudy skies made it feel as though it were nighttime, and the port was shaded. The sun was probably visible only to the men at sea, as the torches were being lit in the city of Hadibu.

The prince sensed that some of his men had begun to gather behind him, waiting for his commands. He turned to face them without delay, drawing his large sword, and ordered, "Prepare your swords, men." His voice was loud and deep, and he roared so all his soldiers could hear him over the winds. And they did, holding their sharp iron blades above their heads. The men on the other ship witnessed the shiny swords being unsheathed in the last light of sun and began to draw their swords as well.

Prince Leith waited for all his soldiers to finish hailing him and his father. He then lowered his sword to his side, signaling all his men to be silent and hear him well.

El Kashef stared in his prince's eyes and sensed his urge for revenge. The seventeen-year-old was no longer after the child. He wanted to do what his father and older brother before him had failed to do.

"We shall not rest our blades until this wretched island of Socotra surrenders to Aad. This island shall be ruled by Erum. *Glory to Aad!*" he cried, and they all cried back, "Glory to Aad."

He raised his sword high again and pointed towards the men at the sails. His ships spread their dark wings and flew above the water towards Socotra.

51

Fad was still unconscious. The stone cell where he and his new friends were imprisoned was normally used to keep the stowaways who were caught upon arrival. It was located on the coastal side, right beside the mouth of the channel, and it had a small window in the door which faced the city, not the sea. Fad and his friends were no stowaways, but they were clearly unwelcome.

Shaf'e continued to look out the cell window and plan their escape and rescue, but so far all his plans had been vetoed by the healer, who did not want to risk failing. Shaf'e had also cursed his luck and blamed his name for their misfortune. "If we had been four," he said, "they wouldn't have caught us."

But the healer tried convincing him otherwise. "We *were* four. You weren't counting his son."

"Then what do you propose we do?" he asked the healer in an annoyed tone.

"I do have a plan. We'll call them in. Then when they're not looking, one of us should sneak out. But…I have no idea where they would be taking the child. And I still can't think of how we could get the child from them; the Noorians seemed to have all the city guards under their command. We'll just be captured again."

"Who are they? What do they want from this man's child?"

"I don't recognize their faces," replied Mudawe.

"They helped us in the boat against the Kattaf-Raffay. They stood firm and spoke with the wind!"

"We can't spare more time for talk," said Mudawe. "If I can reach the Protector of Socotra, I'll explain it all before it's too late."

He then looked down at Fad and towards the door. He knew their cell stood near the waters from which they'd come, which meant the Protector's tower stood on the other side of the channel. He would need to swim to reach it, and he'd surely be caught. But he felt he needed to try. He needed to help the Erumian father, Fad, find his son.

...

A few months earlier, he had been serving an exquisite healer in Babylon named Esagil. Esagil maintained the health of two Babylonian kings and was known to own thirteen healing jinn connected to a tree he had brought back from their realm. Thus, no one dared to challenge his knowledge or skill. Nor did he share his secrets easily.

By the time Mudawe met him, he had aged a lot and had begun to teach many other scholars his physical and metaphysical skills, though only those he rewarded with a special "stone"—actually a seed from his jinnic tree— were named as his successors.

Mudawe had served him for more than a year and a half, and Esagil had never shown any signs of accepting him, for Mudawe was more of a physician than a *saher*. Mudawe believed in herbs more than the power of jinn. He had once described Esagil's jinnic tree as "just a tree"!

One day, a diseased man had come to Esagil for a remedy. "My skin is like bread, and my urine shines red like wine. My eyes are always wet, and when I sleep, I snore like swine. When I walk, I trip, and every night I cry. I came for your help. Release me from my pain, or I soon shall die."

Esagil had recorded everything he had heard. But first, he had gone through the famous routine he used with every patient. He had taken the man to his fenced barn and given him a rotten fig. In the barn, there were many pigs of many colors. A few were white, some were brown, lots were gray, and two were black.

The sick man had known to avoid the black pigs. He had thrown the fig near the white ones, but they had moved away while it was still in the air. Only when it rested in the sand had the pigs raced back towards it. And unfortunately, it had been a black pig who had eaten the fig.

"You will face certain death in less than a year," Esagil told his patient. "Healing you is a waste of our time."

The poor man lowered his head and walked away, tripping after a couple of steps, weeping in agony and cursing his fluke throw of the fig.

Esagil's students had observed and nodded, but Mudawe had not been convinced. He had followed the doomed man and stopped him for a talk. "What do you do every day?" he had asked.

"I mine during the day, and at night I cook the food for the miners."

"It is the mines that made your skin hard," Mudawe had told him. "And your nose is blocked, so you breathe from your mouth and swallow the lead dust; thus, your internal organs are infected and your urine is red. Your eyes are wet from the fumes of what you cook, which is why you cry at night, and smoke from the fire has irritated your nose, which is why you sound like swine."

The patient had wept more and cried, "You may be right, but what is the cure? I shall soon meet death, as you have seen, for my fig was swallowed by the ugly dark boar."

"Do not go into the mine for the next two or three weeks," Mudawe had said. "Go to the river every morning instead. Wash your skin and drink plenty of water; then rest under the sun. Do not cook your food, but eat it raw, and eat more greens than meat if you can. And I will pray for your health."

The man had hugged him and thanked him with excitement and broad smiles. He had needed hope and had promised to follow this advice at once. He had nothing to lose and so decided to try.

Mudawe had noticed Esagil watching from afar with an angry expression and had feared then more than ever that he would never be rewarded with a successor's stone.

The sick man had eaten nothing but greens that day and slept early in order to wake early. The next morning, he had walked with optimism all the way to the river to wash. He had dipped in to wash his skin, but the flow had been strong, and he had found it too hard to swim. He had drowned that day, and when he had been found near the banks, everyone had learned his tale and trusted more in the figs and the pigs.

"Take this." Esagil had given Mudawe a shiny red stone—a blessed seed with a mark engraved on it. "You have earned it and now can leave to be a successful healer."

"But—" Mudawe had eyed the stone in his hand and wondered whether it was another test from the old teacher. "I failed to heal the man. I killed him instead."

"You healed his heart. He died with hope after he had lived in sadness, weeping every night before he slept," Esagil had said. "Therefore, his soul will forever rest in peace. And that has earned you the Stone of Esagil-Kin-Apli, the highest reward, the healers' stone of Babylon. Grow the tree and nurture it well. It is a blessed seed from another world."

All the other students had removed their turbans and bowed ritually to accept and congratulate their colleague in his success. Mudawe had thanked them all, bid them well, and traveled back to his aunt in Socotra. But on the way, he had met Fad and felt bound to help him find his son and heal his saddened heart. *No man deserved to suffer the pain of having his child kidnapped.*

...

Now, after sitting in silence beside Fad for a while, he pressed the man's chest and then opened his eyes suddenly, looking at Shaf'e. "Call out for the guards," he said urgently. "Fad is dead!"

"What?!" Instead, Shaf'e froze in his place, filled with shock and fear.

"Have you forgotten the plan?" Mudawe whispered.

"Which plan?" asked Shaf'e.

"Call them in," he replied, "and I'll find a way to sneak out from behind them. Keep them distracted. I need to reach the Protector."

"Right; I do remember."

Shaf'e cried out for the guards to open the door and let them bring Fad outside.

But the guard at the door showed no sympathy to a Guardian from Erum. "So? If he's dead, he's dead. Opening the door won't bring him back to life."

Shaf'e and the healer looked at each other in silence, each waiting for the other to suggest another plan.

"He isn't dead yet; he's dying and needs to be healed!" Mudawe cried. "But I can help him if I can get my herbs." He thought that if they escorted him out, he thought he might try to escape them. It would be a lot easier than the first plan.

"It'll soon be dark," replied the guard. "Then all three of you will be free to leave. These are the orders we have."

Loud cries began to ring out before the guard had finished his words. "Prepare for war! Prepare for war!"

The healer and Shaf'e sensed the guard who had spoken to them had run away. They sprang to the door and peeked out.

"What is happening?" Shaf'e asked the Socotrian healer.

They could see only men running back and forth and many others standing in organized formations facing the sea. "The last time I heard these cries, Socotra was at war!"

"It's getting dark sooner than we thought it would," Shaf'e said. "We won't have time to save Fad's son."

"The sun is setting behind the western mountains. But from where we stand, you're right; I fear we won't be able to save his child!" The healer continued to observe from the small opening in the door. A familiar figure caught his attention, and he raised his eyebrows in surprise. "The Protector! Even he's out with his axe."

Shaf'e remained silent as they both continued to observe the events from the port side. They sensed trouble but had no way of knowing about the two battleships heading their way.

"It's coming fast!" cried the Socotrian troops.

Interpreting the cries outside, and hearing the waves growing louder, Mudawe figured it had to be a battleship heading towards the channel. "It will be crushed if they do!" Mudawe feared for the crew of the ship.

Although a man of healing and remedies, he had some knowledge of the new defense systems that had been developed after the last war with Erum. Most Socotrians knew.

The channel had once been deep for big ships to float over easily, and its waters had been calm. But that all had been in the past! The Socotrians had poured sand in the channel to make it shallower and covered the bottom with spikes that could be raised by ropes to form a defensive barrier against any attacking ship.

They'll sink at the mouth of the channel! Mudawe could imagine the battleship smashing into the spikes. As he thought this, the waves began crashing louder, and men began to ready themselves for battle. The Protector raised his red axe high above his dark head and cried, "Now!"

Other cries of "Now!" and "Pull!" echoed from all over as men began to raise the spikes, triggering the trap meant to sink any unwelcome ships.

When the ship crashed, Shaf'e and the healer heard it clearly. Instead of simply sinking in its place, the ship pushed forward a bit after it crashed, turning towards the land. Once it came to a full stop, it began to tilt, creaking, and fell on its side with a loud crash. The irregular bangs of a giant wooden structure on land filled their hearts with unfamiliar fear.

Fad opened his eyes and cried out in pain, holding his head. "What happened?" But the other two did not hear him. The turn of events outside, and the loud noises now coming from directly above them, made them tense. Although they had noticed Fad awakening, they stood still near to the window and impatiently observed the roof. It felt as though the ship's sail had tilted and was above their heads. Strange cracking noises came from above: the loud wailing sounds of winds pushing a gigantic sail, or sails, like a flag snapping on a windy day, the creak of a large mast tipping to its side right over them to separate itself from the half-sunken hull, and the escalating sounds of all the shrouds, ropes, and chains breaking, allowing the weight of both the mast and sail to fall aside.

After the last of the main ropes snapped, there was a mere moment of silence, followed by the whipping sound of the mast falling like a tall tree directly over their cell.

The healer and Shaf'e pushed their backs to the walls. On the other side of the cell, Fad remained silent and in anticipation as well.

The mast broke the roof above them, demolishing their mud-walled cell. It split the room in half, and they all ducked low to prevent being smashed like bugs. Luckily, the roof was made of dry palms and haystacks mixed in a thin layer of mud.

They opened their eyes to find themselves blinded by the large sail that covered them all. They called one another. Mudawe found Shaf'e first, and the two crawled under the sails to reach Fad. Outside, they could hear Socotrian troops storming the area and attacking the ship. They needed to escape fast, before they were caught in the midst of the anarchy.

They crawled their way under the sail and reached the fallen mast. Still no sign of Fad.

"Fad," Mudawe cried, but not loud enough for the troops to hear. It was more a loud hiss than a cry.

"I can't see anything," said Shaf'e from behind him.

"Fad," Mudawe called again, a bit louder than a whisper this time. He heard footsteps coming near them.

"Help!" A voice came from under the crumbled wall, not far from where they were. It was Fad. The walls on the other side of the cell had fallen over him.

They sprang to help him out. They couldn't see his face well, but his dark green tunic appeared under a beam of wood that kept his arms from moving. It took effort from all three to push the beam aside and free him.

"Thank you," he said and slowly raised himself to their crouched heights.

"Are you hurt?" the healer asked.

"I'll be fine."

All three turned their heads at the sounds of footsteps coming their way. "We need to run," Mudawe said. But it was too late. A man appeared before them. It was Behas, and he was so surprised to see them that he drew his dagger in defense at once. "You!" he said at the sight of Fad, lowering his Guardian's dagger in relief.

"Behas?" Fad said in amazement. He had thought the man was dead near Lake Darbat.

"Did you find your child?" Behas asked, approaching them and lowering his dagger further.

"It was the Noorians. They took him from us."

The flash of a lightning strike illuminated the sail above them and was followed by a loud rumble of thunder.

Behas raised his dagger again and continued his way past them. "We haven't got much time," he said worriedly.

"Where are you going?" Fad asked as he followed him.

"To find your child."

52

The Socotrian troops approached the wrecked hull of the sinking ship, but no one came out to meet them. The ship was empty! Aside from Behas, who had been hiding in it and fled earlier from under the sails, no one was there.

It was a decoy used by the Guardians of Erum to destroy the defenses of the channel, allowing the second ship to anchor safely behind it. Luckily, it had done a great deal to clear the traps in the shallow waters. And, having collapsed on its side on the port, it also provided a good cover for the Erumians, who were able to disembark and gather safely on the docks.

The plan was to storm the barricades and capture the weaponry and treasury. The falling mast had done them a great favor by destroying one wall of the barracks. Now they didn't need to break it.

From the other side of the channel, the Socotrians continually stormed the ship with arrows, but it was difficult for them to aim in the dark. And even if their arrows did hit someone, they were weak and made of shark bones, not iron.

"Into the barracks," the Protector ordered after realizing Erum's plans. He had made a big mistake when he first saw the ships coming by ordering most of his men to stand outside the barricade.

The barracks had actually been built by Erum twelve years before, when Aad had captured the city of Hadibu, but he had never succeeded in establishing control over the whole island of Socotra, and Hadibu had been recaptured by the Socotrians. The barracks were laid out the same way as the ones in Erum, which gave the Erumians an advantage over the Socotrians, for they knew where to go once they were in. The first batch of twenty men stormed in, killing any Socotrian in their way, and headed straight to the main gate to block it. The second group were ten men who aimed to rid the rest of the barracks of any living troops.

Prince Leith then entered with his seven Guardians, Hadaus, and El Kashef. The last group of men, who carried food and medicine, entered last and worked on piling up rocks and wood to close the gaps in the walls they had come through. Both ships were now empty.

The prince's plan went well; the main gate to the barracks was blocked, and any Socotrian troops who had remained in the barracks were killed without mercy.

Lightning flashed and thunder roared above their heads from time to time. It hadn't yet begun to rain, but the clouds above them looked heavy and strange that night. El Kashef had never witnessed anything like them in his life. They were gray and humongous, like mountains floating above. The most terrifying thing about them was their glowing heart. A strange bluish-green glare emanated from the center of the sky, illuminating everything. El Kashef felt it was supernatural. It was as if the clouds had swallowed the bright full moon that night. Every Erumian and Socotrian was busy with the battle and ignored it. El Kashef felt like he was the only one amazed at the sight.

Every time a bolt of lightning struck, he felt it behind him and jumped with fear. For a long moment, standing in the courtyard, while everyone else was busy following orders and preparing themselves for their attack, he continued to stare above into the strange abyss until something flew across his sight. Several black lines arced high above and hung in midair before gliding down towards them. "Arrows! Arrows!" El Kashef cried in warning.

The men dodged them all, and even those who were hit weren't really injured. It was probably the winds that had slowed the arrows and made them fall harmlessly on the soldiers, thought El Kashef. He then checked one and found the tip was made from a shark's tooth.

"Are the men ready?" Prince Leith asked the commanders who had joined him from Sumhuram. They were four commanders, and each one of them commanded nine soldiers.

"They are all ready, my sheikh," they replied.

"Take your positions and wait for my signal to open the gate. We'll allow them to storm in before we exit and attack."

The four commanders nodded and left at once. The gate was still being banged by the Socotrians, harmless arrows continued to fly in from above, and El Kashef remained in his position next to the prince.

Hadaus came to El Kashef after helping the soldiers. He looked more worried than the prince and all the soldiers in the barracks that night. "We need to leave and find the child before it's too late," he whispered to El Kashef.

"Has the sun not set yet?" El Kashef responded, remembering the warnings he had received. It was as dark as night.

"Not yet, but it soon will. We need to reach the mountain soon. Their cave shouldn't be far, if I recall correctly."

The prince noticed their side talk and worried looks and came near. "The child," he said to Hadaus. This had been his primary objective ever since he had received the letter from his older brother Zufar. "You said you knew where he would be?"

"I believe I do, my sheikh," Hadaus replied. "But we need to leave now if we want to save him," he continued, after pausing for a thunderclap.

"Abed," the prince called to his advising Guardian.

"Yes, my sheikh?"

"Once the men are done with the preparations, help El Kashef and the Noorian escape through the back," he ordered. "Take enough men to keep their passage safe from behind, and follow the Noorian until he finds the child."

"I will, my sheikh."

"Abed, the child must return alive!"

The prince then turned to face El Kashef and Hadaus. "We will be waiting for you here. Good luck."

"Indeed, my sheikh." Hadaus nodded.

El Kashef might have wanted to stay instead, but his choice had been made for him. He followed Hadaus, Abed, and four other Guardians out the back. There, they faced six Socotrian troops, who were no match for them. Hadaus killed more with his bow and arrows than the Guardians did. His determination was clear to El Kashef, but the other man wondered why the Noorians had sent only one occultist, although the woeful tidings he brought were evidently serious. El Kashef's task had begun with solving a crime in Wadi Dawkah, but that now became insignificant to everyone, even to him.

Now he found himself chasing after a Noorian and caught in two wars, one between Erum and Socotra and another between occultists and sahers.

...

Back in the barracks, the main gate opened, and the Socotrians stormed in, believing they had succeeded in breaking it open. Prince Leith had never fought in battle before, and that night, he surprised both the enemy and the Erumians with his brilliant strategies.

He used every oily substance found in the food storage at the barracks. Ghee, butter, olive oil, and even honey were spilt around the entrance to the courtyard, creating a slippery pool. The first line of Socotrians tripped in it, and the rest tripped over them. The few who remained standing were shot with arrows—iron-tipped and deadly arrows—by the Erumians, as were their fallen comrades.

Then the Erumians set loose a batch of twenty goats and six cows that were kept in the barracks. These were animals confiscated from sailors who had broken Socotrian laws. Each beast carried the heads of Socotrians who had been killed when the Erumians entered the barracks. The Socotrians saw familiar faces, and other body parts, hung on the horns of goats and cows that pushed through their ranks. The sight frightened some of them, causing them to break formation. Following the beasts, the Erumian soldiers burst out with raised swords, killing any frightened or brave Socotrians in their way.

The Protector could see his men being beaten and slaughtered. He had only about a hundred men. Although that was double Leith's force, he estimated he had lost thirty or more since the gate was opened, while fewer than ten had been killed on the Erumians' side.

He continued to observe the port and barracks from a high vantage point, trying to develop a counterattack before it was too late. His men at the gate were now gaining ground and on the offensive, but something more needed to be done, he thought.

He then saw the second batch of Erum's army storming out of the gate, and one was a giant. *A son of Aad!* he thought with surprise. "Let's strike him down. If he falls, they all will. Get me my horse."

Unlike kings and sheikhs, whom men would die to protect, the Protector of Socotra was willing to die instead for his men and island. He intended to gallop through the lines and face the prince. But just before he began, one of his troops told him the back wall of the barracks was open again.

"Great!" said the Protector, and he and a few of his men galloped their way through the alleys to enter the building from the seaside.

El Kashef and Hadaus, seeing them from far, thought at first that the Socotrians were coming after them but then noticed them turning down the opposite side of the path, towards the broken wall. Hadaus stopped. Even if he found the child, it would be useless if Erum lost its hold on the barracks before he returned. "Go back!" he told the five Guardians escorting him and El Kashef. "We'll manage ourselves. Protect the sheikh from them."

...

The Socotrians were on horses, and they had reached the barracks earlier. Most of Erum's soldiers were outside the barracks, fighting alongside their sheikh. A few had stayed inside to guard the weapons, but they failed to alert the rest and were killed by the Socotrians. The Protector could see the prince's unprotected back from behind enemy lines. *He's dead.*

"Once I am out, close the gate. We shall corner them like sheep who've lost their shepherd." He stood on the horse with his back bent, ready to leap high from it, and held the axe in his right hand. He was aiming for the giant prince's head. The horse maneuvered the dead bodies, beginning to gallop once it was outside the gate. "Son of Aad!" cried the Protector, yelling the name "Aad" loud and long enough for the prince and all his soldiers to hear. He wanted the Erumians to turn in time to see their prince lose his head.

The prince turned on cue and found the Protector leaping through the air towards him, with his axe raised high. He tried to tilt his head away from the blow, but the axe fell on it quickly and sliced down the right side of his face, starting from his eyebrow. It cut away parts of his cheek, ear, and chin.

The seventeen-year-old giant prince trembled and fell to the ground, holding his bloodied face. He was a young lion who had challenged another for the throne of Socotra but now suffered for it.

The Protector fell as well but quickly rose to his feet to command his men. "Kill them all!" The gate behind them shut, and the Socotrian troops charged, cornering the Erumians.

The Protector raised his axe again and ran towards the wounded prince, who screamed and cried in pain. Two of the Guardians who had come with him from Wadi Erum stood above him to push the Protector back and spare their sheikh from any more blows. The soldiers helped drag the giant prince back to the closed gate.

All the other soldiers who had managed to stay alive fell back towards the closed gate. They had created a circle around Leith, but they were falling one by one. By now, the force was nearly down to half of what it had been when they came.

Two of the healers came out to tend to their sheikh. They had been in a few battles and had seen some blood and injured faces before, but nothing of this magnitude. They had limited resources, and the lives of their sheikh, all the Guardians and the soldiers, and themselves were now in their hands. The prince could not die. And they had to go back inside the barracks, which were now closed from inside.

The Protector hid away behind his troops. He was proud of his heroism. "I wish Aad could see another of his sons dying here in Socotra. He shouldn't have underestimated us again," he said to some of his men. "After this is done," he went on, raising his axe, "I will make sure this axe is sent to Aad as a gift."

53

Behas ran through the streets and alleys of Hadibu as if he were a Socotrian shadow that knew the place better than its own inhabitants. Fad, Shaf'e, and Mudawe tried as best as they could to follow him.

They now ran uphill towards the mountains, towards a cave on the western side where Behas had pointed earlier.

No one tried to stop them except a single gatekeeper on the outskirts, whose job was to keep wild animals from entering. Behas knocked him out when he tried to stop them from running. Fad and the others who ran behind, trying to keep up with Behas, found the unconscious young Socotrian guard beaten to the ground but not dead. Fad took a spear from the knocked-out guard, Shaf'e took a lantern hung over the fence entrance, and Mudawe closed the wooden gate behind them as they continued to follow Behas.

The plains and the sparse forest of dragon-blood trees were dark that night. Although the full blue moon illuminated parts of their path and lightning flashed from time to time, no light passed through the branches and twigs of the dragon-blood trees. The green crowns were like small clouds below the gray shadow of a greater thunder-filled cloud.

Shadows under shadows, thought Fad. It would have been easy to lose Behas's trail in the gloomy forest, as the saher always ran in the shadows, but they could see the mountain above, and the cave entrance was easy to spot, lit by torches, and standing high on a short cliff. It wasn't far anymore.

The cave came closer and closer as they continued through the woods. Fad noticed shadows of men standing guard at the entrance, and he felt they had noticed the travelers coming and were prepared for them. He clutched the spear in his hands and grew angrier. He would fight them alone if he needed to in order to save his child.

But when they all got close to the cave, Fad and his company noticed Behas had stopped and was staring at the tip of the mountain. They paused beside him but did not notice anything unusual. Fad did see the clouds were greener and more illuminated, moving awkwardly from different directions and interlocking into a single mass above the mountain. But he did not feel their significance until a huge bolt of lightning struck the top of the mountain, illuminating the whole area.

He could see the men by the cave clearly now, and their number seemed to grow. A loud bang of thunder erupted in the air, followed by the sound of falling rain which had not yet reached the earth. More lightning sliced the darkness above, and Fad could see the water drops falling towards them.

When the showers poured over their heads, they moved together two steps and stood under a dragon-blood tree for shelter. Behas remained in his spot.

"We're late!" Behas said, his eyes still focused on the clouds.

All three stared at him in silence, waiting for his next words. "The sun has set, your child has been sacrificed, and the beast has been summoned." He turned towards Fad and said, "I have to go." He then moved to travel back down but stopped and turned to add another word before leaving. "And as for your child," he said, eyes filled with grief and anger and fixed on Fad, "I am sorry, but he is most probably dead now. Save yourselves. Go back."

Behas disappeared at once. It was the last any of them saw of him for a long time afterwards.

"What do we do now?" asked Shaf'e.

Fad stared blankly, feeling lost and distracted, angry and rebellious, grieving and afraid. Mudawe noticed it all and answered Shaf'e for him, hoping to heal Fad and direct him towards what he thought was right.

"We shall climb to the cave. It is closer to us now than going back," Mudawe said. "If we find your son alive, we might be able to save him. But if he is dead, those who stole him shall pay for what they have done!" His words were like added fuel for the fire of rage in Fad's heart.

"We have no weapons," said Shaf'e. The lantern he held had gone out, though their eyes were adapting quickly to the dark.

"I'll climb alone," said Fad, remembering the bad luck he had been warned about. He should probably carry on alone.

"We will climb with you," said Mudawe.

"No. Go back. I shouldn't be helped. I must go alone," said Fad, but he was interrupted by Mudawe.

"We will follow you," Mudawe said. "They have no right to take your child from you. We witnessed it, and we did not stop them. No man deserves to have his child sacrificed to evil jinn. I have seen and heard from many men and women who have lost their children to dark rituals or had them kidnapped. We are not following you just to help you, Fada. We are here to do what is right."

"You are right," Shaf'e added. "We have to stop them."

Shaf'e grabbed two hand-sized round rocks. "Hold this," he said, giving one to Mudawe. "Let's go without any more delay. We must hope the child is still alive."

They climbed wet mud and rocks. The slope was not too steep nor the cliff too high as they worked their way around it to prevent themselves from being seen and so surprise their enemy.

Fad crept near the edge and crouched below a rock to see the cavern's entrance. The cave did look deep and dark, lit by only a few lanterns and torches.

"I see five men inside, some with daggers only," whispered Fad, using his fingers to point out the number, since the noise drowned out his voice. "We'll all attack at once. If they hold on to their weapons, kill them. If they surrender, spare them." He wasn't sure whether they had heard him or not, but he did see them nodding. "Try to get their weapons, too."

He then allowed the other two to get a look before jumping in. Once they had all nodded their readiness, they sprang out by the side of the entrance, each running towards one of the nearby guards.

They were fortunate that a battle had taken place at the port, and only inexperienced guards had been left to escort the three occultists.

...

At that the exact moment, back in the port of Hadibu, Prince Leith and his men dropped back to the entrance of the barracks, which had been shut against them from the inside. This was an evil and smart move from the Protector, who had injured the prince severely, almost splitting his head in two. Luckily, the prince had been able to avoid taking the full blow, only losing part of his face and not his head.

As the prince lay on the ground, being treated for his injury, his men banged the gate hard, trying to open it, but it was no use.

"Are you done with my head?" he spat angrily at the men aiding him.

"Yes, my sheikh," they said. Seeing him push himself to stand, they tried to stop him, but they couldn't. "But you need to rest it, my sheikh!"

With only one eye, but standing tall enough that he had a good view, he could see his men fighting the enemy with everything they had. The Erumians were stronger and more experienced in battle than the Socotrians, but they were outnumbered, and out in the open. He turned towards the gate to help his men open it. Pushing with all his strength, he felt the painful heat of blood rushing to his half-open head. He knew he would faint.

Inside, the five Guardians led by Abed arrived and found the Socotrians holding the gate. The Guardians did not hesitate and began to shoot them with arrows.

As the prince and his men pushed it from outside, the gate began to crack from inside too. Leith pulled his giant body back and threw it hard against the gate, crying out in rage and determination. The wood was strong, but the hinges lost their hold after the last push, and the gates fell flat over the now-dead Socotrians behind them, crushing their bodies under its weight.

"Fall back into the barracks," cried the prince. The Erumians all rushed to enter, and then raised the gate to close the entrance again. They leaned it on the stone wall, allowing only a small opening.

The Protector gave orders to push the gate and break in, but the prince and many of his men pushed back against it, holding it firm.

The prince had lost his sword after he fell, but he had come prepared with more large weapons to match his height, which the Erumians had left in the barracks with the rest of their goods. He called his men to fetch his swords, and this time a spear as well.

His Guardians feared he'd go out to fight again. "My sheikh, we need to get back to the ship. We'll push them to make room for you to escape." To them, their sheikh's safety was more important than everything else.

The sheikh ignored them. He held the sword in his right hand and the long spear in his left while leaning his back against the gate. "Protect my back this time, Guardians," he yelled.

Then he ordered the others to let the gate open.

From the other side, the Protector saw his men burst in, but they quickly fled back, away from the entrance. More specifically, they fled from the giant lion, Prince Leith, who was swinging his man-sized sword back and forth, slicing two or three of them in half with every blow as he advanced ahead of his men.

"Protect his left side and back," cried one of the four commanders from Sumhuram to his men. "Do not let them touch your sheikh."

But the lion needed no protection this time. He was driving through them like they were grass. Even those who managed to escape his sword were stabbed and slain by his long spear.

The Protector decided to attack him from the front this time. He climbed his horse with the axe in his hand and galloped straight on, calling for his troops to stand aside.

Leith waited for the horse to be at a suitable distance. This time, the Protector did not stand on his horse; he probably wanted to throw the axe instead. But the prince didn't wait long. After his last swing, he raised the large sword over his shoulder and then threw it at the galloping horse. It flew like a lightning bolt, too fast for anyone to see coming. It was also too dark for the prince to aim properly, but the blade did cut the horse, which fell to its side, sending the Protector down to the wet ground.

The Protector gathered his strength and leaned on his axe to push to his feet. As he turned to face the prince, he found the giant running towards him, holding his long spear. He froze in his place, knowing he had met his end, and opened his eyes wide as Prince Leith drove the spear in between his chest and hip. The head of the spear came out of the Protector's back, ripping his spine into two. The prince continued to run, raising the impaled Protector high for everyone to see and then dropping him down, sticking the spear on the ground with the Protector's dead body on it.

"This is our land!" A cry for everyone else to surrender by the prince ended the battle. All the Socotrians sheathed their weapons and knelt before their new ruler, Prince Leith.

54

While Leith fought the Protector, Fad was fighting his own battle. When the three entered the cave, surprising their enemy, Fad ran ahead and stabbed one of the guards in the shoulder. Mudawe, who ran behind Fad, knocked the guard out with the rock and grabbed his dagger. Shaf'e targeted another guard, knocking him unconscious and grabbing his dagger as well, but another near him surprised Shaf'e and brought him down to the ground. Shaf'e did his best to dodge the guard's swings. Fad saw him and ran to help him, stabbing the crooked enemy in his side. Shaf'e used the dagger to kill him.

They both turned to find Mudawe fighting two on his own. One of the guards was bleeding from his forehead, where Mudawe had sliced him, but was still fighting. Fad and Shaf'e ran to help their friend. Fad kicked one guard away, and Shaf'e killed the other. The one Fad kicked fell far and, when he stood again, he found the spear's head had disappeared through his stomach; Fad killed him without hesitation or regret.

Three Noorians and two other guards remained, standing at the deep end of the cave, where the ritual was taking place. Mudawe and Shaf'e attacked the two Socotrian guards as they came near, while Fad ran towards the Noorians and his child. One of the Noorians carried on with the ritual, crying loudly and saying strange words as he stood above the child, while the other two Noorians came running towards Fad.

Before Fad could act, he was shoved by the red-haired Noorian he had seen on the boat, falling flat on his chest. The older Noorian grabbed Fad's spear and pointed it at him from where he stood. "Kill him, Saffron!" cried the older Noorian.

"I should have pushed you out when we were on that boat, Guardian of Erum," Saffron said, pushing Fad's head down and holding a dagger to his neck. "Tonight, Erum will pay for what it did to us."

"Let him go, traitorous occultist. Let him be." Mudawe and Shaf'e had been able to knock out the last two guards. But they couldn't move forward after seeing Fad was held down, threatened with a dagger to his neck. They were too far away to save him now.

Fad struggled, feeling the sharp blade getting closer and almost touching his neck. But before it ended him, the Noorian above him, Saffron, fell backwards off Fad.

Hadaus had intervened at the right time, with an arrow from the dark to save Fad.

Once he found himself released, Fad jumped to his feet, but he froze in his place as the other Noorian held the spear against him.

"Kill the child, El Sarabi," cried the Noorian, Fattir, after he saw his student, Saffron, die. "Finish the ritual!"

By then, Hadaus had pulled another arrow, and he shot Fattir dead.

They all turned their eyes to El Sarabi, who stood far away from them all. El Sarabi raised the Mystic Dagger, preparing to stab the boy and end the ritual.

Hadaus pulled another arrow, his last. He aimed it quickly and shot it at El Sarabi, but it missed him!

"No!" cried Fad. He ran towards El Sarabi, but he was too far.

El Sarabi finished his ritual and locked gazes with Dil. "This is for Socotra."

And just as he was about to swing the Mystic Dagger to kill Dil, Yam appeared in front of him with a rababa in his hand.

El Sarabi was horror-struck, and everyone else was astounded! But Yam acted fast. He swung the rababa and broke it on El Sarabi's head, knocking him backwards and forcing him to drop the Mystic Dagger.

Still not sure how in the world Yam had appeared before him out of thin air, El Sarabi tried to stand and get the dagger, but Yam kicked it away. El Sarabi then noticed Fad, Hadaus, Mudawe, and Shaf'e were all running towards him. He picked himself up and ran to the other side, escaping through a hole in the back of the cave.

"The child!" cried Mudawe, pointing to the far end of the cave, where he saw Dil moving his hands. Fad sprang to get his child.

Hadaus cared only about the Mystic Dagger, and he went to pick it up. He hoped he could find El Sarabi, but the traitor had disappeared. He then walked towards Yam, who had given him the biggest shock he had ever imagined.

"How did you…?" Hadaus did not even know what to ask Yam.

Yam, remembering the man who had killed his master, decided to ignore him and keep his distance. "We saved the child!" he exclaimed, turning away towards Dil.

Fad thanked him dearly. He never forgot that day when Yam had appeared in a blink of an eye, just in time to save Dil. In fact, everyone there that day was astonished by it and remembered it forever—Mudawe, Shaf'e, Hadaus, and El Kashef, who had left Yam near Jibjat!

They found the child surrounded by torches on a tilted stone slab, motionless and moaning quietly in pain. His tiny hands and feet had been poked with the dagger, making wounds from which his blood dripped and pooled on the blank slab, then streamed to one side and dripped down into an endlessly deep hole. Dil was left bleeding to death. His breaths could be seen, and he was alive, but his eyes remained closed.

By then, El Kashef had arrived—late, as he couldn't keep up with Hadaus. He had witnessed some of what Fad and his son had been through and decided to help the outlaw with his child first.

"What have they done to him?" Fad expressed his fears. Everyone could hear the sadness in his voice. He blamed himself for being late, though he was thankful his child was still alive.

"What should we do?" Fad asked Mudawe. "Can you heal him? Will he survive?"

Hadaus answered instead, holding an open pouch in his hand and green paste in the other. "Help me close his wounds," he said, and he and Mudawe tried to heal the child. The paste dried quickly and stopped the bleeding, but the child remained wet with blood and looked dull and unresponsive.

"He's lost a lot of blood; he won't make it," said Hadaus.

"No," Mudawe replied. "We'll take him back to the Red Temple. We have the necessary remedy for children there. My aunt can help. We can save him."

"It is still raining heavily outside," said Hadaus. "And the city is far! The child's cuts must stay dry."

"We'll hide the child under my leather garment," El Kashef offered. They agreed. All—except for Hadaus and Yam, who followed later—left the cave and headed towards the Red Temple.

When Fad and the others had gone, Hadaus walked over to the broken rababa to examine it. It was broken in three parts and looked severely damaged. Yam picked up what was left of it, making sure he got every broken part.

"Who gave you this instrument?" Hadaus asked.

"It is not mine. It belongs to the Chief Guardian, El Kashef. He lent it to me," Yam concluded and walked away, escaping any sort of conversation with Hadaus.

...

Early that morning, Yam had been in Jibjat, waiting his turn for a bath. He had closed his eyes, pictured his mother, and played the rababa. He suddenly felt the air around him change. Opening his eyes in a panic, he found himself miles away from Jibjat, sitting in his mother's room! She was surprised to see him and welcomed him back.

He had not understood what had happened or exactly how, but he knew that it must have been the enchanted rababa. And so he had spent the whole day trying to use it again, picturing Jibjat in his mind, but it hadn't worked at all. He had then decided to picture another person, and he had thought of Dil. Yam had kept playing the rababa, accidentally summoning his own type of jinni—an air jinni! And at the right time, he had appeared out of thin air and saved Dil from El Sarabi, just as he had saved him from Behas's snake before.

...

They all walked back swiftly under the rains and through the forest to reach the streets of Hadibu. The path back was wet and dangerous. The rains did let up when they neared the city, and they faced no issues other than the guard whom Behas had knocked out at the small gate, the gate which was meant to keep wild animals from entering the city. The gatekeeper was conscious when they arrived and scolded them for leaving the gate open. Mudawe had closed it; Hadaus and El Kashef had been the ones who left it open.

"And which one of you smacked me down to the ground?" the gatekeeper asked angrily.

Hadaus got angrier. "We found you on the ground when we passed here." He pushed the gate hard to open it for the rest of them to pass, almost breaking it.

"Calm down, big man," said the gatekeeper as he shrank in his place. "You'll awaken the whole city."

Fad apologized for stealing his spear, and Shaf'e told him about the cave so he could send men there to bury the bodies and help the unconscious guards, which he did.

Led by Mudawe, they reached the Red Temple. The healer woke his aunt, Mother Sekina, to help the child.

Mother Sekina brought all her potions. She applied some red oils to the child's chest and forehead and used some other liquid on his wounds. The child turned red from all the dried blood and dragon-blood oil.

Taking out a very small silver bottle, she poured a tiny drop of liquid onto her finger, whispered strange verses, and rubbed it inside the sleeping child's mouth. He swallowed it, grimaced in disgust in his sleep, and began to cry loudly. That sound made everyone happy to know that he was still alive. His nursemaid, Jelila, rushed to feed him.

Sekina assured them that the child would live. They would feed him well and help him regain his strength after he had lost so much of his blood.

"His skin, though," Sekina said to Fad, "might become weakened. I used a strong potion on his heart and body. It was important to keep him alive. Other diseases might follow, but they can be studied and cured later."

"Thank you for everything, my lady," Fad said. His eyes filled with joyful tears.

"You must forgive us. The child was brought to us by the occultists; I trusted them. We did not ask them whose child he was, and they told us he was a jinxed child whose mother had died giving birth to him. I suspected wrongdoing when I first saw the scar on his face, but there was nothing we could have done." She then smiled and looked across the room to where Dil was being fed, saying, "I will name him El Ahmar." *The red one.*

Fad smiled, thanking her and Mudawe again, and then left to sit beside his little reddish child.

Shaf'e was pleased when he met Sekina that night and witnessed her skills. He explained his mother's condition to her, and Sekina gave him instructions and the things he needed to heal his mother.

Yam came by and sat beside them. They all expressed their gratitude and praised his heroism, and they all were curious to know how he had done it.

"Yam," Fad smiled, "I cannot thank you enough. You saved my child twice. You appeared tonight the same way my child disappeared. How did that happen?"

Yam laughed and told Fad everything, about Nada and Faseela, who were probably now terribly worried after he had disappeared from Jibjat, about El Kashef and the rababa. Fad told him where he had gotten the rababa from and was pleased to know that his wife was healed in Jibjat, but he became worried about how she might be, not knowing her husband and child were safe.

"I wish I hadn't broken the *rababa!*" Yam thought out loud. "I might have been able to take you to Jibjat with it right away. And since it is your rababa, I am sorry that I broke it."

Fad laughed. "Have no worries, Yam. You can keep the rababa; I never cared about it in that sense. If it hadn't gotten to you, who knows what would have happened? My child might have been killed."

Mudawe and Shaf'e agreed.

"And as for my wife and Faseela, I will head back to them as soon as I can," Fad hoped.

Yam thanked Fad for the enchanted gift. He did think about getting it fixed and using it again later. The use of jinn to help others was allowed by Erum.

"Where will you be headed later, Yam?" Fad asked him.

Yam took Arkin's flute from his pockets. "Well, I still remember Arkin. That kind man changed my life. I will use the silver he gave to me and travel to his hometown, Ibri, to find his daughters. They deserve to know how great their father was."

"If you needed anything from me," Fad said, "do let me know. You know where my farm is."

After a while, El Kashef came by. "Fad," he said, "may I have a word with you in private?"

"Certainly," Fad said, getting up and following him to an empty corner of the Red Temple. Everyone could still see them, but the noise of rain covered their voices.

El Kashef related all of what Daheen's cousin had told him about the first night after he left Wadi Erum on his journey.

"I cannot deny nor confirm any of what you have heard," said Fad. "I don't remember well what happened and what didn't." He then continued to tell El Kashef all of what he had seen. "But sometimes I see flashes of the events. It is true that it might have been me who burned one of the sacred trees. It must be the reason why they became angry and came after us that night. But I would never kill Bessel like they told you. And I did not know that their cousin died because of me. He threatened Bessel with a spear, and so I reacted without thought and smacked his head to protect Bessel."

El Kashef also discussed the rababa and how he had found it. Fad was heartbroken to hear about Qamaria's father. They both hoped Qamaria was all right, but later they both learned about her death as well.

El Kashef then told him about what he had seen near Jibjat and shared Daheen's description of Fad as a jinn master who summoned the wild hyenas that night.

"I do remember that night well, and I do remember who summoned the hyenas." Fad went on to tell El Kashef about the second night of his journey, when he got caught by the Guardians and Laeem appeared with the red substance.

El Kashef then related to Fad what had happened in Wadi Teyq during the third devastating night. Fad was deeply sad and sorry to learn about the poor men who helped him in Wadi Teyq. "It was Behas's idea to steal your Prime Ring and use it to lead an army against Socotra," Fad explained. "I never wanted to trust that jinn master, but I had no choice. I needed to save my son. Behas led us to the cave where my son was, but he disappeared before we got there. He told us, 'The beast has been summoned.' He said my child was most probably killed. But I thank Mudawe and Shaf'e, whom I met on the sailboat. The two helped me and did what an army might fail to do."

"An army has been dragged to this island, if you must know. Sheikh Leith, son of Aad, is fighting the Socotrians in the port. He is here for the sake of saving your son as well. I hope nothing bad happens to them." And that concluded the report of the fourth night, which had ended with Dil being rescued at last.

"You are still a suspect in Bessel's death, and you are in trouble for helping Behas steal the ring," El Kashef continued. "But there are other questions I have not yet found answers to. First, I still do not fully comprehend the strange behavior of Behas. He first came in an effort to kill your child, and then he managed to escape his execution. And as I learn from you, he helped you escape Wadi Teyq and guided you towards Wadi Darbat. You also say he came to the island and led you to where the child would be.

"Until I find the proper answer to all of this, I will consider you only a suspect. You are free to move inside the borders of Erum's dominion, but I need to know where you will be all the time."

"I will not object to whatever conclusion you make," Fad said. "I have told you all about my encounters with Behas and Bessel. If ever you will need me for more answers, I will always be at my farm near Wadi Erum."

El Kashef spoke that night to Fad, Yam, the healer, Shaf'e, and Hadaus as well. He learned a lot, but there was one man left for him to hear from before he could conclude his case: Behas.

...

That night, a man interrupted the peace in the temple and entered abruptly, without knocking. He was a regular Socotrian who, it appeared, had come to find Sekina.

"Socotra has fallen. The Protector is dead, my lady," he cried. El Kashef, being the only one in a Guardian's uniform, did not enjoy the Socotrian's hostile gaze upon him.

"The son of Aad has claimed authority over the island," the Socotrian went on, "and all the sheikhs of Socotra are ordered to pledge allegiance and submission to him in the morning. Word has spread that a Guardian from Erum will be named the new Protector of Socotra. Can you imagine?"

El Kashef couldn't hear Sekina's whispering. But she looked as calm as a dragon-blood tree, still and motionless. El Kashef noticed from her gestures that she was trying to calm the guard down.

"It was horrible, Aunt Sekina. I saw it all. I saw my father killed before my own eyes."

Mudawe heard the news, and he too was saddened, for the man was his cousin, and the Socotrian guard who had died was his uncle.

Fad blamed himself, feeling responsible for all the calamities. But Mudawe explained to everyone that Fad and the Erumians were not the ones to be blamed. It was the occultists' guild in Socotra, who called themselves the Noorians of the Dragon, who had caused all the trouble.

El Kashef had heard enough and walked towards Hadaus. "Should we go back to the port? It seems that the young sheikh has gained control over the whole island."

"Indeed we should. It would be better to rest the night there than in this temple." Hadaus brought out a white stone of frankincense and offered it to El Kashef. "Want one?"

"No, thank you," El Kashef replied.

"What about the child?"

"Let him feed and heal for now. The father can bring him in the morning." El Kashef told Fad that the two were leaving, and Fad promised to meet them in the port the next morning.

55

It continued to rain the next morning, slowing only a little in the afternoon. All the tribal sheikhs gathered to pledge their allegiance to their new Protector, Abed, a Guardian of Erum to whom Prince Leith had given the Prime Ring that day. His main objective was to ensure that life in Socotra continued until the Prime Sheikh, Aad, confirmed the appointment or assigned another Protector.

The seventeen-year-old prince ordered a rectangular pillar to be erected near the barracks as a symbol of the rule of his father. A green sail and a flag were raised on the pillar, ones like those found in all the ports ruled by Aad.

"This I will take to my father," he said, ordering his men to load the Protector's axe to the ship. The axe that had injured his face was made of a carved red stone and was the same one that had killed his older brother thirty-nine years before. El Kashef saw pride in Leith's bandaged face that morning, and he thought the prince had earned it. He had achieved two great things on his journey: He had retrieved the child safely for his brother Zufar, and he had conquered Socotra as a gift to his father.

...

They all reached Sumhuram the following day. The rains there were heavier than the ones in Socotra.

Fad, Dil, and his nursemaid, Jelila, were allowed by the prince to leave for Jibjat and find Nada. He ordered an escort of guards to ensure their safe return to Wadi Erum after they reached Jibjat and found Dil's mother.

The prince prepared for his own convoy to depart for Wadi Erum, but El Kashef excused himself from the journey.

"I still need to find answers for the traitorous acts against Bessel," El Kashef explained to the prince. "I might find other clues that will prove the farmer, Fada, is innocent."

"Can we offer you any help?" asked the prince.

"My horse and hound are with me, and they are all I need."

The prince prayed for El Kashef's success and left at once, disregarding the heavy rain.

Prince Leith and his party took the mountain path back to Wadi Erum. Their journey took four days because of the rains, which poured heavily from time to time, forcing them to stop for shelter more often than walk. Only when the rains stopped were they able to march on straight to the city.

On their way, they found all the dams had been damaged due to the storm, which had led to catastrophic events in Wadi Erum, as well. They reached Erum after the chaos was over. Only when they arrived did they come to learn that a great flood had filled the lower parts of Wadi Erum. Many lives had been lost during the three days the storm raged.

The lower parts of Wadi Erum were still filled with water when Leith and his men arrived, but it wasn't all dangerous anymore, and the upper parts of the wadi were safe.

Prince Leith kept his face wrapped when he entered his father's sabla, but the news of his success in Socotra reached them before he did, and they all praised him that evening. His father ordered his finest healers to replace the lost parts of Leith's face with gold. And ever after, he was called Leith El Thahabi, the Golden Lion.

His brother, Prince Zufar, enjoyed his success and return the most. He was also glad to hear that the child had been saved, and he ordered the sages to bless the child and have him protected spiritually in Somood's temple like any Guardian of Erum would be. Zufar carried Dil himself and raised him before the head of Somood, and Zufar saw the stone smiling back like it never had before.

Aad's sons remained in the east, as the war carried on near the borders of the sheikhdom. When the prime prince, Shaddad, learned about the flood, he ordered Zufar and his army's swift return to help keep Wadi Erum safe. But when the sabla later learned that the execution of Behas had been faked, Aad was forced to send Zufar into exile. Aad did not want to punish his son, but these were his own rules. To reduce the punishment, he ordered that Zufar would represent his father in Sumhuram, and the whole Province of Salalah would be under his control. Some called the decision unfair, feeling it was a reward rather than exile, but no one could question Aad's rulings over the sabla.

. . .

The day El Kashef stayed back in Sumhuram, he needed help from Hadaus before he could leave in his search for Behas.

"Hadaus," he called to him while he remained at rest in Sumhuram. "The Mystic Dagger—you told me it belonged to Behas."

"Indeed it did."

"May I borrow it?"

"Never. What do you need it for?"

"I need to find the saher. My hound, Kashefa, is skilled. She can find him using the dagger. I need to ask him about everything that occurred."

It surprised Hadaus to learn that Behas was still alive. "You will not need the blade to find him," Hadaus said. "Behas hides only from his enemies; his all-knowing jinni warns him. But for your cause, you can ask the villagers in the eastern lands, and they might direct you to him. Start with villages that praised him. And be more careful than ever. He can be misleading. I myself would never trust him to be honest."

. . .

El Kashef went to the markets of Sumhuram to fill his sacks and bags with enough goods for his next journey, but he did not predict its length accurately.

It took him seventeen days to find Behas. He had to ask in many towns, villages, valleys, and even cities he either passed by or rested in. Finally, he found the saher far up the northern coast, resting in a small barn and disguised as a peasant. Only two or three of the locals knew his identity.

"Behas." El Kashef spoke his name while he sat under a lone tree. The man didn't show any signs of welcome. "I found you at last."

El Kashef was not wearing his Guardian's tunic, and his beard was much longer than it had been the last time Behas saw him in Wadi Teyq. But deep inside, El Kashef felt that Behas knew him well.

He looked up and waved a hand for El Kashef to sit on the other side of the rug, where a stuffed pillow lay.

El Kashef sat after he had tied his white horse and his black hound.

"You have traveled far. What is it you seek from me?"

"Answers," El Kashef replied without delay, but he paused a long time when he noticed the old man's eyebrows twitch.

"Answers?" Behas prodded.

"Yes, answers. The child born under the Serpent-Neck star, the one you failed to kill." El Kashef paused again, waiting for a reaction, but there was none. "I haven't introduced myself to you. My name is—"

"I know you well, Rasheed, son of Masc. And I know that whatever I tell you about that child, you will not understand. I risked my life to save Wadi Erum during that calamitous week. I could have been executed. I was chased by wicked beasts. A Noorian poisoned me to death. I could have drowned or been caught in Socotra. I…" He stopped for a thought. "I saved a lot of lives. I saved Wadi Erum from an unstoppable peril. But I will always be perceived as the enemy, like my mother and father before me. I have my reasons for keeping Erum safe, but no man will ever understand, not for now, at least."

"Then for the old man's sake, speak," El Kashef said, referring to his grandfather, a man Behas had known well a long time before, when he had served in Erum. "Answer my questions. I am not here to question your intentions towards Erum, Behas. The events surrounding the child cost many lives. We know what or who caused most of the deaths, but I have been tasked by the Prime Chief Guardian, Qassas, with finding out who killed our Chief Guardian, Bessel.

"Once I hear the story told from your view, I might find the answers we seek. Start at the beginning, from the night you came to Wadi Erum seeking the child," El Kashef said calmly, with a smile.

"For the old man's sake, I will speak," he said with a sigh. "My all-knowing jinni can identify where a child will be born under the Serpent-Neck star. And my jinni can do so, because I myself was born under the same star. That star is the most hated by the evil jinnic lords in the jinnic realm. Killing such a child on his twelfth sunset as an offering can grant one great wishes from the greatest evil jinnic lords."

El Kashef shook his head, for he had never heard such tales.

"The only way to stop such an evil is by killing these newborns before they fall into the wrong hands. And I would have succeeded, if it weren't for the child's father and Arkin's student. When I was imprisoned, I needed to find a new plan. I told Prince Zufar what I believed would happen, though he was not convinced at first. But I also knew that the Noorian queen would try to keep me alive. She wanted me to show her how the Mystic Dagger could be used. And when Arkin convinced Zufar, the prince decided to help them, not me, although he knew his father would object to it."

Behas continued to explain what had happened near Jibjat, outlining how he and Fad had escaped and were almost killed by Hadaus near Wadi Teyq.

"When I met the farmer, he told me he was accused of killing Bessel. And later, when I hid in the battleship on my way to Socotra. I became curious, and I asked my all-knowing jinni if he knew how Bessel died. He told me Fad had been possessed by an evil jinni that night. The farmer acted unwillingly; the jinni made him sleepwalk and burn the tree. The jinni wanted the farmers in Wadi Dawkah to come and kill Bessel. It wanted only Bessel to be dead. It did not care much about the farmer."

El Kashef's hair stood on end, and he felt his face turn pale. This was not at all the answer he had come for. He convinced himself not to trust all of Behas's words. "Why would an evil jinni want to kill the Chief Guardian of Palace Affairs? That makes no sense!"

"The jinni was sent by someone who wanted Bessel dead. Bessel might have had his own enemies," said Behas, "strong enemies who could summon such an evil jinni from the jinnic realm. Perhaps one was an experienced jinn master my all-knowing jinni could not identify."

"I still cannot understand it," El Kashef said. "If the jinni wanted Bessel dead, why couldn't it have possessed him instead and made him kill himself? Why did it possess Fad?"

"Because it cannot possess a Guardian of Erum. They are spiritually protected. But the farmer's soul was weaker and easily taken over."

"Then couldn't the jinni just use Fad to kill Bessel in his sleep? Why go through all the trouble of burning the sacred tree?"

"A jinni does not control your body but your mind. It manipulates the ideas in your head. The farmer would never think about killing Bessel, so the jinni wouldn't be able to make him do it. But because the two were aiming to stay warm and they had worked on lighting a fire, the jinni planned to get them in trouble with the farmers. And since it had achieved its purpose and was sure that Bessel was dead, it left, leaving the farmer in trouble."

El Kashef remained silent, trying to digest it all. "Why that night in particular? Why had the jinni never tried to kill Bessel on any other day?"

"The jinni had probably chosen Bessel as a target a long time ago, but since he was the Chief Guardian of Palace Affairs, I would assume he had never left Wadi Erum, a city protected from any evil jinn powers. It had probably waited for a night when Bessel finally left the protected city, and it was fortunate to find him riding with a weak soul. It did what it did to accomplish the goals of its jinn master."

Who would that jinn master be? El Kashef wondered. He was still hesitant to accept Behas's words.

"Did you get the answers you came looking for?" Behas asked.

"Well, as an investigator, I do need evidence that can strengthen your story."

Behas smiled. "You never asked why the farmer had a weak soul, which made him easily possessed by the evil jinni."

El Kashef raised his head in wonder. "Because he isn't a Guardian of Erum?" he asked.

"No! Every man and woman has a strong soul, not only the Guardians."

"Then how was Fad's soul weak that night?"

"Only those who offer their souls to the jinn weaken them."

"Why would Fad ever offer his soul?" El Kashef asked.

"It wasn't him; it was his neighbor. I believe you have met with her," Behas explained.

Faseela? El Kashef couldn't believe it at first.

"Make her confess," Behas said. "That will be your evidence. Do you still have other questions?"

El Kashef smiled. "Yes, I do have one last question. I am curious. The ritual in Socotra—what kind of calamity did you warn about? You even left Fad and never went there to stop those who performed the ritual, yet you claim that it was you who saved Wadi Erum!"

"We were late. The beast was summoned. No one was able to see it; all they saw was clouds above. But I saw the spirit of the old dragon, Socotra, flying high up out of the mountain. It swam up in the clouds and stirred the storm towards Erum. I had to leave them and stop the beast.

"It was difficult to do so without my Mystic Dagger, which the Noorians had taken from me. It also took a while for me to find a white donkey in Socotra. Finally, with the help of Zuhal, we were able to summon a flying jinni. It flew me above the clouds, and from there I climbed over Socotra's head. The beast squirmed and flew randomly up, down, and around, trying to topple me off, but I held on to her and managed to crawl to her ear and speak with her. I couldn't kill her without my dagger, so I tamed her instead and convinced her to stop. She agreed and withdrew her fury and rage against Erum, she flew me back home, and Erum was saved. The storm she created in the skies stayed for days, and if I hadn't tamed her, the rains would have stayed for months until Wadi Erum sank below the earth."

...

El Kashef didn't believe him at first—not until he traveled back to the wadi and learned from the people there that a storm had flooded the wadi and caused great perils for all of Erum. Later, Behas spoke more about the calamity to El Kashef, who wrote a book to record the tale. He called the book *Taming a Wind Dragon*.

56

When El Kashef first arrived near Wadi Erum, he went straight to the palm groves. He asked and was directed to where Fad's neighbor, Faseela, lived. He wanted to ask her first and confirm Behas's tale before he made his report to Qassas.

He noticed a boy of seven years old and called upon him from outside their farm. The little boy raced to the fence. His head was covered with a turban that was too large for him—probably his father's. He held the grip of a dagger wrapped on his waist. It was also bigger than his size, and probably also his father's. El Kashef was pleased to see the new generation of boys wearing daggers

"Where are your mother and father?" he asked him.

"My father is resting, and my mother is sewing," the boy said.

"Well, call your mother for me please, young Guardian."

The boy eyed El Kashef's uniform and realized he was talking with a Guardian of Erum. El Kashef could also tell from the look on his face that he enjoyed being called a Guardian.

"Yes, master. I mean, Guardian," the boy agreed, then raced away through the palms to get his mother.

"El Kashef! What a surprise visit," she said. "Please enter."

"I will be fine standing here, Faseela. Where is your friend, Nada?"

"She's staying in Erum; it's safer there. In the upper valley, of course, not the lower one. She wants to raise her child there. As you know, it's not safe for him here after the incident, and the child is sick and in need of care. You do know where her father's house is, right?"

"I do. But to be truthful, I came here looking for you, not her."

"What is it that you need?" Faseela asked, smiling.

El Kashef leaned near the mud fence so only she could hear. "I know what you did, Faseela."

She stepped back. "What?"

Behas had told him everything, and El Kashef did not waste any time. "You offered their souls to a seer in Ubar, didn't you? What will happen to you if I tell your friend, Nada?" El Kashef asked. "I wonder if she is your friend at all!"

Faseela swallowed her tongue in shock. El Kashef continued scaring her. "You should be punished in the market so everyone can witness your traitorous acts against your friend and neighbor."

Faseela almost fainted with fear at what he said. "No, please, Chief Guardian. I meant no harm for her at all," she wept. "I love her like my little sister. I knew how much she wanted her first child from Fada to be a boy. All I wanted was to help her.

"I went to Ubar intending to see a seer and guarantee that her first would be a boy. All the seers I asked wanted money in return, and I could not afford what they asked for. Except for one. He was willing to tell me if I would offer him their souls in return. I was eager to know if her first would be a boy or a girl, so I brought the seer what he asked for.

"I secretly took a hair from each, Fad and Nada. He also needed their spiritual acceptance, so I asked them if they were willing to give anything to have a boy, and they both said yes. When the seer assured me that their first would be a boy, I raced to tell them, and they were both very happy to hear it. The seer promised me he wouldn't harm them. He did. I should have never trusted him. I was tricked.

"Oh please, Guardian of Erum, forgive my mistake. I have spent the last days with Nada trying to help her recover from it. I was glad to know that both Fad and Dileel were safe. I was so relieved that she was still alive, too. If anything had happened to them, I would never have forgiven myself. Never."

From afar, her son noticed her whining and ran to get his father. El Kashef noticed it too and decided to end the conversation there and leave before creating a scene. He had come with the intention of scaring her, not punishing her.

"Fine, I will spare you any punishment," El Kashef interrupted her. "But under one condition."

"Anything," she cried desperately.

"You will first help us identify the seer from Ubar so we can punish him and force him to return whatever he took from Fad and Nada. Then, you will confess your wrongdoing to everyone you know, including Nada. You need to warn them against making the same mistake."

Her eyes grew wetter, and her husband came up beside her. "What is happening, Guardian?" he asked in worry. "What agony have you brought upon my wife?"

El Kashef greeted him with a confident gesture. "Your wife, Faseela, will tell you everything," he said, and noticed her eyes grow wider. "But first, allow her to rest and think before she can speak."

She nodded, and El Kashef thanked her for her bravery and honesty in agreeing to warn everyone she knew about the lessons she had learned. Never should free women or men sell their souls to any jinn masters.

Later that day, she did explain her mistake to everyone she knew and asked for their forgiveness, and everyone did forgive her unconditionally. Even the head of Somood at the temple smiled back at her, and she felt it was the first time that it seemed to be doing that.

...

"It then took me another ten days to travel back to Wadi Erum. And here I am before you, Prime Chief."

As El Kashef finished relating Behas's tale to Qassas, he eyed the last specks of sand passing down the hourglass. Exactly an hour had passed since he had started reporting the whole story of Bessel's death to Qassas.

"By Somood, El Kashef," said Qassas with a sigh. "You've spent the whole hour I allowed you exactly."

El Kashef nodded with astonishment as well.

"And why didn't you capture him when you found him?" he asked.

"I am but an old and crippled man, Prime Chief."

"Very well. Do tell us where he was. We will send bounty hunters to kill him for us," Qassas said to El Kashef. "Karbi," he then called to his second-in-command.

A large Guardian, one no younger than Qassas, entered the room. "Here, Prime Chief," Karbi said. Crumbs of bread flew out of his mouth as he spoke.

"Do you ever stop eating?" said Qassas. "The rumors of Behas and the fake execution are true. Keep your men on high alert. We shall inform the sabla tomorrow. And prepare a platoon for tonight. You will storm the dark alley in Ubar. Put any saher or seer who matches the description El Kashef will give you in the dungeons."

The chubby Guardian forced himself to swallow. "It shall be done, Prime Chief."

And that concluded the report regarding the traitorous murder of Bessel, who had been killed by an evil jinni summoned by one of his enemies, an enemy neither El Kashef nor Qassas could condemn. Fad had been only a tool used by the jinni; he was not to be blamed for that or for stealing the Prime Ring, as he had gone and done only what he needed to do to save his child.

Many had died in less than one month because of the events: eighty-nine men and one woman, starting with the death of Bessel and continuing through to the men who had died in battle in the port of Hadibu. And then, because of the Socotrians who had planned revenge against Aad, another ninety innocent souls had died in the great storm that drowned the lower valley of Erum. Forty-three women, twenty-two men, and twenty-five children had lost their lives in the resulting flood. And to be honest and grateful, all of Erum would have drowned if it hadn't been for the one who called himself the *true* Guardian of Erum, Behas.

Later that day, El Kashef went to meet with Fad and to inform him that all charges against him had been dropped and that he and his family could live in peace.

...

When Fad and Nada returned with Dil from Jibjat, their parents were filled with joy to see them and their special grandchild safe and well. The young couple stayed for a while in Nada's parents' house before moving back to their humble farm. For generations to come, people told the story of the first couple from Wadi Erum to regain their child after he had been kidnapped by jinn masters. They had four more children, whom they gave names with meanings relating to stars or planets in the galaxy. Dileel meant "guide," as in a guiding star. A daughter they named Najma, meaning "star." A second daughter Fad named after the woman who had helped him escape the spearmen in Qairon Heriti, Qamaria, which meant the "girl of the moon." They gave their youngest daughter, Shamsa, a name that meant "the sun." And their little boy they called Satee, meaning "bright." All these names were anchored in the meaning of Fada's name—not "emptiness" but "the galaxy," as he had learned from Shaf'e. And he and his family lived happily ever after.

He and his father continued to take their harvest to Sumhuram, but before reaching the port, they would stop by in Wadi Teyq and give the tribes there half of their dates as a gift, in recognition of the sacrifice the tribesmen had made when they helped Fad save Dil.

Dil enjoyed an extraordinary life, one filled with love, joy, and adventure. Until the age of ten, he was known as El Ahmar. Later, when his skin began to develop strangely, as Sekina had warned him it would, he became known as Yeld Elhai, or just Elhai, meaning "serpent skin" or "serpent," for his red skin would occasionally get irritated, stiffen, die or molt like animal skin, shed, and grow anew. It was a strange phenomenon that many healers who came across him studied him to try to help. Mudawe helped him as well, with a herb he found in Africa called the Abba. It never fixed him, but it helped Dil bear the pain and relax his skin in periods of shedding or regrowth.

Evil jinn masters no longer chased after him. In fact, he chased after them. He grew up and joined the Guardians of Erum, becoming a jinn tamer. After he learned about the events that had occurred when he was born, he dedicated his life to helping keep Erum and its people safe from the darkness of the jinnic realm.

BLOOD LINE OF AAD AND HIS SONS

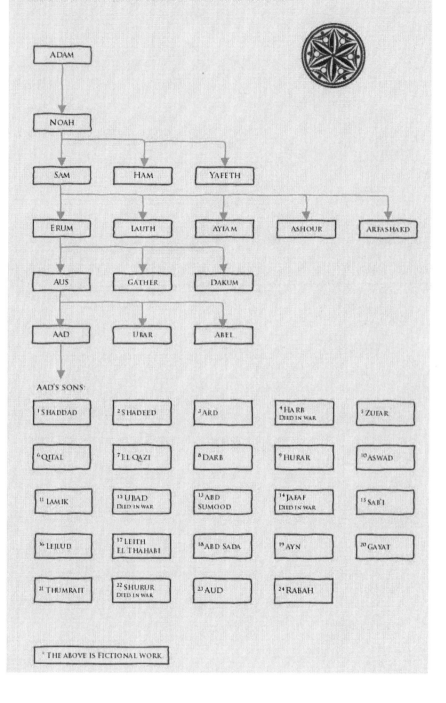

ADAM

NOAH

SAM | HAM | YAFETH

ERUM | LAUTH | AYIAM | ASHOUR | ARFASHAKD

AUS | GATHER | DAKUM

AAD | URAR | ABEL

AAD'S SONS:

[1] SHADDAD	[2] SHADEED	[3] ARD	[4] HARB DIED IN WAR	[5] ZUEAR
[6] QITAL	[7] EL QAZI	[8] DARB	[9] HURAR	[10] ASWAD
[11] LAMIK	[12] UBAD DIED IN WAR	[13] ABD SUMOOD	[14] JAFAF DIED IN WAR	[15] SAB'I
[16] LEJLUD	[17] LEITH EL THAHABI	[18] ABD SADA	[19] AYN	[20] GAYAT
[21] THUMRAIT	[22] SHURUR DIED IN WAR	[23] AUD	[24] RABAH	

* THE ABOVE IS FICTIONAL WORK

EPILOGUE

Twenty days after he saved Dil in Socotra, Yam spent all his silver coins to reach Arkin's hometown, Ibri. He asked and was directed to where Arkin's house was. He met with the man's daughters, Rakia and Taiba, and he gave them their father's flute.

He told them the whole story, and he and Arkin's daughters decided to work together to honor Arkin's small guild of occultists and keep it alive. Their first mission was to fix the enchanted rababa. And from there, Yam's adventures as an occultist began!

TO BE CONTINUED...

AFTERWORD

I chose to write this book in hopes of revealing some of the hidden jewels of Southern Arabia. The first uncommon aspect of the story is the time in which it is set. I intended to explore the ancient pre-Islamic era in Arabia, which is very astonishing because it is not pure legend, myth, or a fairy tale made up by our forefathers but a realm which all Muslims today believe once existed.

The advanced civilization of giants who ruled Arabia once before—the people of Aad, as they are named in the Arabic and Islamic scriptures— built and inhabited a wondrous land: *"Erum of the pillars. The like of which was never created in the land." (Quran 89:7–8)*. The Erum in my book, and its people and rulers, are inspired by the many descriptions of them in the scriptures. There, the Erumians are presented as a tribe that dominated the lands and had all the riches and resources and power, but they misused them by oppressing weaker men and were therefore punished by God and buried under the desert: *"Will you continue to build on every high spot monumental buildings for fun and show? And make for yourselves great castles, (as if) hoping that you might live forever? And when you strike and seize [others and their goods], strike and seize in the style of tyrants?" (Quran 26:128–130)*.

The second hidden jewel of Southern Arabia is Oman. I set my tales in several locations in the southern province of Dhofar in Oman, trying as much as I could to use locations that are now tourist sites and that the reader can explore. Especially during the first months of autumn, when the dry land turns green and is filled with life, Salalah is an inspiring paradise facing the Arabian Sea.

Finally, the events in the book are inspired by the many fairy tales and folk stories that circulate in Oman and Southern Arabia. Some of the most common kinds of stories are the tragic tales that relate to the kidnapping of newborns and sacrifice of innocent souls as offerings to the unseen jinnic lords. But I rather chose to keep most of the jinnic world, and the opposing spiritual power of occultists, who do exist in the Islamic world even today.

There are still those who call themselves jinn masters and who are visited by dark-hearted people who pay for them to cast harmful spells against others. On the other side, there are many men and women today who call themselves healers, or occultists, as I named them in my tale. They oppose the dark use of jinnism and work hard to break its evil powers. A part of that war between good and evil is revealed in my story, but it is not the main focus, as I intend to keep it unknown and hidden. Most of my ideas come from local culture and old traditions and beliefs. The protection spell or metallic stone that keeps Wadi Erum safe is one example. Did you know that a minority of people in modern-day Southern Arabia sleep with silverware under their pillows so no evil jinn can come and harm them in their sleep?

Many questions arise from that realm itself. How can you become a jinn master or an occultist? Do you need to perform a trick or use an instrument, as Aladdin did with the magic lamp in the *Arabian Nights*? Or is there some sort of practice or ritual you can use to gain access to such powers? Most of the jinnic powers and skills in my tale are also inspired by the Arabic and Islamic scriptures, and I hope to focus on that area in another book, as Yam explores the jinnic realm further and tries to understand it more deeply.

…

Here I leave you with one of my inspirations from the Islamic scriptures, a story which discusses the use of an air jinni and its ability to teleport things through thin air in the blink of an eye:

[The Queen, having received his message, decided to visit Solomon (at his home). Knowing of her journey,] Solomon said [to his council]: "O you nobles! Who among you can bring me her throne before they come to me in submission?" One strong and cunning among the jinn said: "I can bring it to you before you rise from your council. Surely I have the strength and skill to do so, and I am trustworthy." And one who had some knowledge of the Book said: "I can bring it to you in the twinkling of your eye." When Solomon saw the throne set in his presence, he said: "This is out of the pure grace of my Lord, that He may try me whether I give thanks or act with ingratitude. Whoever gives thanks, gives thanks only for [the good of] his own soul; and whoever acts with ingratitude, [let him be aware that] my Lord is surely All-Wealthy and Self-Sufficient, All-Munificent." *(Quran 27:38–40)*

ACKNOWLEDGMENTS

Dear reader, my first thanks are to you. In this age of many things to do and many books to read, I am forever gratified that you have spared some of your precious time to read my story. If it weren't for you, who made me think throughout this whole process, "Is it worth their time? Are the readers going to enjoy this tale or learn from it?" this might not have been a good story. As you've reached the end, I sincerely hope that you did enjoy it and that it was worth the time you've spent reading it.

Next, I thank my parents for making writing my hobby in one way or another. I would never have loved being a reader if it hadn't been for my mother, who forced me to come back from school every week with books borrowed from the school library, and I would never have found joy in writing if it hadn't been for my father, who constantly praised Dan Brown. Am I writing to impress my father, I wonder? I also thank my wife, Shammah, for her endless support and patience throughout my writing process. I thank my brothers and sisters for being the first fans of this story, and I thank my high school English teacher, Jason Potter, who advised me to try to write what was in my mind as a foreign person wanting to learn the language. My warmest thanks are to my dear friend H.E. Eissa Al Fahim for his never-ending encouragement and positive energy.

In the making of this book, from inspiration and research to the editing stage, my thanks are spread equally to Dr. Ismail Al Zadjali for all his knowledge-sharing, support, and full access to books and studies on Oman's history; to Dr. Aisha Al Darmaki for her insightful works on Oman's folkloric literature, folkloric arts, and folkloric traditions and beliefs, which, along with many elements of the story, inspired the main plot—parents who suffer losing their newborn and are kidnapped by jinn; to Dr. Abdulaziz Al Musallam for his book *Encyclopedia of Superstitions: Creatures in the Emirati Heritage*; and finally, for all the editorial and professional proofreading services and endless support I received, to Luke Palder, founder of ProofreadingServices.com, and his team of experts—whom I would highly recommend to my fellow self-published authors and writers.

ABOUT THE AUTHOR

A. Ali Hasan Ali is a transport planner who started writing mystery and crime fiction during his high school years as a hobby and a tool to help him learn English. Inspired by Arabia's ancient history and folklore, he wrote and published his first novel, *The Guardians of Erum and the Calamitous Child of Socotra.* He lives in Abu Dhabi.

Contact: theguardiansoferum@gmail.com

Made in the USA
Las Vegas, NV
29 July 2023

75406860R10208